Critical acc...

JA...

'Jack escapes death more ... ...t
to find the traitor in the ...

... ... *ph*

'Vigorously imagined, dashingly done espionage adventure with
newly retired military man, Jack Absolute . . . New territory for
spy fiction, but utterly convincing in its period and ethnic detail.
Few comparisons unless you go back to Fenimore Cooper's *Last
of the Mohicans*. Quite bloody, thoroughly gripping, intensely
readable' *Literary Review*

BLOOD TIES

'With *The French Executioner* Humphreys established himself
as a quality purveyor of historical crime fiction with a heady
blend of historical detail and vigorous action . . . This unusual
storyline is dispatched with consummate skill, and the conflict
between father and son has an intelligence and sophistication
that transcends the narrative' *Good Book Guide*

C. C. Humphreys excels as ever in the throat-in-mouth action
and knows instinctively how to keep a reader pasted to the
page . . . This novel shows a writer reaching ever upwards and
I can't wait for Humphreys' next novel. If you like Bernard
Cornwell's *Grail Quest* series, you'll love *The French Executioner*
and *Blood Ties*. To my mind, Cornwell is good, but Humphreys
is better' Sally Zigmond, *Historical Novels Review*

THE FRENCH EXECUTIONER

'Falling somewhere between the novels of Bernard Cornwell and
Wilbur Smith, C. C. Humphreys has fashioned a rollicking good
yarn that keeps the pages turning from start to finish'

John Daly, *Irish Examiner*

'. . . how he fulfills his mission is told with enormous zest in this
splendid, rip-roaring story . . . a fine addition to the tradition of
swashbuckling costume romance of which Robert Louis Steven-
son is the incomparable master'

George Patrick, *Hamilton Examiner*

C. C. Humphreys was born in Toronto, Canada, and grew up in London. An actor for twenty-five years, leading roles have included Hamlet and the Gladiator, Caleb, in the miniseries *Anno Domini*. He also played Jack Absolute in Sheridan's *The Rivals* in 1987. His plays have been produced in the UK and Canada. His first novel, *The French Executioner*, was shortlisted for the CWA Steel Dagger for Thrillers 2002 and has been optioned for the screen. The sequel, *Blood Ties*, was published in 2003. His third novel, *Jack Absolute*, is the first in a series about the master spy. A schoolboy fencing champion and fight choreographer in the theatre, with this, his fourth novel, Chris has continued pursuing his love for all forms of bladed weaponry. He is married and lives in London. Visit his website at www.cchumphreys.com.

By C. C. Humphreys

NOVELS:

The French Executioner
Blood Ties
Jack Absolute
The Blooding of Jack Absolute

PLAYS:

A Cage Without Bars
Glimpses Of The Moon
Touching Wood

SCREENPLAY:

The French Executioner

THE BLOODING
– OF –
JACK
ABSOLUTE

C. C. HUMPHREYS

McArthur & Company

TORONTO

First published in Canada in 2004 by
McArthur & Company
322 King Street West, Suite 402
Toronto, Ontario
www.mcarthur-co.com

This paperback edition published in 2005 by
McArthur & Company

Library and Archives Canada Cataloguing in Publication

Humphreys, C. C. (Chris C.)
The Blooding of Jack Absolute/C. C. Humphreys.

ISBN 1-55278-510-6

I. Title.

PS8565.U5576B57 2005   C813'.6   C2005-903260-X

The publisher would like to acknowledge the financial support of the
Government of Canada through the Book Publishing Industry Development
Program, the Canada Council, and the Ontario Arts Council for our publishing activities. We also acknowledge the Government of Ontario through
the Ontario Media Development Corporation Ontario Book Initiative.

10 9 8 7 6 5 4 3 2 1

To my very own Roaring Boy –
Reith Frederic Humphreys,
born 2 February 2004

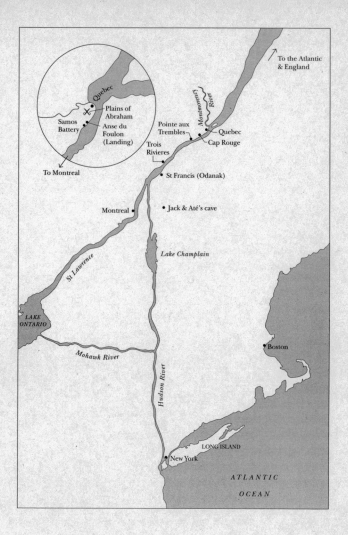

— PART 1 —
Youth

– ONE –

Cain and Abel

Cornwall, September 1752

The End of Time came on a Wednesday – and Jack was missing it. There was rage and riot in every corner of the realm, all because the Papists, led by some downser named Gregory, had stolen near half of September. He didn't really understand how that could be, how True and Christian Englishmen could let a Pope tell them what to do; but the Government had ordered it so, surrendered to the will of those beyond the sea: Froggies, Italians and the like. Jack had never met any but he knew they wished him no good. And, like any other native of the Isles, he wanted to join his voice to the others, cry out, 'Give us back our eleven days!' The word had spread, just ahead of the flames. In Exeter, they'd burnt down the Court House. In Plymouth, seafarers from Naples had been tarred and feathered. And anything they could manage in Devon – where the people were known to have wishbones where their backbones ought to be – the Cornish would top. They'd be kicking up a dido all around and Jack had plans to join in, wasn't going to rest content with a little fuss in the village. No, he and some of the other Zennor lads were bound for the big town – Penzance. Three hours across the fields, if they took it at a clip. He'd been there twice, never seen anything so vast. All sorts lived there, including, no doubting, foreigners! They'd get what they deserved. And Jack would be there to see it.

Except he wouldn't. Not unless he could shift these bonds.

He strained against them, again to no effect. It was Lutie Tregonning who had tied them and Lutie, when he wasn't digging for tin in the Absolute fields, was a fisherman and knew his knots. Though he'd shaken his head and muttered while he did them, he'd had his commandments from the squire and did a proper job. His liking for Jack didn't extend to risk losing his livelihood.

The hempen coils were passed through an iron hoop, which was driven hard into the wine cellar's wall, then anchored to a barrel. The length of cord meant Jack could stand, crawl to that barrel, even draw some wine out from its spigot. He'd tried to console himself with that, had lain underneath the tap and sucked. But the wine had gone off, its foul sharpness still coating his mouth an hour later. An old pint pot lay under the tap for catching drips and it gave off an acrid, vinegar smell, its surface thick with tiny black flies.

Something moved in the house above. Someone coming for him? He tipped his head. Through the door came only the same muffled shouts, snatches of song, banging of tankards. His uncle was still celebrating some change in the family fortunes. Duncan Absolute was not renowned for being sober – indeed, he was universally known as 'Druncan' – but this debauch outdid even the King's last birthday. His cronies from the Plump Pigeons had arrived three days before and never left. This annoyed Jack. When his uncle was this drunk he was easy to elude. So how was it that he'd been caught?

Jack spat into the corner but sourness clung to his tongue. He knew how, knew his betrayer. Duncan's son, ever mindful of a chance to do Jack down, would have stayed watchful. So when Jack, forbidden to leave the house, ordered to slave doubly hard on all the guests' horses and carriages, had snuck from the barn on his way to the rendezvous of the brave boys bound for Penzance, Craster Absolute was waiting.

Craster. The image of his cousin's smirking face, peering from behind Duncan's back as the man raved and frothed, made Jack tug again against his bonds until the skin at his wrists bled, still to no avail.

Another sound distracted him, the faint booming of the surf beneath Zennor Head. Jack listened, to the long roll, the crash as the wave smashed down. He didn't need to see it to tell that the tide was running strong and it made his imprisonment all the worse. If he couldn't be in Penzance, he could at least be there, plunging into those waves, he and Treve Tregonning, hurling themselves ahead of the walls of water just before they peaked, riding them to the shore line, their bodies straightened out like arrows, neck bent up, hands thrust ahead to steer. In the chill, pulsing water, the shock and the thrill of it, timing it just right so that you were in and on and of the falling cliff of salt, using its power till the very end, gliding gently onto your belly in the sand, to leap up, turn, run in again and again, until you were blue and shaking and had to stop or drown. Some had, Billy Wits last year, and the activity was strictly forbidden ever since – such prohibition making it all the more delicious.

That *was* a sound now. The door above opening, feet on the stairs. Jack tried to guess whose footfalls it could be, how he could prepare for whoever was coming through the door. Duncan had promised to return to punish. Craster would be there to watch and gloat. The key shrieked in the lock. The door swung in.

'Morwenna!'

If Jack could have moved, he would have leapt to the ceiling in his relief. For in the doorway, filling it, was the comforting, near-spherical shape of the housekeeper of Absolute Hall. Morwenna Tregonning, Lutie's wife, Treve's ma, and the only woman in the world Jack loved.

'Ah, there's the dear of him.' Morwenna raised a chubby finger to her lips, thrust out beside the lamp she held. 'Hush now, my lover, and no fuss, see.'

She put the lamp on a barrel top, pulling the two huge jugs dangling by their handles off one forearm. Straightening, she let out a sigh and rubbed at the small of her back.

'They've finished them casks they dragged up bevore. Now they want beer vor their terrible thirsts. Then it'll be the brandy again. Tis a circle I can't see closing this side o' Sunday.' She came over and bent again, her hand pulling his thick black locks away from his eyes. 'How are 'ee then, Jack?'

'Proper,' he replied, and tried to smile.

'Ess, look proper too,' she said sadly, lifting the bound wrists, her finger lightly touching the reddened skin. With a sigh she lowered herself to the floor to sit beside him, pulling his head over so it could rest against her considerable chest. 'Can't stop long, vor they'll be missing the beer. But I brung you this.'

From a cloth bag at her waist, she pulled out a pear-shaped object. Jack, who had not eaten in a day, leaned forward excitedly. 'Figgy Hobban,' he cried.

'Was makin' a batch for the squire and his friends so I snuck one off the tray. I've orders not to feed 'ee but if you sup up every grain, so none 'ull see . . . now, I bain't able to free your poor hands—'

'I wouldn't want you to.'

'But mayhap you can feed yesself if I holds it here.' She held the delicacy in her cupped palms and Jack bent over them, biting off the pastry plug, chewing swiftly to the sweet raisins within. As he chewed, Morwenna talked.

'Oh, Jack, you'm daft as a carrot half-scraped! Why could you not have bided? They're drinking and drinking, o'man, like the drink's about to end for ever and they better get it down. And though it's all "Damn the Jacobites!" and "Health to the fair maids" now, it'll be blows bevore supper. And I fear's them's to fall on 'ee, sure enough.' As Jack had guzzled more than three-quarters of the pastry, she was able to remove one hand to stroke his head. 'I told 'ee, sure: the more you meddle with an old turd, the worse 'ee do stink. And your uncle's reeking foul now.'

Through a mouthful of dough and raisin, Jack spluttered,

6

'When Druncan's that gone, his switch arm tires fast. I'll be right.'

Morwenna hesitated, taking her lower lip between her teeth, chewing at it. Finally she said, 'Trouble be, I just heard 'un say it's time his son and heir had the correction of 'ee.'

Shite, thought Jack, and felt the first real prickle of apprehension. Craster was two years older, big for eleven and strong with it. He'd beat Jack till his arm fell off.

To counter his fear, Jack sought his ready bravado. 'Anyway, "son and heir" is a big name for such a coose downser. He may be the son but he'll be no heir. Craster Absolute's a bastard, just like me.'

Morwenna hit him lightly for the cuss words for though she swore as hard as any miner's wife, she made to curb it in the young. Then she stroked where she'd struck, continued, 'And didn't think any less of 'im than we did of 'ee. But this party is not for nought, o' man.' Her voice dropped to an excited whisper. 'There's tin found on the Absolute lands, a brave keenly lode, they say. T'will make Duncan Absolute rich.'

Above them, the noise got louder suddenly, the cries of 'Where's that damn'd ale,' coming clearly down. Then a door was opened above. Jack leaned away and spat dough and raisins behind a brandy cask, running his tongue over his lips to wipe away any trace that might betray Morwenna's kindness.

'Mind that step, Father.'

It was unmistakably his cousin's voice, that new and strange quaver in it as if it sought to settle. Its caution was ignored for a roar followed hard upon it, a sound of slipping, a series of guttural oaths.

'Here, Father, I'll help you up.'

'Leave me alone, boy. I am more than capable of aiding myself.'

These words were spoken slow and measured, the phrasing precise, in contrast to the curses. The man on the stair was mastering himself and Jack and Morwenna looked at each other in mutual horror. When Duncan Absolute was roaring he was least capable of harm. When he was drunk and attempting not to be so, he was dangerous. Jack had switch scars on his back that testified to that.

Father and son lurched there, the wavering lamplight giving their faces an equally grotesque cast. They blocked the doorway, for the Absolute blood tended to produce size and Craster had filled out in the last year, his head coming up above his father's shoulder now. But he still had a boy's face beneath his thick, red-gold hair and his features were coarser than his father's, wider at eye, thicker of lip. His mother had been a milkmaid at the Hall and Morwenna had hinted more than once that there was coercion in the coupling. She had died giving Craster life while Duncan had acknowledged the only child he'd ever produced, raising him to be Jack's plague.

In their stance at the doorway, the boy imitated the man in the stare down the prominent nose but what was inherited in the face of the son was corrupt and bloated in the father. Duncan's skin was a web of broken vessels while greying hair spilled out beneath the heavily powdered and ancient periwig, whose curls had unravelled to reveal patches of pink and flaring skin. He had a habit of rubbing the coarse horse-hair across his head, the regularity of the activity increasing the need for it.

He was doing so now, while his eyes roamed from Jack to Morwenna and around the cellar. Craster simply stared at his cousin and while Jack tried to stare back, the weakness of his position, squatting and hog-tied made him drop his gaze at last. It settled for a moment at his uncle's side and moved on swiftly and too late. For clutched there, in Duncan Absolute's right hand, was a bundle of thick and springy staves.

Jack swallowed, trying to get moisture in his mouth. They would break one stave on him in their enthusiasm. Even two would mean the punishment would be over soon enough. But there were at least five in his uncle's grasp . . . and that did not bode well for his arse.

8

'Mrs Tregonning,' Duncan continued in his formal and steady tone, 'why do you dally here, when I have guests above who thirst? You do not bring any succour to this villain, do you?'

Morwenna had stood as soon as she heard the foot on the stair and now waited with head bowed. 'No, sir,' she muttered in a small voice, 'was . . . was . . . just trying to remember which ale you required.'

'Why, the strong, of course, Mrs Tregonning. You would not have me insult my guests with small beer?'

'No, sir.'

'Then about my business, if you please.'

Morwenna curtseyed and went to fill the jugs. Craster moved into the room, stopping before Jack, taking in the bonds, the raw skin beneath them. Then he gazed past the prisoner, to the floor behind him, and stopped suddenly.

'Crumbs, Father.'

'Crumbs?' Duncan peered.

'And . . .' the boy raised a finger to his eyes, squinted, 'and a raisin.'

'A . . . *raisin*?' As Duncan spoke, chillingly calm, Morwenna froze, then bent again to her task. She'd begun the second jug.

'A raisin,' Duncan repeated. 'Seems to me that we ate raisins just now, did we not, Craster?'

'We did, Father. Figgy Hobbans. You commented that they were over-dry.'

'Ay, yes. They were. And did I not also say – nay, command – that this wretch was not to share any of our food this day?'

'You did.'

'Well,' said Duncan Absolute, his voice beginning to shake, 'it appears I have been disobeyed.'

The second jug was full and Morwenna, just replacing the spigot in the barrel, was bent over, facing away, when Duncan crossed the space between them and kicked her. His stride was unsteady and so perhaps the blow was not what it could have been but it was with the toe of the boot and Jack could see it

9

hurt. Morwenna gasped, staggered forward, head banging into the barrel, beer slopping from the jug.

'Leave her be,' Jack screamed.

Duncan turned and cuffed him with the back of his hand. 'Take that beer to my guests, you disobedient slut,' he bellowed.

As she scurried out, he aimed another kick, missed. Morwenna paused in the doorway, looked back at Jack, as if she would say something. He managed to look into her eyes, to shake his head. She nodded, turned, went. Nothing she could say would aid him now. Quite the reverse.

'And now, you whoreson . . .' It was Duncan's most used endearment, yet reserved only for Jack. 'So you would riot with the peasants of Penzance. You would bring more disgrace to the Absolute name than your father has already done since he got you on your doxy of a mother. Well, I have methods here to correct you. Five good and true methods.' He raised the switches into the air and Jack could see them clearly for the first time. They were cut from young birch, springy, hard to snap. His cousin's work. He shuddered. 'Turn him, Craster.' His uncle laid four of the sticks down on a barrel head. 'Turn him and hold him fast.'

Surprisingly, the boy did not move. 'May I remind you, Father, of your promise?'

'Promise?' Duncan growled. 'Just do as I say, boy, or I'll save a switch for 'ee.'

Craster stood still and for a moment Jack had a little hope. Duncan's temper was like any of his moods, it could change direction like a breeze off the sea. It could blow into another sail.

'But I only remind you, Father, to spare you effort. Why tire yourself and remove yourself any longer from your guests' company and the fine ale you've just ordered up?' As Duncan licked suddenly parched lips, Craster added, 'Let me do the beating.'

All hope fled in Jack, taken by the sudden smile that came to his uncle's face.

'I did promise you his chastisement, did I not, boy?'

'You did, Father.'

'And since it is a special day for the Absolutes, a day of change as well as celebration,' Duncan's voice had again become measured, 'and since you will be an Absolute in all ways soon enough, you should begin to take on some of that honourable name's responsibilities.' He hiccoughed loudly. 'To . . . to have charge of the . . . distaff side of the family.'

'It would be my honour to fulfil my duty.'

Father and son smiled at each other. Then Duncan handed the switches across, formally, as if he were passing over a symbol of his office. 'Punish him well, boy. Give him a most excellent thrashing.'

'Oh, I will, Father.'

Without another glance at Jack, Duncan left the cellar, the same step that had given him trouble on the way down catching him again. Spitting curses, he stumbled beyond reach of their ears.

The slamming of the door above still echoed as Craster turned. 'Well, cousin.' Smiling, he sat down on a barrel and, in the accent he used with everyone but his father, said, 'You'm fitchered and no mistake.'

Jack tried to think of something to say, some defiance to cast back, but his speech was stoppered by the sight of each switch being lifted, bent back, laid down in a row on the barrel head in a gradation of suppleness and strength. Jack found he was gauging each one's merits almost as keenly as his cousin.

When the fifth had been placed between numbers two and three, a choice Jack found himself disputing to himself, Craster stood, yawned and began to take off his jacket. 'I don't blame 'ee, Jack, wanting to go see the fun. They's kicking up such a dido at Penzance, they says, anyone with a uniform is in for a duckin', at the least. Teach 'em Pope's arse-kissers, eh?' Craster sighed, attaching the coat to a hook on the door, reaching for the knot of his stock. 'I'd be over to there myself, 'cepting I didn't want to miss the celebration here.' The stock was pulled from round the neck, laid over the top of the jacket. Even in the pale lamplight Jack could see the excitement in the other boy's eyes. 'You've heard? A keenly lode, they say, biggest in these Hundreds for fifty year, more. The Absolute family fortune made, tis said. Well, part of the family.' He smiled and reached for one of the switches.

'Which part?' Now his cousin looked ready, Jack needed to delay him as long as possible.

'Mine, boy.' Craster bent to bring his gaze level with Jack's. 'Don't they say, "The Devil shits luck for some but when it comes to 'ee, he's hard bound."' He dropped his voice as if confiding. 'Know what's going off up there?' He raised his eyes to the ceiling above through which the sound of a drinking song came faintly. 'The curate's there, along with a few of Father's other friends. His cloth don't make him no less drunk than t'others. Maybe it makes him more so. But he's come to share in the family good fortune for Father will get the living over to Morvah out of mortgage. He'll have to give it to someone. Someone who's done us a favour. Someone who has filled in a marriage registry form.' The voice had now dropped to a whisper, their heads so close Craster's lips were almost on Jack's ears. 'Someone who has sworn he married my poor ma and Sir Duncan Absolute before I was born.'

He straightened, swished the stick through the air with a delighted laugh. 'Sure enough, Jack, you'll be the only bastard left on Absolute lands. Till I start gettin' a few of my own, course!'

Jack winced, but not from the sight of the switch still cutting the air. The pain of a beating, however severe, would pass, its scars mend. But what gave him the little status he had was that both Absolute boys were bastards; neither could crow over the other, though Duncan was the elder and held the baronetcy of Absolute Hall, while Jack's father, James, was the younger, the wastrel soldier with a mistress and a life of sin in London.

The thought of these people – doxy mother, debauched father – whom he had seen only twice in his life, the last time so long ago – three years – that he could barely remember them, though he could recall the wren-egg green of his mother's frock, pressed to his face, the day they departed Zennor again without him. The idea of them now, leaving him as the sole bearer of shame, suddenly brought water to his eyes. He turned away, not swiftly enough.

'What's this?' Craster grabbed at Jack's shoulder, pulling him around, lowering himself to eye level. 'Cryin'? Cryin', is it? Thought I'd never see the day when Jack Absolute deigned to cry.' He pushed himself off with a hoot of laughter. 'Well, have to take 'vantage o' that.' He stepped back. 'Tell 'ee what I'll do, Jack,' he continued, that strange quaver in his voice still making it go up and down, 'seein' as good luck has come for us, I'll pass some onto you. You show us your arse and I'll beat only 'un. Break the third stick and it's over. Don't, and I'll use all five on 'ee.'

Jack looked up, gauging the offer. Three sticks wasn't a bad one; even Craster'd tire after two. But when he saw the triumph in his cousin's eyes, when he heard the echo of his own sole bastardy proclaimed, he knew he couldn't do it. He'd make no pact with the Devil. He had to beat him.

'I tell 'ee what *I'll* do, Craster Absolute. I'll fight 'ee, here and now.'

The stick paused, lowered. 'Now why should I do that, when I already have 'ee tied like a hog for the knife?'

They had known each other all their lives. They had fought, one way or another, a thousand times. With luck, and space to move in, he could outmanoeuvre the bigger boy, for he spent more time with Lutie, learning the wrassler's ways. Yet in a cramped cellar, where he'd have to stand toe to toe and punch, his bulky cousin would have the edge. And that gave Jack his little hope – for he knew that Craster knew that too.

He could see him weighing it now, and pressed home. 'I pinned 'ee last week with a·flying mare and made 'ee shout for terms. Can do it again too, even in a cellar.'

Craster's eyes flicked around, measuring the room. His

voice was not all that had altered in recent months. He was a foot taller than Jack now and many pounds heavier.

Jack waited and watched and, when his cousin took the bait, kept his smile to himself.

'Done. If you vow that when I beat 'ee, you'll tell all how I did it.' There'd been an audience for Craster's humiliation the week before, Treve and some other of the Zennor boys.

'Done.' Jack said it a little too quickly and he saw Craster hesitate as he bent to Jack's knots.

He straightened again. 'But just so you can't try any of your cheatin' ways . . .' He formed a fist, the middle knuckle sticking out and punched Jack hard in the centre of his upper right arm. As Jack twisted away, he punched him with equal force on the left. While he cried out, his cousin bent again to the knots. 'Evens, eh, Jack?' The fisherman's knots proving too testing for his impatient fingers, he drew a small knife from a sheath at his side. As the slashed bonds fell and Jack rubbed life back into his wrists, Craster ran his foot back and forth over the floor. Stepping behind the mark created, he adopted the stance of the prize fighter, left fist forward, right back, weight on his rear foot.

'Come on then, you little bastard,' he smirked. 'Toe the line.'

Jack's arms burned. The blows had been well placed and he wondered desperately if he would be able to lift them at all. For lifting them was a vital part of his plan. He needn't get them as high as Craster's; but he'd need them up all the same.

He stretched them out to the side, groaned, heard his cousin's gratified laugh. Then he began to stand slowly, making to stagger slightly to the side while he was still low down to the floor. This brought him near to the cask that held the befouled wine, close to the chipped pint pot that caught the leaks.

With movement as swift as his previous had been slow, Jack snatched the glass from the floor and dashed the contents into Craster's face.

The wine-turned-vinegar had its instant effect. Craster shrieked and spun away, heels of hands pressed into his eye sockets. As Jack ran past him, his cousin made a grab for his legs. Jack twisted from the grasp, kicked back, catching Craster on the shoulder. Another howl pursued Jack as he took the stairs two at a time.

The cellar door was a small one set into the mansion's main staircase. Accompanied by the shrieking from below, now resolutely high-pitched, Jack burst out into the entrance hall . . . and straight into the voluminous folds of a dress.

'Lawks!' yelled Morwenna, tumbling backwards, landing with a thump, Jack on top, the empty beer jugs launched from her hands. One dropped beside her, bounced, didn't break; the other skittered and slid backwards to thump and smash into the half-open door of the parlour. The force of it knocked that entranceway open and Jack, spluttering up from the skirt, looked through the gap. Half a dozen men, with red faces, yawning jaws and sagging jowls, looked back; and the reddest one there, once the glazed eyes had focused, began to bellow, 'The whidden! Young whelp bastard! Where's 'ee to? And where's my Craster?'

Behind him, Jack heard his cousin's slipping footsteps on the cellar stair, his voice alternating pain and fury. Before him, red-faced men were struggling up, Duncan throwing back his chair, using the table to rise. Jack's weakened arms did not seem able to push him out of the engulfing folds of the dress and his toes scrabbled for purchase on the polished floor.

'Jack!' hissed Morwenna. 'Kitchen.'

He turned to it. The door there was ajar and past the flames of the range, the steaming pots, the chickens on their spits, Jack saw something more enticing than the food his stomach craved. He saw freedom; for the back door of the Hall was open and beyond the yard were the fields he knew so well.

He heaved himself to his knees. His uncle, still roaring, was shoving aside a bulky man in the cloth of a cleric who squawked and fell against the table. Behind, Craster had just gained the top of the cellar stair. Pushing himself off the floor, Jack began to run, his legs weak at first, gaining strength with every step. By the time he was halfway across the kitchen's flagstones, he was flying.

The roar built behind him, a discordant sing-song of question and response, Duncan's bass harmonizing poorly with Craster's erratic alto. It faded as Jack rushed through the door and into the yard, then built again as he sprinted across its cobbles. He was vaulting over the gate when his uncle's voice came clear again.

'My hunter! Whip out my hounds!'

If Jack had discovered before that fear could weaken the legs, he learnt now that it could also do the reverse. He raced the three hundred yards up the pitted Hall lane to where it intersected with the road. To the right led to Zennor; to the left to St Ives. Houses, with places perhaps to hide, but both a fair way and if he could move fast on a roadway, horses and dogs could move faster. He could turn part back on himself and sprint for the cliffs, to the path down to his beach. But since there was just that one way onto and off it, he'd be trapped down there.

As he hesitated, the yelping of the pack, the clatter of hooves on cobbles, carried clearly. He had to decide! Ahead were fields, bisected by streams and little stands of bush, criss-crossed by walls of piled stone, all Absolute land. Even if there was a slim hope the horses would tire from the jumping, he knew the dogs would not. They would not hurt him, for he knew them all by name, but they'd lick him to death when they caught him, and hold him with their pressing bodies.

He scrambled over the first of the walls. This field was long, full four hundred paces across, sloping sharply down. He took it at speed. The stream at the bottom was swollen by the early autumn rains and he had to run up it a little way to find a point where he could leap, his foot plunging into mud on the far bank. As he drew it out, the sucking sound was topped by a shout.

'There! There's the whelp! Get 'un!'

Glancing back for the briefest of moments, he saw Craster peering over the wall. His uncle's grooms rushed to the gate, flung it open. Dog, horse and man charged through it.

The field beyond was the reverse slope of the valley and steep. Jack's breath came hard as he struggled up it but he was pushed on by the 'Halloos', the hounds giving tongue, the snort of horses. Someone had brought a bugle and played it now off-key. Craster probably, his musicianship as unsettled as his voice. The memory of his cousin from the cellar, the legacy of his dead arms, the thought of his gloating spurred Jack as he neared the summit of the hill.

I may be a bastard, he thought, but I'm a bastard that can run!

He gained the summit. At his feet three fields lay like a spread fan. One was filled by a small copse; hard for riders, yet riders could dismount and the hounds would pen him in. The second was full of after-grass, not yet gathered, swept up in drams, long piles that curled like snakes from wall to wall. About half Jack's height, he could burrow into them, remain hidden for a while. And he could see coneys hopping between the rows, sight and sniff to distract any dog. He nearly ran into one . . . until he glanced into the third and largest field to his right. This looked different from when he'd last been there and it took him a moment to realize why. When he did, he immediately began sprinting towards it.

This third field was pitted with new shafts. This was where they'd found the keenly lode of tin, which would make the family rich again. These were test shafts and they'd be deep. Horses and dogs could not go down 'em and men would little want to. Jack could, would, for he'd played down such holes all his life despite the prohibitions. He'd get in a deep one and worry about getting out of it later.

His dally had let the pursuit gain. Jack glanced back. Hounds flowed over the wall behind him and, amongst them, hunters jumped, five at least, Duncan and Craster prominent at their head. The look back cost him. He stepped into a divot, one of thousands in that chopped-up ground, tumbled, rolled, was up and sprinting in a moment. But the fall had been seen and the yelling behind him doubled in volume.

He was not going to make it! They were closing fast and the nearest mine head was still a hundred paces off. Suddenly, he jerked to a stop. The land was cleft before him, a jagged rent in the earth where someone had begun to dig, then abandoned the effort. It had been a while before as the grass had grown over it again. If he hadn't been looking he'd have plunged down. The rent only went for six feet in length and a dozen across, maybe as deep. He ran its edge, straightening to head for the shaft again. Maybe there was a chance still, maybe if he ran flat out, maybe he could beat them there. He knew it was a faint hope; but he'd not surrender until all his hope was gone. There was no mercy to be expected from his relations. He was a fox now; and Craster would be blooded.

The first dog ran by him, nipped playfully at his hand – Demelza, a favourite and fastest of bitches. The others would not be far behind. She leapt before him, blocked him, happy with the game. He could only slow, fifty yards from his hope. It was over. Then he heard different sounds. An animal shriek of terror, followed by a human one.

'Christ!' screamed Duncan Absolute, and the scream was still in the air as Jack turned to see his uncle and his mount arrive at the concealed gash in the ground. The stallion must have seen it late, its forelegs were scrabbling in the grass, gouging trails as it sought for purchase. The suddenness of its attempt to halt had shot its rider forward. Duncan's feet were out of the stirrups, his hands still clutching the reins but under his stomach now, his body halfway along the horse's neck. The animal's eyes were wide and white, its ears at the alert. They proved no obstacle to the man as he slid over them, down the long nose. His feet jerked, his hands came free, reached, found nothing but air as the animal's rear legs, scrabbling furiously, countered the slide for a brief moment,

18

while the man's momentum propelled him ever faster and finally into a fall.

Duncan Absolute tumbled screaming into the earth. One moment he was there, the next vanished. The horse he'd left, lightened in its load, looked as if it had won its fight against the drop until its rear legs slipped from under it on the mud at the hole's edge. Its rear came down hard, its front legs whipped out. With a shriek almost indistinguishable from its master's, it followed him into the pit.

The wail that came from below was swiftly cut off and replaced by the hideous screeching of an animal in agony.

Jack, frozen by the sight for those extended seconds, now reacted to the sound. He ran back, through the pack of hounds that surrounded him. The other horsemen were struggling with their mounts who were whirling, heads jerking, huge-eyed. One turned and bolted, the rider unable to halt him as he galloped straight back up the field, clearing the stone wall there in a jump. As it disappeared, another shape came over the stones. It was Lutie Tregonning, who ran down towards them, followed by half a dozen hands from the farm.

As Jack reached the lip of earth, so his cousin managed to regain control of his mount. Immediately he hurled himself off it, staggered the few yards to the hole, dropped to his knees. The two boys stared down.

Into horror. The pit was not that deep but it was narrow and there was nowhere for the stallion to move. Besides, Jack could tell in the instant that at least one of the beast's legs was broken. Above ground, a horse would go still when that happened but its situation would not let it here. Not when it was lying on a human body.

Back and forth the beast rolled, Duncan Absolute rolling beneath it.

'Father! Father!' Craster cried, his hands reaching down towards the crumpled figure. Then they went up in vain effort to block out the terrible animal screams.

Lutie Tregonning ran up, looked down, cursed, then turned

back to a horseman, one of Duncan's cronies, only now bringing his mount under control. 'Your gun. Quick, man.'

The man fumbled the pistol from his saddle holster. Checking that the pan was primed, Lutie lowered himself into the pit. 'Hoke, hoke, hoke,' he called to the stallion, as he would to cattle in the fields. But the animal was lost, in its agony, in terror. With a grimace, Lutie pulled the hammer to full cock, placed the muzzle right between the beast's eyes, fired. With a last jerk, the stallion reared up, then collapsed, its limbs twitching.

The sudden silence was somehow as awful as the noise that had preceded it. The acrid tang of powder filled Jack's nostrils while his sight was half-obscured by smoke. When he could see clearly again, he watched Lutie reach beyond the dead horse's neck to the man's. Fingers pressed there for a long moment; then he looked up at the curate and shook his head.

'The Lord have mercy,' said the man of God.

Jack found his legs would no longer hold him and he sank down like his cousin, directly opposite him on the pit's edge. Lutie's son, Treve, Jack's sometime playmate, now ran up, with several of the servants from the Hall. 'Treve,' said his father in a voice suddenly calm, 'take the boys over to that shaft. There's a small derrick there, do 'ee see it? Dismantle it and fetch it here.'

Craster, pushing himself up, nearly slipped into the pit, staggered back. 'That's right, Lutie. Father's fine. Needs a doctor, is all. Hoist that beast off 'un. He'll be fine.'

Lutie looked away, glanced back to the curate, who stepped up to the boy, dropped a hand onto his shoulder. 'I'm afraid . . . Craster . . . I'm sad to tell 'ee . . .'

'No!' Craster shrugged the hand off, stepped away, eyes wide and glaring. 'Father's alive. He's hurt, but he'll be proper when we get Thunderer off 'un.' He looked down into the pit in desperate appeal. 'Tell 'em, Lutie. Tell 'em.'

Lutie's voice was soft but clear. ' 'Ee's dead, Craster. I be sorry. But that's God's truth. Gone to a finer place, 'ee has.'

'No!' Craster's eyes were now ranging all round, settling on faces that bore it for a moment then turned away. All except one. When his cousin's gaze reached him, Jack held it.

'I'm sorry. So sorry.'

He meant it as condolence, nothing more. But Craster took it as something else.

''Ee done it,' he yelled, a quavering hand raised to point. 'Jack killed 'un.'

Lutie had heaved himself from the pit. He went to Craster now. 'No, boy. T'was accident, nothing more.'

Craster shoved aside the hand that reached out to calm. 'No! He killed my father. Led 'un to this field deliberate, led 'un to this pit to die.' The quavering voice rose to a shriek. 'Seize 'un! I'll swear a warrant and you'll be witnesses, every one.' As no one moved, he screamed, 'If Father's dead, then I'm Master of Absolute Hall and all your livings come from me. I'll turn each out of their cottage and your families can starve this winter. Seize 'un! Get a gun and hold 'un.' When no one moved still, Craster turned and ran to where the horses were held. There was a second pistol in a saddle holster there.

Lutie turned to Jack, gazing at him across the pit. 'Will 'ee come, boy?' he said softly. 'All know that such a charge won't hold. You'll only be kept awhile. And . . .' here he coloured, ''ee could be our new master.'

One of the other men, hearing Lutie's words, began to step around the pit. 'Ess, boy,' he said, 'you'll only bide a time.'

Craster had fumbled the gun out of the saddle. 'We'll hold him for the magistrate. Take him. Take him to the cellar.'

Until then, Jack had been almost too numb to think. Tired too, and scared, and wanted nothing more than to be back with Morwenna in the kitchen eating soup and curling up before the fire. And he didn't want to cause any trouble for his friends, Lutie and Treve and the rest. But as soon as his cousin named the place where they must take him, he knew he couldn't go. He'd bided in that cellar once and had just escaped a terrible thrashing. He knew that what faced him there now would be far worse.

So Jack ran. The pistol roared behind him but he did not think the shot came near. He soon crested the hill and was down the other side, out of sight. Not sound though. His cousin's strange, cracked piping came clear to him.

'You'll hang for this, Jack Absolute. By Christ, I'll see you hang!'

— TWO —

Reunion

Jack came along the track at a steady lope, thinking about Time. The Papists had won, it seemed, despite Englishmen expressing their displeasure, in flame and riot, the length of the land. Time had stood still. So though Jack had been hiding for near three weeks now, by some trick only ten days had passed on the calendar. He and Treve, his only contact, had scratched their heads a lot, especially when considering if they were now younger than they'd been. If that was true, it was not good. He needed to get older as fast as possible, for with age would come size and strength and these were requirements for the hard life promised.

Or mayhap it was the lack of food that was curbing his reason. It had been a day and a night since last he'd rendez-voused with his friend and Treve had brought what little his mother Morwenna could spare. Since then, Jack had made do with a fish he'd found washed up on the beach. That had made him sick, probably because he'd been unable to cook it properly.

Jack halted. The track plunged into a gully whose steep sides, lined in thick bramble, would be hard to scramble up. He might need to for two reasons. Firstly, the effects of that fish made frequent halts a necessity and he didn't want to be stuck with his breeches down on a track this close to Absolute

Hall. Secondly, Treve had warned that Craster was once again hunting him, after the period of restraint that had followed Duncan's funeral. Treve's dad, Lutie, and many of the others had tried to persuade his cousin that Jack was gone, had joined the fishermen in Penzance or even set out for the clay pits over Austell. But Craster was determined. A warrant had been sworn, blaming Jack for his father's death. In fact, since that day, it was said that Craster Absolute had changed, had taken on attributes of the dead man. His voice had settled deep, he cursed Jack day and night, and he had begun to drink.

Jack's bowels calmed, enough to shift his feelings to his stomach and its emptiness. He hoped that Treve lay up ahead with perhaps a pasty or another of his mother's Figgy Hobbans. The memory of that last one – three weeks, or ten days before, whichever it was – now made up his mind. He hastened down the gully.

Rounding the bend, he saw Treve there before him. But his joy in the sight died fast as he saw that his friend was not alone.

'Seize him!'

Craster's voice had indeed settled low. He sat astride his horse and pointed. Men from the farms moved in on Jack and held him. Lutie was the first and his grip was firm enough to hold but not hurt.

'Don't blame the boy, Jack,' he whispered. 'Your cousin caught him sneakin' food out. 'Ee'd have had us out our cottage if 'ee did not give you up.'

Jack nodded. At least it was over. Whatever happened now, wherever they took him, he'd have something to eat there.

His cousin dismounted slowly, handing his reins to a servant. He had a riding crop in his hands, his father's, ivory-handled, a forearm's length of leather furled tight. He bounced its looped end against his hand as he walked over to where Lutie held Jack. They watched him approach and Jack wriggled a little in the grasp.

'Well, cousin,' said Craster, 'at last!'

He lifted the crop, struck down hard with it. Jack managed

to turn his shoulder, Lutie letting him slip, but the blow still landed and it stung.

'Hold him, there,' shouted Craster, 'hold him while I give him the beating he deserves.'

Instead of obeying, though, Lutie stepped back, releasing his grip. 'Come now, Master Craster,' he said, his voice placating, 'we's catched the boy for 'ee. Baint it now the magistrate's turn?'

Craster's face mottled, purple spreading over it. 'His *turn*? I'll tell 'ee, Tregonning, there's no "turns", not while this whelp is on my land. So you'll hold him or face the consequence.'

Jack watched the conflict on both the Tregonning faces, father and son. Saw the anger harden, not soften, knew his friends were about to take a stand for him, one that could cost them the very walls they lived within. He could not allow that.

So he stepped up to his cousin, stood toe to toe and clouted him, a swift one to the stomach. It may not have been the hardest punch he'd ever given but it doubled Craster over, had him staggering back. A hand descended again as he made to pursue, Lutie's voice following. 'That'll do, Jack.'

But Craster had straightened swiftly. 'Let him go,' he screamed and at the same time leapt forward. Jack, off balance, was knocked to the ground, his cousin falling on top of him.

'Shall separate 'em, Lutie?' one of the other men said.

'No,' he replied. 'This reckonin's been a long time comin'. Let 'em be.'

The men formed into a rough circle. Jack was under still and Craster was trying to pin him, his knees moving up to hold Jack's arms while leaving his own fists free. Whipping both his legs to the side threw the boy above slightly over. Whipping them back, he tipped Craster, who was forced to remove one of his gripping hands to stop himself falling. Jack reached up then, grabbing an ear, twisting hard. With a cry, both Craster's hands came up. Jack threw his legs again, knocking Craster off.

Both boys rolled away, came onto their feet, breathing hard.

They glared at each other but a moment and then they leapt together, like stags butting, arms out, seeking a grip. Jack went high, then dropped low, to grasp Craster around the waist, lift and twist him, throw him as hard as he could upon the ground. But his cousin anticipated it, dropped low himself, wrapped his arms around Jack's shoulders. The two locked together and they spun and twisted, now one tipping down, now the other.

It could not go on that way for long. His cousin was heavier, older and even at his strongest Jack would find it hard to take him in a plain grapple. Weakened now by his hunger, he needed more than ever to break away, to gain space for the throws that required not weight but timing, which Lutie had trained him to do: the foreheap, the foretrip, the flying mare. But now he was locked in there, and no matter how much he jerked and twisted, he couldn't break his cousin's grip. The older boy had managed to link his longer arms. He'd begun to squeeze and Jack could feel less and less air getting in. It could not go on for long.

'. . . And this, my dear, is the very thing I was telling you of. It's known as "wrasslin" in these parts.'

The voice intruded, partly because it could have been heard in the next Hundred, partly because the accent was so strange coming from outside the county, beyond even the next one. Jack wondered, as Craster's grip relaxed on him, if the accent did not come from as far away as London.

He used the slight release Craster's surprise gave him, broke the grip, staggered away. His cousin did not pursue, just stood like Jack, hands on hips, breathing heavily and staring up the gully where the slope crested and two intruders were silhouetted against the sun.

The fighters, all those down below now, raised hands to shelter eyes against the glare and look at the man and the woman on horseback. The man wore a coat of palest blue, his waistcoat a contrast in vivid red, reaching to midway down the dark breeches. These were tucked into knee-length boots, gleaming black where they were not bespattered with mud, which was not in many parts. The horse also bore signs of hard riding, its chest caked brown, foam flecked.

The woman's horse was equally muddied, her crimson riding habit as spotted, especially where her legs curled around the riding horn of the side saddle and a flash of a yellow petticoat could be seen. But, unlike the man, her face was unblemished by dirt. Narrow eyebrows curved down as if pointing the way to the firm, straight nose. The eyes made the blue of the man's coat look gaudy, false. Her hair was held up under a bonnet but the ride had loosened some strands to fall across the high forehead. Staring up at her, Jack thought he had never seen anything, anyone, more beautiful in all his life. And he was discomfited to find this vision suddenly focus her attention back upon him. Those eyes widened, the crop she'd rested on her shoulder now reached out to tap her companion on his, then point at Jack. The gentleman looked and nodded.

'He has your nose, James,' she laughed, some lilt in the husky voice adding a musical run to the words.

'He has,' the man grunted. 'Fortunately for him, he is compensated for it with your eyes.' He descended, reaching up to pluck the woman from her perch. Everyone in the gully, up to that moment, had been frozen, hands raised, jaws dropped. Now, men began to move, hats slid off heads, bows were given. Taking her hand, the gentleman led the lady down, to pause before Lutie.

'Mr Tregonning, my dear. Do you remember him?'

'I do indeed. We are grateful to you for the message you sent.'

'My duty, your ladyship.'

'Duty to friendship, Lutie,' said the man, thrusting out his hand, 'and I thank 'ee. You be well?' For the first time there was something other than refinement in the gentleman's voice.

Lutie smiled took the proffered hand. 'Proper, Jamie . . . Sir James. Proper.'

The lady had moved swiftly on, stood now before Jack and

27

he knew not where to look, except down, into the mud. 'Do you not know us, Jack?' she said, softly.

It was hard. A moment before he'd been fighting flat out with his cousin. His breath was still not back. His guts were once more reminiscing on half-cooked flounder. And now the most beautiful person he'd ever seen was bending before him, regarding him with interest . . . no, with something more than interest, something he could not recognize, because he had never seen it before.

'Can you not speak, boy?' the gentleman said, somewhat sharply.

He could not. So Lutie did. 'G'awn, Jack. Say how do to your mother.'

It was too much. He knew them, these people he'd longed for all his life, had prayed for whenever he'd remembered to pray, had cursed far more often for leaving him with those he hated, who hated him back. And now they'd arrived too late. For now he was a criminal, had a warrant out for him, people to swear he'd killed his uncle. Too bloody late and their fault, this man who'd abandoned him, this woman who'd bred him to that sin.

What had Duncan always called her? What title had he always borne? He was her son and she, in her red dress with her fair face, was what they'd named her.

'I know 'ee right enough,' he shouted. 'For you're the whore what bore me.'

She flinched and her face blanched. There was a gasp from all there, even Craster who'd stared as silent and awed as any. Only one man moved. He swept down on Jack where he was standing furious and defiant, readying more words to wound as he saw he had just wounded. But the man did not give him the chance. A fist swung down from on high and sank deep into Jack's stomach.

Jack had been hit before, hit hard, by boys and men. But he had never been hit as hard as James Absolute hit him then.

He collapsed onto the ground, his breath all gone. His father leaned down and said, in a low tone meant for only him,

'Remember this, boy, and you and I will rub along well enough: you will show nothing but respect to your mother and to myself. Is that clear?'

It wasn't, not really, they were just words. Nothing was clear, for a time, while he attempted to find air, that search rendered harder by the woman, who'd gathered him up and clutched him deep into that dress, an extensive string of surprisingly crude curses aimed at the man who'd delivered the blow. His one consolation, as he stared out from the red folds, was that he wasn't the only one shedding tears. Craster Absolute had begun to cry, too.

Jack sat on the beach watching near-perfect waves sweep in; yet he made no move towards the water. He'd always loved this place in the morning, the sun barely risen, reddening the whitecaps as they foamed and formed far out, then surged closer, disappearing for a moment only to be re-made nearer the strand where he and the others could snare them, adapt their bodies to the curl, ride them to the shore. Those he observed now were as good as any he'd seen, not so large that they'd spin you over and round so you'd go under and not know which way was up until you saw the bubbles climb; but large enough so that, with the timing right, you could be folded under the lip of the surge, drive along it at an angle, before it, yet within it, too. It was a freedom he never found on land – except maybe on a fast horse.

His knees drawn up to his chest, his chin on them, staring, wanting, still he did not move. He wouldn't now, because once he began it would be the beginning of the last time and that was unbearable to consider. For when he was forced from the water, by cold and tiredness, freedom would end. He'd climb the cliff path, he'd walk back to Absolute Hall, he'd put on the new clothes they'd sent for, he'd ascend into the carriage and, with his parents, he'd ride all the way to London. And though he knew little of London, he did know it had no sea, just a stinky brown river. There'd be no waves on that.

Behind him, someone started down the path; he heard it in the slip of shale, the curse. He smiled because many had ended up on their arses on that slope. Then the smile went as he recognized the voice.

His father was coming for him. Jack found it hard to think of Sir James Absolute as such, the term having no place in his world. Other boys had fathers, Treve, even Craster. Jack was always the little bastard nephew, an error dumped in the country, the outcast. Father and this other term – Mother – were foreign ideas. And yet in the week his parents had been there they had changed his world for ever.

At least they had ended the nonsense of the warrant. It collapsed under Sir James's swift interrogation while the pretence of Craster's legitimacy had been as easily punctured. Jack had heard that his father had dragged the curate by his ear to the church where the registry was examined by a local magistrate summoned from St Ives. It was found to be recently and poorly altered and, with Duncan dead, witnesses now came forward who testified that the maid died the night of Craster's birth and was most certainly unwed.

It didn't matter much to Jack. There'd always been two bastards at Absolute Hall and there were two still. Except one was leaving. Him. And it now appeared the man who was taking him away had negotiated the cliff path, better than most unfamiliar with it, and could now be heard in the squeak of boots along the sand. Still Jack stared at the perfect waves he'd left it too late to catch. The man on the beach meant that decision was another thing beyond his power.

The boots had halted behind him. 'Did you not hear us shouting for you, boy?' came that gruff voice, flecked with its ready anger.

'Nay, sir.'

'Deaf, are you?'

'Nay, sir. The waves make hearing hard.'

He expected the man – his father, he should get used to thinking of him as such – to order him up, grab him by his scruff when he was tardy, perhaps even strike him as he had that first day but not since. So he ground himself into the sand to make it harder. Yet instead of a blow, there was an exhalation as a body dropped down beside him. Jack would not look at first, just kept staring out. As the silence continued, he glanced quickly. Sir James Absolute sat beside him, staring straight out, too.

'A fine morning,' his father said at last.

'Tis,' replied Jack.

The silence returned. A cloud of terns changed shape over the water, diving and rising as one, from fan to flask to arrow. Thus formed, they shot away, their bodies skimming the whitecaps.

'You know, tis time, boy. If we're to make Truro by nightfall, we must away.' James had picked up a line of seaweed and was engaged in pressing the rubbery balls, bursting one after another. 'Your mother and cousin are packed, the horses in the traces.'

This turned Jack. 'Craster does not come with us, do 'ee?'

'Aye. Can't leave him here, an orphan now.'

Jack, feeling the colour rush to his face, turned it angrily back to the water. They'd left *him* there! He'd waited for these people for ever and now he was going to share them as Craster had never shared Duncan? It was not fair, yet another knot in the string of unfairness that was his life.

Yet his father, as if sensing the broil within him, went on. 'But he'll not bide with us in London. He'll go to school, like you. But not with you. He's for Harrow and he'll be a boarder there. It's far from us in the town and you'll only see him on holidays, and mayhap not even then.'

This was better, but it raised another question. 'And where am I to?'

His father dropped the seaweed. 'You'll attend Westminster School, where I went.' He smiled. 'Once you learn some ABCs and suchlike. You're a powerful way behind other boys of your age.'

31

And whose wrong is that? Jack thought, anger arriving again. It was amazing how easy it came to him. Craster had had some learning from the curate. But since the cousins could never bide in the same room for long without blows, Jack was usually expelled. Such knowledge he'd gleaned came from Morwenna. Half of that was Cornish and her little English learning was little indeed.

It was as if his father was still reading his thoughts. 'Three weeks ago, before Lutie Tregonning got word to us about Duncan's . . . tragedy, we couldn't have bought you the grammar you'll study from nor the cap for your head. Not with the earnings of a half-pay officer and an actress without a season's contract. And now,' he laughed, a rich sound, as rolling as the waves, 'now we can hire a carriage to take us back to London, put two boys into school . . . and much more besides. Oh yes, much more.' He chuckled again.

Jack had wondered about that. All he'd ever heard about James was from Duncan, the elder brother accusing the younger of being a wastrel who lived with his whore.

'Is it so very rich, sir, the mine?'

'So they say. I became soldier just so I would know little of these things and care to know little more now. So long as the profits come my way. But I've made Lutie Tregonning into my cap'n and he'll see me right. He'll move into Absolute Hall, with money to do her up. There'll be gold enough for that. Tis like alchemy, boy, as rich a seam as they say this is, pure alchemy. For it turns tin into gold.'

Jack couldn't help himself. It was the question that had harried him since the moment he'd heard of the riches to be dug from the earth. 'And who will get it after you, sir? I know Craster's a bastard again so . . .?'

'Craster?' James interrupted, puzzled. 'Craster's not my son, anyway. For better or worse, and may God help us both, you are my only offspring.'

'But a bastard's a bastard and, I'm told, cannot inherit. T'was what my uncle was trying to change.'

'Aye, and I soon put a stop to that cozenry.' James's puzzlement had not left his face. 'But who says you are a bastard, boy?'

'Tis known. Tis a fact.'

'Tis?' James smiled. 'Well, I know you was there, boy, but I don't recall you taking in much except great gulps of air to deafen us with. Or you'd perhaps recall that I was there too, despite the outrage of the midwife. I was there because I'd come back from the war in Germany the very morning that you decided to kick your way into the world. I knew naught of you or your coming, so when I found out I came to the attic where your mother bided and I dragged a clergyman with me. There was he and me at your mother's head, taking the vows at a gallop between screams and there was the midwife at your mother's legs, sliding you fast into the world. Vicar'd only just pronounced us man and wife when he added the title of parents.'

This was impossible! He'd lived all his life as one thing, held this title of shame. 'So . . .'

'So you're an Absolute true, Jack, and heir to the family fortunes. If I leave you any to inherit. Which is far from a certain thing.' He winked.

Jack turned back to the sea to hide the saltwater that ran from his eyes. He didn't know if he'd been in time. Beside him, his father rose, scraping sand from his breeches and coat-tails. Jack rose too. Looking up at his father, he saw that he was staring out to the water again.

'You know, when I was about your age, boy,' he said, after a long pause, 'before I was sent off to school, Lutie Tregonning and I would come down to this beach and we'd climb atop of waves like that and ride 'em.' He looked down at Jack. 'Don't suppose you do anything like that?'

His father's voice, so refined in all the talk so far, had suddenly taken on a very Cornish tone.

'Might do,' sniffed Jack, 'now and again.'

James looked to the cliff top so Jack did too. Someone was

waving a cloth up there, summoning them. It looked like Morwenna. They turned back to the sea.

'Bollocks,' said James suddenly. 'Redruth's got inns too and changes of horses. If we only make it that far tonight, that'd be proper.'

His father was suddenly pulling at his clothes, dropping each beautifully tailored item with no ceremony to the ground.

'C'mon, boy,' he said, hopping as he tried to pull off one boot, 'bet you a gold guinea piece I ride one further than 'ee.'

'You never will, so done!' yelled Jack. His few clothes came off fast, and together and naked the Absolutes rushed into the sea. His father's cursing at the cold taught Jack several useful new words whose meaning he could only guess at. For an old man of nigh on forty, he wasn't too bad, if a little unused to the trick of catching the wave just so. A few pointers from his son and he was managing fine. Not enough to win the bet, mind.

Later, with the feeling gone from his feet and barely able to stretch out his arms, with his father waiting for him on the beach, Jack launched himself ahead of what he knew would be his last wave. He didn't begrudge it, now. Endings were beginnings, too, he reckoned and, as he steered himself down that final enfolding tunnel, he thought that even if Time had ended and they'd stolen eleven days from his young life, he still had a few of them ahead.

The Challenge

London, April 1759

The situation was as perilous as any Jack had faced. One by one, his comrades had been brought down. Any weakness was swiftly exposed, then exploited, any defence soon overcome. Jack, watching them crumble, had come tardy to the field where usually he would have led. His shoulder was still sore from a tumble he'd taken in a chase the week before. Still, he had halted the rout for a time, even regained some of the ground lost, he and Abraham Marks, the Jew able to best most of his Christian tormentors in this ancient combat. Yet finally, even he fell, not noticing that the most deadly of their enemies had positioned himself just where he could dive and catch the ball before it struck the ground. Marks's bulky figure had joined his white-clad team-mates amongst the gathering, dark-suited crowd. Word had spread of the rally and nearly all of Westminster School was now crowding the edges of Tothill Fields where Westminster and Harrow were playing their annual cricket match.

For a while, it was beyond Jack's control. He struck when he could, notching up a reasonable Hand; but his companions made only the odd run before falling. Even Theophilus Ede could add only a little. A worthy ten and he was gone, to be replaced by Nicholas Fenby. And by his own admission Fenby was no batsman, his skill in the delivery of the ball rather than its receiving.

Still, somehow the partnership held, the notches rising up the board, stationary when Fenby patted the ball away, steady when Jack faced it. He had a Hand of 47 now to Fenby's 7, and had restrained his usual tendency to batter and smash. He knew that if that was partly due to his shoulder, it was mainly because of his opponent, Harrow's best player, who'd caught Abraham so spectacularly, bowled out Ede and taken six of the other seven wickets with deliveries that had both pace and twist.

He'd been swiftly dubbed, in whispers, 'The Man' and it was an appropriate term. For if he's a Harrovian, I'm from Mesopotamia, Jack thought, scowling at the fellow. He stood a good six inches taller than most of his team-mates, as many inches more around his chest. A shadow of beard thoroughly darkened his chin and cheek. Harrow had lost this match four years in a row and they'd taken measures not to lose an unprecedented fifth. Though it was more than common in matches between counties and dukes, Jack hadn't heard of such a fellow – one paid well for his skills – being deployed by a school before. And it wasn't the thought of losing the gold they'd all inevitably wagered on the outcome that most rankled with Jack. It was about honour. Yet that same honour dictated that Westminster could not challenge this hulk's credentials.

All they could do was win. And despite how impossible that had seemed when Ede had fallen and Fenby staggered in, Westminster had steadily advanced ever closer to Harrow's total. One ball was left in the over. All Fenby had to do was hold steady, leaving Jack his end to deal with The Man.

He's good, thought Jack. But so am I.

The other Harrow bowler delivered a straight ball, a grubber and easy to pat away, which Fenby, with a nervous shuffle, duly did.

'Over,' declared the umpire.

'Score, sir?' Jack called to the scorer crouched over the wooden block, his chisel in hand. The schoolboy looked up. 'Harrow have 112, Westminster stand at 108.'

'Play up, Westminster,' came a deep voice from the edge of the field and Jack recognized it as the headmaster's, Dr Markham. He affected to despise all games, believing solely in the virtues of Virgil, Homer and the birch rod. But the annual match against Harrow was different and an unprecedented fifth victory in a row had lured even this learned man from his study. His voice, penetrating the hitherto respectful silence, broke the dam.

'Forward, Westminster.'

'Up, Harrow, up!'

To the cries now coming from all corners of the field, Jack strode up the wicket to Fenby who met him halfway. 'That's four for a draw, five to win it.'

'D . . . d . . . d'ye think you can do it in this o . . . over, Absolute?' Fenby was squinting up at him over his spectacles. His stutter always became more pronounced under pressure and the last thing Jack or Westminster needed now was for him to crack. He had done well, defended doughtily for his seven notches. But he was no batsman and Jack knew he must not let him face the bowler again.

'Aye, I think I can. You've set me up, lad.'

'Even . . .' his friend glanced nervously back, '. . . against him?'

Jack looked. The Man stood there, casually throwing the ball up in the air and catching it behind his shoulder without a look.

'Oh, I think I must, don't you?' he said with a confidence he did not quite feel. 'Just follow up smartly, eh?'

Fenby nodded, began to walk back to his stumps, passing The Man, who came forward, ostensibly directing the placement of his fielders. Jack decided to wait for him. When The Man drew level he stopped and for a moment it was as if they were quite alone. Hitherto, he had been silent as a Benedictine through all his triumphs but now, leaning in, he whispered, 'Ay's goin' to spread ye, ye bastard.'

The stretched vowels confirmed Jack's suspicions. The voice was western, but not as far in that direction as Cornwall. He undoubtedly did not attend Harrow. He probably attended upon one of his team-mates' estates.

Jack let his tone and level match the other's. But he also let the accent, the one he'd been forced to restrain at Westminster in order to survive, come again into his voice.

'You'm goin' to try, ye downser. And you'm goin' to fail.'

The Man's eyes narrowed, puzzled for a moment, then the scowl returned. He grunted and walked back to position. Jack waited until he turned, until he had the man's gaze again. Then he deliberately went to his crease and put his legs square before the stumps. They would protect his wicket; but such protection came at a price. He would not be out if the ball struck his leg. But if the ball struck his leg with the force that this man could bowl, it would hurt.

It was a challenge and it was taken up, the underarm chuck making the hard leather come fast and straight. Jack's bat defence was mistimed and the ball thumped into his shin.

Probably the only two people who did not groan at the crack it made were the bowler and Jack. He walked away, restraining both limp and yelp. And when he took up position again, he called down the wicket. 'The midges are out early this year.'

The next ball came, if anything, even harder, just as straight. Again it missed Jack's bat, to crack again into the shin, almost in the same place. Jack made sure his voice had shed his agony before he looked up and smiled. 'No, seems I was mistaken. They've passed away.'

'Less talk, young man, if you please,' the umpire growled.

They had disdained the fashion for playing six in an over, had stayed with the legal four. So he had two balls to face, two to finish it. Yet the next one went wide, too tempting to flay at it and yield up a catch. He left it. Jack looked at the bowler again and wondered if his provocations had worked. The Man had, after all, been chucking them down all afternoon and, with these three fast deliveries, he was tiring. The ball would come fast again but perhaps not as fast, straight . . . but maybe not quite so straight.

To encourage him, Jack stepped deliberately one pace to the side. Once more the twin stumps, their bail perched atop them, were temptingly exposed. The challenge was given.

Taken. Unfurling those heavy shoulders, The Man let the ball fly, and Jack was wrong both about the speed and its accuracy. It pitched once, short, which Jack wanted, but it came on perfectly hard, perfectly straight, which he didn't. It demanded safety, a patting away, a wait for something less deadly. And Jack couldn't wait, wouldn't let Fenby face the bowler again. He needed five runs, five times his battered legs must carry him up and down that wicket. And the short outfield where the spectators encroached was usually only worth the four. Yet Jack had played this field for years, knew all its little secrets – unlike the bowler. There was one place where the ground dipped and ran into a clump of scrub bush, a place where fives could sometimes be found. It was off Jack's right shoulder, forty-five degrees behind him. So now, as the ball came straight, hard but short, he angled his bat toward that place. A miss and he was out, and he and Westminster had lost.

The ball hit the tilted bat with all the ferocity The Man had put into it and took off, Harrovians in pursuit. Jack didn't even look. 'Run,' he roared, and Fenby, backing up well, passed him before mid-wicket. His legs felt stiff but as he turned at the opposite crease, the sight at the field's perimeter gave him impetus. The ball was disappearing into the shrubbery, two white-clad boys in close pursuit.

'Again,' he cried, striding to meet and pass his partner. The crowd was hallooing both chaser and chased. 'Two!' came the universal cry. All knew what was required.

'And again,' Jack yelled above the tumult, making his third run. Turning, he saw the boys still rooting frantically, others rushing to their aid. So they took the penultimate run required, leaving just the one more to win. But at the very moment that his bat touched down in the crease, even as his breath came in gasps and his legs became as stiff as the stumps before them, even as he was turning to go for that last wild sprint, a boy emerged from the bush, ball in hand.

He could stop, let his team-mate face another over. That was the safe and sensible thing to do. The scores were level now so even if Fenby got out, as was most likely, the match was a draw.

'Again,' Jack bellowed instead and, as the Harrovian bent to throw, Jack began to run.

With ten paces to go, Jack sensed, rather than saw, the ball above his head, sensed it in the tensing of the receiving fielder, none other than The Man who'd sprinted down, anticipating this final play, shoving aside the boy whose job it should have been. His eyes were up, he took a step back as Jack closed the distance to five yards. A leap, a hand shot high, one moment a bare palm, the next it filled with dark leather. Three yards and Jack began to dive, but stretched ahead of him as his arm had stretched ahead to take a wave in Cornwall. No watery softness to cushion him here, just hard ground from a dry spring. His eyes were on that ball as The Man brought it from on high, flashed down. As the tip of the willow bat reached the crease, the bail was struck from the stumps.

'Out! Out, by God!' cried all of Harrow.

'In! In, by God, and safe!' rejoined Westminster.

And all there looked at the umpire, crouched low and intent a few yards away. He was a neutral, an usher brought in from St Paul's School due to some rather unfortunate rioting at a close and disputedly biased decision a few years previously. In a sudden silence that seemed eternal, under the prone Jack's desperate appeal, beneath the threatening, outstretched hand of The Man, the umpire slowly straightened.

'In and safe,' he said, briskly. 'That's stumps, gentlemen. Victory to Westminster.'

Jack lay where he had fallen. It was only when he was lifted from the ground and hoisted onto the shoulders of his team-mates and their supporters that he looked once more at his opponent. The Man was standing, still holding the ball against his muscled chest. And as he saw Jack looking he did some-thing else that confirmed he was no Harrovian. He spat on the ball, threw it high into the air and, without watching where it fell, walked away.

The Inauguration of the Mohocks began late due to the necessities of triumph. Though Jack refused at least every second bumper during his processional through a gauntlet of back-slapping hands, he still discovered the stairs, when he finally reached them a good hour after stumps, harder to negotiate than normal. He climbed them now to a room that Matthews, the proprietor of the Five Chimneys on the edge of Tothill Fields, had set aside specially for them. He was fond of Jack, even fonder of the way money seemed to follow him, and this had been another epic day for the landlord's coffers. In gratitude, he had even provided a stableman to hold the door against over-enthusiastic attention. Nodding to the burly ex-seaman, Jack pushed into the room.

His three friends were bent over dice. Abraham Marks was on 'spot', shaking the dice in his huge hands, muttering prayers, leaning over the table, dwarfing the others, especially the small, neat Nicholas Fenby who stared up through thick lenses, provoking the big man with insults and doubt. Between them, a tankard raised, was the Honourable Theophilus Ede, as slim as Marks was broad, as pale as Jack was dark.

Unnoticed, he took pleasure in watching them for a moment. The Jew, the Scholar and the Nobleman – with Jack something of a mix of them all. An outcast like Marks when he'd arrived at Westminster six years before with his broad Cornish vowels; studious like Fenby when he chose to be; a baronet's son if not a duke's. They'd all been singled out from the beginning, persecuted for their various differences, and had discovered, equally early, that strength lay in unity. If one was bullied, the bully would find himself isolated against the four some dark night in Dean's Yard. If a monitor was over-enthused with his tanning rod, something queer would often befall him playing football on Tothill Fields. Even the ushers were known to withhold punishment ever since one of their number had taken a January tumble into the Thames. They had been known as 'The Froth' in the Under Petty, 'Roaring Boys' in the Upper. But now they were in the Upper First they'd decided they needed a new name. Hence their gathering there that night. They were to become, they had decided, Mohocks.

As Marks threw and lost, as Fenby yelped in triumph and Ede snatched up the dice for his turn, Jack stepped forward. 'Ah-ha-ah-ha-HA-HA-HA!' he cried.

'Ah-ha-ah-ha-HA-HA-HA!' the cry was returned.

He was especially pleased with this battle cry. He'd got it from an old soldier in Derry's Cyder House one night, a veteran of the wars in Canada who had himself learnt it at the campfires of those savages who fought for the British against the French. It had a plunging, up-and-down cadence and an expectoral punctuation that was hard to master; but under the stimulus of many a tankard of arrack punch, the former sergeant of Foot was happy to coach Jack in his rendition. Mastered, he then taught it to his friends and though none attained his level of terror, they were bloodcurdling enough. They'd then decided it was far too fine a thing to share beyond their circle and the only possible recourse was to form an esoteric club around the whoop. With further research by Fenby, the scholar, and tales from Jack, who'd acquired a tattered manuscript entitled *Slave to the Iroquois: a Tale of Rapine, Lust and Murther* by *One who Experienced all Three*, the friends soon had the information necessary for a proper constitution. Jack was named chairman or, in this case, war chief. All that was to left was to settle on suitable initiation rites. Ideas had been mooted, set down on parchment. This meeting would finalize their choices.

With the cry still in the air, Jack closed the door on the stableman's startled face. 'So I ask you, lads,' he said, smiling, 'why are we gathered here?'

The response was immediate: 'Who has not heard the Scourers' midnight fame? Who has not trembled at the Mohocks' name?'

Tankards were slammed down in unison, beer froth foaming onto a table surface already awash, then raised and drained. The aspirant Mohocks – this tribe having been selected from the Six Nations of the Iroquois as the most vicious – had decreed a fast for the night, despite the victory celebrations: 'No injurious spirits to be imbibed.' It seemed appropriate to the holiness of what they were about to undertake. Brandy and punch were thus excluded. Beer, and especially the Five Chimneys Fine Porter, was, of course, another matter.

While Jack poured another round from the jugs and Ede carried on singing the rest of John Gay's verse in his fine tenor, Fenby went to fetch a large sheet of parchment from a satchel. It had been carefully burnt around the edges, to give it an ancient touch, a feeling added to by the Scholar's laborious copperplate. Pushing his thick glasses onto the crown of his nose, Fenby said, 'Shall I re . . . re . . . read it, Absolute?'

Excitement or fear made his stutter worse but he was always game to struggle against the affliction. Jack thought he would spare him – and them.

'But, fellow,' he said, kicking a leg of Marks's chair, who'd leaned back and now shot forward, 'our friend here will be asleep if we do not give him something to do. Besides, those of the House of Mordecai chant as a natural part of their religion. Why not let him recite our new creed?'

'And what do you know of my religion, Absolute, you who have none of your own?'

Marks's face creased into what passed as a smile, indicated by his huge eyebrows meeting fiercely. 'Give it here, then.'

'A moment.' The chair on which Ede had been leaning back

so precariously now came crashing down onto its two remaining legs and the Honourable reached across the table for his tankard. 'I should be the one to read it. I am he, remember, who played Quontinius in the Latin Play, a role you all coveted and failed to secure. Only I can give our principles their proper . . . gravitas.'

'Gravit . . . arse,' said Marks, rising belligerently, Fenby an irate shadow at his side.

Jack sighed. They were destined for debate, which, given their natures, could be interminable. Then he noticed something that would end all argument.

'Manus Sinistra,' he said, pointing, delighting in the horror on Ede's face as he looked at the full tankard in his right hand. Rules of Honour declared that, on cricket days, one could only drink with one's left. Harder and harder to remember as the pints slipped down.

'Drink,' came the universal cry, and Ede, with a careless shrug, duly did. Jack almost felt sorry for him. He was as slight as Abe was solid, as tall as Fenby was short, and so fair that Jack's darkness made him seem as if he was made of air. They could almost see the black liquid slipping down that white throat as if it filled a translucent vessel. As he drank, the table was thumped. It took twelve knocks, six more than was usual with the Honourable. At last, he laid the vessel carefully down and settled back into his chair.

'Apologies, apologies,' he said, and belched. Then he joined in the thumping of pewter tankards upon the table again as Marks, unchallenged now, stood, raised the parchment before him and declaimed, ' "Let it be known—" '

It was as far as he got. It had taken till then for them to realize that theirs was not the only percussion in the room. As they quietened for the words, they noticed that the door of their chamber was being kicked, irregularly and hard.

As Jack stepped towards it, it flew open. On the other side, the burly stableman who had kept guard was lying on the ground. One man was on his chest, another pinioned his arms while his legs, free, still kicked out. A blow from these had opened the door, though it looked like the force of each kick was weakening. This was probably due to the efforts of the third man who bent over the doorman with two hands round his neck.

Suddenly aware that he had an audience, this third man straightened, turned. Smiled. 'D'ye know, this fellow had the cheek to tell us you were not to be disturbed. So we felt we had to reprimand him. Can't let someone of his station sunder us, can we, dear cousin?'

'Hallo, Craster,' Jack said, and swallowed.

He hadn't seen his cousin in six months and then only briefly and glimpsed across a packed and baying tavern from which Jack had slipped quietly away. He had contrived to see him as infrequently as possible and, since they boarded at different schools – Craster at Harrow – he had largely succeeded. There were a few family events when there could be no avoidance, the last a year ago at his mother's birthday. Now, with this uninvited chance to study him, Jack could see that Craster had changed. He was just gone eighteen and if he was always big, he had grown huge, his chest thrusting out of a lime-green, brocaded waistcoat whose buttons had been much altered in a losing struggle to contain it. Thick, red-gold whiskers corkscrewed along his broad cheeks, matching the heavy curls that burst from under his tricorn hat. If he lacked the Absolute hair colour – Jack and his father were hell-black, as had been Duncan – he had the family nose, as prominent as Jack's, yet streaked and mottled as Jack's was clear. Indeed, the skin of the face was everywhere puckered; the inoculation had not helped Craster avoid the smallpox, unlike his cousin. His lips were fleshy and full, his eyes, set too close together, porcine and mean.

Craster's cronies rose from their task and their victim pulled himself up to wheeze against the doorframe. Jack pushed his chair back, gave himself what space he could. Behind him his friends did the same. They had heard tales of Jack's cousin.

'Shall we send this dog for some more of their watered-down ale, cousin, and toast the Absolute name?' Craster had taken one step into the room, immediately making it seem too small. 'After all, you added to its lustre today with your fine Hand. Well done, old fellow.'

The congratulations came from such a constricted throat it told Jack something. 'You didn't make the mistake of backing your school against your family, did you, Craster?'

The other grunted. 'I may have risked a little gold, aye.'

'How little?'

'Enough.' The voice lost any pretence to civility. 'I thought the odds were against you, to be sure. We seemed too strong.'

There was something shifting in the eyes, something behind the words. 'You didn't take any measures to affect those odds, did you?'

'What do you mean, sir?'

'I mean, sir,' said Jack, 'the inclusion in a school team of someone who is not a pupil?'

'Don't know what you are talking of,' Craster muttered, turning away. But any further blushes were spared him by the recovery of the doorman who lurched up, gave his assailants a baleful look and staggered down the stairs. He seemed to be trying to summon help, noises emerging from his chafed throat.

'I think you may wish to consider leaving and swiftly. Matthews doesn't care for his men to be assaulted. He don't tolerate it from a Westminster, we are forever banned from the Tavern. From a Harrovian he may take stronger measures.'

Craster stepped closer to the table, lowering his voice. 'Then I will be brief, sir,' he said. 'You would not deny Harrow a chance to get even, would you?'

Jack frowned. 'I think another cricket match might take a little arranging.'

'I do not speak of cricket,' his cousin interrupted briskly, 'but of another game in which you are also reputed to excel. Billiards.'

'I am indeed . . . fond of the game.' Behind him, Fenby sniggered. Jack had been Westminster's champion for two years now.

'As am I.' Craster's eyes gleamed. 'Care to take me on?'

Jack hesitated. He'd heard, because his mother had complained about it, that his cousin was spending much time in the company of rogues of the baize, men who could fleece an unsuspecting fellow of the shoes he stood up in. And Craster's clothes, now Jack examined them closer, were finely tailored indeed, quite beyond the purse of one on the sixty guineas per annum Jack knew his father allowed Craster. Perhaps he was supplementing his living another way.

Craster butted into the silence. 'Frightened?'

It was Jack's turn to colour. 'Of you, boy, never.'

His cousin's cronies hooted at that. Craster said, 'Well then, the day after tomorrow, the Angel. Noon.'

There was no hesitation now. 'Agreed.'

'And a little wager perhaps?'

'Of course. How little?'

Craster grinned. 'Oh, say . . . one hundred guineas.'

Ede whistled, the sound cut off by Marks's elbow. It was a lot of money, far more than either schoolboy would have. But no doubt, as in the cricket, each school would back their side.

'Done,' said Jack.

The triumph was clear in Craster's eyes as he reached out a hand and they shook with no squeezing for dominance, just a quick agreeing shake. They would have competition enough and shortly.

From below came the sounds of boots on the stairs, the muttering of angered men. Craster glanced back casually, then down onto the table. 'What's this?' he said, spinning the Mohock Charter around. Ede stepped forward to seize it but Jack waved him back. He let Craster read.

'Revival of the Mohocks, eh? I have heard of that crew. Do you think you have the spunk, you four?' He said it with a contempt that indicated his beliefs.

'We shall see,' Jack said evenly.

'And the rout planned for tomorrow night, eh?' He smiled. 'Well, do get to bed at a reasonable hour, dear cousin. For you will need all your faculties the day after next.'

Five workers of the Inn had appeared on the stairs now. They were carrying cudgels and headed by the irate doorman and the landlord, Matthews. The latter called out, 'Mr Absolute, these curs have abused my man. If you have no objection, sir, we'd like to teach 'em some manners.'

It was tempting to step back and let justice have its way. And for a moment Jack enjoyed the unease that came to his cousin's face and those of his fellows. But blood was blood in the end. And his father would not forgive him if he heard that he'd not stood up for an Absolute.

'I would take it as a special favour to myself, Mr Matthews, if you would accept their apologies this one time. And perhaps a guinea to let liquid soothe your man's injured throat?'

The seaman's anger relented somewhat at the suggestion. Craster's seemed to increase but he recognized he had no choice. Not with five before him and Jack at his back.

'I'll get it back on Wednesday, never fear,' he muttered, before turning to the men blocking the door and handing over the coin. 'And now, if you wouldn't mind . . .'

The three were jostled a little as they made their way down but were allowed through. His men scurried on but at the bottom of the stair Craster paused and called back, 'A good turn deserves a reply, cousin. I was at my dear uncle's house this noontime, paying birthday respects to my aunt. They said they were seeing you at suppertime but, sure, they must have mistaken the day . . . for do they not dine at six? And is it now not half past that hour?'

With a final smirk, he was gone. Jack flushed. He didn't know how it happened but he was always incorrigibly late. As the landlord and his men passed down the stairs, Jack seized coat, hat and stick. 'Zounds. Bloody damnation and hell,' he cursed, 'I must be away.'

'But, Absolute,' Fenby had snatched up the parchment, 'do we not have to settle on the Initiation Rites?'

'You three do it. I'll agree to all you devise and see you tomorrow. Five o'clock at the Old Hummum Hotel.' He was at the door when he turned back. 'Marks, you'll raise the stake, yes?'

'I will.' Marks's skill at dicing and an eye for winners in the cockpits meant he had a syndicate of Westminsters who would back him. A hundred guineas was a large sum. But once it was known that school honour was at stake . . .

Jack took the stairs three at a time. Behind him, the Mohocks' war cry rang out again but this time he did not join in. For now he had to reckon with something far more savage than a savage. He had to deal with Sir James Absolute.

— FOUR —

A Quiet Supper

Jack ran. His legs, sore from his exertions at the crease, were
wobbly at the start and combined with a stomach – and brain
– still awash with the Five Chimneys' Fine Porter, to make the
placing of his feet on the slick cobbles of Horse Ferry Street
rather tricky. There were crowds outside the Cockpits in James
Street, his constant dodging and weaving accompanied by the
shrieks of birds in battle, so he did not really get into his stride
till he was past Buckingham House and onto the grass of
Green Park. He had, of course, been strictly forbidden to go
there at night for darkness transformed it from a fashionable
strollers' promenade into an arena for other forms of exercise.
Indeed, it seemed to Jack that every second bush was being
shaken vigorously, giving forth groans, giggles and the occasional curse or scream. The worst part of the Park was on the
edge of Piccadilly, where the two-penny bunters could dispatch clients in one moment and be back on their pitch a
moment later. But it was the most direct route home and
although he was still several streets away, he imagined he could
hear his father's roar.

Down Street took him up. There was a cut through Collins
Court, a fence to jump that brought him out onto Brick Street
and the gardens. Though these were diminishing in size,
swallowed by the houses and white stone mansions of an

ever-expanding Mayfair, there were still a few hold-out tenants who grew vegetables to sell and kept their animals. Jack had often used this back way into the house and it was his only hope now. Hoisting himself over the fence, he failed to shush the sheep that scattered from his path. Someone shouted from an open doorway but he did not pause. A wall was vaulted and he was in the back garden of Absolute House. Light came from the scullery and he made for it. More light came from the room above, the glister of a hundred candles. The birthday celebration was underway.

The Absolute cook, Nancy, was bent humming over a steaming kettle and did not notice him. He warily ascended the stairs, gained the ground floor and the steady rumbling that had accompanied him since he'd made the garden grew clear.

'Misbegotten . . . kiss-my-arse . . . wastrel . . . jackanapes,' were just some of the milder epithets that nicely covered Jack's climb up the somewhat creaky main stairs. Once in his room, it was a matter of moments to strip off his cricket clothes and pull on a fresh lawn shirt, his emerald waistcoat, mauve coat, green breeches. With a quickly-tied blue stock, a glimpse in the mirror told him he was both fashionable and presentable. The only problem was that someone appeared to have removed all his shoes. So slipping back into the ones he'd arrived in, he descended.

The roaring had subsided, replaced by a vigorous slurping. Nancy exited as he arrived at the door, gasping at his sudden appearance, then giving him a warning look. But since there was nothing to be gained from timidity he took a deep breath and marched into the room.

'Mama,' he cried, heading straight for her, 'congratulations on your birthday!'

Lady Jane Absolute, née Fitzsimmons, rose from her chair, her face summoning up the complexity of emotions that had made her such a sought-after actress in the days before she became a Lady. There was delight within the eyes, a spark raised by the recognition of her only child. A mother's love showed in the lips, which looked as if they would frame words of thanks and welcome . . . were it not for the anger spreading like flame from two spots on the cheeks to the high forehead, in a red almost as deep as the framing curls. Yet if there was a storm within the beauty, it was as nothing to the tempest that erupted at the other end of the table.

'You dog!' Sir James yelled. 'Where have you been?'

'Upstairs, Father.'

It was not the answer expected, the word swallowed and sticking in the older man's throat. 'Up . . . stairs,' he gurgled.

'Aye, sir. Composing an ode on Mother's birthday. I heard you call, of course. But Mama always tells me that when the Muse descends, one must listen and never turn away from her, howsoever pressing the summons. And I believe I have been visited this night. Oh, let me recite it, pray. It begins, "In fairest lands, the fairest do display—"'

It was as far as he got, further than he expected and he was thankful for the interruption. Extemporizing was not his strength.

'Ode!' His father's already florid face had grown purple with the effort of expelling the monosyllable. However it was the sole impediment to the flow that followed. Sir James's language had been bred in the country and expanded in the barracks. It included oaths in all the languages he spoke, for he had served in three other countries' armies as well as his own. His periwig slipping further and further back over his greying stubble, his words drew him from his seat the better to level his volleys at Jack. He seemed as wide as the table end, his powder-blue coat spreading around him like the tail feathers of an enraged peacock.

Helpless before the storm, Jack looked to his mother for succour. The anger was still there in her colouring yet had been displaced by something else in the eyes, something that disturbed Jack even more. He could withstand the fusillades from Sir James, so long as they were confined to words and not actions – he may have grown taller than his father in the last year, but he had not one half his strength – but what he found harder to take was what he saw in his mother's eyes. Disappointment. He had hurt her, she whom he loved more than any in the world.

So he stood silent, head bowed. And when the storm abated while Sir James took a deep drink of punch and drew breath to continue the assault, he spoke.

'I am so sorry, Father. And Mama, a thousand apologies for this rudeness. It was only my regard for you that delayed me, determined to get my poem right. If I may be permitted to continue with it to show that my lateness has not been all waste?'

He calculated on his father's wrath – and hunger. Sir James was not a man who brooked delay once sat at supper, and his idea of poetry was his hunter clearing a hedge. At a pinch, Jack could produce a recently conned love poem from Ovid – a schoolfellow had bought some of the more scurrilous verse from a 'print' shop in St Giles. He thought he could adapt it and they might not know it. Not always certain with his mother who was fiercely well read. But he had calculated his father's reaction perfectly.

'Damn your poem, sir!' he shouted.

'Sit, Jack,' his mother softly said. 'We can discuss poetry later, methinks, when the soup does not grow cold.'

There was always something in her voice, as if all the words she spoke were taken straight from a ballad. The music came from the Irish lilt that yet lingered, the delivery on a breath that had carried whispers to the furthest gallery in the largest theatre in the realm. Sir James had confessed one night, when mellowed by a fourth bumper of claret, that it was the voice that first entranced him. 'Could lure a fleet to the rocks and the sailors would drown content,' he'd declared.

It contented now. With a subsiding growl, he sank back into his seat and reached for his spoon. Jack, under cover of the renewed slurping, took his seat, set, he noticed thankfully, closer to the female end of the table.

Silence accompanied the turtle and punch. A few words of a strained and general nature were exchanged over the soused eels and Rhenish. His mother spoke of the latest play she'd penned, a one-act farce containing a veiled attack on the government she hoped would slip by the Chamberlain, while they cleaned the bones from the Pigeons Fricando and sipped at a Calcevella. Jack merely picked at the Attlets of Fat Liver – he was not overfond of oysters – but the accompanying Porter was as good as at the Five Chimneys and led Jack, by association, to describe, in some detail, the cricketing victory and his part in it, remembering to say that the game was played the day before to maintain his 'ode' alibi. This finally drew Sir James out of his grouch, for he had been a Westminster too and a keen batsman, before a never-explained incident had led to him leaving school for the army at the age of fourteen. By the time the Veal in a Sharp Sauce had been washed down with an excellent Claret and even more so after the Duke of Cumberland's pudding had been flamed, consumed and enlivened with a Lunel, the conversation had become general and boisterous. His mother's hair had slipped down in places and she leant with her elbows on the table; Sir James had thrown off his coat and three times Nance had had to put it on the chair back as she brought the next dish in. At that third time, she was encouraged to sit and take a glass of port as reward for the splendour of her feast. Jack observed again how there were few airs around the Absolute table. His father had spent more than half his life in barracks before his valour on the field at Dettingen had earned him a battlefield knighthood from King George and the death of his brother Duncan had given him the baronetcy. Whilst Jane had risen from the streets of Dublin on the strengths of beauty, the singing voice of a goddess and an instinct that told her the traditional way of acting – the rolling, roaring declamation of the old Stagers – was a thing of the past. A talent that James Quinn had recognized when he brought her from Dublin to Drury Lane.

This was when he loved his parents best, away from the public gaze, unafraid of being themselves. Yet even as he watched them laugh and flirt – they had a highly embarrassing way of appearing still to deeply desire each other – he was aware that the fun was transitory. It could not last. There would be a return to business, there always was since he boarded at school and saw his parents but rarely. Recently they had never failed to discuss the subject he most dreaded – his future.

It was the brandy that did for him, as brandy usually did. It followed the final course, sorbets conjured from the ice house beneath the cellar. It was a luxury, a treat for a birthday, for the Indies lemons, together with the smuggled French brandy, may have cost as much as the rest of the English-supplied meal altogether. Both made Sir James think about money. And money made him think about Jack's future.

'So, boy,' he said, beginning his campaign as he licked the last of the lemon ice from the bowl and reached for his bumper, 'have you thought more on our last discussion?'

'Discussion' was an odd word for the diatribe loudly delivered a month before to the effect that Jack's allowance and the fees at Westminster were bleeding the Absolute coffers near dry and that, now he'd turned sixteen, he should be out and earning his own living in the world.

'And what discussion was that, James?' His mother had placed her own glass down as her husband's rose. She spoke mildly, her elbows coming off the table to settle at her side. Her husband recognized the war-like stance.

'The boy expressed an interest in the army, is all,' he muttered.

It was a palpable untruth as all there knew. Jack cleared his throat to begin his defence. But his mother was quicker. 'The army? That is the first I have heard of it.' Another lie but she didn't leave a pause. 'Yet I thought all this was settled, James, dearest? We agreed, didn't we? He is to make use of the brains that God has given him.'

She was using her voice to manage him, and a memory that was selective at best, but brandy always rendered him unmanageable. '*Brains* my arse!' he said, his voice rising. 'Too many brains never did a man any good. Look at me. Never had a use for 'em in my life!'

'You are being disingenuous, sir,' she replied.

Before she could continue, Sir James guffawed, 'I'll tell you what use brains are, shall I? For I've seen enough of them spilled on the battlefields of the world to know whereof I speak!'

He glared at them triumphantly. Jack and his mother exchanged a look of mutual incomprehension. After a long pause, Jane ventured, 'Your . . . point, my love?'

'My point? Ah yes, my point.' He leaned forward, a finger thrust at his son. 'My point is easily made.' He stabbed with his digit on all the main words. '*Brains* are of little *use* when you are *wiping* them off your *sleeve*. Eh? *Eh*?'

Since this was directed straight at him, Jack could not just ignore it. 'I am still not quite clear, sir, what—'

His father breathed deep, drew himself up. 'Ye Gods! Am I speaking Hindi? It's obvious, isn't it! Life's a fragile thing, gone in a moment. Certainly its sudden absence takes many by surprise. So you seize the opportunities life presents to live before you die. There is no better place to do that than in the army. Now,' he leaned back, chin raised and pointing at them like a gun barrel, 'I have been speaking to an old colleague who is raising a regiment for Canada. It will cost me, of course, but to get my only son on the ladder . . .' he smiled, waved a hand, '. . . least I can do.'

'I am still not quite clear, husband.' Jane's voice was frighteningly calm. 'Let me see if I have it. In order to utilize our son's brains, you would send them where there is the best chance . . . of a savage stoving them in?'

Sir James flinched but did not withdraw. '*Stove* my arse! Our country fights a war against our oldest foe, madam. The Absolutes have always fought, I and my father before me, in a line back to . . . for ever. My father died at eighty and I do not doubt that I will live just as long to plague you both. We are thus talking, madam, of duty.'

'Well, I have no illustrious ancestors to conjure from my past, to be sure,' said his wife, her voice returning to Dublin. 'I have only myself and what I have done with my life. Those experiences have taught me that one's highest duty is to oneself. A man need no longer lurk in the barbarous shadows with the herd. Man has taken his rightful place, solitary in the sunlight.'

'And woman too, Mama,' Jack added, knowing his mother's inclinations.

'Of course. I was speaking generically.'

'*Generica . . . lize* my arse!' James bellowed, turning puce with the effort of adding the unknown word to his favourite curse. 'You and your . . . *philosophies*, madam. They've over-ruled your reason and they are castrating our son. What duty would you have him perform, eh? That of an Unitarian minister dispensing tea and witticisms in the country? A coffee-house dandy in the town?'

'I would have him be true to the gifts that God has given him. There are better ways to serve your country than having your brains extruded for it. Nay! Jack, as he and I have discussed, will compete for the Election to Trinity College, Cambridge.'

Sir James was having a little difficulty breathing. He pulled at his stock. 'Cambridge. And pray, madam, what will he do there?'

'Study the Classics, of course, Latin and—'

'Latin? Latin? He needs one word only of that. One word, along with its declination.' Sir James now rose and began thumping the table like a war drum. ' "Bellum, Bellum, Bellum, Belli, Bello, Bello. War! O war! A war! Of a war! To a war! By, with or from a war!" ' He beamed, triumphant. 'That, madam, will suffice for his Latin while the only other language he needs is French. To read the great military texts in that tongue. To converse with his prisoners.' He turned to Jack. 'You are still religious in your attendance at your French classes, are you not, boy?'

'Oh yes, Father.' Since they did not bother with such fripperies as living languages at Westminster, they had to be sought outside. Sir James had arranged for Jack to attend a French jeweller in Soho, as well as fencing and riding lessons, to complete a more martial education. These latter he under-took enthusiastically enough, but French was his passion, his attendance 'religious' for reasons his father must not know, for they had little to do with the Frenchman and all to do with his daughter. As he thought of the divine Clothilde, his heart gave a leap. But his mother's next words brought it swiftly to earth again.

Lady Jane had used her husband's draining of a glass to interpose. 'What he studies is immaterial. It is whom he studies with, do you not see? At Trinity, he will mingle with the future great of our land. He will then use these connections to get elected to the House, to join like-minded radicals in Parliament, to actually bring the philosophies you deride to our benighted land.' Jack sighed. His mother came from a family of rebels and espoused the rebel cause in all things, and she had aligned herself with a group forming around a ranter named John Wilkes to the continual disgust of her husband, a Tory of the old school. Her writings and satires supported that cause.

Sir James, meantime, reacted to more than the politics. 'The House?' he began to stutter in his horror. 'Do . . . do . . . do you have any idea, woman, how much that would *cost*?' he finished in a roar.

The heat of this old battle was building between them, both now standing at their chairs and Jack may as well not be there; indeed, he could probably slide from the room now and neither would notice. But victory to either side might lead to consequences that he would only have to deal with later. For he had a very clear idea of what he wanted in life. And it had nothing to do with either war or politics.

'Actually, parents both, I know myself the course I would pursue.'

They turned. Under their fierce attention Jack wilted slightly. But this was his life they were deciding upon, after all; so taking a breath he stated his desire: 'I wish to be a poet.'

The silence that greeted this statement was profound, intense and twice as terrifying as the tumult.

'Um . . . with perhaps, some . . . uh, dramatic works thrown in?'

This last was aimed at his mother. Still they stared, held in their previous attitudes of combat. The words had lodged in his father's throat as effectively as a pigeon bone. So it was his mother who spoke first, subsiding into her chair. 'Jack, dearest,' she said, not unkindly, 'as I am sure you have observed in my life and from my associates, no one makes a living from the playhouse.'

Aware of the storm about to burst upon him from the other end of the table, Jack rushed to secure an ally. 'But this is why I shall write poetry, too. And articles for the journals. I had that small piece in the *Gentleman's Magazine* last month, remember?' It had been more in the nature of a notice but it was Jack's first words in print and he'd been thrilled. 'And like you, Mama, I wish to use my pen to persuade, to agitate, to subvert.'

During her career on the stage, Jane had been flattered by the very brightest in the land, from very different motives. She had not succumbed then and would not now. 'Jack,' she said gently, 'you are too young. You have nothing to write about.'

This outrageous idea now halted Jack's next words. *Nothing to write about?* Were not his journals full of his life, with characters he encountered, scrupulously observed? Did he not have a sheaf of poems on every subject whose style had been compared favourably by an usher at school with Thomas Gray's? Was he not halfway through his first play: *Iphigena or Lost Love Lamented*? Well, he'd written the first scene and that a cracker. His mother was talking nonsense. It was not that he had nothing to write about. It was that he had too much!

Of the two male Absolutes, his father recovered his voice first. As so often was the case, he was three sentences behind the conversation.

'Poet . . . poxed . . . poltroon!' he roared. 'D'ye think for a moment that I am going to pay you an allowance so you can sit in a room and . . . versify!'

'So long as I have pen and paper, what need is there for money?' Jack replied, loftily, 'I may live on air.'

It was odd how arguments took these turns. It must have been the liquor – his parents' standing order to water down each glass having been ignored since the age of fourteen – but it was strange how often it made his tongue say the thing most likely to provoke his already overtaxed father.

It did. 'You puppy!' Sir James was up now, his chair smashing to the floor behind him. 'By God, you sneer at me, sir, at the money I have spent educating you, turning you from the Cornish peasant I found into this . . . simulacrum of a gentleman. And here I have been offering to spend yet more to get you a commission and you . . . you . . .' He was swaying alarmingly and staggered back, only to lurch forward and around the table towards Jack, who hastily leapt up and moved away behind his mother. 'Damn me if I don't disown you, lodge three and fivepence with the trustees and make you live on the interest, take you from your damn, Whig-gish school and get you an ensignship . . . in the Artillery! I'll be buggered if I don't disinherit you and leave my all to Craster!'

This invective had accompanied three journeys around the table, Jack preceding him on every one. At the beginning of the fourth, however, his father's toe caught on the rucked-up rug; he pitched forward and, missing the table, crashed onto the floor.

'Husband,' cried Jane, moving forward.

'Father!' Jack bent down.

'Sheep shit,' declared Sir James. From his prone position by Jack's feet, he sniffed again before his son could step away.

He looked down. Indeed, his shoes were stained a vivid and reddy brown.

'Ah,' said Jack.

Sir James rose to his knees. 'Ode in the bedroom? When the Muse descends one must listen? Well, you can kiss my arse, 'cos you've just snuck in through Taylor's garden.'

He was up now and steadier than he'd been and Jack knew what that steadiness foretold. Lying was the ultimate vice and there would be only one victor on this battlefield. As Sir James took another step forward, Jack made a bold brush of it . . . and fled.

— FIVE —
Ode

Jack awoke from a dream of love. Though the images vanished with the opening of his eyes, their lingering effect was clear before him. He'd thrown off the heavier coverlets in the night and only a sheet lay atop him, in the nature of a tent held up by a single pole.

Jack reached down and grasped the structure in both his hands. To be alone in his bedroom at Absolute House and not in the dormitory at Porten's where he boarded, with the dozen beds shaking each morning under their occupants' exertions, this was a rare joy and he immediately thought of taking advantage of it. Hidden in his armoire were some quite extraordinary prints that Sommers, a schoolfellow who had developed a talent for the purchase and purveying of such choice items, had supplied. It would be a matter of moments to fetch them, study and learn, lie back . . .

Then, an image from his dream did come back to him and it halted his motion out of the bed. A face appeared in his mind's eye, sweet, pure, unblemished, framed with the palest of fair hair formed in corkscrew curls. Clothilde! He was to see her today. And he could not, would not sully his thoughts of her with any actions now.

And yet . . . There was another whom he also planned on visiting this day, one whose face – and body – had also haunted his sleep and helped cause his by now quite painful physical display. She would be more than delighted if he used her in such a way. So long as he recounted every detail of it. Fanny liked details.

He groaned, then levered himself out of the bed. No. He knew a piss would help ease the strain and indeed, all the milk he'd drunk in Nance's scullery the night before – a fine way to prevent the morning headaches, he'd always found – was taxing him now. He'd hidden there from his raging father until he'd given up the hunt and retired. Pulling the chamber pot from its drawer, he set to. There was relief in one sense, little in the other but, having decided, he would hold firm . . . or rather, not.

What he needed was to divert his thoughts, not away from the two faces of his dream but towards them in a different way. To utilize these feelings. For was that not what a poet did with his Muses? *Nothing to write about, Mother?* he thought. *Ha!*

Pulling the sheet off the bed to cover himself, he sat at the small writing table. Both his inspirations would require verse from him . . . but in quite different styles.

It was the labour of an hour. When the knock came at the door, he jumped and the sheet fell off him. Since he'd written Fanny's sonnet last, the purity of his sentiments in his ode to Clothilde had been displaced by somewhat grosser thoughts. He'd returned to his waking state. And that was the moment that Nancy chose to walk in with a cheery, 'Mornin', young Master.'

He snatched up the sheet just in time. 'Ah, Nance! What . . . ah . . . what time is it?'

'Straight up midday and a fine bright one it is.' She set a basin of water on the side table and dragged open the drapes. Sunshine streamed in.

'Midday?' Jack groaned. He was already late for his French lesson. Again.

'Aye. Your ma's gone to the theatre and your da's still asleep. So quietly now, my lad, up and out.' She bustled about the room, straightened furniture, lifted the blankets from the floor, dumped them on the bed. Then she grabbed one end of the sheet still wrapped around him. He held onto it as she tugged.

'Nance! Leave go, I'm—'

She looked down at his bare shoulders. 'Nothing I haven't seen before, young Jack.' When he'd been brought to London and before Westminster, Nance had had the care and washing of him.

You've never seen this, he thought, and held the sheet tighter.

'Why, Master Jack!' she said, coyly, still tugging gently. 'What have you got to hide there from your Nance?'

He stopped pulling but didn't let go of the sheet. Then with a hoot, she whipped it off him, turning away as she did, her laughter accompanying her out of the room. 'There's a note from your ma there, boy. And I've some cold meat and tatties in the kitchen for ye – if you can get your breeches on!'

Her laughter disappeared with her down the stairs. Jack looked around then saw it. Nance had laid a piece of folded paper down on his desk. As he took it up he reflected that it was just as well that she couldn't read because his morning's efforts were proudly on display. She might not have disapproved of his 'Ode to a Merman' dedicated to Clothilde. But Fanny's sonnet beside it, 'On a Religious Conversion by Candlelight', would have disturbed her.

His mother's note was merely a reminder that he was expected that evening at eight sharp – the 'sharp' underlined three times – at the Assembly Rooms in Dean Street where her play, which they'd discussed the previous night, was to be premiered. Away from the Garden, she had more chance of her satires escaping the Lord Chamberlain's notice.

Jack sat on the edge of the bed, note in hand. He had forgotten this rendezvous with his mother, was late for his French lessons. Wasn't there something else the day held, aside from his two, poetry-inspiring assignations?

Then memory came in a rush. The Mohocks! Tonight was the night for the Initiation. Yet the clashing appointments did not perturb him longer than a moment; they'd agreed that most of the Rites were to take place in Soho anyway so he would have time to attend his mother's play during them. The interlude might even help in his other plan – to be restrained in all things despite what the other aspirant Mohocks might do. For another memory came: Craster's challenge to billiards at noon the next day.

Jack rose and splashed his face in the basin of warm water Nance had set on the side table. He was excited, for it was to be a day of adventures. Yet there was also this need for moderation.

Yes, he thought, nodding to himself in the mirror above the basin, *I will be moderate in all things*.

Due to the lateness of the hour, he'd had a choice: breakfast or dressing. Since the former rarely delighted him and the latter always did, he spent some of his precious time in selecting suitable attire for what would be a long day. In the end, he settled on something new yet robust – a coat so dark in its green it was nearly black but with shining buttons and gold embroidered holes; a waistcoat of a crimson that was almost military and whose studs fastened into openings that were wreathed in gilded oak leaves. He chose black breeches and stockings, since the London streets were unforgiving to white; a pair of plain and solid square-tipped shoes – Nance had returned his collection, polished, while he slept – albeit with a brace of fine silver buckles. He toyed with stocks but he had enough black on him and any other colour jangled with the waistcoat. Besides, as he had discovered on his last outing into Covent Garden, people could grab you by the stock.

His thick, dark hair was, as usual, untameable. There was little chance of visiting the switzer in Half Moon Passage, the restraint of a cerise tie would have to do. Snatching up his silver-topped stick and squeezing the tricorn on his head, he looked himself up and down. He was so glad he'd persuaded his mother to buy him this full-length mirror. It reflected back a young man of the Town who would do. Who would do very well.

Then he was out onto the street. Since it was near one o'clock, it was crammed with people – though the hour made scant difference; it seemed to Jack that Mayfair was now always crowded, day or night. It had changed even in the few years that Absolute House was bought and built. Formerly, his route to Berkeley Square would have encompassed many more gardens like Taylor's but now every paddock sprouted a house or was in the throes of doing so. Builders scrambled up the wooden scaffolding, hammers beat in nails, bricks were slathered and slammed down, plaster slapped onto walls. Prosperous men stood about studying plans, gesticulating at the rising edifices, scarcely seeming to notice the thick dust that settled everywhere and gave them the appearance of ghosts. Jack coughed, cursing this dulling of his finery, glad every house and hostelry had a brush in the hallway. Yet, as always, it was the noise that struck him most forcefully. At Westminster, in the environs of St Peter's Abbey and the cloisters of the school, all was calmness, in the twinned dedications to religion and study. Here, aside from the construction, there was that dull roar that was the very sound of the Town, made up of the thousands – hundreds of thousands – of voices, competing to be heard. In his first hundred paces' stride down Curzon Street, a dozen different street sellers noisily hawked their offerings. It mattered not that this was an area rising in gentility, for the offal seller pushed his barrow of neats and lights past a blind stationer and his penny-priced memorandums; a ballad singer's fair soprano clashed with the harsh cries of the Oyster-and-Eel wench; while a pudding vendor warred with a pieman in the extolling of their wares. Any who travelled in pairs – and several who walked alone – declared their business or opinions in bullhorn voices aimed at convincing not just the person beside them but anyone standing in Hyde Park as well! The scent was as assailing as the sound with the smoke gushing from the various building plots, the clashing of cooked and raw fishes and stewed meats, the horses leaving their deposits on cobbles already besmirched and steaming; while the miasma rising from hundreds of people, perfumed and unwashed and moving rapidly about their so-important errands under the warm spring sun, was the strongest odour of all.

It was farmyard, factory and food shop. It was the main hall at Bedlam with the inmates unrestrained. It was London . . . and Jack loved it.

Late as he was, he had two obligatory stops. In Berkeley Square, the Pot and Pineapple was the best confectioner's in the town and here he purchased half a pound of crystallized fruits and four peaches in brandy. It left him little change from ten shillings but he had shared in the winnings of Westminster at the cricket and, anyway, it was money well spent. Clothilde's outrage at his tardiness would be swept away in her delight at her especial favourite sweetmeat. And Fanny . . . well, Fanny loved laced peaches.

His second stop was down an alley, just where Brewer Street turned into Knaves Acre – an apt name for an ill place. So dark and dank it was that spring's heat and light barely penetrated. Jack had found the little shop on some ramble. Part apothecary, the extent of strange potions, liquors and philtres was extraordinary, but it was the Curiosities that had drawn Jack into the gloom. Skulls hung from the ceilings, reputedly of well-known heroes, highwaymen and traitors to the realm, the proprietor, a wizened Portuguese, claiming that half the Jacobite Lords from the '45 dangled there. Artificial eyes rolled in bowls, teeth, both human and animal, were threaded like rosaries to hang from the beams. False limbs were stacked around the walls, piled up like the endeavours of a particularly drunken surgeon after a battle while the taxidermist's pride was displayed with native animals like lynx and fox mouldering beside more exotic beasts from Africa and the East. It was among these that Jack had discovered the most curious of all. A half-crown had secured it for a week, his purse light before his prowess at sport could fill it. Now he had returned with the guinea he required to make it his and delight the heart of his own true love.

From Knaves Acre, it was but a short walk to her door. He took Compton Street, as he had had enough of alleys for the while. Turning left onto Thrift Street, in a dozen strides, he stood before his destination – the House of Guen, the goldsmith's trade proclaimed in the gilt scales and model furnace that swung above the entrance.

Four years I have been coming here, Jack thought. Four, since his father decided his inevitable military career required French. But only in the last year did he enter this house with anything other than a schoolboy's reluctance. Only in the last year did he bound through the door. And the stimulus was not a language at which, admittedly, he was showing much improvement. Unless it was a different kind of language . . . *la langue d'amour!*

The bell rang as he pushed into the shop. It was empty. '*Bonjour*,' he called and was answered from the room beyond.

'Monsieur?' It was not Clothilde's father who emerged, but his apprentice, Claude. He came out wiping his hands on a polishing cloth. On seeing Jack, he threw it down. '*Ah, c'est toi, Jacques. Mon brave, comment vas-tu aujourd'hui?*'

'*Très bien, merci*, Claude. *Et vous?*'

'*Bien. Il fait beau, non?*'

'*Très beau.*'

Jack eyed the apprentice, hoping this exchange of formalities would be an end to conversation. He was late and had little enough time as it was. He wished to spend all that little with his beloved. And this Claude . . . what was it about him? Only a few years older than Jack, he had recently joined his uncle in London and for the same reasons that had brought the family there ten years before: the persecution that had been driving the Huguenots from their homeland for decades now. While

68

he had every sympathy with a man fleeing the foul despotism of the Bourbon to breathe freedom's pure air in England, the fellow was still . . . well, French. Jack was not prejudiced in the least, of course, his closest friend was Marks the Jew, and he had lessons in pugilism from a Negro at Angelo's school and never grumbled at the pummelling he took. But the French were different, his country at war with them again . . . yet this Claude showed not the slightest gratitude for the sanctuary provided him while maintaining an air of familiarity –'tu' indeed! – that was not quite decent. Jack would mix with any man, peasant or poet, that was the English way. By God, he considered the King to be not much more than one of his elected representatives! But he expected a man who was, essentially, a servant in his tutor's house, to have a little more respect. Not only to him; he had also observed his attentions to Clothilde. They were familiar to the brink of flirtation. And his face, even in the context of Frenchiness, being thus rather prettified, annoyed Jack.

Fortunately, he was spared any more of the man's insolence. '*C'est* Monsieur Absolute?' a voice trilled from above and Jack's knees gave at the sound.

'*Oui, cousine. Il est arrivé.*'

'*Dis-lui à monter.*'

That was unusual! They always had their class on this lower floor in a little room at the back, close to where Monsieur Guen and Claude laboured. Delighted, Jack made for the stairs, Claude giving way a little reluctantly. He paused by him.

'Monsieur Guen, *il est* . . . he is out on business?'

'*Oui.*'

Better and better. 'Gone for how long?'

The other man's reply was a shrug.

'Then . . .' Jack dug into a waistcoat pocket, pulled out a silver sixpence. 'See we are not disturbed. Tricky conjugations to learn today, eh? *Vous comprenez?*'

The man did not take the coin immediately and when he did he seemed reluctant. '*Oui*, monsieur, *je comprends . . . très bien,*' he said at last, nodded his head – it was not a bow – and stepped from the path. Jack took the three flights at a clip.

She was by the window, silhouetted against the sun, but were the day stormy Jack could not have been more dazzled. It was only two weeks since he had last seen her yet she seemed to have aged, in the most delightful way, continuing in that steady progression from the day the year before that Jack remembered so well. He'd arrived then in an ill humour, dragged from a game of tennis at his mother's insistence. He'd been told that the daughter of the house would conduct his lesson that day and not the father, information that had deepened his temper, for his dealings with her had been that of any boy of near sixteen to a girl two years younger – brief and rather rude. But any temper had died when she'd walked in – for Clothilde Guen had started to become a woman. He was hers from that moment on.

And yet if it was her beauty that caught him, it was the rest of her that held him, kept him coming back ever more enthusiastically to her side. The girl who could still take a childish pleasure in such simple presents as Jack could afford to bring her was also the woman who was learning, as Jack was learning, more adult delights: the pleasure of lips pressed to a palm, the colours that came to a face with a whispered compliment; while behind that face was a mind alive with ideas. Clothilde was as well read as Jack, better in many ways, for his schooling dwelt only on writers long dead. It was Clothilde who introduced him to the contemporaries whose ranks he aspired to join; half their lessons were spent translating Thomas Gray or William Collins into French, study and sentiment combining to make hours pass in moments.

And her transformation had continued. She stood now, golden hair up and held with tortoiseshell combs. Her dress was waves of ivory cloth, sweeping down to pink and delicate shoes, a glimpse of whitest stocking. Her almost almond-shaped face now held hints of colour that came not only from her youth, but from some external means, delicately applied, while her thick eyebrows had been tamed, teased and darkened. These were raised against him now; together with the hand that lifted as he advanced, they prevented any contact.

'You are late, again. *Toujours, toujours en retard.*' The delicate lips – a trace of colour there too, Jack saw – drew into a pout before she carried on in that mix of language they used before the lessons proper began. 'You do not care that you spend so little time here. Your lesson – pft! *ça ne fait rien. Moi, aussi*!' She turned back to the window.

'*Non*, Clottie, *je suis desolé. J'étais . . . très . . . très . . .* busy. For you. *Pour toi. Regarde*!' She faced him again as he reached into his satchel. 'I have three gifts—'

'*Trois cadeaux*,' she corrected, coming away from the window, eyebrows still raised.

'*Oui, trois cadeaux. Le premier . . .*'

She squealed when she saw the Pot and Pineapple's distinctive paper cone. '*Les fruits au sucre?*'

'*Naturellement.*' He handed them over, content to watch her revert to the girl she still could be, especially as the woman he'd kept waiting now retreated. She offered him the cone, smiling up at him, those reddened lips now smeared in crystallized white, but he declined. It was more fun watching her unobserved. When she'd finished, she took a handkerchief and delicately patted at her mouth before raising her pale-blue eyes again. '*Et le deuxième . . . ?*'

The second present, procured at the curiosities shop, required a touch of the theatre.

'*Ferme les yeux*,' he ordered and went to the mantelshelf, moving aside the little china shepherds and milkmaids there, reaching again into his satchel. Just before he opened the Hessian sack though, he glanced back. '*Ferme*!' he bellowed, in mock anger, and with a little giggle she complied.

When he had put the object in position, he went back to her, behind her, laying his hands across her eyes. She gasped, and her own hands rose to cover his. Behind her like this, he could feel the heat of her body, rising from the ivory folds, could just glimpse within them the rounding that was another sign of her encroaching womanhood. He knew he shouldn't, mustn't linger on that view, on those thoughts. So he opened his hands.

Her reaction was everything he'd hoped it would be, for she shrieked, staggered back against him, he had to hold her to him as she fought both to turn away from and regard the horror on her shelf.

'*Ah, Dieu! Dieu! C'est horrible! Qu' est-ce que c'est?*'

Her voice was frightened, her stare undeniably fascinated. She had often confessed a love of monsters. Now he had brought her one of her own. '*C'est . . . c'est . . .*' He had no words for this in her language. 'It's a merman. Caught in the Sea of Japan. Half man, half fish. *Un . . .* er *. . . demi-poisson?* See.' He tried to lead her forward but she resisted so he went to the creature. 'It has the head of a man but look at its teeth . . .' he put his fingers into the gaping mouth and then cried out, jerking his fingers back at her scream. 'Ah, like daggers,' he continued, smiling, sucking at his forefinger. 'It has the arms of a man too and fingers, *regarde . . .*' He bent one back. 'But look at the tail – pure fish.'

She came forward a step then. 'How . . . why is it so . . . dry?'

'Mummified.' He tapped the tail and it gave out a hollow note. 'Probably hundreds of years old. Maybe thousands.'

She came close now, reached up a finger to touch it. 'It's terrible,' she said, fascinated. 'And how . . . how do you think he . . . they . . . is there a mermaid too?'

'Where there is one, there has to be more. I think this poor little lad has been wrenched away from his love.' He watched her eyes widen – delectable sight! – as she stroked the scaly tail. 'And that . . . that is my third present to you.'

He led her to the chaise, made her sit. Then he reached within his bag again and pulled out the paper he'd laboured so hard on that morning. He took up position just beside the creature, adopted the prescribed pose for tragedy as gleaned from the works of Le Brun, and began.

ODE TO A MERMAN
In distant seas I sought my love
Through reeds below and shoals above
And there, by man, was t'aen.
With my last breath, Clothilde, I cried,
For thee I searched, for thee I died
For thy sweet love was slain.

Jack glanced at his audience. Tears had filled her beauteous eyes, a hand was raised to her lips. He continued.

So here I sit, sans love, sans life
And dream of you, my half-fish wife
Who swims on all alone.
Yet mantelshelf contains me not
In dreams I seek our blessed plot
In reedy beds I moan.

He had turned side on to her, staring as if through fathoms of water to a heaven denied far above, a hand raised before him as if he would soar from those depths. He held the pose, waited for the sound of her tears falling, as they must.

A snort. *Poor lass*, he thought, *so overcome that she releases so indelicate a sound.* He turned to her.

'Fishwife?' she said, her lower lip thrust out, her brow distorted in a frown. 'You compare me to a fishwife?'

'What?' Jack turned, lowering the paper. 'No, no, not "fish-wife". It is "Half-fish . . . wife"! The hyphen, see where it is?'

He showed her the paper and she squinted down at it. '*Ah, je comprends. Je suis* "the mermaid", *la Petite Fille de la Mer. Comme lui*, half fish. *Un moitié poisson.*'

'*Exactement.*'

73

Her frown clung as she scanned the sheet. 'I think the terms might be better . . . *en français*.'

Of course! Everything always sounded better in French!

Surely, it was fairly clear. He didn't mind someone analysing his endeavours, indeed he always welcomed criticism, but surely she could have shown the emotion first and saved the commentary for later?

'Clothilde,' he said sadly, 'do you not like the poem I wrote for you?'

'*Ah, non*, Jacques. *Je l'adore*. I love it. It's so . . . so . . .' She studied the paper for inspiration.

He didn't think he could bear another comment. And there were other things that needed attention. 'And does the poet not deserve a fee?'

She looked up then, all pretend innocence. 'What fee?'

He lowered himself beside her, took her hand. They had been in this very position two weeks before. He had kissed each of her fingers then. He had something more ambitious in mind now. 'This,' he said, and leaned forward.

'Jacques!' She turned her face but did not pull away. Not far enough, anyway. His lips reached her cheek, touched her. 'Jacques,' she repeated but in a different tone and turned her face back. 'We mustn't. My father—'

'Gone out,' he said hoarsely, 'and Claude has silver to warn us of his return.'

'Claude . . .' she said, her voice concerned, but he could not let another man's name rest on her lips. So he kissed them, his hand behind her back so that he could help her resist her initial impulse to pull away. It worked, for she tensed, then relaxed and they stayed joined for a delicious age. Her lips were as sweet as their promise, as sweet as they had been in a thousand dreams. He was sure that had nothing to do with the crystals of sugar that clung to them.

He could, would have stayed like that for weeks, content only with that. Clothilde, though, had begun to lean further and further back so that to maintain contact he had to lean forward. They reached the balance point and toppled over it, she falling, him on top. Suddenly he was pressed to her at more points than just lips and he realized that she had indeed grown into a woman.

'Clothilde,' he said, huskily.

And then came the sound of boots on the stairs, coming up fast. Jack was across the room to the mantelshelf in a moment. Clothilde rushed to the window, trying to puff out a skirt that had been somewhat flattened. They reached their respective positions just as the door burst open.

'Monsieur Guen!'

'Monsieur Absolute!' Clothilde's father stood in the doorway. Though of smallish stature he was broad in the shoulder, with hands surprisingly large for a man who did such delicate work in gold. These were clenching and unclenching now as he looked from his daughter to Jack. 'I did not think you were coming today, Monsieur Absolute, you were so late. That is why I was not here to greet you.' He entered the room slowly, looking around as if he expected someone else to be lurking there. Behind him on the landing stood Claude.

Jack glared at the apprentice for a moment then turned his attention back to the goldsmith. 'Yes, I am sorry, sir, I had . . . business in the town that delayed me.'

'Business?' Her father had reached her at the window and Clothilde was not doing well under his gaze. '*Ça va, ma petite?*' he said, then continued, turning to Jack, 'Do you not think my daughter looks a little fevered, sir?'

'Can't say I noticed, Monsieur Guen. But I am fevered myself. Been having the Devil's own time with some conjugations.'

'Indeed? Is my child not teaching you correctly?'

'*Au contraire*, monsieur. She is . . . most agreeable.'

'Agreeable?'

It was a word Jack would have had back. He was sure there

was something similar in French that he meant to say. That was the problem with this bantering in two languages at once!

Monsieur Guen raised a hand to his daughter's brow. 'Hot indeed. I fear for her, monsieur.'

'Papa, I am quite well,' Clothilde protested.

Her father ignored her. 'Would you mind if we terminated the lesson for today to let her rest?'

'Oh no, Papa, why?'

Jack struggled to veil his disappointment. He had thought of little but Clothilde since waking and now to have only these brief moments with her? But the goldsmith looked immovable.

He swallowed. 'As you wish, monsieur.'

'Same time, next week then, But downstairs, *hein*? Where I will then make sure I can keep an eye on your . . . conjugations, yes?'

Jack collected his satchel from near the fireplace, his hat and stick. Straightening, he winked once at the merman, then turned.

Clothilde's father had the poem in his hand. 'Fishwife?' he enquired.

As his mother said, these days every man styled himself a critic. It was best to ignore them. 'Monsieur. Mademoiselle.' He bowed to each of them then proceeded to the door where a smirking Claude stepped aside. Jack gave him another glare. There was no doubt that the fellow had gone to fetch his master back, despite the sixpence he had retained. There was nothing that Jack could do about that now. But he'd pay him for it one day, nonetheless.

Gaining the street, plunged immediately into the hurly-burly, Jack leaned in the doorway and took stock. Disappointment still held him. But then the second of his morning reveries returned and he remembered what his satchel, lightened by the removal of the merman, yet contained.

'Chair!' he called out and immediately two fellows stopped beside him. It was not a long walk but the streets were crowded and the cobbles made slick by a small shower. Besides, he wished to conserve his stamina. He suspected he would need it.

Climbing in, he called out his destination. 'Golden Square.'

− SIX −

Sonnet

There was a mews that ran from Warwick Street along the back of Golden Square and it was at the entrance to this that Jack got the chairmen to set him down. He was not allowed to enter the house from the front, for the lady was assiduously re-building her reputation and a handsome lad dashing up the front steps and not leaving for hours would not help in that. So he paid the men off, then entered the cobbled cul-de-sac. Carriages were being readied, for it was near the hour that calls would be made. Thus occupied, no man paid him attention as he went to a small entrance, unlocked it with a key hidden for the purpose above the lintel, and slipped inside. There he paused, back to the door, staring down the garden to the rear aspect of the house.

His first delight at seeing her, stood before her fireplace, changed swiftly to chagrin when he saw that she was talking to someone, ire increasing when his hope that it was merely a maid was dashed by a man who approached her – touched her dress! – before disappearing again out of sight. In that glimpse, Jack confirmed it was not Lord Melbury; Jack had calculated that, as Parliament sat, His Lordship would not visit his mistress before it rose and thus he was safe in this surprise. But a stranger – and young from the glance of him! Jack would not be so churlish as to be jealous of the man who paid for the house and everything inside it. But any other rival he would not brook.

Jealousy spurred him forward. He could have gone through the rear door, up the two flights to the salon. But a wrought-iron balcony gave onto the room he sought and a sturdy vine was as good as a stair. Swiftly he climbed. As he did he heard laughter – hers, so distinctively husky, so full of pleasure – and the man's. Lowering himself carefully over the balustrade, he moved to the open window.

'You cannot mean it, sir,' came her voice, 'you wish me to clutch it . . . thus.'

'Exactly so, madam, yet fingers closer to the tip . . . yes, now thrust it forward and a little more on the side.'

'Like so?'

'Just so. Yes, madam, yes! That is . . . exquisite!'

It was the man's groan of delight that brought Jack from his hiding place and into the room with a bellow of indignation.

'Pox!' yelped the man, stumbling away, nearly bringing down what Jack saw to be an easel. Clutched in his hand was a palette and knife.

'Jack,' yelled Fanny, 'what the . . .' She gathered her full hooped skirt and marched towards him. 'What the Devil do you think you are up to?'

'Um . . . thought I'd surprise you. Didn't know you had company.'

He was aware how pathetic it sounded. Fanny took charge, just as she always did. 'You will apologize to Mr Gainsborough at once for your japes.' Turning to the artist, she said, 'I am so sorry, sir. My brother lives in the country and does not know the rules of the town. Such as using the customary entrances.' She turned and glared.

The artist had righted himself and his easel. 'Not at all, madam. I was . . . unaware that you possessed such a thing as a brother.'

'Half-brother, actually.' Jack had stepped forward on Fanny's look and allowed his accent to slip into some of the wider vowels of his youth. 'My sister's kind enough to narrow the gulf between us. I'm only up for the week, see. Lawks, what a time I be havin'.'

'Indeed? And what part of the country are you from?'

Deep into a lie, Jack thought he might as well continue. 'Somerset,' he said with the suitable 'zeds'.

'Really? I am off to Bath myself shortly.'

'Sure, I've been bathing myself since I was four,' he said, and let out a hoot of laughter.

'Pay no attention to this idiot, sir. The distaff side of the family, you know. T'was ever mad.' She glared again at Jack before continuing, 'Mr Gainsborough means he is off to live and work there. I was fortunate enough to waylay him as he passed through London. And before his reputation is so established I will be unable to afford his time or pay his fee.'

'Ah, Miss Harper,' the artist replied, 'there is always time for such beauty.'

Fanny beamed, while Jack thought, *notice he didn't snub the money!*

'Still,' Gainsborough continued, 'I am sure you wish to visit with your brother. And my hand will shake somewhat after that . . . ha, ha . . . shock. So perhaps we will leave it here for this day.'

'Oh, sir. And just when I got this into the correct position for you.' She raised the porte-crayon in her left hand.

'We will remember it for next time.' He was packing up his things. 'One more session should accomplish it.'

Jack and Fanny waited, side by side, while the artist finished gathering. Then he carefully laid a cloth over the easel, stepped back and bowed.

'I do see the familial resemblance now you are together. Perhaps, next time, a double portrait?'

'We would be zo honoured, sir. Zounds, we've a site for such a one 'bove the old fireplace in Harper Hall.'

His accent wandered around the West Country during this sentence and her nails dug in so hard he barely restrained a yelp. Gainsborough smiled and left the room. They heard his tread down the stairs in silence and the front door close.

'Idiot!' Fanny hissed.

'Fanny,' he laughed, 'I'm sorry.'

'Oh yes, you seem it.' She stood, hands on hips, glaring. 'Here have I been working to restore my name and you jeopardize that work with your schoolboy antics.'

Jack felt chastened. It had been, for Fanny, a long path back from the nadir of appearing, five years before, in *Harris's Book of Ladies*. It was just after her husband, Thomas Harper, the actor, had sued her for 'criminal conversation' – her adultery with a fellow player. The divorce had sent her into a decline but Harris had been premature – she had never 'traded' in the way that most of the girls in his list did. In the gradation of bought love, she had never sunk even as low as a 'Lady of Pleasure'. And now she was a 'kept mistress', why, she was almost respectable. Nonetheless, 'The Harp' as she had been known, had been written up in alluring terms indeed. Jack knew them well. After their first . . . encounter, he had found an old copy and had clipped the page to stick within his Greek Grammar. It was more enticing than any Ovid.

And this Venus had chosen him! All because Lord Melbury had been too busy to escort her home from the theatre three months before and had sent the schoolboy Jack in his place. She had drunk a little and fondled him in the chair. At her house, she had invited him in and, within minutes, had taken what he had long sought to give away.

'Well, young Jack,' she'd said then, lying back and laughing, 'you do have much to learn.'

And for the three months since she had taught him. She only had three rules: cleanliness, cundums and kindness. So he bathed. He bought his engines ('for only the man who keeps me here may come to me unarmoured!' she'd declared). And he learnt how to take his time and return the pleasure given.

And for these lessons, he repaid her with jealousy and threatened exposure?

'I am so sorry,' he said. 'I am a fool, a jealous fool. Please forgive me.'

'Don't know that I shall,' she huffed, moving to the table on which were set a decanter of port and some glasses. She conspicuously poured just the one and stood there, side on and ignoring him while she sipped.

This is not going to plan, thought Jack. He couldn't stand more disappointment, not after Clothilde. And though the merest thought now of that purer love made him flush a little with guilt, he forced himself to remember that it . . . *he* was different with Fanny. And to enjoy those differences he would need to redeem himself. The poem he had written for her was in his pocket but he was determined not to produce that too soon, it would be doing what she had been strenuously teaching him not to – reaching the climax too soon. He needed something else first, to build toward it.

It was her profile that gave it to him. Moving around the easel, he lifted the cloth from it. She turned at the noise, said, 'No, Jack, I forbid—'

His raised hand halted her words, timed with the gasp he let out. 'Oh, madam, it is . . . extraordinary.'

Indeed his reaction needed little in the way of pretence. Jack was no student of art, though his mother had forced him to accompany her to various exhibitions, but even he could see that this Gainsborough had something special. The rigidity of pose and line that seemed to dominate in most portraits of the day was absent. The hooped dress flowed in its cascades of lilac silk, genuine fabric not sculptured marble. This was a woman, not a statue, and the artist had achieved the same effect with the skin, must have seen the passionate transformations that occurred there as Jack had. Indeed the expression on the face seemed to be not a pose at all but a translation direct from life, as if she were caught just before some intemperate or seductive speech.

Jack had been prepared to flatter by rote. Now he had no need. 'Fanny! It is you. You to the core.'

'Really? Do you think so?' She approached now, peering over his shoulder at it. 'I was thinking he was making me a little dull.'

'Dull?' Here was dangerous ground. Over-praise of the artist might count against the model. Under-praise him and it would be a condemnation of her judgement and thus purse. 'Not so. He has the very colour of your eyes and the thick veils that guard 'em. He has the ripeness of your lips, parted as if ready to speak forth some wisdom. He has the slant of your gentle nose, the strength of your chin, the perfect symmetry of your ears. All that nature has provided you, he has captured. Except . . . yes, now I look closer, he has not yet quite managed the exact shades of faun that make up your wondrous hair. But he said he was to return tomorrow, did he not? Then perhaps he will stay up half the night attempting to mix together some pigment that no one has yet discovered, unseen on canvas till now.'

He wondered if he'd gone too far. But her sigh reassured as she tipped her head now this way, now that in contemplation. Then a hand came up to rest on Jack's shoulder. 'You do not think something too . . . too forward in the expression.'

Jack looked again. It was hard for Fanny to appear anything other than sensual. But what she wanted to hear was that this portrait, which would be seen around the town, especially if it was exhibited, added to the reputation she was re-establishing. All would know she was a rich man's mistress. But there was a large difference between a courtesan and a demirep.

'It will make you in the Town, that I am sure,' he murmured, reaching up, taking her hand, kissing it.

'Sweet boy,' she said, turning her wrist so that he could kiss her palm. He was only too happy to oblige. Three months before he would undoubtedly have galloped on apace, sought lips, tongue, breast, and all in rapid succession. But he had been a good student. So he led her around to the table, poured them both a glass of the port, clinked glasses before draining his, then whispered, 'Stand here, I have something for you.'

'A gift?' she said as he returned to his satchel, which he had dropped by the window. When he returned with the jar of brandied peaches, she sighed, 'So sweet! But I've told you, Jack, I want for nothing so you should not spend the little you have on me.'

'Those are a token only.' He pulled out the papers. 'This is the real gift and the only expenditure is from my insufficient self. Have pity, for it comes from the heart.' It was not quite true. Other parts of the body had inspired Jack in his endeavours, together with the memory of a night the week before and a quite extraordinary lesson.

'"On a Religious Conversion by Candlelight,"' he announced. 'Shall I?'

'Please.'

Clearing his throat once, he began.

When I first run my tongue down your smooth thigh
Just like a priest, I kneel and bend to pray
And gaze with his same fervour for on high
My altar calls and sweet scent guides my way.
On both our passions candles cast their light
But his reveals nothing save pure gold.
A richer treasure far is in my sight
Whose soft and flowing red is warm, not cold.
Then with my stubbled chin I lightly climb
The full perfection of those luscious slopes
And kiss, so soft, yet building up till Time
Itself takes pause and hangs upon our hopes.
I suck you in, your flesh explodes in me,
Your moans, Love's music set in sweetest key.

He had not assumed one of the prescribed positions from Le Brun as he had for Clothilde. The subject matter here was not a monster from the east; this required nothing but the slight husk that came naturally to his voice as his words mixed with his memories. Lost within them for only a moment, it ended when he looked up to see that she had half-closed her eyes, had leaned back against the table, as far as the hoops of her dress allowed her.

'Oh, Jack! That is indeed a gift worth receiving. And yet . . .' she reached down and grasped folds of lilac silk in her hands, 'yet it seems it is a gift only half given.'

Jack looked down. The hands were now engaged in pulling the material upwards. Already the silken fringe had cleared the lowermost wooden hoop. Suddenly dry-mouthed, he took a step toward her, then another, trying not to rush.

'Your bedroom,' he said, in a voice gone quite thick.

'No time.' She matched him in huskiness, as the material rose still higher. 'I am expected at Lady Dalrymple's rout in half an hour and it took me at least one to get into this dress. Besides,' and here the white silken shift beneath the gown cleared the knees and Jack had the first glimpse of her cerise silk stockings, 'your poem speaks of more accessible delights. So, kneel to your devotions again, Jack. Let us see if you have truly learned your catechism. And if you have, a further lesson awaits you. Or should I say reward. For I shall show you the way I really like to consume peaches.'

At that, she popped the lid off the jar, slid her fingers into the depths and produced one soft and succulent segment. Sliding it into Jack's mouth, flooding it with fruit and cognac, her wet hand then disappeared up within the gown.

'What was it, Jack? "And sweet scent guides your way . . ." Here.' As she reached fully up, her eyes half closed again while her other hand snaked behind Jack's head, applying a little pressure.

Jack had prayed for this from the moment he awoke in his bedroom that morning. She had managed to raise the hoops so they concertinaed a little, just enough for her to rest her buttocks on the table's edge and for him to slide under the rings of wood. Cotton encased him, it was like a cave with a treasure at its limit, delight beckoning him towards it. But the poem was in his head and he turned aside, his lips finding the stocking on her left thigh. Running its length he came to the tie that held it there, a bow, a single simple knot. Putting his teeth to it, he jerked it free and, in the little gap created, inserted his tongue between thigh and silk.

He heard, as if from far away, the groan. Thinking where once was good, twice was better, he switched to the other side, teeth seeking, finding, pulling again. This lace was longer, his head reaching back till it was pressed against a hoop. Twisting freed it, and once more his lips found a paradise that, until recently, he never knew existed – the softest skin near the top of a woman's thigh.

This groan came louder through the folds. This high the cave had become darker, and there was little air. It made him giddy, the lack of it, and what there was so rich and dense. The undergarments ahead of him were, of course, not joined, something else he had not known before he'd embarked on that first exploration the week before. Thus he only had to part the fold of these smaller shifts which he did with gentle fingers. His palms spread to the side, pushing out the thighs just a little, before his face pushed forward once again. He was nearly there, nearly drunk with the closeness and the glorious, now brandied, musk of this place. Turning his head to the side, he nipped, very gently, that last fragrant inch of flesh then reached forward . . .

He was nearly knocked backwards. Fanny had suddenly pushed off the edge of the table. As it was unlike her to rush so, he was just about to mention it when the near darkness became complete, with the concertinaed hoops suddenly unfurling again and the swathes of material dropping to the floor. She had stood up and he was crouched inside the tent of her gown.

'Fanny! What . . .' he gasped and then received a blow to his head through the silk that made him wince. But he didn't attempt to speak again, halted, not by the pain nor even the lack of air, but by heavy footsteps.

'That idiot Carthew chose today of all days to have a stroke.'

Lord Melbury's voice was trained to overcome the protests of the Opposition raised in the House. It easily pierced the layers of cotton and silk.

He could not move. He was frozen there, on his knees, his arms now dropped and held to his side while Fanny pressed on him from above. Glancing down, in the little light that spilled under the fringe of her dress, Jack could see that she was standing on her toes. Scrunching his neck allowed her to at least settle. But she was still, essentially, sitting on his head.

'Ah, my dear . . . I . . . I . . . am so delighted to see you.'

'Yes, well, I cannot stay long. Lord Wolvermere's backbone needs stiffening over supper. Infernal idiot wants to back down on the Naval requisitions. I must away to White's in . . . one hour. Plenty of time. Hallo, what's this?'

Jack's own backbone stiffened. He saw the shadow of feet moving past Fanny's and he prepared for discovery.

'Pot and Pineapple peaches! Did I send you these?'

'You did, my love, ever thoughtful.' Jack marvelled at the calm in Fanny's voice. She was quite still above him, had not moved since she settled.

There came the sound of slurping. 'And I have excellent taste. Marvellous things. Uses good brandy rather than bad, that's the key.' There was a pause while more peaches disappeared noisily. Then he said, 'Why are you standing there like that, Fanny?'

'Why? I . . . I thought I might recite to you.'

'Recite? I had something rather different in mind. No time, d'ye see?'

'Oh, only a short poem. I wrote it for you. Thought it might, uh, stimulate you. Knowing your love of such verse.'

'Ah?' The salacious tone of the monosyllable was clear. 'Well, why not then? Long as it's not too lengthy, eh?'

'Sit, my dear. Sit.'

Jack felt Lord Melbury moving away. He had met him on several occasions as he was a great man of the theatre and patronized a stable of playwrights as others might own racehorses. Lady Jane had once been favoured until she failed to acknowledge the patronage with something other than words. He was a big man, but nimble with it. He was also renowned as one of the best pistol shots in England. A thought that made Jack freeze even more despite the growing pain in his legs and neck.

The sofa squeaked as His Lordship sat. 'Very well. You may begin.'

Jack wondered what she was going to do. Recite something? She had been an actress after all. Or extemporize? She certainly had the wit. But what she did do, Jack had not expected. For she suddenly leaned away from him as if reaching back, then straightened again. Her voice, when it came, was quite clear.

' "On a Religious Conversion by Candlelight," ' she announced.

Jack's first thought was . . . Plagiarism, by God! The damned woman had claimed this as her creation! Then, as she began to read, he had two other distinct feelings. One at his groin, which had never really gone away since he'd woken up. And the other higher up, in his throat.

Jack began to giggle. What was the woman playing at? He hadn't written an epic poem but a sonnet. Sixteen lines, no matter how slowly she took them. Sixteen and then Lord Melbury would seek the place that Jack had been denied by this interruption, no doubt further inflamed by the sentiments he'd so skilfully rendered into verse. The more he tried to stop the giggles – and he could tell by the poem's increased volume that they were audible – the more they came.

Her rendition of the poem had become positively dirge-like.

'Pick it up, girl, for Christ's sake, I do have a supper appointment,' came a bellow from the room.

Absurdity was mastering him. Air was scant enough in his cave and he was trying not to breathe too much as he feared it was fuel to his laughter. He feared he was going to fall or faint.

He assumed she must have a plan for the sonnet's end. He needed to stay conscious long enough to react to it.

The poem ended. Lord Melbury clapped. 'Bravo, my dear, bravo. Exquisite sentiments, beautifully expressed. And you were quite right as to their . . . effect.' The floorboards creaked as he stood. 'And now . . .'

It was then Fanny screamed. 'Ahhh! What is that?'

'Damn, what? Where?'

'There, my Lord. There on the wall *behind you!*'

The emphasis on the words was an unmistakable hint. And as she said them, the hoops were ratcheted up and Jack was exposed to the light. He saw that his Lordship had taken the bait, half-turned away. The window was open. He made to rise . . .

And fell. The cerise stockings, which had slid down, had somehow become entangled around his ankles. Jack thumped onto the carpet.

Lord Melbury turned. His face, which had often been likened to a fish in the broadsheets' caricatures, took on an aspect of salmon now, lower jaw dropping to his chest. Jack, half in and half out of the dress, smiled up. He couldn't think of anything to say. No one could, for what seemed like minutes but couldn't have been more than a few seconds. Then everyone talked, or shouted at once.

'Young Absolute!'

'My Lord.'

'Of course, I can explain . . .'

But, of course, she couldn't. Fanny had been a fair actress in her day but Peg Woffington could not have got away with this one. Lord Melbury started forward, his face dangerously mottled and his large hands clenching and unclenching.

'You puppy! By God, I'll . . . I'll . . .'

Fanny stooped, whipped her stockings away from Jack's ankles. 'Go,' she hissed. 'Go!'

Jack needed no further urging. He scrambled to the window, was through it and over the balustrade in a moment.

The vine provided handholds, though he eschewed nearly all of them, sliding most of the way to the ground. He exited as he had entered; though now, as he ran down the garden, a furious voice followed him.

'I know you, whelp, you and your mongrel family. And you will pay for this! By God, you will pay!'

— SEVEN —
Night of the Mohock

'. . . and let all ye who know, live with that knowledge in fear, for we – Wolf and Bear and Snake and Hawk – do this day, the twenty-eighth of April in the year seventeen hundred and fifty-nine, declare the Ancient Order of Mohocks, that terror of the London Streets in the reign of our late White Mother Queen Anne, to be revived.'

'Ah-ha-ah-ha-HA-HA-HA!'

Marks's deep voice soared. 'We shall be as wild as our forebears who stalked from the Garden to the Mall. And we shall honour those savages who dwell in the forests of our Colonies whose name we take.'

'Mohocks!' came the cry.

'How shall we honour them, Bear?' Jack shouted.

'By performing their savage rites, Wolf,' Marks replied.

'Name them!' Fenby and Ede – Hawk and Snake – called.

'Rite One,' Marks continued, 'is already accomplished: "Purging in the Sweat Lodge." '

That had been Marks's idea. They had chosen the Old Hummum Hotel on the Little Piazza of the Garden to sweat, drink sherbets. They had stayed a long while – the faces of three of them still testifying to the fact – before repairing to the room set aside for them a cobble-stone's throw away across the Great Piazza at the Shakespeare's Head tavern. Jack and Marks glowed a deep scarlet, while Fenby was forced continuously to take off his glasses and wipe away the steam. Only the Honourable Ede had returned to his normal pallid hue. Nothing affected his porcelain countenance for long.

'Rite Two: "Feast upon the turtle."'

Fenby came up with that one. No one prepared turtle soup like John Twigg at the Shakespeare's Head and they eagerly awaited his entrance now.

'Rites Three, Four and Five: the Stalking of the Squaws in the ancient hunting grounds of Soho; the trapping of the same and then—'

The climaxing rite remained undeclared, due to the sudden opening of the door and the admittance of all the noise of the crowded tavern. Each looked eagerly to what they hoped would be a soup tureen. But the hand of the man who entered was filled with nothing bulkier than a slim book, bound in finest calico.

'Gentlemen,' the man croaked, 'I think I have here all your hearts – and your loins – could ever crave.'

Jack stood, pulled out a chair. 'Mr Harris, would you care to join us in a cup?'

'Too kind.' The voice near a whisper, the head inclined, he slid into the proffered seat. It was always a confused area of etiquette where this man was concerned. He was, after all, the head waiter here; but he was also one of the true powers of the Piazza and thus of London. He claimed to be an Old Westminster, his word on it never challenged, certainly not by Jack and his friends who benefited so much from the association. The Shakespeare's Head was one of the most popular of taverns, yet Harris always found them a room – for the sake of the Old School.

'Some ale, Mr Harris?'

A thin, white hand was raised palm out before the face. 'No ale, indeed. When one is a martyr to the Stones, as I am, one watches one's volume. But I have taken delivery of a fine Armagnac, if you gentlemen . . .'

Ede gasped, for he was especially fond of such distillations and Harris was known for smuggling in only the best from the country with which England had been at war for three years. But Jack interposed. 'No hard liquors, thank'ee, sir. As you know, we need clarity for what is ahead.'

'Ah, yes, the Initiation.' The way the word was breathed out between scabrous lips made Jack shudder slightly. He had no doubt as to the cause of Harris's 'martyrdom' for his so-pale face was studded with eruptions that the thick, rouged powder only highlighted, the visual expression of an internal malady. The man was plainly poxed; which, given his honorific title – 'Pimpmaster General of London' – was scarce surprising. It reminded Jack to sift all advice given; for if Harris had been before, he wanted none of his Mohocks to follow after.

'Yet do not let us stop you.' Jack signalled to a boy servant in the doorway. 'A glass of Armagnac for Mr Harris and more . . .' He indicated the empty jugs.

'You are kind. Yet I cannot stay long. Tonight, in the Burbage Room, there is a gathering of the Senior "Cyprians" and they will demand my attendance.'

All there knew to what he referred, for Harris hosted a weekly meeting of the top whores where all 'matters pertaining' would be discussed, interlopers dealt with, gentlemen with bizarre requests found a willing partner for a suitably high fee. A fee from which Harris would take a considerable cut.

'An opp . . . opp . . . opportunity, Jack,' declared Fenby. 'We can accomplish Rites Three, Four and Five under one roof. As if we were at F . . . Fortnum and Mason's.' He gave a nervous laugh.

'Oh, gentlemen,' breathed Harris. 'The Cats next door would not serve your purposes so well. They are . . . venerable, to say the least. And Peep o' Day Boys such as yourselves deserve something more . . . succulent. Some fresh tit up from the country, eh? Eh?'

The young servant returned with the porter and Armagnac. The latter was raised while ale was swiftly poured out.

'Gentlemen,' said Harris, regarding them fondly over the lip of crystal. 'To the Night of the Mohock.'

'Mohock!' came the cry as bumpers were swiftly drained, then banged upon the wood.

Harris set his down gently, rose. As he did, he pushed the book toward Jack. 'This is fresh from Digby's Press in St Paul's Churchyard. I will leave you to its perusal. I have taken the liberty of marking, in red, certain entries. I have not got out to visit them myself, alas, given my recent struggle with the Quacks. But my diligent scouts tell me those indicated are the cream of a very fine crop. The cost of the book will, of course, be added to your bill. Gentlemen.' With a bow, he was gone, passing another servant in the door who entered with the turtle soup.

As Marks ladled from the tureen, Jack lifted the book, and despite his eagerness, opened it carefully, spreading out the pages from the centre so as not to break the spine. The volume was worth the care, Digby's finest printer in London. After all, only the best would do for *Harris's List of Ladies*, the *sine qua non* of Whores' Directories, in which Fanny had once appeared.

With the book in one hand, Jack slurped as he studied the listings. Each entry bore at least an initial, though a name often followed the Miss or Mrs. A price range was given, set sometimes by duration, sometimes by peccadillo or speciality. Yet the body of the text was reserved for the delights on offer, delineated in the purplest of prose which seemed to prove that its author, 'John Harris, Esquire', had indeed had a classical education.

They had decided that each would choose for another and drawn their victim's name from a hat. Jack had got Fenby and he swiftly found the perfect entry. He took pity on his friend's nerves by selecting someone who was not so old or experienced that she would terrify the little fellow. But she also had attributes that would turn the encounter into a good story.

' "To all lovers of carrots," ' he read, ' "we recommend this nymph of scarce sixteen. Inclinable to be lusty, she takes her evening excursions on Compton Street where her clients may put their case to her either in a tavern or in her own apartments." '

Hoots enfolded little Fenby, as he coloured and sought to speak.

'A red-head, Fenby, with a temper to match, I'll be bound.' Marks slapped the smaller man on the back, causing him to spit soup.

Ede had the last word. 'At least you will not be able to fool us as to the accomplishment of Rite Five. Assuming she is a true Carrot.'

He took the book, selected one for Marks whose main virtue was 'a most consummate skill in reviving the dead', necessary, Ede declared, because Marks was known to fall asleep standing up in a crowd. She also was said to be 'fit for keeping by a Jew Merchant', and though Marks scowled at the implication, he had expressed a desire to find and set up a regular mistress. Ede was thus helping his friend.

Marks returned the favour by searching through the book for 'a Lady in Mourning', as Negresses were designated. It amused Marks to think of that most ivory of Honourables contrasted with an ebony. That she had 'as pretty a pair of pouting bubbies as ever went against a man's stomach' was incidental.

That left Jack. Fenby seized the book and, in a spirit of vengeance, tried to force him to visit one Miss Bird who was 'short, fat and corpulent', spoke in a northern brogue and was 'too often in a state of intoxication'. 'Let's see you compose an Ode to her, Sir Poet!' he'd exclaimed. Jack had eluded the choice as this particular bird roosted in Brydges Place off St Martin's Lane and the hunt had been strictly designated for Soho. While the argument continued, Marks flicked through the pages and suddenly thrust an entry before Fenby who peered at it through his spectacles then beamed.

'Yes. Oh yes!' He cleared his throat. ' "You have admired this student of Thespis on the stages of the Garden and the

Lane. Any who saw her Juliet would want to be her Romeo and claim his dawn's delight. The mysteries of Miss T, who always wears a mask, will be revealed only to one who can raise both a gold guinea and his own Love Dagger."'

'An actress!' Jack exclaimed. 'You can't make me go to an actress. What if I know her?'

'Exactly!' yelled each of his friends and this time there was no gainsaying them.

Jack scowled but there was little he could do. At least the location was perfect; for she laboured in St Anne's Court, a nasty lane of rookeries that ran between Wardour Street and Dean Street. Jack had other business on the latter thoroughfare that his fellow Mohocks need not know of – attendance at the Assembly Rooms for his mother's play. Since their rendezvous to report was set for midnight, he had four hours to both perform the Rites and still be a dutiful son.

It was all settled. The jugs were emptied, the tureen drained. As they stood to leave, Marks reached into the pocket of his coat and threw the contents onto the table. Four sachets of yellow silk lay there, tied with a red ribbon.

'Cundums!' came the cry as the packets were snatched up.

'Not just any, my warriors. Look at the label.'

Ede lifted a packet to the tallow candle. '"Mrs Philips at Half Moon Alley".'

'But, M . . . Marks,' said Fenby, 'I've brought my old stalwart. Soaked in vinegar these three days.' A thin and mottled piece of linen emerged from his pocket.

Jack hid his smile. To Jack's certain knowledge, because he had heard the confession, his friend's 'stalwart' had seen action just the once and that very, very briefly.

Ribbons were pulled off, contents examined. 'Gut, by God!' said Jack. 'Must have cost?'

Ede sniffed, grimaced. 'Not . . . pig, is it?'

Marks glared, his eyebrows melding. Jack interceded. 'Never fear,' he declared, 'Mrs Philips only uses the finest sheep's intestine.'

To another 'huzzah', the cundums were put away. Jack took up his, in a spirit of clansmanship though he already knew that, however his fellow initiates fulfilled Rite Five, he was not going to use it. If his liaisons with Fanny produced a certain guilt regarding his emerging love for Clothilde, any visit to a whore would have been quite unacceptable, and, given Fanny's freely given delights, unnecessary.

The thought of these two produced a sudden feeling of concern. He knew Clothilde was safe within the walls of her father's house, but Fanny? He wondered if she had been much abused by Lord Melbury, if she yet retained her position. He had hopes that sometime during that evening a moment could be found to return to Golden Square and find out. If she'd been thrown out . . . well, as the cause of that, he had an obligation. She must be provided for until she could again provide for herself. If his allowance would not run to the expense, his skill with the billiard cue must; perhaps, he remembered, as soon as tomorrow, in the match arranged against Craster.

With another raucous tribal ululation, the lads leapt down the stairs. The three others set out ahead, racing in different directions, for each would travel separately to their hunt, solitariness being a necessary state for a Mohock stalker. Jack, last to leave as he settled their bill, was tapped on the shoulder near the door.

John Harris was behind him. 'A word, Mr Absolute?'

'At your service, Mr Harris.'

Because of the noise in the corridor, with waiters clattering past bearing liquors and soups and a party of men just beginning a rendition of 'Nan Dawson' in the main room, Jack was led by the arm into a snug where the only occupant, a hefty young gentleman in a salmon-pink jacket, snored, his face obscured by his tricorn hat.

'You know I am fond of you, sir.'

'I have always relished our acquaintance too, Mr Harris.' Jack kept any distaste from his voice, ever the actress's child.

He was concerned that Harris was going to offer him some particular tip from his book. But the words that came were more alarming still.

'Watch your back this night,' came the whisper.

Jack pulled away, looked into the other's eyes. 'What do you mean?'

'I have heard a rumour. One hears them in my position. No names, you understand.' A thin finger was raised to tap those poxed lips. 'But there is someone in the Town who wishes you ill.'

Jack felt a flush to his neck, the hairs there rising. 'Lord Melbury—'

'Shh!' Harris pulled away, glanced down at the sleeping youth. 'I said, no names. I can neither confirm nor deny. I can only warn, as I have done. For the sake of the Old School.'

With that and a squeeze to the forearm he was gone. Jack shivered again, then went out onto the Piazza. It was pell-mell as ever, especially on the south side where Tom King's three coffee houses stood. Jack made for the middle one, the Green Man, stood in its entrance looking back to the Shakespeare's Head. People came and went and it seemed the entire tavern had joined in the chorus of 'Nan Dawson':

> *Of all the girls in Town*
> *The Black, the Fair, the Red and Brown*
> *That dance and prance it up and down*
> *There's none like Nancy Dawson.*

A huge cheer went up. The pink-clad youth, who'd snored in the snug while he and Harris conversed, emerged, talked briefly to someone inside, then strode along the porticos, disappearing up James Street. Was there something familiar in his gait? Yet fear yielded neither memory nor a name.

As Jack moved off across the Piazza, the bells in St Paul's church struck eight. Late again. Jack rolled his shoulders, shrugging off the feeling between them of being watched, which, now Harris had mentioned it, had seemed to reside there most of the day. It was all nonsense! Lord Melbury, one of the country's most powerful politicians and senior member of the Duke of Newcastle's cabinet, would not waste his time over a boy such as he, surely?

Increasing his pace, Jack headed up James Street, the same one the naggingly familiar youth had taken. Even if it led through the notorious rookeries of Seven Dials it was still the swiftest route to the Assembly Rooms in Dean Street, Soho.

He was still late, of course. A fact his mother noted the moment she saw him at the theatre entrance, her anger bringing that touch of Irish to her tongue. 'And how many times, sure, must I underline the word "sharp" after the hour for you to recognize it?'

'A thousand apologies, Mama. I was studying for the Trinity Election and quite lost my way in Cicero.'

An arched eyebrow indicated that he was not believed; but the sight of him seemed to placate enough for her cheek to be offered, which was duly kissed. Standing back, he noticed a man behind his mother regarding the reunion with a smile.

'So good to hear youth is still diligent in its studies,' the man said, thrusting out a hand. 'And I understand you attend the very place that gave me my start in learning.'

Jack's hand was gripped, held, another coming over to make it fast. Jack had no desire to break away, for the man's mellifluous voice, his steady eye, captivated.

His mother spoke again. 'This is a friend of mine and a fellow playwright. Jack Absolute . . . meet John Burgoyne.'

'A mere pretender to your mother's throne.' The man's eyes searched Jack's face. They were deep-set, of a grey that pushed to blue, his hair a brown that stopped just short of black. It was exquisitely, unostentatiously styled, making Jack wish to run his fingers through his own ill-laid hedgerow. Burgoyne's clothes were of an equally simple elegance, rich material precisely cut, brilliantly dyed. He exuded a scent of sandal-wood and musk, undoubtedly made only for him by some parfumier in Bond Street. The total effect was almost perfect, could have led to accusations of foppishness. But John Burgoyne, in his grip, his gaze, had an authority that would belie any such imputation. In that one moment, Jack wanted to be the man's friend, even as he was aware of the absurdity of the idea. Burgoyne was ancient, thirty-five if he was a day.

'Yes,' murmured Burgoyne, 'I can see your father in you, too.'

'You know him, sir?'

'Not well. We have encountered each other. Both Dragoons, d'ye see? Indeed, I am raising a regiment now.'

Ah, that's it, thought Jack, *that's what's beneath the finery. A military man.*

Jack's hand was released as Lady Jane began to push through the throng towards the stage. He could see two boxes beside it but knew his liberally-minded mother would not be heading for them but for one of the front benches. She preferred to be in the Pit, among the people.

'I am surprised,' said Burgoyne as he and Jack trailed through the gap his mother rather forcefully created, 'not to see Sir James here this night.'

Jane gave a rather unlady-like snort. 'You *can't* know him that well. My husband has never learnt how to behave at one of my plays. He does not understand the,' she waved at the raucous audience, 'collaborative nature of theatre. If someone were merely to cough during a line, he would attempt to thrash them for the disrespect.' She indicated the stage where, as always, benches had been provided for the wealthier audience who liked to be close to the action. Jack could see that the Harlequin and his Pierrot, engaged in an entr'acte, were having difficulty executing their romantic dance between two rowdies more concerned with the actress's supple legs than the art before them, lowering themselves with loud guffaws to the floor to look up her short dress. Jane continued.

'These fellows would be assaulted in a moment. No, it is best for all that he keeps away.'

She gave a sigh. Yet within it there was something affectionate, almost proud, that made Jack shudder. Though he knew that when he and Clothilde were at last united, their love would continue, undimmed, a thousand years, there was something disquieting in parents displaying the same passion.

The dance ended, and they made their way to the benches. Three fellows in apprentices' smocks rose, accepted the sixpences Burgoyne placed in their hands, touched their hats and gave up their seats. There was a brief interlude as a cloth dropped, indicating a bucolic scene with a farm cart wheeled on before it.

'Is this yours, Mama?' Jack was a little puzzled. His mother usually wrote for an urban setting.

'Mine,' said Burgoyne, leaning forward and rubbing his hands together. Jack was surprised to see the footlights reflecting in the sheen on his brow. 'Mine,' he said again, and swallowed.

Music struck up. Given the financial limitations of the Assembly Rooms, this was not the orchestra to be found at the large venues but merely a drum, French Horn and fife. Those limitations were noticed again in the cast that eventually entered, for the Harlequin of before was here transformed into a rubicund country gentleman with rouged cheeks, while his Pierrot returned as a simple country maid. Jack, who had noticed not much more than her stockinged legs before, now saw that she was indeed rather pretty, with a beauty spot nestled next to lips both full and rosy. A hitherto unseen younger gentleman entered and the piece began. Burgoyne leant forward eagerly, his mouth mouthing the words along with the players . . . until a sharp elbow from Lady Jane made him desist.

Whereas his mother used the obscurity of the Assembly Rooms to sneak her anti-government satires past the Lord Chamberlain, Jack knew that many playwrights saw them as a proving ground, aspiring to the larger houses with plays as conventional as any that would be seen at the Lane or the Garden. Just such a play was Burgoyne's. The country maid, the impoverished noble who loved her, the lecherous guardian who 'would have her or none would!' all interspersed with the bursts of country dancing and song required by the form. Yet this was, at least, better crafted than most and with a simple story that struck Jack's heart. For he saw himself in the smitten youth, Clothilde in the sad maiden, even – and this was a reach, he knew – the smirking Claude in the squire's leers and lust. And when the young man, upon his knees, told of the maid's immediate banishment to a far land and declaimed, 'I will follow thee over all the seas in heaven and through every flame in hell,' Jack, reminded of his own watery poem recited only that morning to his love, was held on the line, as hooked as any merman.

He raised his hands to applaud. But just as he did so, someone threw something from the right-hand box where, up to now, only shapes had moved in the shadows. A piece of orange peel hit the kneeling youth in the forehead. He jerked back, his mouth opening and closing. Someone laughed, then someone else and, very distinctly, Jack heard one word emerge from the box.

'Now.'

Lady Jane, in a harsh whisper, said, 'A claque, John. It seems your enemies have found you.'

Jack had been around enough with his mother to recognize the term. Theatre, like cricket, drew partisan support and one player succeeding meant less acclaim for another. There were two other new playwrights on that night's bill aside from the more established Lady Jane. One of those novitiate's patrons – for as in cricket, nobles sponsored their favourites – had organized a claque to ruin Burgoyne's debut. The peel chucker opposite, no doubt.

One of the youths on stage – an especially pimply-faced, unkempt fellow – had obviously taken the thrown peel as a signal. 'I've paid a florin for this,' he shouted, 'And it's not worth a farthing.' One of his hands was thrust out toward the audience in appeal, the other was engaged in trying to reach under the dress of the actress who, frozen by the interruption, now thawed to slap the hand away.

A few in the audience concurred, hooting their derision, while several others yelled, 'Sit down, ye dog!'

Burgoyne, who'd risen, looked as if he were about to climb up and intervene. Yet it was Jack, with the alacrity of youth, who beat him to it. Perhaps it was that a friend of his mother's was being gravely insulted; perhaps the ale working within him; or perhaps the feeling that it was his Clothilde under threat by the groping drunk. Whatever it was, Jack was on the stage in a moment.

'Hello, cocky,' he said, advancing to the youth and seizing his arm, 'fancy a spin?' He grabbed, pulled the fellow tight to him. He was slighter than Jack, for all the peacock puffery of his clothes.

'Unhand me, sir,' cried the youth, trying to slip from the hold. 'What the Devil are you about?'

'This,' said Jack. Dipping the fellow towards the musicians, he said, 'Strike me up a jig.' Though startled, they did, Jack taking the man's feet entirely off the stage and three-stepping him over to the wings. Burgoyne meantime had begun to clap in rhythm, as did Jane, and soon almost the entire audience had joined in, drowning out the appeal of the second youth who yet attempted to disrupt the play. Out of sight, against the wall of the theatre, Jack still held the squirming bravo in his grip. 'Now you . . .' he whispered. 'Behave!' And on the word he tapped him with some force, forehead to nose. Not enough to break, just enough to bring water to the eyes. He released him and turned back to the stage where the other was now waving at the clapping audience, trying to command silence. When it wouldn't come, and Jack approached, he hung his head and darted to the opposite wings.

The clapping changed at the song's end into pure applause,

the players took up their positions to recommence and Jack slipped down the side of the stage and retook his place on the bench, several backslaps accompanying his journey.

'A hero, your Jack,' said Burgoyne to Lady Jane, seizing Jack's hand and pumping it, 'and every inch his father's son.' Turning, he said, 'I am in your debt, lad, and will consider myself under obligation until I can repay it.'

'T'was, nothing, sir. I . . . I was enjoying your piece, is all, and . . .'

'Well, you have gained a friend by it. And, I fear, an enemy.' Burgoyne nodded at the box opposite. 'I wonder who the leader of their claque is. If only he'd emerge from the damn shado . . . oh. Oh, of course. Well, it seems my noble Lord's dislike of my politics now extends to my plays.'

Jack turned now to see of whom he was speaking. The man in the shadows of the box had indeed leaned forward but he wasn't looking at Burgoyne, he was looking at Jack. And as he met Lord Melbury's gaze, for the second time in a day, he saw His Lordship mouth, quite distinctly, three words:

'You. Are. Dead.'

— EIGHT —

Last Rites

If his mother was surprised when he bolted at the very climax of her play, in the moment before the applause, she did not have time to show it. A squeeze of her shoulder, on the word, 'Excellent,' the barest touch of Burgoyne's hand and he was gone. In the crowds beginning to disgorge from the Assembly Rooms there was the shelter of the herd. For it was now obvious – Lord Melbury was having him followed. Those eyes he'd felt on his back all night, the warning from Harris; men had been hired to dog him down some Soho alley, to thrash him . . . or worse. His Lordship's mouthed words could not have been clearer.

Jack was not sure what to do. The only true refuge lay at his school or his home. His boarding house was not expecting him, he and the other Mohocks having contrived a simultaneous two-night exeunt for a variety of reasons, medical, educational, familial. He could return there early; but Mrs Porten's door was hardly stout and the old retainers unequal to any tough of Melbury's. He could go home, sneaking in the back way again. But the sneaking irked, while his father's company and accompanying lectures held little appeal. Besides, there was the Initiation to consider, rites yet unfulfilled, rendezvous to keep. How could he let down his friends?

Fuck Lord Melbury, thought Jack, as he elbowed his way to

the entrance. He'd wager he knew the shadowy recesses of Soho better than most. Ever since his father had ordered him there for French classes, Jack had delighted in exploring the maze of alleys and courts. He'd lose any pursuit within it and bide till he could fulfil his mission.

Refuge was found in a hedge tavern, that lowest form of alehouse. There was one that delighted him in Meards Court, where the top floors were a brothel, as indicated by the spread fan above the door, while in the warren of rooms below an illegal still provided powerful spirits to any who craved them. Jack found a suitably dark corner and ordered only ale from a serving wench who desired to offer him much, much more and continued to renew and expand her offers each time she fetched him another tankard.

Politely refusing everything save beer, Jack bided the hour necessary for any pursuit to have been given up. True to his vow, he was moderate in consumption, choosing only porter. Thus he was surprised when he stood up to stagger a little. *Must be the smoke*, Jack mused, as he pushed his way to the door through clouds of it. He was not a pipeman himself, the inhalation affecting him in a disagreeable way liquor did not. He found the smoke also caused his eyes to misglance for as he moved through the second room he was almost sure he saw again that fellow in the pink jacket who'd snored in the snug at the Shakespeare's Head. But as he stepped forward to verify, one of the Cats rose from a table and entwined him in her arms. By the time he'd disengaged and gained the street, the figure had disappeared.

St Anne's Court was but a short stumble along Wardour Street but Jack's progress was slow down a thoroughfare crowded with revellers, swaying from tavern to coffee house. Vendors competed, with both their shouts and the scents rising from their barrows and trays, and Jack, suddenly realizing that he'd eaten little beyond the bowl of turtle soup, became instantly famished. A hot pudding man offered one for one-and-sixpence but two for half-a-crown, and Jack took the bargain. The first disappeared in an ecstasy of shovelling fingers, the second was wrapped in a broadside, the subject of which Jack saw to be a highwayman's execution the month before. Tucking it carefully into his satchel – the man had assured him it was near all meat and would not leak – a much fortified Jack moved up the street, certain that no one could have followed him from the hedge tavern, the crowds being too extensive.

His sanguinity lasted until the moment he turned into St Anne's Court. Whereas on the main thoroughfare at least one in every five householders had observed his civic duty and placed a lamp above his doorway, the denizens of this court had no such scruples, their activities perhaps requiring less light. One lamp spluttered on its last oil at the Wardour Street end but when Jack reached the dog-leg halfway down, even that paltry glow vanished and nothing at all shone in from Dean Street to replace it. It was beyond mere night, for the shadows fell like curtains from the roofs almost conjoined above and mist rose to meet them from such slick cobblestones as remained in place. Yet if light had been sucked away, noise had not. It was muted here as befitted the dark, dank mantle laid upon it, but as in the rest of London, sounds never ceased. Something was scratching in a doorway he'd just passed on his left, the regularity of the nails on wood making Jack believe it was an animal . . . until a voice whispered, 'Yes, yes, there!' and another voice groaned. That drove him three steps on, further into the murk, halted by a growl, a high-pitched squeal, a snap. Reaching out till he encountered a doorway, he leaned into its scant protection, raised his stick before him. The crushing sound moved nearer, then went by him and, in the faint spill of light at the building's corner, he saw a small dog, a terrier, a broken-backed rat still squirming in its mouth. With a final twist and chomp, the writhing ceased, the dog moved on and Jack suddenly felt the chill of the April night he'd previously ignored. Shivering, he considered immediately following the animal and its prey back to light and life. The Mohocks would understand; none would wish him to die in this dark passage. He even took a step away from the doorway until a moment of recognition came. The door he sought was the one he'd taken shelter before.

'Well, if it's locked,' Jack muttered, 'there's no more I can do.' Half hoping, he stepped toward it, shoved none too hard. The door gave and, when footsteps suddenly slapped on the cobbles down the alley, Jack stepped inside and pushed it to behind him.

At first he thought the darkness within more complete than that without; but then he perceived light both beneath the doors on either side of the entrance and through their unevenly joined slats, heard a slurred laugh, someone clapping slowly, a whisper. When a floorboard creaked and a footstep approached, Jack quietly climbed to the first landing, just turning the corner as the left door opened. 'Nothing, I told you. No one,' a well-bred voice declared. 'And now, my dear, shall we continue with . . .' The conclusion of the proposition was cut off by the door closing. Jack breathed deep, then began to climb cautiously on, hand against the wall, feet reaching carefully, each floor giving him its own variation of sound and seeping light. The top floor, Harris's list had said, was where the masked actress resided.

So attic-wards Jack went. And when he could go no further, he stopped and felt around him, touch his only sense for no light gave its slight comfort. He found the entranceway, sure enough, traced its outline; yet it was dark and when he tapped lightly upon it, got no response.

Then a door downstairs opened, closed. He knew it was the outside one and not one of the rooms because the opening brought a trace of noise from Wardour Street, instantly cut off. Whoever came in, paused; for there followed a silence so deep that Jack thought his breathing a roar, the floorboards, as his weight shifted, a shriek. When he settled, so did the silence but only for a moment . . . just until the sound of footsteps began.

There was nowhere to flee whoever ascended. The one window was glassless, boarded tight and the door, tested again, still locked. He could only press himself and hope that the darkness was as engulfing for the climber as for he, that whoever approached would not see him trying to be as small as possible in the corner. Then, as the creaking of steps reached the first floor, he realized that they would indeed see him for one obvious reason – they were looking for him. The man who climbed steadily had followed him all day and into this night, wore a pink coat and had Lord Melbury's gold in one pocket, a cudgel or a pistol in another. And all Jack could do was press himself against the wall and thrust his stick before him.

The last stairs began their chorus of creaks and Jack could wait no more. 'Aaah,' he screamed, swooshing the stick from on high, encountering nothing but air until he reached the floor with a force that jarred his arm. 'Aaah!' came an equally forceful cry from below, though this was decidedly female.

Jack held the stick high but didn't let it fall again. 'Who's there?'

Silence for unutterably long seconds. Then a woman's voice, but in a shriek. 'Keep away! I've a knife.'

'So have I.'

More silence, except for breaths sucked in. ''arris?' the woman said at last. Jack couldn't think what to say to that, so he didn't. The voice continued, 'I've promised you the money, 'arris, I've got it for you, really I 'ave.'

'I'm not . . . 'arris. I'm . . . a customer.'

'You're . . . what?' Silence came again, shorter-lived. ''ow did you get in?'

'Um . . . the door was open.'

Another pause. 'Who are you then?'

'Jack—'

The voice was sharp. 'Jack . . . 'arris?'

'No, I've said. Jack, just Jack!'

'And you mean me no 'arm?'

'None, I swear!'

There was a longer silence. Then, 'Well, Just-Jack, why don't we get inside and get a light going? Then I can take a look at you.'

'That would be . . . yes.'

The steps creaked again, a key entered a lock. Jack stayed in his corner until he heard the door opening, took a step. 'Wait a second, there's a poppet,' came the voice. The door was shut, locked. Jack stood in the darkness, debating whether to run. Surely he had dared enough. One rite unfulfilled . . . then, just as he decided to, the door opened again, light shone out. Standing before the lamp was a woman in a long purple dress and loose bodice of yellow. Covering her eyes and nose was a feathered mask.

'Come in, dear sir, come in,' she said, in a voice quite different from the one she'd used on the stairs, richer, deeper, certainly from another class. She stepped aside, her arm descending in a flourish to wave him in. 'I am Matilda. And you?'

'Jack . . . Harris . . . son! Jack Harrison. Ha!' He entered. The room was an odd shape, much smaller than he'd expected, little bigger than the bed that occupied most of it. A small table, which held the oil lantern and a porcelain basin, took up most of the rest of the space. He then saw why it was under-sized – the walls weren't walls at all but screens, wooden-framed and paper-panelled, with stays and stockings dangling from their crests. The real walls of cracked plaster and bulging horsehair were just visible above.

The door closed behind him. 'Your stick, sir. Your hat. Please!' She gestured and Jack took off his tricorn, placed it on the knob of his stick, leaned both against a screen. When he straightened and faced her again, she had stepped closer to him. She was tall, her nose level with his neck.

'Now, sir,' she said, making a little curtsey, her voice still husky, 'what is it I may do for you?'

Her eyes were hidden beneath the gold and the feathers of her disguise so it was her mouth he looked at. Not so much the lips, which bore some purplish stain, but an exquisite little mole to the left of them. And as he studied it, he realized he had seen it before and that very night and just as he recognized her, her eyes at the very same moment widened. They spoke as one.

'I know you—'

'I saw you tonight—'

They both paused. The woman moved back, the eyes still upon him. She went on first. 'You were the gallant who intervened when those boobies would upset the play.'

He nodded.

'You were a hero, sir.'

'Hardly that.'

'To me you were. And I'm sure also to the author for . . . wait, were you not sat beside Burgoyne? You are his friend?'

This was not the time to go into why he was there. He'd told the Mohocks that this would be a danger, picking out an actress for him to visit. The last thing he needed was for this story to become theatrical gossip. And get back to his mother.

'I am.'

Matilda had stepped back closer to him. 'Colonel Burgoyne is fortunate in his friends indeed. So brave, so handsome.' She reached up and pulled the mask from her face. 'No need for that precaution tonight. You know me already.'

The uncovering revealed something slightly different than Jack expected. The maid of the play was not a blushing sixteen but at least ten years older, the face not unblemished perfection, but full of the little lines and signals of a hard life. The paint that had smoothed all under the soothing stage lights looked thick and cracked by lamplight. She was still pretty, or would be were not an underlying tiredness the primary look in her eyes. Nevertheless, Jack said, 'But a man always desires to be reacquainted with such beauty, madam.'

She clapped her hands, laughed. 'So gallant. You are not . . . I have heard that the Colonel has one or two . . . indiscretions, who usually reside in the country. Are you perhaps . . .'

'One of Burgoyne's country indiscretions? No indeed, madam.'

Jack was rather alarmed to find that he was blushing as he spoke, a colour that deepened when a hand reached up to rest on his face. 'And you sport the badge of youth,' she said, laughing again.

Now that he was here, Jack felt two things equally keenly: the first that this encounter, a mere pistol shot from Thrift Street, was hardly worthy of one who loved such an innocent as Clothilde; the second that what had sounded marvellous when concocted as the fifth Mohock Rite at Tothill Fields was ridiculous in the Town. How the rite was performed was up to the individual warrior, but any thought Jack had had of taking what he wanted by sudden surprise or subterfuge had vanished in the mutual recognition.

'Why the disguise?' he asked, as she finally removed her hand and reached past him to hang the mask on the screen. Their bodies were very close, she was leaning forward and the loose bodice flopped forward, revealing two rather large but finely shaped breasts. She appeared unaware of the effect the sight had on him, yet took her time leaning back.

'Though it is too late with you, sir, I will rely on the gallantry you have already displayed to keep my secret. I took on this extra . . . profession when times were especially hard and it was that, starve or return to my Methodist mother in Barnstable.' She shuddered. 'But though the two trades are thought to be interchangeable, it would not do me much good when contracts at the Garden or the Lane are being discussed, if "whore" was atop my list of recent credits.'

He flinched slightly at the word, the venom with which she said it. She noticed, smiled again. 'But do not fear me, young sir. This contract at the Assembly Rooms means I can dispense with my second occupation. And I'd asked Harris to remove me from the new edition of his book. He said that it had already gone to press and that he would be by to collect his money soon. That's why I,' she gestured to the door, 'was a little afraid when you appeared at my door. I haven't been here for a fortnight, see. I only came by tonight to pick up my things.'

Matilda kicked at a leather case that Jack had not noticed as it was wedged in under the bed. 'I have played this stage for the last time,' she continued, stepping close again, bending forward again, 'but since I *am* here and since you are a friend of Burgoyne, a man who will write many more lovely plays with many more lovely roles in them, perhaps . . . perhaps . . .'

She was so close. And Jack had always loved actresses, been around them ever since he'd come to London and his mother, prevented from acting by acquiring the title 'Lady Absolute', had started writing her plays and satires. And, after all, he had been on heat all day, torn from Clothilde's embrace, forced to flee from Fanny's . . . In three other rooms in Soho he was quite sure his brethren were facing no such qualms now.

So he bent and kissed the perfect imperfection of that mole and though she sighed and pressed against him and yielded tongue for tongue, yet there was something . . . studied in the giving, with none of the fearful anticipation of his French love, or the complete hunger of his mistress. As he probed, he warred within himself, but what he'd drunk still fired him and a woman's body was pressed close. And then the bells of St Anne's, Soho, sounded. He pulled away.

'What's wrong, Jack?' she whispered, trying to re-engage. So he held her at arm's length and told her what he'd really come for. She asked him to repeat it. He was scared she might be angry. He knew many women who would be. Instead, she just laughed. 'Well, I've had a lot of strange requests in my time but that . . .'

Then she stepped away from him and began to roll up her loose dress, taking her time, her eyes on him. He watched the dress rise in circular folds, passing up the stockinged legs that he remembered so admiring earlier that night.

'Come then, Mr Harris . . . son,' she breathed, 'my gallant, my hero. Come and take your reward.'

Jack reached into his satchel and, when he was quite ready, leaned forward.

Bob Derry's Cyder House in Maiden Lane, the Mohocks' rallying point, was misnamed, having neither Cyder nor Maidens – not so far as Jack could see out of the one eye that remained open. It was all Cats and Jig girls, all arrack punch and gin, and though one small part of his battered brain kept reminding him that, for some undoubtedly important reason, he had vowed to stay with brewed liquids, sup nothing fermented or distilled, yet he only ever remembered this when he'd already taken a gulp of whatever was placed before him. With an exclamation, he'd dash the remaining contents to the floor, invert the mug, shout, 'No more, damn ye, not one drop more!' But then he'd turn, the pewter would be brimming, he'd take a gulp, swallow, gag, swear, dash, invert . . . and the whole ghastly sequence would begin again.

His friends were of no use. Marks refused to sit, just loomed and swayed and occasionally crashed his forearms down upon the table when he wanted to contradict some particular point. Their little table in the corner of the main room had space around it despite the crowd for he would not confine his arguments to his own set. His last sober moment had been on his arrival when, quite solemnly, he'd handed Jack a purse.

'A hundred guineas – for the match against Craster,' he'd said, winking profoundly. Jack had spent the next ten minutes trying to get him to take the beastly thing back. It was the first of the arguments and the trigger for many more.

Ede made up in recumbence for his friend's verticality, being stretched full out on a bench and, though prostrate, was going through every nuance of his recent triumph in the Latin play at Westminster.

In one corner of the vast cellar, two women were raging. Clothes had been torn, bosoms revealed and ripped by flaying nails and teeth, hair jerked out in chunks. They were surrounded by screaming partisans and neutrals placing bets. An equal crowd had gathered around another scrap, this between a man and two women in the main, though others would join in when appropriate, when one side had gained an upper hand. To Jack, the fight, which had been going on for at least fifteen minutes, was turning in the favour of the women, who had pinned the man to the floor and were taking turns raking him with long nails. Yet even as he watched, another man stepped in and hauled one of them away by the hair while the man on the floor bucked the other one off. The crack her head made on the table seemed in no way to daunt her for she was up and on him again and, with seconds out, battle was re-engaged.

It was all quite diverting, though there was one worry that drew Jack's one eye occasionally to the door: Fenby was an hour late at the least and in that part of his brain still functioning, Jack was concerned for his little friend. Then, just as the woman picked up a pewter mug and was narrowly restrained from smashing it on the prone man's skull, Fenby appeared.

'Here, here!' Jack leapt up, pushed past spectators and combatants, seized Fenby's arm and dragged him back to the table. Marks finally sat down, Ede up, and all regarded, in some horror, the Last of the Mohocks.

He was a sight. Both lenses of his glasses were stoved, pushing in like starburst fireworks, and both eyes were swollen, appeared to be blackening, while one had the added problem of a trail of blood running down from the scalp and pooling in the socket.

'Damn, man,' said Ede, 'what have you been about?'

'Did some ruffian . . .' Marks was rising again, his big hands thrust before him.

'No, no,' said Fenby, 't'was no villain, I assure you, t'was . . .' He reached up to touch his glasses and as soon as he did they crumbled off his face, ending on the table in four pieces. He sighed, produced some wire to attempt repairs. 'I was trying to f . . . f . . . fulfil the Rite, see.'

'And did you?' said Jack. They had none of them discussed their success or failure that night for they had agreed all tales must be told together.

'Well,' said Fenby, after a long pause, 'can a m . . . man not get a drink to wet the whistle?' Punch was poured and Fenby gagged, spat, took his time drinking again, looked up.

'So?' said Marks impatiently, 'did you hunt the Big Carrothead?'

'I did.'

He sipped again. The other three sighed in exasperation. 'And?' said Jack.

Fenby put down the mug. 'What could I do? I have not your g . . . g . . . gift of speech, Absolute, nor Ede's alluring nobility, nor Marks's courage. I could only use subterfuge. But when I finally made the attempt the result was, well, as you see.' He indicated his face, his shattered spectacles, wincing and smiling simultaneously.

'And was this the only result, Fenby?' said Jack. 'Tell us now: did you complete the Last Rite of the Mohocks?'

Fenby looked at each of them in turn; then, very slowly, he reached into his coat's inner pocket. First, he pulled out a piece of scrap paper which he carefully unfolded in the centre of the table. He reached again and produced, this time, a silk sachet. All recognized it, for it had formerly contained the cundum that Marks had handed out at the night's commencement. However, no engine of love fell out when Fenby shook the sachet over the table. Something else did, drifting down to settle on the page.

'As you can see, I did indeed complete all the Rites. For I hunted, I trapped, and finally, I . . . scalped. And as you can also see, gentlemen . . . she was indeed a true Redhead.'

The other three leaned over. There, sitting in the centre of the table, tiny but unmistakable, was a tuft of pubic hair. Ginger.

The yell that went up, the cry of 'Ah-ha-ah-ha-HA-HA-HA!' was so loud, so triumphant that it caused even the scrappers and their audience to cease for a moment, to turn and stare.

'A bumper, a bumper for the first Initiate to become a Full Blood Mohock – Fenby, the Hawk!' Jack turned, seeking a servant. But before anything else, he saw a pink coat just disappearing into the mob.

'A moment,' he said, and swayed off in pursuit.

His quarry might have eluded him again had not the fights, paused at the Mohock cries, recommenced with double vigour. One of the women leapt on the back of the single man who twisted and bucked. When these tactics failed to shake her, he began to spin, roaring the while. Just as the pink coat was passing the fray, she was dislodged and landed pretty much square on Jack's quarry. Jack reached the fellow as he was endeavouring to rise.

'Need a hand?' he said, and, reaching down, he grabbed the man by the collar and jerked him to his feet. It was only when he had him upright and was looking up into the face – an unaccustomed angle for Jack – that he recognized it.

It was The Man from the Harrow–Westminster cricket match.

'You!' Jack's grip tightened, despite the fellow's efforts to dislodge it. 'I know you.'

'Indeed, sir? Where from?'

'Where from?' The rising, walking, lifting had sent the blood to Jack's head again and he swayed slightly, using his hand on the fellow's collar to keep himself erect. 'Don't attempt to cozen me, you dog.' He swayed towards him, swayed back. Jack was not sure which of them was moving. 'You are a schoolboy impostor and played for Harrow yesterday.'

'Oh, that!' The man managed to slip from Jack's grasp and when Jack leaned forward, placed a hand against his chest.

'And you've been dogging me all night. Melbury's man.'

The large red face creased. 'Melbury, sir? Don't know who you mean. I've been drinking around the town, tis true. Thought I sees you once afore. But I bain't be doggin' nobody.'

Jack glared, sought a response. At that moment, a voice beside him said, 'Trouble, Absolute?' and he looked to see Marks and the other Mohocks clustered behind him.

'Yes, this fellow's been following me around all night. Up to no good.'

'I bain't, gentlemen, honest.'

'We know him, don't we?' said Ede.

'We do.' Jack nodded slowly.

There was a silence. 'Damn fine bowler,' Fenby said at last.

'Not a bad bat,' added Marks.

'But you gentlemen is even finer,' said The Man, hurriedly, 'for you gained a fair and fine victory. Can I buy yous all a drink?'

'You can!' came from three of the four voices and his friends led their rival back to the table. Jack, still muttering his suspicions, followed. But he couldn't keep his ill temper long, especially since Horace – as The Man was called – proved a splendid fellow, swearing innocence in such a bluff, true way that he reminded Jack of his old Cornish friend, Treve Tregonning. And he insisted on making amends for his imposture the day before – an imposture, he pointed out, that had singularly failed due to their collective skills – by ordering bumpers of arrack punch. Jack had truly sworn off the stuff, despite the several glasses that had slipped inadvertently down, but he could hardly refuse the toast Horace proposed.

'I take it all back, sir. There be no doubt that you made that last run, that you were "in". So, gentlemen, I propose Mr Absolute's last notch. I doubt I'll live to see a finer.'

The toast was to him so he alone stood. While he tipped the tankard back, the Mohocks thumped the table and ululated their war cry. When he reached the end, he suddenly found that he was sitting down again without any memory of making the descent. Indeed, little thereafter stayed with him. He had an idea that new fights began when the old ended; that one of the combatants, a wickedly attractive young lady, joined them at Horace's request and seemed immediately and immensely fond of Jack; that his friends' laughing faces flickered in and out of vision and that later one of them was pressing him to go; that he resisted this disgraceful idea strongly. And that the last thing that impinged was his late sporting rival and new-found friend leaning over him and saying, quite distinctly, 'You're Out!'

It was the snoring that roused and, for a few moments, reassured him. He woke to such tunes every morning at Mrs Porten's, his boarding house fellows supplying an orchestra's variety of notes, mainly from the brass, a bassoon here, a trumpet there. This from beside him was higher, a piccolo perhaps, but that was no cause for disquiet, for boys from eight to eighteen all shared the same long room. All it meant was that he was safe, that somehow he had made it back. He had no recollection of how, whether by chair, wherry, or Shanks's Pony. Indeed, no memories of the night before came at all and he did not care. He was safe and, with luck, had yet a few hours to sleep off . . . whatever he'd done to himself the night before.

He sighed, turned his head . . . and it was as if someone had taken a mallet and driven a wedge from under his jaw to the top of his scalp. His yelp, which manifested itself as nothing more than a rattle in the desert of his throat, caused a dam of hot, viscous liquid to crack open and surge . . . In a moment he was upright and leaping towards the bucket kept in the corner of the dormitory.

He never made it for three reasons. The first: his foot was caught in a roll of bedclothes that held his lower body fast while the upper fell. The second: when his shoulder slammed into the floor, what he would give to Porten's bucket would not be contained and burst from him in a torrent that hit the junction of wall and planking a good four foot from him. And thirdly: he was not *at* Porten's.

This realization was confirmed by the whisper that came from behind him.

'Awake, sweet'art?'

Something terrible rose from where Jack had just been lying. It was loosely covered in a shift that, even in the palest of light that was seeping under the shutters into the room, Jack could tell was filthy. He yelped, again tried to struggle away from the terrifying vision. But his foot was still caught and the more he struggled the tighter it seemed to be bound. As the figure continued to rise over him, even reach out a hand, his struggles became increasingly desperate. Finally, he placed his foot against the bed frame and kicked hard; there was a tearing and he shot back across the slick floor on what he now realized was his bare arse.

He collided with the wall, shot up. The agony the sudden elevation caused was intense, his head filled with mist and he would have fallen had not the voice from the bed kept him upright in terror.

'Come, lovey. You wasn't so shy last night.'

Whatever was facing him, he had to know it. With another sickening leap he was at the shutters, wrenching them open. Daylight, sudden and vicious, streamed in.

The vision on the bed gave a cry, held up a hand across her face. 'Eh, you fuck, what you doin' that for? Shut it! Shut it I say!'

Jack half closed them, letting in enough light still to see. The room was dingy, with peeling walls and dirt-encrusted floor, the only furniture a bed and a washstand with a basin and towel as filthy as the bedding. A half-empty bottle of gin stood beside it. It was not a habitation, it was a place of business and with that recognition Jack turned his attention back to the proprietor. The voice had told him it was a woman and he saw now that her face was so heavily painted, and that paint smeared, that it was impossible in the half-light to tell her age. She could have been sixteen or sixty. Something in that voice though told Jack that she was probably closer to the latter.

'Who . . . who are you, madam?'

The woman sniggered. 'Ooh, such a polite young gent – 'ceptin' 'ee don't remember Little Angie. And you wouldn't leave off sayin' the name last night. Rhymin' it with all sorts of things.'

She sniggered again and Jack's eyes, getting used to the light and the sensation of wakefulness, got more acute. He looked, looked again, verified. The woman only had one eyebrow; though that one compensated for the absence of a mate by being extensive and bushy. Of its twin there was no sign. But there was an abundance of hair above, though this was slewed at an unnatural angle across the forehead and of a reddish colour not found on Nature's pallet.

She noted his study. 'Lawks,' she said, and reached up to adjust. 'Tha's your fault, that is. Pawed me about so I'm all askew.'

Jack felt his stomach heave once more into his throat. With an effort he quelled it, tried to keep his voice level. 'Are you saying . . . Angie . . . that we . . . that you and I . . .'

'Don't'cha 'member, lovey? Can 'e not 'member your sweet girl who rhymes with ever so many things?'

For the life of him, Jack couldn't think of any rhymes for Angie, except 'mangy', which seemed ungallant but horribly true.

'So . . . we . . . we . . .' He gestured to the bed.

'Ashully, to be 'onest,' she said, 'you wash that far gone that . . .' She seemed suddenly to be having difficulty speaking, circling her jaw in a strange manner. ' 'alf a mo', dearie.' A grubby finger was inserted in the mouth, rooted for a moment, then there was a distinct click. 'Dere,' she said, pulling out a set of teeth, 'dat's betta.' She looked up at Jack and began bending some wires. 'Now, where wash we? Oh yesh, you wash that far gone, I 'ash to work hard. Very hard. Lor, I earned my money.' She smiled up at him gummily. 'You seemed to enjoy yesshelf even if there wash no true wakin' of the dead. Still, it'sh early.' She set her feet down on the floor, reached a hand out towards him. 'Your friend paid, said it was for an 'hole night. So 'ow's about 'avin' the rest of it now?'

Jack looked into the abyss. There were two teeth in there that were her own. He spun to the window, threw back the shutters and vomited again. It seemed to go on for ever, retching when there was nothing left to expel save the foulest bitterness. As he leaned there, a bell nearby tolled. By the tenth and final stroke he still had not recognized its note. He wiped his mouth, turned back, was greeted by another click.

'Where,' he said, trying not to look again at the mouth that now gleamed at him, 'am I?'

'Vinegar Yard. That's St Mary's in the Strand you just 'eard.'

The Bell. Ten in the morning. There was something nagging at his much abused brain. Something he must do.

'Friend?' he suddenly said.

'Wha'?'

'You said my friend paid.'

'Yus. Said to give you the best time.'

No Mohock would have done this. 'What did he look like?'

The one eyebrow moved centrally, indicating concentration. 'Nah, can't 'member. But I 'ad been in Derry's since eight so . . .' She cackled. 'But 'e 'ad a lovely pink coat.'

The Man. Horace. An impostor for Harrow. Harrow versus Westminster. Harrow . . .

'Craster!' He had two hours – less – to pull himself together. Less than two hours before he faced an almost certainly well-rested Craster Absolute across the baize. Despite the pain it caused him, he began scrabbling for his clothes. These were all soiled, soaked, patterned with things he could not contemplate. Then, hopping into his breeches, he remembered something else, something far more important. He stood with one leg in his breeches, one out.

'Where's my damn money?' he gasped.

'Money?'

'My gold. Damn, where are my guineas?'

His voice had risen to a roar, startling her. 'You didn't 'ave none. Pink gent paid.'

'No!' he bellowed. 'Please God, no!' and spent a desperate

minute ranging round the room, shouting as he scrabbled at floorboards and pushed into the rotten plaster around the beams. But there was nowhere to hide anything and Angie's fear at his sudden rage was genuine, she was too frightened to lie. She'd been well rewarded for a night, a guinea piece Jack would swear.

Pink Gent had paid with Westminster gold.

– NINE –

Duel on a Green Field

There was no question of going home. The walk to Mayfair and back – for the Angel, venue for the contest, was a porter's chuck from the Garden – would have consumed Jack's little store of time; and that had to be spent in repairing the irreparable: his clothes and body.

He went where he could get credit – the Old Hummum Hotel, where the previous evening's Initiation had begun. Mendoza, the proprietor, was as surly as ever, rendered more so by the demand for help. This was the time of day when the Cats who entertained there till near dawn were curled up at the top of the house and the lower floors of the Hummum were cleansed in preparation for the night to come. But one of the small bagnios, the last to be vacated, was still rich in heat and the first of the day's water was on the stoves. Grumbling, he let Jack in, assigned a servant to him, conspicuously marked his slate. He even arranged for another servant to take Jack's clothes and attempt some salvage, though the pronouncement on them was not good.

Jack then began a regime of purge, plunge and cleanse. Firstly, he drank some milk still warm from the cow, the first mug of which stayed down no longer that it had taken to come out. He persevered, put down the rebellion in his guts to master a second, then ordered a quart of ox-cheek broth from the stall in the Great Piazza. While he awaited it, he went to the heat, evil-smelling sweat coursing from every pore, the pounding between his temples redoubling till he could bear it no more and he plunged into a bath of cold water, forcing himself to remain till his fevered red had turned to blue. The arrival of the broth, fortified with a slug of sherry, revived him a little. A further alternation of heat and cold and he could at least open his eyes without squinting, somewhat necessary for what lay ahead.

A small vat of coffee and a stale Chelsea bun was the limit of the treatment. He had now moved from crippled to merely prostrate and lay propped up on a divan while the servant brought him cool cloths that muffled his head yet were not thick enough to exclude the sound of St Paul's bell tolling noon.

'Christ!' said Jack, shooting up, the suddenness of the movement nearly undoing all his good work. 'My clothes, dammit!'

They were fetched, the servant charged with their renewal protesting that he had not had the required time. They were indeed a deranging sight – stained, slashed and sopping. The cleansing that had partially corrected one problem, created another: they were soaked. Yet he was already late, as always. Despite a chill April wind that had reappeared to cut through London's streets, he had no choice. Shivering already, he slid into dankness and as he did, begged one last favour from the landlord who grumbled, but eventually complied. Metal tokens were used in the Hummum, handed over for any 'services', tallied in chalk on a slate to be collected at night's end, for clients with no clothes stored their money behind a stout grille on the first floor. A bagful of these metal disks was collected now and given to Jack in a maid's cap.

'I will bring these back when I return to pay you later, Mendoza,' Jack said, as he scurried out the door.

'You had better,' the Maltese called after him, shaking the slate which was chalked to an outrageous nine shillings, 'or your reputation is lost.'

My reputation, thought Jack, is already buggered.

There was only one way to redeem it. To make the Angel before St Clement's struck half past and he forfeited the match. And then, of course, to win. For if he did not . . .

The metal tokens clinked in the maid's cap as Jack shrugged into the bitter wind.

St Clement's tolled the half-hour as he walked through the Angel's door. Though the room was crowded he saw Craster immediately, for he was silhouetted against a pink jacket. Horace was standing behind his employer, arms folded, while Jack's cousin harangued an elderly gentleman in a dark-blue coat and grey waistcoat.

The room was crowded, a feat considering its size for it occupied the entire first floor of the large tavern. A sea of mainly dark wool was broken by islands of green – the baize of half a dozen billiards tables. Five were in use while the sixth at the centre of the room was surrounded by the arguing men. Jack, unnoticed at the door, began to push through.

He arrived in time to hear Craster declare, 'I say again, rules cannot be gainsaid. Straight up noon was the time agreed but the half has tolled and the challenged is not here. Westminster must forfeit.'

Cheers outweighed the boos; the Angel was Harrow's tavern in Town and barely a dozen Westminsters had forced their way in. Three of them were Mohocks though and Marks especially had a carrying voice and the mind of an aspirant lawyer.

'Mr Absolute displays his ignorance with his every utterance. The noble game of billiards has no "rules". It has laws!' The Westminsters jeered and cheered. 'Show me what *law* has been broken here. Give me chapter and verse or, by God, I say we give my friend till one.'

'There's precedent, sir,' whined a Harrovian, one of the hulks Craster had brought to the Five Chimneys two nights before. 'And English law *is* precedent.'

'Precedent, my arse. Name 'em, every whore's son of 'em,' thundered Marks.

'Gennelmen, some restraint, pray,' the elderly gent, obviously the umpire of the match and, from his accent, a professional of the baize, interposed. 'There's unnerstandins in our sport, wivin and wivout the laws. Now, it's true to say, that if the Challenged has not shown by now—'

'But he has.'

Jack's voice, quiet enough, still pierced the hum. 'Jack,' Fenby cried. 'You are here. You are alive.'

'Yes to both.' He turned to the umpire. 'I am sorry, sir, to have delayed you. Business. Unavoidable.' He looked at Pink Gent Horace, who stood agape, then shifted his gaze to Craster. 'A temporary inconvenience, I assure you.'

Craster's large mouth was opening and closing like a trout jerked suddenly to the bank. Finally he spluttered. 'And the stake?'

Jack scratched his chin. 'The stake? Hmm. The stake. Now where . . .' Then reaching inside to the sodden inner pocket of his coat, he pulled out the maid's cap, shaking it till it clinked. 'Sorry about the receptacle . . .'

The umpire smiled. 'Was that your business, sir?' On Jack's shrug the whole company laughed, save for Craster and his shadows. He'd turned to Horace, who shook his head quite definitely.

Craster turned back. 'I think we need to count it.'

This drew a hiss, and not only from the Westminsters. 'Do you question the gennelman's honour?' the umpire asked Craster. Turning to Jack, he said, 'You are a gennelman, ain't you?'

Jack replied quietly, keeping his eyes on his cousin. 'I am.'

'Then a gennelman's word shall not be questioned. Not while I preside.' He glared at Craster who flinched. 'Your stakes, if you please.'

Two bags were handed over and if Jack's weighed lighter than Harrow's guineas the umpire did not indicate it. The

Westminsters then pulled Jack to one of the settles that paralleled the long sides of the table, while the Harrovians did the same with his cousin.

As Jack sank with a groan, his friends crowded around. 'What happened to you, Jack?' said Fenby.

'What happened to *you*? You deserted me.'

'Not fair, Jack. Marks was snoring, Ede had disappeared with some . . . woman,' both fellows had the decency to look ashamed, 'while you seemed much enamoured of our new friend over there. You matched him, b . . . b . . . bumper for bumper. Then he whispered something and you said, "Lead me to 'em," and when I tried to dissuade you, you d . . . d . . . damn'd me for a half-blind, one-handed stoker and left. I tried to follow but you were out of my b . . . broken sight in a moment.' Fenby pushed his second pair of glasses, old and much entwined with thread, up his nose.

Jack rubbed his forehead, sighed. 'I'm sorry, lads. The Devil got inside me. That Devil,' he said, looking across to where Craster was muttering to Horace. 'The foulest of tricks was played upon me,' he shuddered at the memory of his awakening, 'and worse.'

'Worse? What could be worse?' queried Ede.

Through his fingers, in a low tone, Jack said, 'Our bag of guineas? It's not.'

'What do you mean?' said Marks, alarmed.

Jack shook his head, first in exasperation, then in pain. 'What do you think I mean? Those who stole our night, stole our gold.'

The gasps were sensibly muted but distinct. 'Then, if you lose, we're b . . . bug . . .' stuttered Fenby.

'Quite,' said Ede. 'So . . .'

'So I must win,' said Jack. 'Yet even if I do, my cousin knows no guineas lie within that cap. Win or lose, he'll somehow force a look.' He shushed the alarm. 'So at match end, be ready to make a bold brush of it.' His head indicated the door. 'We'll need to leave with both bags and fast.'

'Gennelmen, your positions, please,' the white-haired umpire called.

Jack rose with a sigh, his head throbbing again. He leaned toward the rack, pulled out cue after cue, sighting along them, rolling them on the baize until satisfied, then turned back. 'Fetch me water, boys, a bucket of it.' Something bubbled up from his stomach and releasing it, he added, 'Make that two buckets. One empty.'

He walked carefully to the centre-side of the table. The umpire began to lay down the conditions of this match. Best of three games: two to one hundred points, the third, if required, to the man ahead at a half-hourglass. While he explained other limits and variations – for billiards' laws could vary according to the house – Craster spoke from the side of his mouth.

'You're a cheating dog. Shall I tell the company I know your cap's as vacant as a Jew's heart?'

'And shall I tell them how you know? That you got yon man to dog me all night, put a tot in every one of my pints, drown me with arrack punch, leave me with a whore?'

'You've no proof. Whereas I will have when you open that purse.'

'And that I'll never do.'

'You'll be forced to when you lose.'

The age of this conflict suddenly caused Jack to speak from an older tongue. 'Ess, boy, but I bain't goin' t' lose, see.'

The umpire stepped to them, coin in hand. 'Your call, sir,' he said to Craster.

'Heads.'

The coin spinning through the light made Jack's head hurt.

'Tails! Your choice, sir.'

Jack shook his head gently, regretting even that much movement. His vision was adding a slight corona to every object he regarded. He looked at the three balls on the table, trying to bring double images into one. At the far end, the single red ball was on its dot, while before him the two white balls were behind the inked line that marked off the top third of the table, both balls within the 'D' at the centre of that line.

Leaning forward, he picked up the white ball that had a black spot and dropped it into his pocket. 'After you,' he said. Making Craster commence was only partly to put pressure on his opponent; he wanted to remind himself how the game worked, such knowledge seemingly driven from his head by the excesses of the night.

As Craster placed his unmarked white ball within the 'D', sighted, shot, Jack's eyes closed. Thus it was not the vision of white on red, nor the balls' subsequent trajectories around the table, that brought to his mind a sudden clarity. It was the sound. The 'clack', the sweetness of ivory on ivory, brought several instances to mind, from the moment his father first introduced him to the game, through every subsequent hour which, if added together, would total months of his young life. *That sound!* How he had sought it out in houses both private and public, in St James's clubs and taverns much like this one; more often in these, for in these murkier waters the sharks swam and once they had realized his enthusiasm and his limited means, they would usually play him for the price of the table and a stake that would still buy them a port and pie.

Other sounds came, the shot was either fortunate or a sign of high skill, and each half of the partisan crowd reacted accordingly.

'Three points for the pot-red hazard,' the umpire declared, fishing the red from its pocket and resetting it on its spot. Craster must have mistaken Jack's closed eyes for apprehension, for when they opened he raised his eyebrows before settling for his next shot. This was easier, a straight pot and he missed it, leaving both balls a foot apart and away from the top cushion.

'Your innings, sir,' said Craster, through a tight mouth.

Jack placed his ball, stood back, thought as he chalked his cue. His opponent had opened brilliantly with a difficult shot and failed dismally with an easy one. Craster had shown he was perhaps over-excited and not a little surprised at having to compete at all.

Jack had no doubt he could match him in flashiness. But, as he bent to the table to do just that, the sudden change of elevation reminded him in surging blood that his head was precariously positioned on his neck and brought the words of a sharper who'd been teaching him tricks one afternoon: 'Tricks is easy, once you know 'em, and every fool can play 'em. But it's a simple game at bottom, young sir. And simple knows best.'

So he played the simplest shot in the game. The more tricky shot would be to hit both balls, the 'cannon hazard', striking both the red and his opponent's white ball with his own, then continue to play them, racking up a score. But it was a difficult initial shot. So he went for the red instead, taking it on a thick edge so as to bounce it only a little off the top cushion and send his own ball off it into the top pocket.

'In-off red,' said the umpire, digging out his ball, rolling it back down the table to him. 'Three points.'

All there knew that Jack had chosen safety over adventure.

'He's feart,' said Pink Gent Horace, his Somerset accent strong. 'You'll take 'un fast, zirr.'

Jack smiled, bent carefully to his next shot. Since they were playing for totals and not against the clock in this game, he could, within reason, take all the time he desired and, with the simplest shots, keep Craster off the table.

A combination of simple hazards – in-off his opponent's white; in-off red; pot-red – meant that Jack chalked up a score of forty-five before a little error off the cushion left him a tricky shot that he missed. Fortunately, he did not have long to dwell on his malaise for Craster only made a break of ten before an attempted cannon failed and left Jack in a fine position, with all three balls bunched up in the corner. To play them all was now the simplest shot available.

'Fill your boots, Absolute,' Marks called out.

'You know,' said Jack, 'I rather think I shall.'

He nudged all three balls around the corner of the table, spurning any opportunities to pot, striking each ball on each shot. It was dull stuff, the voice of the umpire reflecting that with his metronomic, 'Two. Two. Two.' But it delighted Jack and his friends to see their opponents' shoulders slump ever lower.

At ninety-seven, he doubled the red into the top pocket. 'That's three points for the pot-red hazard and game to Westminster,' called the umpire. Jack laid his cue gently on the baize before he was engulfed by enthusiastic back slaps of the Westminsters. The treatment was not salutary, and Jack lowered himself into the settle as swiftly as he was able. Once again, away from the baize and its challenges, he was immediately reminded of his condition in jabs and lurches.

'Water,' he gasped.

'All right, Jack?' Fenby looked at him anxiously as he passed the bucket.

Jack's mouth was so rank he could not form words. He drank deep. Usually he avoided water but this seemed sweet enough. 'Have you a plan for a sudden exeunt?' he whispered hoarsely.

'The beginnings of one, aye,' Marks said.

'Then find an end, too,' Jack muttered, 'and fast.' The pause had reminded him of his frailty. He didn't wish to play a third game.

The umpire called, 'Time, gennelmen,' and Jack moved to the table. Harrow had used the little break to discuss tactics, for a cacophony of coughs greeted Jack as he placed his ball within the 'D' and sighted on the red.

Fuck them, he thought. There was a shot he could play to open that, if successful, would put Craster on the back foot immediately. It was one that, if he practised it a hundred times, he'd make about eighty of them, and involved bringing both the red and his own white back down the length of the table, and leaving them behind the baulk line. His opponent was not allowed to play his first shot behind that line and would have to play up the table, try to hit on a rebound. He'd miss. And Jack could once again 'fill his boots'.

It required speed and angle. He had the second but not the first. His own white fetched up sweet and close to the cushion. But the red settled just in front of the line.

'No score,' said the umpire as Craster stepped up. He did not smirk now, his heavy brow scrunched in concentration. And he'd learnt, for he did not try anything fancy. A straight pot-red and he was away.

Jack was allowed back on the table just twice. Both times, a developing tremor cost him. Third time on the table, Craster never forsook it.

'That's game Harrow, and all square,' called the umpire to loud acclamation. Jack laid his cue down, went and sat, head in hands, sheltering his eyes from the window-glare that had grown as the sun moved around. It had become hot, the smells within the room rank; someone threw the tall window open. The Westminsters, even his friends, were silent around him. Gulping more water, he allowed himself a groan.

'Gennelmen, that's one game apiece, and the third to be decided on time.' The umpire held up a half-hourglass. 'Winner is the player ahead when the sand runs out. But I'll have no shiftin', you understan'. Be brisk in your strokes or I'll pull you off the green.'

The Mohocks were clustered close. Through his fingers, Jack said in a low tone, 'Have you finalized the plan?'

Fenby blinked. 'We think so, J . . . J . . . Jack. The rest of the lads are ready.' He indicated the other Westminsters engaged in returning the jibes of the Harrow men opposite. 'First we'll—'

'Don't tell me, Fenby,' snapped Jack. 'Just do it.'

'Mr Absolute,' said the umpire, coin in hand, 'your call, I believe, sir.'

The silver shilling spun up. 'Tails,' Jack called.

'Tails it is. Will you begin, sir?'

He didn't feel like standing just yet. 'Oh, why not let my honourable opponent?'

'Delighted.' Craster strode to the table, the confidence of the last game still carrying him. He placed the ball in the 'D' and, as he bent and the umpire inverted the half-hourglass, he turned to Jack, winked, turned back, struck. Hard. It was the same shot that Jack had attempted in the previous game, one to leave his balls behind the line and Jack having to play forward. But where Jack had failed, Craster succeeded.

A whoop went up from Harrow, a groan from Westminster. Jack felt his stomach shift and not just from the agonies of the night before. He rose, went to the table. He had to rebound off the top cushion and strike one of the balls. Strike and try not to leave his opponent well positioned. But the throbbing in his head had redoubled and the geometry of the angles kept shifting. He chose a line, struck . . .

'A miss. Two points to Harrow.'

His ball had finished near the red. Craster saw the opportunity, took it. Kept playing his ball onto the other two, the umpire marking each double-click. 'Cannon: two. Cannon: two.'

He took his time to reach thirty, warned twice by the umpire to speed up. At least half the sand had run out before he made an error, sending Jack's white close but not sinking it. Nevertheless it had settled around the knuckle of the pocket, flush to its curve. No target ball was thus directly in Jack's line. He either had to play up the table for a rebound, a repeat of the first shot he'd already missed or . . .

As Jack stood to contemplate his options, Craster whispered, 'That's it, you cur. I'll be on the table next shot and I'll never leave it. Time'll run out, we'll take a look inside the bag and find you are no gentleman.' He smiled. 'So play your finest shot. And prepare to lose your name.'

Jack looked into his cousin's pocked face, saw again the shades there of Duncan Absolute in the fleshy lips, the porcine eyes, the heavy jowl. Heard again his uncle's nasal whine, almost felt the hand on his shirt, the other raised with some instrument of pain. There were no words that could sum up what he felt, none that would answer the triumph in his cousin's eyes. There was only this piece of wood he gripped and a way of using it.

So he moved to his ball, looked at the geometry. There was a simple shot to play . . . one that would gain him a little. Not enough. The phrase came again into his head: *Simple knows best.*

Bugger that, he thought.

Raising the cue almost vertical to the table, butt end pointed to ceiling, he struck sharply down on the ball's right side. It spun out around the knuckle of the pocket, straightened to meet the red. When they kissed, the red responded by moving away, sinking into the end pocket with the groan Jack so loved to hear.

'Pot-red, three points,' called the umpire, re-spotting it.

The room hummed, voices raised in shock, delight, anger. Craster did not move, cue gripped tight in his hand, so Jack had to sidestep him every time he moved around the table. It was just one of the things he shut out, along with the voices, the sunlight, his body's jabs and gurgles, the corona expanded around each ball like the edge of an eclipse, the two bags at the table's end, one of tokens, one of gold. And the final thing he had to shut out was the sand slipping noiselessly down the glass, the only goad he needed to push him ever faster around the table. He had almost no time to calculate the angles, had to see them on the instant, make his shot, see the next one as he made it, make that. And as his score mounted, even the drone-like quality of the umpire's calling disappeared, the tally coming sharper to the rhythm of the balls.

Cannons, pots, in-offs, they were all interspersed and if he made a slight error on one shot, he somehow corrected it on the next. His target was thirty-one, a single point more than Craster's total.

And then a groan – Fenby's – forced him to look away from the green.

The top of the hourglass was nearly empty. And because he

looked, he looked back and shot too fast, missed pot, in-off and cannon. Let his enemy back on the table, with ten points still ungained.

'No delay, please, sir. Toe the line.' In his excitement, the umpire had borrowed the phraseology of pugilism and indeed it had become a fight, both men reeling, blow after blow. Even Craster felt it, stepped up, did not hesitate. For Jack's last shot had left Craster's white and the red in a line with the centre pocket, about a foot and a half away.

Three points for a pot-red and Craster would have it, his tally beyond anything Jack could achieve before the last grain fell.

He bent, sighted, his cue ran smooth, the balls kissed and parted, the red moving slowly, sapping the sand, towards the centre pocket. If not perfectly straight, it was straight enough to hit the knuckle. From there it could have drifted in or out.

It settled before the pocket.

'No points,' said the umpire, a trace of sadness in the voice. Not, Jack knew, because the ball had not disappeared but because Jack still had ten points to make and perhaps ten grains of sand to make them in. His white was level and six inches from Craster's, almost on the baulk line, and the red was on the centre pocket. There was only one shot.

He drove hard, Craster's white crashing straight into the top end pocket. 'Two points,' yelled the umpire, all calm gone, as he followed, like everyone there, the progress of Jack's ball up the table, off the side cushion, off the end cushion, towards that red hovering by the knuckle of the centre pocket. It travelled fast and struck the red edge hard and shot it in dead centre.

'Cannon: two; pot-red: three,' the umpire shouted, needing to shout now over the cries from all around. The clack had taken the sting from Jack's white and now it drifted slower, rolling on towards the other top end pocket.

'Time,' screamed Craster as the last grain dropped.

'Ball in play,' croaked the umpire. Thus Time paused once

again in Jack's life while all watched the white ball move slowly to hit one knuckle, bounce off, hit the second, roll away to hover and, finally, drop with a groan beyond Jack's most fantastic imaginings, into the pocket.

'In-off, three points and that's match Westminster,' came the words, though they were barely heard under the rising cry that seemed to come from one voice, though from a hundred throats. Craster was stationary, still held by Time's cessation, as was Jack, the only people not moving, until the Mohocks jostled around him, began pushing him towards the open window and Fenby, who stood on the ledge in a wall of sunlight.

'Now!' he yelled, and Jack, emerging from the daze of his last shot, looked to Marks and Ede, who stood at the table where the two bags, one of tokens, one of gold, had awaited a victor to claim them. Both bags now rested in his friends' hands.

'*Promptus?*' shouted Marks, his deep voice piercing the hubbub.

'*Iace!*'

Harrow's gold was duly hurled over heads to the window where Fenby took the bag straight to his midriff, dropping it out the open window, turning to receive the tatty maid's cap that held Westminster's secret.

'Stop them!' Craster's scream was directed at Horace, who stood halfway between window and table, where he'd stood the entire game, holding Craster's spare cue. As Ede lobbed towards the crouching Fenby, The Man who'd nearly defeated Westminster two days before due to his skill with a willow bat, proved he was just as adept with an ash billiards cue. Raising it swiftly above his head, Horace brought it sharply down into the centre of the flying bag. The thin cloth split instantly under the impact and the tokens of the Old Hummum fell like metal hailstones onto the crowd below.

Jack, like many there, was hit; unlike them, he had no need to catch and verify what he already knew. He also did not need

Craster's cry of, 'Damn cheats! They've culled us, by God!' to accelerate him towards the window. Despite being in the press of the enemy crowd, no one tried to halt him. They didn't have the time.

He mounted the window ledge beside Fenby, turned back. Marks and Ede, empty-handed now, were running for the door, along with the dozen other of their schoolfellows. Their rivals, still held in the shock of it, only now seemed to be reacting to Craster's yells, to the falling tokens. Looking at the angry faces raised towards them, Jack shouted, 'Where now?' and in answer Fenby just stepped backwards and tumbled from the window.

Jack, looking down, saw what his friend already knew; a throwster's cart was directly below, full of spun silk bolts. Jack was not fond of heights but the growling rising behind him left him little choice. As his friend rolled off, he too dropped, sank into the softness, tumbled off the cart, sprawled on the cobbles. Fenby, grasping his collar, jerked him up.

'*Vedeamus?*' he said.

'Yes,' replied Jack, 'and fucking quick too.'

Marks and Ede burst out of the front door of the Angel. Snatching up the gold, the Mohocks sprinted, laughing, down the street.

— TEN —
Violation

In the sanctuary of his room, Jack had to resist the near-overpowering urge to go to sleep. His bed's siren-sheets lured him, could not have tempted more had Fanny, Matilda and Clothilde rested between them, each willing to share him. To lay down alone, to see off the remaining bodily effects of the night before, to sleep till nightfall and then finally to descend to the kitchen for one of Nance's famous soups . . . it was a vision of paradise . . . and it could not be his. Not when Craster and his cohorts would be close behind. Not when men waited at both front and rear doors, men he'd just managed to elude by a complicated route over a neighbour's roof. And especially not since he'd read what had been within the envelope placed upon his pillow. One of those men outside had no doubt delivered it.

Jack picked up the black-bordered card again. The name and title of the sender was printed in gold above three words in black ink, the identical words mouthed at him last night at the Assembly Rooms under the name of the man who'd mouthed them:

LORD THOMAS MELBURY
YOU. ARE. DEAD.

Jack dropped the card back onto the pillow, rubbed his fingers as if to remove some taint, then continued dressing. This was swift, no agonizing over colour or fabric. He put on the simple attire he wore for school, everything black and woollen, stockings, waistcoat, jacket. He was alarmed to find he had to make five attempts to tie the stock, so violently were his hands shaking, and though he tried to steady them with a shot from the brandy flask he kept hidden in his armoire, it did nothing but scorch his throat and empty stomach. Spluttering, he went to the mirror, tried again. In the end the knot he resorted to was of the simplest, most impoverished kind.

He regarded himself in the mirror for a moment. He had another sanctuary to find, somewhere, anywhere, to see out the day, to allow the chase – chases! – to pass him by. Only then could he creep back to Westminster. There, the Election for Trinity commenced on the morrow and the ushers were rigid in barring all strangers from the grounds. Rarely before had Jack had reason to bless their over-watchfulness but if they would keep the pursuit away from him till the passion of it died down – as he was sure it ultimately would – then, by God, like many a Westminster before him, he would leave them a generous bequest in his will!

This sudden morbid thought had him scrambling again. His shoes were swiftly buckled on, his cloak grabbed from its hook. He was halfway to the door when it burst open. 'Aaah,' he cried, reeling back, leaping the bed, putting it between himself and the thick-set figure that rushed in, bellowing.

'You wastrel cur! Where have you been?'

Jack, from between his raised hands, let out a yelp of relief. 'Father! Thank God, dear Father! What . . . what joy it is to see you!'

Sir James stood four-square and glowering, taken aback by the enthusiasm of his son's greeting. 'What . . . what's the matter with you, sir?'

'I am just so . . . so delighted that it's you, Papa.'

Sir James had come to renew hostilities. But Jack's genuine

happiness at the reunion was obviously not what his father expected. It confused him – enough almost to bring him near an apology. 'I knocked, of course,' he said, indicating the door, 'but there was no . . . heard a noise, so I—'

'That's quite all right, Father, I—'

'I should think it is quite all right.' Sir James Absolute was never nonplussed for long. 'My house, go where I like. Especially since you use it merely as some sort of dressing room.' He toed the pile of discarded clothes on the floor. 'What's this? And this?' He indicated Jack's school apparel. 'Dump your shite and run, do you, sir?'

'Not at all, sir, I . . .' Jack was glancing around the room, looking for an inspiration. Instead he saw Lord Melbury's card where he had dropped it back on the bed. Hurling his cloak over it, he said, 'I was about to take this washing down to Nancy, sir, and—'

He was bending to scoop up the clothes, but his father was quicker, his knees cracking like pistol shots. 'When I said "dump your shite", ye dog, I didn't mean literally.' His large face wrinkled in distaste as he hoisted the ripped and brown-stained breeches. 'What the Devil have you been about?'

'B . . . bad oyster, sir?'

'Oyster. Ballocks,' said Sir James. Lifting the garment, he sniffed. 'It may be fish but it is no oyster. Smells of perfume. Cheap perfume. You've been with a whore, haven't ye?'

Jack's mouth dropped. As it did, there came a memory of gums, a croaking laugh. He shuddered. 'No, sir, I . . .'

'Take care, boy. You know I will forgive almost any sin bar lying.'

As his backside could bear testimony. But what little could Jack tell him of the previous night that would not lead to revealing it all? 'I . . . did spend some time with a . . . young . . . young-ish . . . a lady, sir, but . . .'

'Jack! Did you at least heed my advice at our last talk?' Jack looked confused. His father sighed. 'Did you at least go "armoured"?'

'I . . . did, sir.' Jack had no idea what conversation his father was referring to. They had never discussed carnal matters until this moment.

'At least you showed some sense. "Absolute Sense", eh?' A brief smile came, vanished. 'Boy, you are young and seem to have inherited insanity from my father, for it is rumoured to miss a generation, but,' he sniffed disdainfully, 'aim a little higher, eh?' His expression, ever changeable, shifted again, became stern. He dropped the breeches, continued, 'And now, ye dog, at our last talk you attempted to—'

Jack never found out which sin his father was going to refer to for there came a loud banging on the front door, together with muffled shouts.

'Who the Devil . . .' He turned back to Jack, saw the whiteness of his face. 'Someone for you, is it? Creditors? Or . . . you did *pay* the whore, didn't ye?'

'I . . . uh . . .'

Sir James sighed. 'Boy, you and me need to have another long talk.'

'Could you, Father . . .'

'It will be deducted from your allowance, you may be sure,' Sir James turned as he spoke, raising his voice over the hammering. 'Where's that fat-ars'd bastard who calls himself my footman? Sitting on it, no doubt. William! William!' he shouted, as the bangs on the door grew ever louder.

He left, still shouting, and as soon as he did, Jack snatched up his cloak and crept from the room behind him. Whereas his father went down the main stairs, he went the opposite way, up to the attic. There was a skylight there and from it a short leap to the neighbour's roof. As he climbed, he suddenly remembered a place in London where he could hide. He'd make his way there directly, stay till night, then creep back to school in the darkness. Once at Westminster, he'd not stir again this side of the Michaelmas term. He'd even sit the Election to please his mother. Trinity College, Cambridge had high walls to hide behind, no doubt.

In St Anne's Court, the doors to both the house and to Matilda's attic were unlocked and the room itself empty, as he suspected it would be. She had clearly departed. The gaudy forestage of the screens had been stripped back to reveal the full poverty of the chamber, its patchily whitewashed walls relieved by blooms of blue-black mould, its sloping planks unvarnished and broken here and there with copses of splinters.

Laying himself down, despite the discomfort of the floor and the distractions of the day, he slept.

The bell of St Giles woke him too late to count the hour but St Anne's followed hard upon it and he found, to his surprise, that it was seven in the evening. The shutter, raised, admitted the last of the day's light. He had a flask of ale and a pie with him and now made a supper, delighted that it brought him pleasure not revulsion; he resolved to buy more of the same on his walk back to Westminster. By the time he'd finished, full night had taken the town and, rising and brushing himself down, he set out.

Since he had resolved to bury himself at school, there were two farewells he had to take. He had no doubt that both buildings would be watched by Melbury's jackals, but he would approach both carefully; no one would notice him standing briefly outside them, nor the silent kisses he'd dispatch between his raised cloak and uncocked tricorn. Though Golden Square lay on his route out of Soho, Jack decided he would visit there first. He adored Fanny; but he recognized that the adoration lodged more in his loins than his heart. Since Clothilde held the supremacy in that organ, he would make his final farewell there.

The coaching mews that led to the rear of Fanny's house was still busy with the industry of stables. But shadows between their open doors let Jack flit by, swift and unobserved. He had thought merely to hoist himself upon the wall and gaze upon his mistress. But something made him reach up to see if the key – their key – was still in position. It would be a sign that, despite everything, Fanny still desired him to visit.

The key was indeed there but it did not rest alone above the lintel. It was wrapped in paper and, squatting on the edge of a spill of lanterns, Jack unfolded the sheet and read: 'Vauxhall. Tonight. I *must* see you. F.'

The 'must' was underlined and Jack traced his finger along it. Of course, she 'must' see him! She would wish to make amends for their all too hasty separation. Perhaps his Lordship had proved adamant in anger and thrown her out. Jack was almost tempted to go to the Pleasure Gardens at Vauxhall; he was concerned for her. But he knew he could not help her with some bravo's knife in his guts. Safety now dictated he stuck to his plan, and stayed in School till the furore died down. After the Election for Trinity, in ten days, two weeks perhaps, he would emerge and see Fanny again.

With a sigh, he retreated back into Soho. 'Clothilde,' he whispered to himself. After all the women he'd had dealings with in the last days – Matilda, even Fanny and especially the nameless Cyprian he'd woken beside – Clothilde shone, a beacon of purity. He didn't know why he'd entangled himself with these others when his 'little mermaid' was the only one who had true possession of his heart. How he longed now just to sit beside her, tentatively reach for her soft white hand, gaze into those blue-green eyes. How peaceful would that be. For now, it had to be a paradise postponed, but no one would stop him gazing a last time upon the Promised Land.

He knew something was wrong before he'd turned the corner. Something pierced the street vendors' cries, rose above the shouts and guffaws of the taverns' clientele, a wail of such agony that it even rode through the roar of London; and there was something in that wail, so familiar that the pudding he had just purchased was thrown down upon the cobbles. Jack began to run.

The house of Guen was far enough away still for Jack to

believe that the pack of shouting people was gathered before another door, that the cries came from another throat, the neighbour's daughter, not hers, not hers. Yet when he reached the edges of the crowd, he knew. Close-built and slim though these Soho houses were, there could be no doubt – something terrible was happening in Clothilde's home.

The backs before him did not want to give so he forced them to, using an elbow here, a shove there, a collar caught and yanked. The voices were angry already and that only increased with his treatment of those who stood before him. Blows were aimed, some landed, but they delayed him not at all. Every obstruction cleared made the sounds ahead sharper, the girl's cry – Clothilde's cry! – counterpointed now with another note, a man's bass bellowing in rage and distress.

The final crowd, standing deep on the stairwell, was harder to thrust through but he did it, losing his tricorn to the mob, which thinned on the last flight. Two men, with arms spread like nets, held back the surge. But they couldn't hold Jack, who dodged their grasping hands and fell up the last few steps, halted finally by the scene there.

Claude, the apprentice-cousin, lay on his back on the top landing, a man crouched over him, pressing already bloodied towels to his head. His face was pale, though beneath the eyes and at the throat, startlingly blue. Indeed all the colours were vivid set against that chalkiness but none more so than the scarlet of the blood which seemed to have poured in quantities beyond credit upon wood, cloth, skin. The man was alive, Jack saw, but barely.

There was more blood in the room beyond, the room of wailing that Jack now entered so reluctantly. He saw it straight away from the threshold, even though it was not indiscriminately spread here, indeed because it was quite contained. The contrast was even more vivid than on the face outside for the stain of it against the ivory of Clothilde's dress, the one she'd worn new for him two days before, made it stand out. It was a ripped and shredded thing now, desecrated as a sacked church.

As soon as he saw, he knew. It held him in the doorway as if he'd used all his strength to get this far, had none left to propel him any further, only his eyes seeking something, somewhere else to look at in her room – the spilled chair, the broken porcelain shepherd, the tumbled fireguard. At last the merman, his most recent gift to her, its monkey grin transformed to a scream.

Then she saw him and her cry, which, it had seemed, could not ascend any higher in pitch nor volume, did. '*Non! Non! Non non non!*' she shrieked, throwing herself off the chair, her legs scrabbling against the floorboards, driving herself toward the corner of the room, pushing down against the blood-stained skirt that would rise as she moved. Her father, who had started toward her when she fell, now looked where she was staring and as soon as he saw who it was, he was off the floor, grabbing Jack by the lapels, propelling him backwards to crash against the wall.

'*Violeur! Violeur!*' he screamed, again and again, and though he did not know that word in French, Jack had no need for a translation. He also had no will to resist as he was jerked from the wall, slammed back on each repetition, the watercolours that Clothilde adored falling, the few plates left on the mantelpiece tumbling to smash. Only the merman stood, unshiftable, mocking, as the room shook.

Monsieur Guen was small and Jack large, but the little man did not slacken his assault till Jack slumped further down the wall and could not be lifted. Still the older man tried, pulling at his shirt, popping the buttons there, crying all the time that same accusation. And when Jack reached the floor, in the pause after the last unavailing tug from above, both men at last heard the words Clothilde had been shouting all the time.

'*Ce n'était pas lui, Papa. Pas lui. Pas lui.*'

His breaths coming in huge gasps, Monsieur Guen staggered away to tumble by his daughter. She thrust her face, her muttered denials, into his shirt front.

Jack crawled across the floor to them. He reached out to touch her arm but it was as if he'd stung her, so quickly did she withdraw it. ' Clothilde,' he said, his hand still outstretched, 'my dearest, my sweet . . .'

Still she would not look at him. 'How . . .' he tried again. 'Who . . . ?'

Suddenly she forced her face away. 'I fought, Jack,' she whispered fiercely.

'Of course you d—'

'Look!' She thrust out her fingernails, torn, bleeding. *Regarde!* I . . .' She made slashing motions through the air. 'But there were two . . . three . . . they beat Claude . . . they . . .' The fierceness passed, more weeping came.

'Clothilde, did you . . . did you know him?'

A slight shake of the head. The words, when they came, were muffled yet clear enough and the worst he'd ever heard. 'They look for you.' She did not raise her face when she said it, which Jack thought just as well. If she had looked at him at that moment, he was sure he would have died.

While I lay skulking in a rat hole, they came for her. The thought tore at his guts, worse than any result liquor could have achieved. Melbury had stalked him and failing to find him had traced Jack's haunts, taken his vengeance. While the schoolboy had played at being a savage, the Noble Lord had proved he was one.

Tears came. Through their blur, he looked to the floor, to broken glass shimmering amidst shards of pottery. His mind suddenly too full to think, he could only look, stare . . . here, half a porcelain rose, there a piece of lapis that had once rested on the side of a wine cup. Amidst them all something glittered, something silver. At first he thought it a coin; yet though it was a similar size to a crown, even through his tears he saw the shape was different. Reaching for it, wiping his eyes, he recognized the metal tag he held. It was a season's ticket for the Vauxhall Gardens. He knew it was not Clothilde's for she had been begging him for months to take her there. The front side held a design of the statue of Handel that dominated the south walk. The rear, as Jack knew, held the ticket holder's name.

For the longest moment after turning it over, his mind could not take in what was engraved there. A number, '178', and below that, a name. His family name. But it was not preceded by J, Jack or even John. This token's owner was a 'Mr C. Absolute.'

Craster.

He knew his cousin often frequented the Gardens; knew because his father complained at the expenditure.

Jack wasn't sure how he got up nor when he crossed the room. He was just in the doorway, looking back at the stained dress, the shuddering figures, trying to speak, failing, finding that all his concentration was in his right hand where he was crushing a silver token. Turning, he began to push through those still bunched on the stairs. Yet his departure was very different from his arrival. No one sought to hinder him now.

Perhaps it was his face.

— ELEVEN —

Masquerade

It was a hard pull against the tide from Dung Wharf to Gunhouse Stairs but Jack was grateful for the distraction the exercise provided. Despite the late hour, the river was still crowded with coal barges and cockboats, nightsoil cogs and wherries. The Thames was never at rest. Jack had no flint to light the oil lamp in his bow and had had no will to seek one. He'd wasted enough time in his detour to Mrs Porten's, his boarding house, grabbing only what was essential to what lay ahead: another cloak to replace the one he'd lost at Clothilde's; his sword. But he was well used to the handling of the skiff the Mohocks kept at the dock near the school and if others could not see him, he was aware of them. Using the tide, driving the oars individually and together, he slipped through the traffic and soon was stepping onto the stairs below Lambeth. A rung and a long rope secured his boat. It was not the closest landing to the Vauxhall Pleasure Gardens but that one would be crowded and well lit to welcome the night's revellers and Jack needed to arrive unobserved.

Though the first streets were dark, wharf front and warehouses, the further he progressed the brighter the world became, passing from trade to pleasure. Lamps lit stalls selling everything from quack potions to stewed grigs, while beyond their light, women urged him into the shadows. As he drew closer to his destination, the stalls became plusher, the women prettier. Fans, decorated with the latest events, were offered to him, porcelain figures, charcoal sketches, broadsides, ballads – and masks. Masks were everywhere, rows of them like an audience in the theatre. Jack still had the uncomfortable feeling that he was being watched and these ranks of eye sockets only increased that sensation. But as he approached the entrance to the Pleasure Gardens, the reason for their abundance became clear. Everyone lined up at the gateway was wearing or carrying a mask.

Jack stepped to the side. 'Is it a masquerade tonight?' he asked a stall-keeper.

'It is, sir, aye,' came the reply. 'And you have come in the nick, for I've precious few left.'

Cursing the necessity – for how would he swiftly find his enemy in a place where everyone was hidden? – Jack purchased the simplest of Venetian dominoes, the commonest disguise.

The last of his florins bought him entrance, but beyond the gilt gates there was another problem.

'Your sword, sir.'

Jack tipped the mask up to his forehead so he could look properly at the lilac-coated flunkey who'd accosted him. 'I never give up my sword, sir.'

'You will tonight, *sir*,' replied the man, 'or you'll not come in. We collect for families whose men have died in the war. We do not seek to make yet more widows and orphans.'

Those queuing impatiently behind loudly urged Jack to comply. With a shrug, he did, taking the token, ignoring the coin tray shoved toward him. 'No swords' was becoming the norm in more and more places. Before long they'll ban 'em in the theatres, Jack thought sourly. The only thing that improved his mood was the coolness of metal within his boot, the knife he'd stolen from Mrs Porten's.

Stepping beyond the portico that covered the entranceway, Jack stopped and looked around. He had been coming to the Vauxhall Pleasure Gardens for years, as a child by day with his mother to gaze at the curiosities, later as a young man with his Mohocks to gaze at girls. He had not been lately, the atmosphere tame and cool compared to the hothouse of Covent Garden. Respectable behaviour was expected here where tailors and bankers, jewellers and shopkeepers walked, ate and drank beside the nobility, and kept their excesses in check. The King could sup in a box next to a brewer. But if he wanted to fornicate with his mistress he'd have to do it outside the grounds.

Yet Jack knew tonight would be different. The point of a mask was to conceal identity, leaving the wearer free to indulge hidden desires. The sober burgher, as Bacchus, could drink till he puked. His prim wife could display her flesh as Salome while the rector ogled her through her veils. And a scholar from Westminster could don the domino of Venice and transform into an assassin. He would show Craster as much mercy as he had shown to Clothilde.

But by the time he'd twice trod the Walks, circled the Temple of Comus, lingered at the Cascade where the crowds were thickest, Jack was close to despair. It would have been difficult to distinguish someone amongst these numbers on a normal evening; at a masquerade, it was near impossible. His steps began to drag and, by the time he stood before Handel's statue, his anger was being replaced by exhaustion. He clung to the memories of Clothilde's agony, her shrieks, her bloodied dress. He needed his fury to fuel him; yet the masks – leering eyed, lolling tongued – sapped it from him. Tall though he was, he felt that everyone there was looming above him, bearing down upon him.

Jack sank onto a small stone ledge, pulling off his domino, lowering his head into his hands. What could he do but return to his school, skulking behind its walls to avoid the man who'd left the black-edged card at his house while being slowly consumed by his failure to act, like the Hamlet he'd seen with his mother only a few weeks before at the Lane. What had the fellow said, something about 'dull revenge'?

He became aware of a Pastoral being played, composed by the man whose stone figure loomed above him now, who had also written the Messiah that her father had taken Clothilde to hear at Coram's Fields at Christmas. She had not stopped talking of the experience and Jack, to please her, had attempted to play some of the German's music on his flute. In truth, he had no true skill at the instrument, but she had laughed and clapped and cried for more. And that vision, of her happy tears mingled with the vision of her most recent ones, had Jack up and moving now, his anger bright again, towards the Rotunda. Many did the same, for the concert and dancing there were the climax of any evening at Vauxhall. Everyone would be there in that gaudy room. Craster would be there.

The huge chandelier in the Rotunda shimmered with close to a hundred flames. The walls that circled were studded by sashed windows beneath which mirrors, reflecting the light of yet more candles in their sconces, were angled down to reflect the company back to itself. Pushing just inside the door, pressing his back to a wall there, it was to one of these mirrors that Jack looked, for it reduced the mob to sections.

Fauns mixed with satyrs, Mother Shipton conversed with Punch and Joan, while the wardrobes of the Theatre Royal had been pilfered to recreate Olympus. Jack saw Zeus take a pinch of snuff from Dionysus, the powder snorted up under the plaster mask; a chubby Poseidon used his trident to lift the cloak of Artemis. The next mirror conjured a different scene; at centre, His Satanic Majesty whispering into Caesar's ear. And next to them . . .

Jack started, looked from the mirrors down into the crowd. Once seen, it was unmissable, the focus of the entire room. A woman stood, her pose an agony of embarrassment. Naked. Perhaps not quite, for jewels glowed in her piled-up hair, a scarf obscured her from nose to chin, something silken just covered her loins. But that was all, and men – many men – jostled around her, a special cruelty in their anonymous, masked regard. And then he saw something else, something that had him moving at last, swiftly away from the wall. He saw her breasts. And he knew them.

The orchestra began an introduction to the first dance, a quadrille, and those who would take part scurried to make up their fours, those who would watch stepped away. Jack now had a clear view through to the naked woman, saw Satan seize her hand, place her quite alone, before moving to join another forming four. Her circle of men had not dispersed, were joined now by several women, whispering loudly behind their jiggling fans.

The company had not fully formed. The orchestra commenced another eight bars. Jack moved before her. 'Fanny!'

Her lowered eyes came up sharply. They reminded him of a hunted deer brought to bay. 'You fool! Why did you come?'

'Why your note, it—' Until that moment he had forgotten her summons, his mind so fixed on vengeance for Clothilde. But she gave him no time to dwell on his guilt.

'Leave me alone,' she hissed. 'Go away!'

'But Fanny, you—' He unclasped his cloak, thrust it towards her. 'Take this.'

'No!'

'Why not? You can't . . . enjoy—'

'Enjoy?' Fire displaced the fear. 'This is not to enjoy. This is the first part of my punishment.'

'For what?'

The words came bitter from beneath the veil. 'For you, my dear. For you.'

The introductory bars were ending. They were facing each other, thus half of a four. A man dressed as Priapus joined them and a giggling young woman was thrust forward by her friends. Both raised their hands. Jack raised his.

'No!' Fanny hissed. But it seemed she had no choice. She raised her hand.

The music paused, hovered before its start. For a moment all that could be heard were fans and whispers.

'Why for me?' he said, ignoring the two who leaned close to listen.

'Lord . . . M devised the punishment. "Bathsheba the Harlot." Said that if I did as he asked, he might not proclaim me a whore to the Town, might let me keep my beautiful house, my servants, my . . . position.' A tear ran, disappearing into the filmy covering at her nose and, just as it did, the dance began. The circles moved left, then right. He walked through, passing the other man back to back, bowing at the turn. The women did the same. Then the other couple peeled off to join a couple also parting. He took Fanny's hand to move a few paces to their next position. Their heads now close, Jack said softly, 'But Bathsheba wasn't a harlot. Bathsheba lured David from a rooftop.'

'Just so,' she said, the tears coming faster now, 'and that is the second part of my punishment. To lure you. Then deliver you.'

They had reached their new position. Another couple awaited, their hands reaching out for them, but he did not see them, could only look at her. 'Deliver me?' he said. 'To whom?'

'To me, boy. To me.'

It was Satan who spoke, their new partner in the four. And Jack needed no eyes to penetrate the red plaster of the exquisite, horned mask, for when he'd heard that voice before it had been similarly muffled . . . through the folds of Fanny's dress.

He was dancing with the Devil and Lord Melbury's grip upon his hand was indeed demonic. 'You have two choices,' the deep voice came again, 'a boy's or a man's. If you are a boy, you will consent to go with me to some ground outside where my friends and I will give you the thrashing you deserve, which you will thank me for, thank me as each blow destroys what made you so alluring to my Fanny. Or . . .'

His hand was released. A paralysis had seized him of mind if not of body; his feet kept moving in the dance. He settled, as

Fanny and Artemis the Huntress crossed and twirled between them.

'Or?'

'Or if you claim to be a man, you may meet me on that same ground . . . with a pistol. And then what I wrote upon the card will truly come to pass – for you will be dead.'

He remembered what was said of Melbury. One of the finest shots in the country. So the choice was between painful humiliation and death.

Some shouting drunkard had climbed up onto the bandstand and was trying to seize the leader's bow. The music shuddered then stopped; people paused and called out their displeasure.

Under the Devil's mask, fleshy lips shaped a smile. 'Which do you choose then, Jack Absolute? Are you a boy or a man?'

Even Jack could see an alternative here. 'Oh, neither really,' he said, and began to walk swiftly away through the scattering, angry dancers towards the door.

'Fool!' hissed Lord Melbury. 'Did you truly believe I hadn't thought of that?'

The crowd shifted before him, masks on every side, any of which could have hidden one of Melbury's friends. As he neared the main door, he saw one broad shape step away from it, two others approaching from opposition directions. All were costumed as Hell's Imps, which, to Jack's mind, showed both Melbury's arrogance and his lack of imagination. Immediately he bore sharply away, making for the screen of columns that separated the Rotunda from the Pavilion. There were other entrances there and surely even someone as powerful as Melbury could not have enough men to guard them all?

The press was at its thickest where the rooms joined at a screen of columns; Jack was completely halted. On the columns themselves, plaster boys ascended the gothic wreaths towards the heavens. Thinking that where one boy could go, another could follow, Jack reached, slipped his fingers over a plaster ledge, hoisted himself up. For a moment he hung there and, glancing back, saw the Imps as they saw him. Then he twisted around the column, dropping to the other side. Finding the crowd there much diminished, he began to push speedily up towards the north and west entrances.

Relief was brief. Two large men, in plain dress, stood either side of each of the three entrances. They were not stopping everyone, just those who, like Jack, sported black cloaks and Venetian dominoes. Word had been sent back.

Jack stood on one spot, yet quite unable to stop his feet moving, his breaths coming in ever shorter gasps, his panting causing those nearest him to step away, fearing some contagion. He knew that if he did not move soon, he would not move at all, would stand there waiting, held like a hare in the spill of a lantern, dispatched as easily as one. Yet everywhere he looked, the hunters were closing in. He looked at his hands, shaking as if with some palsy. They would not hold a gun. Yet if they did not he would have to submit to a beating that might leave him crippled.

A noise came from the north entrance, curses and threats. Behind Melbury's men, two flunkeys, wearing the same lilac coats and powdered wigs as the man who'd taken Jack's sword, were preventing a group of bravos from entering, the source of the dispute undoubtedly the flasks they were waving – for liquor could only be purchased from licensed purveyors within. Melbury's men had turned to observe the fracas, there was suddenly a gap between them and at this Jack drove, dipped, smelled freedom in the night air as he slipped past. He started to move quicker, expecting to hear, at any moment, cries of recognition and pursuit. Yet finally it was not sound that halted Jack's flight, but sight.

Standing almost directly before the entrance was a man with the face of a satyr, wearing a jacket in a most distinctive pink. And as Jack slowed, the fellow next to the satyr tore away from a flunkey's restraint with a 'Damn you dogs, I will enter' and strangely, it wasn't the voice he recognized first, slightly muffled as it was by an identical domino to the one he wore himself, it was the white collar below it; or rather, the patch of blood upon it; those, and the three scratch marks that ran beneath the mask from ear to chin.

All fears vanished with recognition. 'Violater!' he yelled, hurling himself across the small space between them. There was no method to it, no remnants of the skills they had learned as boys in Cornwall. Jack was onto Craster, knocking him back, punches flailing down to bounce off raised arms, crown of head, ears. Howling as he struck, no words now, just an outpouring of animal sound.

He was seized, dragged away, not by Melbury's men, but by the maskless flunkeys who served as the Watch of the Gardens, tough ex-seamen in the main. Looking across, he saw that Craster was equally bound, like him had lost his mask in the scrap and, to his fierce delight, was adding blood to his collar stain from his nose and one eye.

'What is this rough housing? Who are these lumber troopers, disrupting the night for respectable people?'

The speaker was dressed in tones similar to the flunkeys but infinitely more richly expressed. He also wore a powdered peri-wig, the only adornment of his head, for he too was maskless.

'Roaring Boys, Mr Tyers, sir,' said the man clutching Craster, ''ad too much gin in 'em by the smell.'

'Gin?' The man's sculpted eyebrows rose. 'All know that such poison is not admitted to my Gardens. By God, I'll banish ye both for life for your temerity.'

'Mr Tyers.' The voice that intruded now came silkily from beneath the Devil's mask. 'Mr Tyers, I think you know me.'

The man moved from wrath to servility in a moment. 'I do, indeed, my Lord M—'

The voice interrupted harshly. 'No names, sir. You know me as a friend and generous patron, d'ye not? I would help you this night, as I have helped you so often before.'

'I would be so grateful, sir. Um . . . how?'

'By removing this . . . offence.' He nudged Jack none too gently with the toe of his boot. 'For he has offended me, too.

I was set to teach him a lesson before he embarked on yet another scape.' He waved a hand over the prone cousins. 'It appears I was too late. But not to make amends. Nothing must interfere with your festivities.'

'You are so kind, my Lord. And if this is a private matter—'

'It is indeed.' He tapped the sailors holding Jack with his cane. 'Allow my fellows to take charge of the miscreant.'

Hands were released, replaced by others equally strong. Jack was jerked up.

A released Craster rose too. 'May I accompany you, my Lord?' he said, pressing forward eagerly.

'And you are?'

'This blackguard's cousin. I've known him all his miserable life. He's always been a villain and I would like to see him get what he deserves.'

Jack, who'd been unable to summon words, found them now. 'The only one who deserves punishment here is him,' he shouted, 'for this day he raped an innocent young woman. Punish me if you will, but call the Watch first. Let him face the punishment of the noose.'

'He lies,' bellowed Craster back. 'The girl he speaks of is a well-known French whore who drew me into the house and then refused to fulfil the business. I taught her a lesson, is all. These gentlemen here are witnesses.' Beside him, his still-masked cronies, the pink-jacketed Horace prominent among them, nodded vigorously.

'You're the liar, Craster Absolute, and a coward too. T'was so throughout your life. You'd stand and watch me thrashed, you'd even get your kicks in. But you'd never stand and face me like a man.'

Quite the crowd had gathered outside the entrance, a line of flunkeys struggling to hold them back. At Jack's words, those unaligned to any cause started crying out, 'Brave lad!' 'Is he a coward then?' 'What's his name?'

Craster flushed. 'I'll fight you any time, boy. Name your ground and time.'

'Here and now.'

Tyers the proprietor spoke. 'We allow no such affairs in Vauxhall! My lord, I appeal to you.'

Melbury's smile had grown under the mask. 'Indeed, this sanctuary must not be violated. But there is ground without which should suit such purposes. And,' he continued turning to Jack, 'since you have now claimed the prerogative of a man, I too will treat you as one. For I am tired of you. So if you survive your cousin's fire, you will face a second flame . . . from me.'

There was no choice. There could be no escaping now should he want to. And in that moment, he didn't. For even if he was to die this day, he would kill Craster Absolute first.

At Lord Melbury's nod, his men released Jack though they stood close by and the whole party began to move toward the Pleasure Gardens' entrance. They had not gone five paces before another voice halted them.

'Tell me, pray . . . where exactly might you be taking my son?'

The party turned. The man who had spoken wore the face of Mr Punch and it was the sum of his disguise. Jack knew the speaker always said that, since he spent so much on his clothes, they would damn well be displayed, masquerade or no!

'Father!' Jack had taken a step back but a raised hand prevented any further approach.

'I know you, sir,' said Lord Melbury.

'And I know you, Sir Devil,' said James Absolute, 'and your ways. As you do in Office, so here. Everything in darkness, nothing in the light.'

Melbury took a step back toward him. 'Do you insult me, sir?'

'Maybe later,' Sir James said evenly, then turned to Jack. 'What is this between you and your cousin?'

Both young men tried to speak, seeking to override each other in their need. Sir James waved them both down. 'It doesn't matter now. All heard your exchange, the challenge issued, accepted. You are both Absolutes and of age and the family name must be respected. But now, sir,' he faced Melbury again, 'what is *your* quarrel with my son?'

'It concerns a lady, sir, and is between ourselves. Your son was offered a thrashing as an alternative punishment and refused. Thus matters have progressed.'

'Thrash my son?' Mr Punch's head tipped to one side. 'Now there was I thinking that pleasure solely mine. So I see why he must fight. Again. Excellent.' He nodded vigorously and made towards the group. 'So let's to it then, gentlemen.' He raised his arms as if to usher them forward, then halted them with a gesture. 'And I presume the proper code is to be observed?'

'Code, sir?'

'Code, sir. Who, for example, is the president?'

'Really,' rasped Melbury, 'this is more in the nature of—'

'A punishment? Yes, you said. But my son's refusal to be beaten like a cur, followed by his challenge, transformed that.' His voice had become very cool, a contrast to Melbury's. 'Have you a president?'

Lord Melbury glowered at the small crowd still gathered around. A fellow in regimental scarlet, topped by the face of a gargoyle, stepped forward.

'Gentlemen, I would be delighted. And my friend here is a surgeon.'

'My next question answered. You see, sir, how easily the code can be accommodated?'

The soldier – for his uniform was too well cut to be anything but the real thing – spoke again. 'And may I suggest that we all retain our masks. No names, eh?' He tapped the gargoyle's warty nose before continuing. 'A public place and the magistrates harsh on such affairs, eh?'

'An excellent precaution. Agreed?' Sir James got a short nod from Lord Melbury. 'Now I presume these are your seconds? And my nephew has these fellows. So where are my son's?'

Lord Melbury said, sourly, 'I am sure you could fulfil the function.'

'You know, I am sure I could. Do you agree, boy?'

'If . . . you . . .'

'Excellent. Wise choice.' He sighed. 'Then according to the custom of these things, as your second I must take on certain obligations, certain duties. I must look to your interests. And the first thing I have to say on your behalf is,' he stepped closer to Lord Melbury, 'that you will not fight two duels in one night.'

'I *will* meet him tonight. Now.'

Sir James' voice was still calm. 'You will not. As his second I cannot allow it. You will choose another night and other ground.'

Lord Melbury roared. 'And allow you to smuggle your bastard out of the country under your *actress* wife's costume? I think not.'

Jack winced. Few people, in his hearing, had ever referred to Lady Jane's previous career without consequence, and none, ever, with the inflection that His Lordship had just given the word. He awaited the thunderbolt. But instead, the knight's voice stayed calm. 'Ah! There! Now you have strayed onto different ground.' His voice lowered. 'You will answer to me for those words. You can take a ball for 'em. Or,' he smiled, 'you can kiss my arse.'

Melbury grimaced. 'When and where, sir?'

The smile broadened. 'Well, we seem excellently accommodated here. Shall we say . . . straight after the lads fight?'

Melbury smiled back. 'Let us. And with you dead, there will be no one to prevent me stamping out the last of your rat's nest of a family.'

The president stepped forward. 'Except for me, sir. I will have no shuffling.'

'Enough. No more talk,' snarled His Lordship.

The conversation had been hitherto conducted on the move. At the gates, most of the small crowd turned back, for their viewing of the duel would cost them another ticket if they wanted to re-enter the Gardens. The few who would follow were dissuaded by Lord Melbury's Imps. So it was only the party concerned that emerged from the gates and began to walk along the Vauxhall Road, past the carriage park toward the open heath land beyond.

The party divided into three. The larger of Lord Melbury's swelled when Craster and his roughs joined them. The president and his surgeon-friend walked between. Jack and his father brought up the rear.

'Father. I . . . I am so sorry.'

Sir James grunted. 'So you should be! How you get into these scrapes I'll never know. Must be the Irish in you. God knows it's nothing to do with Absolute blood, which was ever temperate.'

'How did you find me, sir?'

'Those dogs who beat upon my door in search of you today? Well, that lazy poltroon of a footman was nowhere to be found, of course, so I admitted them myself. They immediately began to threaten me. In my own hallway, damn their insolence! The one ceased talking on the instant, t'other swiftly confessed his allegiance,' he gestured to the Devil ahead, 'and soon after the rest of the plan. So I came to the rendezvous.'

Jack was so overcome he nearly grabbed his father's arm. 'I am much obliged to you, sir.'

Sir James sniffed. 'Should think you are. I'd a good mind to let you die. Teach you a lesson. But Lord Melbury is an enemy to this country, whispering in the King's ear his treasons for an accommodation with the French. It will be good for the realm if I end his career today.'

'Can you, Father? Isn't he—'

'The best shot in England? A rumour largely put about by himself.' He lifted the mask to his forehead and turned now to wink at Jack. 'Besides, never faced an Absolute, has he?'

The party halted a few hundred paces into the open country, just past a series of market gardens newly turned and fertilized for the sowing. A ripe smell came from them, for the nightsoil men of the city sold their collections to the owners of these plots and hundreds like them around London. A strong wind crammed the savour of the excrement into their nostrils, had most there raising kerchiefs; it had also cleared all cloud away, leaving the full moon to ensilver the little that was there, the close-cropped, glistening wet grass, an empty sheep pen with broken staves, the party of cloaked men settling at its edge.

'A fine night for a clear shot, is it not, sir?' said the president, approaching Jack and his father. He gestured to where two of Craster's friends waited. 'The terms, sir?'

Sir James, who had been quietly contemplating the ground, now roused himself. 'Indeed, the terms. But before we talk with them, a word with you, if I may, sir?'

Jack watched the pair walk off, the Gargoyle and Mr Punch, immediately in quiet and intense conversation. Then he looked across to the group and the figure standing slightly detached from it. Craster looked back, for a moment both boys stared, not moving, not blinking. Then each simultaneously turned away, Jack to gaze up into the moon, seeking there the figures from old Morwenna's rhymes: the dog, the cow, the spoon.

In a few moments his father returned. 'That's all settled then,' he declared briskly. 'Both sides agree: the president himself is to have the checking and the loading of the guns for they are his, fetched from his boat here. It is to be one shot apiece and one shot only.'

Jack flushed. 'One? But what if I miss?'

'And he misses you? Why then, you shake hands and walk away and no harm done.'

'No . . . harm?' Jack had begun to shiver, but no longer from cold or fear. 'That . . . scum ravished Clothilde Guen, brutalized her, an innocent, a sweet . . .' A flash of bloodstains, of tears, jammed the words in his throat. He coughed, swallowed. 'I intend to kill him.'

'That may be. There's enmity between you and your cousin I can never comprehend – though I felt much the same about his father. But if you do not put a killing ball into him you will not fulfil your intention this night.' Jack made to speak but his father grabbed his shoulder. 'Look at me, boy. No, look at *me*! This is not about Clothilde any more. If she was harmed as you say, we must allow the Law to deal with that. So this is no longer about vengeance. This is about honour. A man's honour is his life; without it we are nothing, less, and our family name is nought. When you stand facing him, you stand for nothing but that name, just as he stands for it. For all the Absolutes that have preceded you and all the Absolutes to come.'

'But if you had seen her, Father—'

The hand pulled the collar roughly. 'Have you listened, boy? She is a matter for another day, other ground. This day is now only about honour. And whether you live, live crippled, or die, honour *will* be satisfied by a single shot.'

'And if I die . . .' Tears came then, lodged in his eyes, sprung from many sources of anger and fear.

'We are born astride a grave, my boy,' Sir James said softly, looking away, 'live your life knowing that, and you will live your life.'

The president called them to order. Releasing his son's collar, straightening it with a flick, Sir James pushed Jack towards the ground, where the president handed the elder Absolute a pistol. Craster was waiting on a level patch of cropped grass. Jack, his father beside him, walked quickly to stand just behind a cross gouged in the grass, turning from there to face his cousin. He was no more than a dozen paces away.

His father was speaking softly to him again. With an effort, Jack tried to listen to what he was saying.

'. . . my first time . . . a blur . . . body side on . . . reduce target . . . finger off trigger . . . raise . . . breathe . . . sight . . . squeeze . . .'

Words flew at him, words he recognized that yet had little meaning. He found he had stopped breathing and decided to take in air. Then he found he was taking too much, that he suddenly wanted to laugh. How absurd it all suddenly was. The fertilizing shit, the masked men, his hated cousin. How absurd!

With a final squeeze, his father moved away, to rest ten paces back, the same to the side. When he settled, the president began to speak. Again words passed, again he took some in but not all.

Craster's seconds moved away to their positions. Jack looked at his cousin, who stood with eyes downcast, seemed to see every detail of him: his thick reddish hair held down with oil, the scratches on his cheek from Clothilde's nails, the flesh bruising where Jack had struck, these wounds beneath the mask his opponent had replaced, as Jack had replaced his. Indeed all the principals in the action wore them, Gods, Imps and Emperors, standing silently, the wind moving their cloaks, an hallucination by moonlight. Central in the group was the huge figure of His Satanic Majesty, Lord Melbury.

The president was still speaking and Jack forced himself to listen. 'So, gentlemen, I repeat. I will give you three commands: "To your mark." You will step up. "Make Ready." You may raise your guns. I will then call out, "Fire." Once you hear that word, you may act upon it whensoever you please. Not before.' He stepped back. 'Gentlemen, to your mark.'

Jack moved to the cross, scraped his feet into the grass. His father had said something about placing them solidly there.

'Make ready!'

The gun was so heavy! He had barely studied it, had not realized it was such a weight until that moment, until he tried to bring it up. He wanted to use his other hand but knew that was not in the code. Somehow, he brought it level with his shoulder, somehow he pointed it toward the blur Craster had become.

The wind gusted, bringing again that taint from the gardens and the faint sound of the orchestra striking up another quadrille. Was Fanny still there, making a fourth for another dance of humiliation?

'Fire!'

An explosion came instantly upon the word, something struck his face. He would have cried out if there was any moisture left in his mouth to form a sound. He had heard that a bullet entering the body could feel very different on each occasion – a slap, a punch, a mere tickle. This stung and in the moment he believed he had before true pain came, before he was incapable of the action, he placed his finger on the trigger at last and squeezed.

Craster fell with a shriek. It seemed to Jack he fell almost before the ball had been sent, certainly no later than the exact moment of pressure upon metal. Jack was lowering his gun again, slowly, as slowly and with as much difficulty as he had raised it, as if it were on a crank he could only release tooth by tooth. As it finally pointed downwards, a voice spoke beside him.

'Are you well, boy?'

His legs gave, he sank and his father caught him, taking the gun from him just before it slipped from his hand. Thus freed, he reached up to his still-smarting cheek, and rubbed. Bringing his hand away, he saw his fingertips were black.

'Missed you, by God. But he came close.'

Jack croaked, 'Did I kill him?'

His seconds, the surgeon, all had clustered around the prone Craster. The surgeon called out, 'We cannot find a wound. We think . . .' He continued to search through the clothes. 'No! No blood! We think he may have swooned. Here you, fetch me some sal volatile from the bag.'

The bottle was fetched, uncorked, held beneath Craster's nose, now free of his mask. He awoke with another cry. The surgeon looked up. 'He is well.'

The president stepped forward. 'Here's two misses, then. Brave boys and honour satisfied, eh? Will they shake?'

Craster was raised to his feet, Jack pushed towards him. Only now was he emerging from the fog that had sucked him in, though tendrils still clung to him, confusing him still.

Had he missed? Surely, with Craster Absolute before his gun, he hadn't missed?

The two cousins fell into each other, like drunks, like dancers, like wrestlers closing for a hold. Their hands gripped, their faces were close, the others stepping away to leave them to the reconciliation. So Jack only had to whisper. 'I'm going to kill you, Craster. One day. Soon. But you won't have to watch your back. You'll die looking in my eyes!'

Craster looked in them now, his own bloodshot, gummy. He muttered, 'Not if you look in mine first.' Then they were pulled away, their fingers clinging as if reluctant to part.

'Good lads,' said the president. 'And now, sirs—'

'And now,' said Sir James, 'I know how fond you are of the playhouse, my Lord. Since we have had the entr'acte, shall we advance to the play?'

Lord Melbury smiled. 'Indeed, sir. And do not be comforted by our respective masks. Today Mr Punch will be vanquished and the Devil will triumph.'

'That we shall soon know.'

Lord Melbury gestured to one of his servants who stood holding a pistol case open. 'Since you come unarmed, sir, perhaps you would care to choose one of mine?'

Sir James peered in. 'Exquisite. Whitworth's?'

'Indeed.'

Sir James reached, lifted a pistol from the red velvet, together with a flask of powder and a ball. 'I may load myself?'

'Of course. A single ball, yes?'

Sir James nodded. 'I thank you, sir.'

'My great pleasure.'

'And one that he thinks will be all his, no doubt,' he muttered as he moved away to his son, holding up the one ball to the whole company, then giving it to Jack together with the flask of powder. 'It can't be helped. But one should really try to avoid fighting with another man's weapons.'

'Why, sir?'

'He knows 'em too well.' Sir James was squinting inside the

barrel. 'Hmm! Not enough light to see by, but I'd wager it's rifled at the breech.'

'Rifled?'

'Aye. Strictly forbidden but hard to prove without cracking the gun open, a sacrilege to one as beautiful as this. But I am sure my Lordship's reputation is at least partly founded on a rifled barrel. More accurate, see.' He looked towards Melbury, called. 'Do she throw, sir?'

'Hardly at all. An inch to the left, perhaps, at twenty paces.'

'That'll mean two to the right at fifteen,' Sir James said under his breath. He then took the flint out, striking it against the frizzle, replacing it, cocking the gun, touching the trigger, watching the hammer fall and the spark jump. 'Naturally. Trigger set to a hair. Always check it, Jack, because if you shake and set it off, not only may you shoot a spectator or your own foot, it will count as your shot.' He blew in the touch-hole, then, taking the rammer from its slot under the barrel, gestured for the powder, wadding and ball.

Jack watched as his father swiftly loaded the gun. 'You have fought with pistols before, haven't you, sir?'

'Once or twice.'

'And with swords?'

A bottom lip thrust out, a shrug. 'Three or four times. Prefer it, actually.' He looked up and a faint smile came. 'Why do you think I've been sending you to the Academy since you were twelve?'

Jack shook his head. 'I feel I hardly know you, Father.'

Carefully lowering the hammer, Sir James now raised his mask. Jack did the same. 'You don't, boy . . . here,' he said, pointing to his head, 'And never have. But you do here.' He tapped Jack's chest. 'You have my blood and that will tell you all you need to know. If this . . . affair goes against me, just listen to that, to your Absolute blood. And take care of your mother.'

Jack was unable to reply, because the president had called the combatants to their marks – a good pace closer than he had stood facing Craster. He wanted to follow, to stand where his father had stood for him. But he suddenly found his legs would not carry him there. He heard the president reiterate the laws, the words clear this time, the voice coming as if from afar. He wished now that the necessity for these masks was over. All still wore them, because a crowd had gathered from the carriage park, drivers and pillions presenting a shifting backdrop. There was little doubt that some outraged citizen would already have run for the Watch. Yet Jack cursed the necessity; he didn't want to remember his father as Mr Punch.

'To your marks.'

They stepped up.

'Make ready.'

The beautiful, engraved barrels rose to glint in the moonlight. The wind had dropped, as if it too held its breath.

'Fire.'

Both guns cracked, as if they were only one. For a brief, tiny moment afterwards, the only movement was smoke, rising. Then both men staggered. One fell.

It was the Devil who crashed backwards, his bulk shaking the earth as he hit it. Jack felt it as he moved, his long-trapped feet now free.

'Father,' he cried, grabbing at the sinking man who clutched at his son's arm, pulling himself upright.

'I think . . . I think I am well, boy.'

Where Jack held him felt wet. He took his hand away, saw the dark liquid there. 'You're wounded, sir.'

'Aye,' Sir James ran his tongue around his lips, 'but not mortally. Believe me, I've had a ball or two in me and would know the difference. Rip the cloth away there and let us have a look.'

Jack did as he was bid. Exposed, the flesh of the bicep was torn near its extremity; the ball had glanced and left, not entered. Clutching a handkerchief to it, Sir James took his own weight then walked towards the men huddled over the figure on the ground.

The surgeon looked up at their approach, shook his head. When his father pushed through, Jack peered from behind him. Lord Melbury lay half on his side, his breath coming short. His red mask had been tipped up to rest on his forehead, his skin a white contrast beneath it. As Sir James leaned down, the eyelids flickered open.

'Did I miss you, sir?'

'No. I am hit.'

'Thank God. My reputation is preserved, at the least,' Lord Melbury whispered, closing his eyes. And though Jack had only seen it once, years before, when he'd looked down at his uncle in a hole in the ground, he recognized the moment life left.

Someone was tugging at his arm. He looked up, into the gargoyle's mask above the soldier's uniform. The president had one arm each on father and son and was encouraging both to rise.

'I have a boat nearby. This place will not be safe for you shortly, mask or no mask. I urge you both to come.'

They did as they were bid, followed as the soldier and the surgeon – no longer required at the scene – forced through the gawkers who had gathered. More were coming, drawn by shots and rumour, from the carriage park, from the Vauxhall Road.

He led them to the river bank, Jack and the surgeon needing to support his father down the stone steps. They got him in, two servants taking the oars, the surgeon lighting a lantern, removing the handkerchief, reaching into his bag for a salve and some clean linen. The soldier joined them, pushing the vessel off before stepping aboard.

'I have a carriage t'other side. May I suggest the briefest of calls at your house and then the Star and Garter in Cheapside? Coaches leave there each midnight for Harwich and ships from there each day to Antwerp. I have some gold, if you do not keep enough in your house. More can be sent on later. I recommend the Crown and Pineapple in the port. But Williams here knows it and he will go with you.'

'You are very kind, sir. Beyond what any gentleman could expect.' Sir James was squinting behind eyelids lowered now in pain. 'May I ask why?'

The soldier smiled. ' "Mine enemy's enemy is my friend." You have done me a great service this night, sir, for Lord Melbury was certainly my enemy, across a variety of battle-fields. Yet it was not the first time your family has done me a kindness.'

'I would seek to know more of that, sir. But time prods us. T'was ever thus with Absolutes. Yet I wonder if you can extend your thanks with another favour.'

'Name it.'

'There is no doubt that I must flee. Lord Melbury's is too great a name. It would not be the first time and I have friends in Germany, former comrades-in-arms who will shelter me until the vibrations of his fall have passed. But my son's crime is less, no blood was shed.'

'He will be caught up in the larger event. He may be called to witness or even prosecuted still.'

'He's too young for an exile like this. Yet, if he must away . . .' Sir James shuddered against a sudden surge of pain. When his eyes opened again he continued, 'I always hoped he would follow me into the army. He's resisted thus far, with fancy ideas gleaned from too much education . . .'

Jack leaned forward. 'I will do what must be done, sir, if only you deem it wise.'

'Oh, I think,' said the soldier, reaching up to pull off his mask, 'I may be able to help you there as well.'

It took a moment, because the light from the boat lantern was poor and he had only met him once before; still, recognition came soon enough.

The man who steered the boat was John Burgoyne.

— PART 2 —
War Cry

— ONE —
To War

Yet again, Jack was pitched forward, his head only saved from further bruising by a hastily thrown-out arm. As on the open sea, so here on the St Lawrence River. The West Indiaman *Sylphide* disdained its delicate name and sought any and every trough in which to wallow. If Jack had been hoping that the term 'river' would lead to a lessening in the lurching that was the vessel's natural gait, he had been swiftly disillusioned. This Canadian waterway could have swallowed ten of the Thames, while its shoals channelled currents that had him wishing for the relative calm of Atlantic swells. Having mastered his stomach two weeks out of the Old World, he'd had to regain control of it all over again five weeks later in the New World. Such control was essential; he did not intend his new commander's first impression to be of a sickly, green-faced milksop.

As voices erupted from the deck above him – a mix of Kentish curses and the bizarre approximation of French that the river pilot spoke – Jack pushed away from the tiny cabin's wall, steadied himself and returned to the task of creating that impression. Replacing the cracked mirror on its hook, he regarded the least distorted of his reflections. It was the first time he'd donned the uniform since embarkation and it did not hang as well as it had in Portsmouth; he'd inevitably lost weight in the green weeks despite the hearty eating since. His father's generosity, now Jack had submitted to his will, was limitless and included the extra £30 for this private . . . box – it could not be dignified with the word 'cabin' – and a seat at the captain's table. Beevor ate well and so, once he'd mastered himself, did Jack; they'd only had to resort to salt provisions three days before Gaspé.

The red coat, with its lines of gold buttons and embroidered lace loops, hung limply from his diminished shoulders. It would have to wait for a regimental tailor to alter it, but he'd managed the waistcoat and breeches himself with a few stitches of sail yarn in the back. Turning each way, Jack had to admit that the overall effect was none too shabby. His hair was powdered and Mrs Beevor had done a tolerable job in setting it. The ribbon that gathered it was of the same dark blue as the uniform's facings while the collar and cuffs had been further darkened with boot black. His stock was white and fresh from the tailor's crêpe.

Burgoyne had said to him, 'You will be the first of the Sixteenth Light Dragoons to serve in North America. You must be a credit to the regiment.'

Looking at himself, Jack felt he probably would be – at least sartorially.

Burgoyne. He knew how his colonel had protested that they should not be sending someone with a mere three months in the trade. Yet he also knew he was a victim of Burgoyne's own excellence. The 16th Light Dragoons had rapidly become the most fashionable of regiments, that ex-cavalryman King George himself attending the parades and exercises of 'The Queen's', often accompanied by the wife for whom they were named. And when His Majesty's detailed thoughts on the pursuance of the war had to be taken to his commander in Canada, it was obvious his messenger must be drawn from the ranks of these new favourites. Then it could only be decided by the 'last in, first out' law of volunteering; Jack was the most junior cornet, the last to receive his commission and thus the most expendable.

At their final meeting, Burgoyne had again expressed how he would not have it so. Then he'd given Jack a copy of his newly published *Code of Instructions* for officers. 'Read, lad, read all the way across. And if, perchance, there is an old soldier on board, attach yourself to him, let him teach you the other part of a Dragoon's life, the infantry drills we ain't got to yet. For, as sure as shit is shovelled, there's no English cavalry on that continent.' He'd smiled. 'Till *you* get there, of course.'

Jack had taken the advice, read assiduously and found himself a mentor, a foul-mouthed corporal from Yorkshire, William Hancock. He'd agreed – for a far from modest five guineas – to teach Jack the essentials of drill and the use of the musket, throwing in for free a quite extraordinary collection of new curses concerned with southerners' lust for livestock.

From above, a renewed burst of swearing came, accompanying another vicious lurch of the ship. Steadying himself, Jack looked down again. Next to the now tattered copy of Burgoyne's *Instructions* were two letters. The first was from his father and, though he had conned it several times, he picked it up once more. It was worth the study.

It was written from Herrenhausen and dated 1 July, two weeks before Jack sailed. It was the only direct contact Jack had had from his father, though notes had been sent to his mother, and it detailed briefly Sir James's rapid progress to the Royal Palace in Hanover where he had many former comrades, having fought in that country's wars in the 1740s. He had re-enlisted, seeing no swifter way to regain his position in England than by distinguishing himself, once again, against the French. And there was a shortage of experienced cavalry officers.

He had also been informed of Jack's mission.

So both Absolutes are bound for war. I had hoped to be with you in your first encounters, to guide you with my experience and steady you with my own equanimity. But your doting mother and kiss-me-arse schoolmasters had filled your thoughts with too much useless blasted learning and your subsequent follies conspired to deprive me of the opportunity and you of my counsel. But these precepts I would have you mark. Your duty, sir, is to yourself, your comrades, your country and your King and of these, the first two are the most important. In the chaos of battle, listen to your officers and for your drums, watch for your standards; but ride knee to knee with Johnny to your left and Billy to your right. Fight for them; for they will preserve you and you them. Never retreat before they do. Never betray them.

Above all, fight for yourself; for the name of Absolute and the glory that your ancestors have always attached to it. Just as you did on that field of honour against another of the same name, your cousin. I was proud of you then, boy, when you toed the line. I saw the man in you for the first time. I doubt not but that you shall continue to make me proud.

The next passage was written with a different nib, in different ink. His father had moved on.

Now, as to that affair. Because we both go to war with all the peril that entails, I will have all clear and honest between us. Though your honour was at stake that night in Vauxhall, your life was not. Colonel Burgoyne and I agreed that young lives should not be blighted by disfigurement, death or disgrace so your pistols were loaded with powder but not ball. I took the decision for you and do not apologize for it. Yet since you have now proved yourself a man, I will never again interfere in such an affair. Should one arise, which, given your hot blood and general stupidity is almost certain, you are on your own. Again, remember your name.

As you know, your cousin has been dealt with. You must now leave that matter where it lies. And as to . . .

He broke off. *Dealt with*? Though Jack had read the letter a dozen times, his anger at his cozening a little less each time,

178

this was one part he could not, would not accept. Though he'd been cut off from Absolute funds, the last of it used to purchase him a commission in a regiment of Foot, Craster had essentially been pardoned, not punished.

Jack returned to the letter, though the words were scratched upon his heart.

And as to the other matter, your mother informs me that this too has been dealt with. It may not be to your satisfaction but it is best for all – especially the lady concerned. Again, I urge, nay, command you: Leave it lie!

Re-reading this, Jack sighed again, closing his eyes. He had repeatedly tried to see Clothilde but had never been re-admitted to the house on Thrift Street. His mother, however, had. And, a week after the affair at Vauxhall, three announcements had been made: that Craster had emerged from hiding and left for his regiment; that the warrants issued for the arrests of the younger Absolutes had been withdrawn; and that Clothilde Guen was to marry her cousin, the apprentice, Claude Berri, who'd bought a partnership in the House of Guen.

Absolute gold had provided a dowry, allowing her future husband his elevation. On hearing the news Jack had gone immediately to Soho, to howl outside the shuttered house till the Watch were called on him. He'd had no further contact with her until the eve of his departure when a package had arrived at Curzon Street containing all his letters and poems, any trinket he'd ever given her – including the merman, now a crushed and mangled thing – and a short, curt note demanding the return of anything of hers. The feeling he'd had when he'd read that, the rejection he'd felt! And then the very different feeling as something had slipped from the envelope and fallen upon the bed.

Jack reached up now into his shirt, felt to the end of the leather string, touched the object held there, rubbing his fingers along the half-coin's edge, neatly cut by a goldsmith's daughter. He had no need to look at it, a part of a silver half-shilling from Edward the Sixth's reign, nor read again the words that were scrawled on the scrap of paper the coin had been wrapped in. '*La moitié de mon coeur.*'

Shutting his eyes, closing his hand over it now, he held her half-heart and prayed that across the ocean, sometimes, the newly-wedded Madame Berri still held his.

Carefully, Jack began to stow his possessions in his fustian haversack. The very last of them, the only one he hadn't reconsidered was, like Burgoyne's *Instructions*, a book, beautifully bound in a green leather cover, the title incised in gold. He picked it up now: *Hamlet, Prince of Denmark.*

It was Alexander Pope's version, a restoration of the complete text. And it was his mother's parting gift, given at the dockside at Portsmouth at the very moment before boarding. She had insisted on accompanying him, despite his protestations. 'I did not have the chance to wave one Absolute off to war,' she'd said, laughing. 'I will not miss playing that scene twice. And I've just the gown for it!'

Indeed she had, a flowing dress of glorious chartreuse. She'd continued laughing in the coach all the way to Portsmouth, right up to the very ladder of the ship. Only at the very end did the tears come, as she made him give all the promises she, the soldier's wife, knew he could not keep. And at the last, as a seaman urged him aboard, she'd pressed a package into his hand. Later, when he'd looked at it in his cabin, he'd thought it was merely a reminder of a wonderful night they'd shared, seeing Garrick in the role at Drury Lane. But then he'd read the inscription on the inside cover, written in her bold, slanting copperplate: '*All truths are within. Seek them out, sweet prince.*'

He'd read it several times on the voyage, enjoyed it, as a story. But truths? He'd found more to admire in Laertes than Hamlet: 'Your enemy before you, a weapon in your hand?' If he could only have Craster thus. He'd pasted Clothilde's last, brief note on the final page.

He'd just placed the book within the bag when someone hammered on the door.

'Are you ready, there? The boat's alongside and you'll transfer here.'

He'd been told that a flat-bottomed barge would take him the last stage through especially treacherous shoals to the Army's headquarters. They had made that rendezvous. Here, on 11 September 1759, he was about to set foot for the first time upon the continent of North America.

Hastily tying his sack shut, donning his cloak and Dragoon cap, he took one last look in the mirror. A soldier grinned back and stuck out his tongue.

'Yes,' called out Cornet Jack Absolute, opening the cabin door, 'I am indeed ready.'

He may have been ready for them. But the brigadiers of the Army at Quebec were unprepared for him.

'What have we here? Are these Billy Pitt reinforcements at last? Damn me if he hasn't sent us a piece of Chelsea porcelain!' guffawed a man near the head of a table, his gaitered legs upon it, his well-cut civilian clothes open to reveal his frilled shirt. He was eyeing Jack's uniform in an exaggeratedly amazed way and was ostentatiously drunk.

'General Wolfe?' Jack stood near the flap of the large command tent, nervously looking between the three men there.

'Don't know what our Caesar looks like, boy?' bellowed the man who'd first spoken, enormous black eyebrows shooting up into the expanse of his glistening forehead. 'Well, I am sure I have his portrait hereabouts.' He brought his feet off the table and began to root beside him in a capacious leather bag.

'Tush, George,' said a bald, pinch-faced gentleman to his left, raising a restraining hand, 'leave the lad alone. He's only just arrived.'

'Best he knows straight away, what? We should have no disillusions.'

The third man there, who, unlike the other two at least

sported the scarlet of the soldier if without the distinguishing lace of the officer, spoke sharply. 'Murray's right, Townshend. Let's have a bit of dignity before the King's messenger.'

The dishevelled officer shot the man a cold look, muttered something, then carried on with his search. The soldier sighed and turned back to Jack. 'Come in, lad. Come! You may remove your hat. Cavalry, eh? What regiment are you with?'

Jack stepped a pace forward, fumbling the cap off as he came. 'Sixteenth Light Dragoons, sir.'

The still-rooting officer, who'd been addressed as Townshend, said, 'Never heard of 'em!' while the other officer continued. 'And their commander?'

'Colonel Burgoyne, sir.'

Townshend looked up from his searching. 'Heard of *him*. Dilettante! Playwright!' Each word was given an equally contemptuous edge. 'Didn't he fuck up that raid on Normandy last year?'

Jack was not shocked by the profanity but by the assault on his commander. 'I'll believe you'll find, sir, that he was the only officer, Army or Navy, to emerge from that venture with any credit.'

It was said with a heat that caused the man to stop his fumbling and look up sharply. 'Don't like that tone, boy. Here one minute, already contradicting your superior?'

Before Jack could reply, the redcoated soldier interjected. 'Leave him alone, Townshend. Bully someone of your own rank, why don't you?' This caused a return to the searching and the soldier turned back to Jack. 'Don't mind him, lad. I think he's merely startled by an expression of loyalty. It's become rare as plover's eggs in these parts.' He smiled. 'I know your colonel well. A fine man. We were at school together.'

'Westminster, sir? So was I.'

'Indeed?'

'Christ preserve me, another one,' muttered Townshend.

Ignoring him, the soldier stepped forward. 'You have dispatches for us?'

'I do, sir. But I was ordered by the King himself to give them only into the hands of General Wolfe. Are you he?'

'I am not. I am General Monckton. This is General Murray,' the small, balding man raised a glass-filled hand, 'and this is General Townshend. We are Wolfe's brigadiers.'

Before Jack could introduce himself, Townshend gave a yelp of triumph. 'Got it!' he cried, slapping a piece of paper down upon the table, spinning it so Jack could see. It was a caricature in pencil, a very thin soldier in the most impoverished of uniforms, supporting himself on a fusil. Words, too small to be read from where he was stood, were written within a ball that emerged from his mouth.

'There, boy! Now you'll recognize our Alexander when you see him,' yelled George Townshend. The spite in the voice was as cruel as the depiction on the page. Jack, out of depth the moment he walked into the tent, was doubly drowned now. He had no idea what was expected of him, what reaction he could give. He'd been taught that respect for your commander-in-chief was essential. What had James Wolfe done to forfeit these men's?

A voice came quietly from behind him, preventing any utterance. 'May I see it?'

All turned. Stood just inside the flap, his hand still upon it as if it partly held him up, was the model for the cartoon: James Wolfe, Commander of His Majesty's Army at Quebec.

He hung there for a moment, regarding each of them in turn, then detached himself and moved to the table. Leaning heavily, he regarded the cartoon in a silence that Jack was sure he was not the only one to find awkward. The length of it did, however, give him the chance to study his new commander, to try to tally all that he had heard of the man with the reality before him. For Wolfe had been much talked about by excited schoolboys at Westminster, at home and in the short time he'd had with the Dragoons. Jack recalled now what Burgoyne had said when he'd first told Jack of his mission: '*Watch General Wolfe, lad. He is ardent for glory. A necessary attribute of a successful commander perhaps that yet can be quite a danger to his men.*' And that had confirmed what his father had said when Jack had met him once at a coffee house, the newspapers full of Wolfe's appointment, at the age of thirty-two to this command. 'I know him, a little. Fought with him, at Dettingen and at Culloden Moor.' Sir James had placed a finger to his temple, revolved it. 'But you know what the King said when someone was cautioning him against making the appointment. "Mad, is he? Then I hope he will bite some of my other generals."'

Jack now studied the man studying his caricature. The portrait exaggerated but not much for the eyes were very small above a long thin nose, the cleft in his chin was deep, a long, corn-pale pigtail ran from beneath a soldier's plain hat. What the picture could not get, being in pencil, was the extreme whiteness of the skin, emphasized by the two very red and heated patches on the high cheekbones.

The man does not look mad, Jack thought, he looks ill. And closer to fifty than thirty.

At last, Wolfe straightened. 'Not one of your best, Townshend.'

His subordinate would not meet his eye. 'Just a little joke, sir, you understand, to relieve the tedium.'

'The tedium? Ah, yes. I am sorry I have so contrived to bore you, George.' Wolfe spoke in a flat monotone, as if the choice of words affected their delivery. 'But I think I may have found a way to occupy your sword rather than your pencil. Can you be as cutting with that, I wonder?'

At this, the three men, even Townshend, became alert. Monckton, who, Jack deduced from his position at the head of the table, had to be the senior brigadier there, spoke. 'You refer, sir, I presume, to the plans we submitted to you these three days past? That you graciously conceded were both sound and prudent?'

A faint smile came to the bloodless lips. 'Sound and prudent. Now those are words to grace any hero's tombstone, are they not?'

'General, we—'

'Your plans would cost us the campaign, and the King his colonies. I have been out tonight, gentlemen, upon the river. I have come up with a different plan. Less sound. Far less prudent.'

Townshend muttered an audible, 'Jesus spare us!'

The bald Murray's jaw fell open. He stuttered, 'B . . . b . . . but, for pity's sake, man! We all agreed upon it. Studied every other alternative.'

'Not every one.'

'Then tell us, Wolfe. Tell us!' Townshend had stood, his face a vivid red and angry contrast to his commander's.

Yet instead of reacting to that anger, the general now glanced to his right, to where Jack stood, frozen with embarrassment. 'And who, pray, are you?' he said.

'J . . . Jack . . . uh, Cornet Absolute. Sir . . . General! Sixteenth Light Dragoons. With messages from His Majesty. Amongst others. Sir.' For some reason, Jack gave a little laugh.

They all stared at him a moment. Then Wolfe spoke. 'Absolute? Absolute? You are not . . . not related to Mad Jamie Absolute, are you?'

It was not a term Jack had heard before. 'I don't think so, sir. My father is Sir James—'

'Must be the same fellow. Dragoon? Cornishman?' On Jack's confused nod Wolfe continued, 'Mad Jamie. Led the counter charge at Dettingen. Saved me from a claymore at Culloden.' The smile on his face was the first genuine one Jack had seen there and it transformed it. 'Damn me, if I wouldn't rather have an Absolute from England than another hundred grenadiers.' The smile widened. 'I suppose they didn't send me another hundred grenadiers?' On Jack's shake, Wolfe nodded. 'Never mind.'

'Sir, Absolute or not, a cornet cannot be privy to what you have to impart to us now?' Murray had moved around the table, went to take Jack's arm.

'And what would that be?'

'This new . . . *plan* of yours,' Townshend added through a fixed jaw, the emphasis unmistakable.

Wolfe turned back, the smile vanishing, the red on the cheeks heightened. 'And I will not tell you of it now,' he said sharply, 'for you have obviously partaken of too much of my wine and that makes you too dull to take in my commands.' He looked around, at each of them in turn. 'My commands, gentlemen. I have left you without them for too long. Besides,' and here the smile returned, 'I will not tell you of them. I will show you . . . on the morrow. We'll go downriver with the morning tide. Be ready. And wear civilian clothes.' Each of the men looked as if he would protest but Wolfe went on, 'That is all. You will now leave me with the King's messenger.'

There was no mistaking the firmness of the instruction. With a varying degree of reluctance – Townshend's the most obvious – the three men left the tent. Wolfe called out after them, 'Gwillim?' and an officer appeared immediately. 'Tell Captains Delaune and MacDonald I would see them. And Surgeon MacLeod.'

The man nodded and left. As soon as the tent flap settled, Wolfe collapsed into the chair and was immediately racked with a burst of wet and violent coughing. Jack could not help but see that the handkerchief the general snatched out was stained as red as his coat. He immediately filled a glass with wine and took it to the table head. Coughing subsided, Wolfe drank, spluttered, drank again, sank back. His face was a chalky white, all the more pale for the contrasting spots that flamed upon the cheek.

When strength had returned – a process that took some minutes – the general waved Jack to a chair and smiled. 'Your father? Is he well?'

'He was, sir, when last I saw him. He has . . . uh, gone to Hanover, sir.'

'Riding to the sound of the guns. Of course, of course. Jamie could not keep away. Would that he had chosen this theatre of operations and accompanied you. The next few nights would suit his especial brand of lunacy! You've always known he was mad, I suppose?'

'With all respect, sir,' Jack blurted, 'he said exactly the same thing of you.'

Jack didn't know why he said it. Maybe he just hadn't been a soldier long enough. Maybe it was because he'd felt peculiar from the moment he stepped ashore in this land that felt so strange . . . yet strangely familiar too. Maybe it was just something in the man before him, the young man within the old.

But Wolfe, thankfully, laughed, hearty laughter that brought more blood into the handkerchief. During this burst, a man in a blue frock coat came in and went straight to the general, wordlessly undoing the plain black stock at his neck, opening the buttons on his shirt, rubbing some salve from his leather bag. The smell of camphor filled the tent. Wolfe gestured toward Jack's pouch. The dispatches were instantly spilled upon the table and the general, around the ministrations of his surgeon, sought and discarded amongst them. The one with the Royal seal he threw down with a sigh.

'The King will have delivered another military lecture and that I can do without. How he expects to conduct a battle from three thousand miles away, and hoodwink as capable a Frenchie as Montcalm, when he barely succeeded controlling one when he stood on the field at Dettingen is beyond me. Ah . . .' He drew out the dispatch Jack recognized as coming from his own commander, Burgoyne – his letter of introduction. The seal was broken, the contents swiftly scanned. Wolfe looked up. 'He speaks highly of you, acknowledges your courage if tempering it with your lack of experience. He says you are fast, lad.'

Jack nodded. 'Show me the horse, sir, and I will take it to its utmost.'

Wolfe laughed, coughed. 'The only pony you'll find here is Shanks's. You are the only English cavalryman in Quebec, Absolute. Can you run?'

'Aye, sir,' said Jack, thinking of cricket and Tothill Fields.

'That may prove useful.' He glanced down, read on. 'And you speak French, do ye?'

'Tolerably, sir.'

'Then you undoubtedly speak it better than most of my other officers, including myself. And that may be useful, too.'

The surgeon, who was preparing a cup of viscous fluid, now said, 'General, you must rest.'

'Can't,' whispered Wolfe, 'Mustn't.' He sat up straighter. 'I know you cannot cure me, MacLeod. But patch me up so that I may do my duty for a few days and I will be content.'

The surgeon sighed, then lifted the cup to Wolfe's mouth. He drank, muttered a curse, drank on. As he did, the tent flap twitched again and the adjutant appeared again. 'Captains Delaune and MacDonald, as you requested, sir.'

The two men entered. One, dressed as Wolfe, in simple and unadorned scarlet went straight to him. 'Are you all right, sir?' he said, squeezing the hand he'd taken.

'Never better, William.' Wolfe coughed again into his hand-kerchief. 'Well, that might be a slight exaggeration.' He gestured to Jack. 'Cornet Absolute, fresh off the boat from England. Captains Delaune,' he patted the man still crouched over him on the shoulder, 'and MacDonald.'

The other man, small of stature and watchful, was a High-lander, complete with a kilt, stockings and a plaid cloak. 'Absolute?' he echoed. 'He's nae kin to Mad Jamie, is he?'

'His son.'

'May Christ defend me! The sire nearly gave me my quietus at Culloden. Does the cub come to finish the job?'

'You'll have to forgive Donald MacDonald,' Wolfe smiled. 'He fought us with the Royal Ecossais on that Moor. Then joined Fraser's Seventy-eighth to fight for us here.'

'I'd little choice, ken,' the Scotsman growled. 'Rot in Inverness gaol or go where the fighting is. And since the cursed English was the only ones offering . . .'

'Do not mind this old Jacobite, lad,' Delaune said. 'He's as loyal as any of us.'

'More loyal than many,' growled MacDonald. He had seen the caricature upon the table. 'I saw that sneck-draw Townshend a-laughing with his noble cronies. Nae doot at the general's expense.' He picked up the paper and ripped it savagely into several pieces.

'His particular loyalty is to me,' Wolfe breathed, 'for which I am very grateful. I need men like these, young Absolute. Especially now. Especially for this plan.'

With a wave, he dismissed the surgeon's further fussings. The man shook his head, gathered his things and left. Delaune leaned forward. 'Your reconnaissance, sir . . . was it worth this blood?'

'It was, William and several pints more. I have sketches.' He gestured to his record book but as Delaune eagerly reached, he laid his hand on it and looked at Jack. 'You must leave us now, Absolute. Though I am sure you are discretion itself, only these two must know of my plan till the morrow when I shall be forced to share it with my brigadiers.'

'Of course, sir, I'll . . .' Jack saluted, started for the entrance.

'Your time will come soon enough,' Wolfe called after him, halting him. 'He's young, gentlemen, and does not know what to expect in battle.'

'Perfect,' said Delaune.

'Aye,' said MacDonald, 'assuming ignorance holds him, not fear.'

'Mad Jamie's son, Donald.'

'Oh, aye.'

'And he speaks French. That may prove very useful in my calculations.'

'Do he indeed?' The Scot stepped towards Jack. '*Où avez-vous appris votre français, mon brave?*'

'*À Londres*, monsieur. *Avec une jeune femme de . . . de . . .*'

'*De la nuit?*'

Jack blushed. '*Mais non*, monsieur. *Elle était la fille d'un ami de mon père.*'

MacDonald turned back. 'He speaks like a Parisian limmer.

But with a little help he may pass muster, given muckle years.'

'What can you manage in a day and a night, Donald?' Wolfe's voice came in a whisper. 'I'll have him billeted with you, and you can bring him up to the mark.'

The Scot looked as if he would protest; then the import of the general's words drew him back toward the table. As he moved he called over his shoulder, 'You'll find my bivouac in the lines of the Seventy-eighth, callant. Ye can await me there.'

Jack hesitated at the flap, looking back. Delaune had drawn the lamp close and, in the small spill of its light, the three men now crouched over the general's record book. A faint whisper came, but Jack could not make out any words. All he could sense was the excitement as they bent to the task of conquering Canada.

– TWO –

The Blooding of Jack Absolute

He had been cold long before embarkation; now, well into the third hour, he felt like a lump of suet, sitting in an ice house. He had tried to control his shivering at first, fearing that it would be perceived as something else. Yet since everyone around him, crammed on the narrow benches and wedged into the tiniest of spaces, was soon shaking as much as he, he had given in. Only Captain MacDonald, who sat beside him, seemed unchilled, but he was wrapped in a great tartan blanket and had the extra warmth of his pipe, rarely unlit in the hours that they had waited.

At least it had not rained. The clouds that had obscured the sky had dispersed and their absence allowed Jack to see by starlight – there was no moon – as well as by the faint glow of the lamps aboard HMS *Sutherland*. He looked up at the man-of-war now, hoping that the sailor who'd visited twice would return again, bearing his barrel of rum. Jack had refused the first issue, to MacDonald's vocal disapproval, fearing a clouding of his mind. He'd taken the second and it had temporarily thawed him. He eagerly awaited the third. No one stirred up above though, save for the men about the running of the ship. Everything aboard was to appear as normal, so the bells were sounded and the watch went about their usual tasks. Earlier from the vessel's depths a fiddle had been heard, a shanty sung, followed by the thumping of feet in a hornpipe. Lately, the ship had returned to its customary night running. The French sentries on the shore would have nothing to note but normality.

Unless they have the ability to see through wood, Jack thought, peering around. For then they would perceive that the activities on the *Sutherland* this night were far from normal. Lined up along its larboard side, out of sight from the shore, four flat-bottomed barges wallowed, bow to stern, with another line of four beside them attached by ropes. Each one held fifty men.

Jack, in the stern of the first boat, gazed down an avenue of oars that rested across the gunwales, sailors occupying the rowlocks the length of the vessel. Beside them, on the benches and squatted down on the planking of the deck, were the thirty-five soldiers each barge could carry. Around him in the little space of the stern sat the officers of the company, MacDonald to his left, Captain Delaune to his right and, opposite the seaman at his tiller, the commander of the three light infantry companies to go in first – William Howe. When Jack was introduced, the man had grunted and promptly forgotten his name, referring to him by various names beginning with 'A' ever since. MacDonald, in an aside, had told Jack that the man was 'as pompous an arse as England ever raised and not a patch on his unchancy, dear, dead brother. But he's brave for all tha'.'

When they'd boarded, the last of the light had been in the sky so they did not fumble in the darkness and alert the listening piquets on Cap Rouge. Although they did not know exactly where they were to land, they were aware they awaited the turning of the tide to carry them downstream to the City of Quebec. It would come after the one bell sounded. Now the brass note came . . . and there was a perceptible shifting down the ranks. No common soldier talked, that was a privilege reserved for officers. But the men ahead rolled stiff shoulders and necks, shuffled their feet, released their white-knuckled grip upon their muskets only to grip again. Looking at them, Jack was struck again by the youth of all in the boats that were to land first, all volunteers. When he had observed this to Captain MacDonald, the Scot had removed his pipe only long enough to mutter, 'Children will obey blindly and dare where experience dares not.' Jack had heard it whispered that this advance guard of young light infantry was called Delaune's Forlorn Hope. It had not decreased his shivering when he'd heard that whisper. He was among the youngest.

The boats creaked against their bindings. On the next barge, the one flush to the side of the *Sutherland*, the naval officer gave the order for rolled blankets to be lashed to the sides to cushion the collision. Drawn by the quiet command, Jack suddenly noticed the man to the officer's left, whom he must have glanced at a hundred times since he boarded. He suddenly recognized him to be General Wolfe. He was almost inconspicuous due to the unadorned uniform he was wearing and Jack remembered why. MacDonald had not only improved Jack's French in the two days he'd accompanied the Scot, he'd laughed at Jack's elaborate clothing and helped him strip all fanciness from it. 'The Canadian Militia have sharp-shooting men who'll delight in plugging anyone in the lace. Why d'ye think our leaders wear none?' he'd said.

Jack was rather startled to find that the general was looking back at him and since the inner boats were facing down-stream, and his own boat up, they were not very far apart. Jack nodded, tried to smile and was further disconcerted to see the general rise, and clamber between the ranks over to their boat. Hands reached up, as the barges gave another lurch, and Wolfe came over. Room was made for him beside Colonel Howe.

'Can you feel her shift, Billy?' Wolfe said to him.

'I can indeed, sir. And about time too.' Howe replied with a degree of petulance that showed what he thought of mere tides delaying him. He looked at the officer on the tiller. 'How long, um, fellow?'

The man sniffed. 'Be fully turned in 'alf an 'our, more'n less.'

Despite the prohibition of talk, the word travelled in whispers up and down the barge and to all those beside and behind. It was as if the night was suddenly full of starlings until a sergeant's harsh curse silenced them.

'Excellent,' said Wolfe, rubbing his hands. 'And a fine night for it, is it not, Captain Chads?'

'If hell's darkness is fine to steer by, aye,' the seaman grunted then relented when he saw Wolfe's face drop. 'I'll get you ashore, sir, ne'er be feart. Don't know why the Frogs make such a fuss about the shoals 'ereabouts. Swear there be nigh to a thousand places on the Thames more perilous.'

Soft laughter came and with it another burst of coughing from Wolfe. He'd managed to hold it in as he sat quietly in his boat but this would not be contained and the handkerchief was lifted too late to catch all of it, blood darkening on the scarlet coat, snatching the humour away in an instant. Wolfe, busy with bleeding, looked up finally to the concerned faces before him.

'Pardon me, gentlemen,' he whispered and coughed again, the only human sound suddenly as the barges creaked on the rising waters, their sides banging through the muffling of blankets against the warship. From somewhere close to the shore, a bird suddenly called, a sharp cry, almost a shriek, with a dying fall as if its life was being sucked from it. Several of the men before Jack crossed themselves, a movement Wolfe noticed. He leaned forward.

'Come, lads, does anyone here know any poetry? Hmm? I heard a snatch a month ago from our trusty Sergeant Botwood of the Forty-seventh. Does anyone know it?'

Captain Delaune spoke. 'I remember only the title, sir. Tis called "Hot Stuff".'

'Well, zounds, let's send for Ned Botwood himself. The Forty-seventh are three boats back if I remember me own

Morning State.' He had half stood, was staring back along the barges.

'Sir,' said Delaune quietly, 'the good sergeant was killed at Montmorency.'

'Ah. Ah yes.' Wolfe sat down heavily again, such colour as had briefly come there now gone from his cheeks. No man would meet another's eyes, none spoke and there was only the sound again of the water lapping and that bird giving another solitary cry. Jack too looked down. He had not shared in the months of hard campaigning but MacDonald and others had acquainted him with many of their grim details. The landing at Montmorency was the worst of several costly failures to get the British Army ashore so they could seize the capital of New France, Quebec. With each setback, with more weeks spent in makeshift camps where the bloody flux weakened or killed every third man and officer, with Wolfe prostrate in his tent spitting red and Montcalm seemingly invulnerable atop his fortified cliffs, the army's belief in itself and its powers had steadily eroded. And the death of stalwarts like the poetic Botwood in futile operations only increased the despair. Despair plain on the faces of the men looking down around Jack now.

'I know a poem, sir,' he suddenly said.

'Do you, lad?' Wolfe's pale face raised to him, a weak smile came. 'Not Virgil, is it? Can't bear the damned Romans myself.'

'No, sir.' Jack had thought of pulling out the copy of *Hamlet* his mother had given him, the volume carried next to his heart for luck. But nothing in that doom-laden play seemed appropriate – and there was hardly light to read by. 'No, it's Thomas Gray. His "Elegy Written in a Country Churchyard".'

'By God! I have a copy in my tent. It is the finest, the most majestic . . .' Colour had come again to the pallid cheeks. 'Recite it for us, lad. But softly, eh?'

Jack took a breath, cleared his throat, began.

The curfew tolls the knell of parting day,
  The lowing herd winds slowly o'er the lea,
The plowman homeward plods his weary way,
  And leaves the world to darkness and to me.

He could feel the men on his boat, on the surrounding ones, draw in again; yet instead of being daunted by their attention, by this silent audience on this moonless night, Jack felt emboldened. The chill slipped from him, his voice grew stronger, as he used the poet's words to conjure that simple graveyard at dusk, the simple graves that filled it, their unadorned headstones marking unacclaimed men who, for all their anonymity, were yet of the same earth as the men who listened so intently now, that earth of England. Who had strived for that land, as the men who listened would strive that day, the verses binding those in their plain brown coats to these brothers and sons in russet-red who had left those fields to toil for their country in a different way, with different tools, with musket and bayonet not scythe and mattock, with cannon not with plough.

Jack felt it, almost as he thought it, coming not as a subtle caress but a jolt, a surge under the boats that lifted them, banging them once more against the *Sutherland*'s oaken sides. The tide had turned, Wolfe and his officers, indeed all who'd waited so long, shifted, and though he was not near the end of the elegy, he gave them the next verse as if it were the last.

The boast of heraldry, the pomp of power,
  And all that beauty, all that wealth e'er gave,
Awaits alike th' inevitable hour.
  The paths of glory lead but to the grave.

'Yes!' cried Wolfe, 'But note how glory comes *before* the grave! And if she does, I'll lay me in the earth with a thanks. Is that the tide at last, Mr Chads?'

'It is, sir, aye.'

'Then put us upon't, if you please.' As commands were passed quietly along the line of barges, as ropes were cast off from the *Sutherland* – on whose mainsail two lamps were hoisted, a signal to the rest of the armada – Wolfe rose to move back to his own boat. Passing Jack, he squeezed his shoulder. 'By God, young Absolute,' he said, 'I would rather have been the author of that piece than beat the French tomorrow. Well,' he smiled, 'perhaps not quite!'

And he was gone. Beside Jack, MacDonald had reached up to wipe his eyes and even in the dull light, Jack could see moisture on his fingers. Caught, the Scot gave a smile. 'T'was a fine verse, laddie, and finely spoken. I think yon poet must truly be a Highlander. It's rare to find such passionate phraseology south of Inverness.'

The barges swiftly disengaged from the *Sutherland* and each other and the eight were soon scattered by the effects of the tide and the force of the St Lawrence, much swollen with early autumn rains. Perhaps their barge benefited from the superior skills of Captain Chads for they were soon ahead of any other vessel and steering for the opposite, northern shore. Jack had leaned right forward in an effort to pierce the darkness; a hand pulled him back.

'Calmness, young Absolute, dinna ye fash. We've a muckle less than two hours to go and since we're clear of the Cap, the next French outpost won't be for a few miles. Ye can sit and bide.'

The lee of the northern shore was gained, the boat settled in a stream about a hundred yards offshore and was borne along by the swollen river's force, the sailors only using their oars at a rare command from Captain Chads, when his tiller alone could not harness the surge. The land loomed to their left, a dark mass rising to the star-lit sky. Twice they saw lights, lanterns waved from a French piquet placed atop the cliffs. But no shore patrol challenged them and on their boat, no one spoke. Silently, they swept downriver.

Time was hard to gauge without sight and little sound but

Jack felt it was over an hour into their journey that the first noises came from ahead of them.

'Thunder?' whispered Jack, looking up into the now cloudless sky.

'Our lads before the Île d'Orléans,' said Delaune. 'Keeping Montcalm busy. He's convinced we will only attempt to land on the Beauport shore downstream, beyond Quebec. That's where he sits with most of his army. Let's hope this show continues to deceive him.'

The sound brought others almost immediately. Suddenly, a lantern's gate was opened. Though its glow could not reach them, it still seemed like the sun in that thick darkness. A voice called, monstrously loud in the silence of running water, '*Qui est là?*'

MacDonald leaned across Jack, muttering, 'Let the play commence.' Then he called out '*La France!*'

'*Quel régiment?*' came the challenge.

'*De la Marine.*'

A silence followed and Jack was sure he was not the only one who failed to breathe. Then something flared – the lantern had been opened and a taper inserted. They were close enough to see, in the brief illumination, a bearded face with a pipe, a tasselled woollen cap. The sentinel drew flame into the bowl, waved, closed the lantern. Light disappeared.

'Well spoken, sir,' Jack sighed out.

'It wasn't just the accent,' replied MacDonald. 'We had intelligence that the Frenchies were planning on running some supplies down to the city tonight with this tide. They'd cancelled the plan – but seems yon laddie ne'er got that countermand. Lucky for us.'

Captain Chads, the tiller thrust hard away from him to counter the surge, signalled angrily for silence with his other hand. 'Fuck!' he whispered distinctly, peering hard at the shoreline.

'What is it, fellow?' said Colonel Howe, too loudly for anyone's comfort.

'I think . . . I think we've been carried past the Anse du Foulon, dammit.'

'What?' That brought the colonel off his bench. 'Then put us in, man.'

'I am not sure . . .'

'Put us in! That is an order. We must make land.'

The oars were needed now to counter the boat's fast progress. Between Chads and his oarsmen, the barge was soon in water shallow enough for the infantry at the bow to leap in. The tide came to their waists but they soon dragged the barge to ground upon the sloping beach.

Jack, like all the men there, slung his musket behind him and clambered out, keeping close to the other officers as they marched up to the tree line at the base of the cliffs, the company of soldiers forming into ranks. On the shore behind, three more boats grounded, drawn in by lanterns flashed over the water. Chads had come ashore with them and Howe quickly pulled him to one side.

'Well, man?' he barked.

Chads was as dour on land as upon the water. He took his time, gazing up at the tree-shrouded heights before him. 'Aye, we've overshot. Not by much, mind.'

'By not-how-much,' Delaune asked, through a tight jaw.

'I think the path's arse is about two hundred yards that way.' Chads pointed upriver, the way they'd come.

'Then we'll need to get there double-quick, to guide the general and the main force ashore,' said Delaune. 'And if the arse . . . the path . . . up the cliffs is indeed there, that's where we must be, too.'

He looked as if he would be away on the instant, took a step along the strand. But Howe was staring upwards and did not follow.

'Colonel . . .' Delaune stepped back to him with some urgency.

'You go,' said Howe, still looking up. 'Take your Forlorn Hope and assay the path. But I'll wager we can get up there faster by this route,' he gestured up the cliffs with his chin, 'and take any Froggies at the road-head in the rear.'

Delaune looked as if he would protest but Howe had already turned to MacDonald. 'You will accompany me, sir. See if you can't cozen the sentinels up there as you did the one before.' With that he brushed past Delaune, who had no choice but to assemble his company of twenty-five and set off at a run. Howe was back with his sergeants, marshalling his men.

'And you'll bide with me,' MacDonald said to Jack. 'How's your French?'

'Can't remember a bloody word,' said Jack, grinning. In fact, from the moment his feet were again on land, a smile had been on his face. He waved at the darkness above them. 'Can we get up them?'

'Lad, you've obviously never visited Glencoe.'

Howe returned at the head of his men. Like everyone else, he had slung his musket, pulled tight its strap to secure it to his back. 'Forward,' he said, 'for England.'

The moment he put boot upon it, Jack realized the slope was not vertical but angled as acutely as a church spire. As a boy he had climbed many a Cornish cliff, seeking gull's eggs. Those cliffs had been slick with seawater and droppings but they were made of granite, had ledges and outcrops, thus toeholds and fingergrips. This was shale, misshaped pieces of grey-black slate, some the size of supper plates, many like arrowheads. A boot placed full upon them slipped and hands that grasped to steady found only jagged edges that cut but gave no purchase. He quickly learned the angle required to lean against the flow and to kick his instep in, wedge it there while he sought some handhold above. Trees somehow grew on the shale while the carpeting of old leaves was a slick hazard – the tree roots ran close to the surface, and Jack used them to pull himself up. The trunks of the striped maples and ash gave a moment's rest; their fallen boughs were ladders to be swiftly scaled, though these came with a danger too if the deadfall was old and crumbled when grabbed. Beside him, a corporal relied

on one too much and fell away, slipping ten foot and mouthing curses – for the order of silence was upon them, as
binding as any monastic vow. Jack still thought the noise they
were making was like hunted deer crashing through a copse.
But he could not think of who might await them at the top,
only of the next handhold, the next heave upwards.

Despite the encumbrance of a musket that would slip
around halfway through a long reach, the bayonet that would
wedge into a fallen branch, the jagged edges of shale that cut
his fingers, the near-complete darkness under the tree canopy,
Jack felt an exhilaration in the climb, as if his limbs, long
confined aboard a ship, were finally free. Consequently, in less
than five minutes, he was among the first to haul himself up to
the cliff's very edge.

Not over it though. In his enthusiasm he might have done
so had not a hand hauled him back, and a voice whispered one
word, 'Wheesht!' So Jack lay beside Donald MacDonald and
waited, trying to listen beyond the noise of men who had not
yet reached the summit. Howe joined them and a whisper for
all to halt was passed back. Ninety men crouched beneath the
lip and held their breath.

They waited a minute, two. Sounds came – the slipping and
settling of stones behind them; a disturbed bird letting out a
cry that sounded as if it were mocking them for their efforts at
silence. Faintly, a human noise reached them. Someone was
singing somewhere along the cliffs, upriver, back where the
head of the beach path had to be. Since MacDonald and Howe
raised their heads to peer, Jack did too and saw, with them, the
faint glow of firelight through the shrubs and trees that
screened the cliff edge and the mist that was held, like the
finest spun web, between them.

'Sergeant,' Howe whispered down the slope, 'form the men
in one body. MacDonald?'

'Come then,' the Scotsman whispered. As each man clambered over the edge and reached for a weapon, MacDonald
drew his sword, the heavy Highland claymore with its basket

hilt. Jack imitated Howe, unslung his musket and on the third attempt, managed to fix his bayonet. No one had powder and shot in their guns; the order of silence extended up here, even unto death.

The mist had thickened in the time it took them to assemble and it was warmer within it. Jack was certain he was not the only one who sweated inside his redcoat. But a compensating rain fell, a little shower that passed quickly over them as, on a hand signal from Howe, they moved towards that faint glow. As it passed, they heard the sound of boots and a jolly tune, tunefully whistled. A man was coming toward them, invisible in the mist. They halted and MacDonald called out, coarsening his accent in the way he'd tried to teach Jack, '*Eah, qui est là?*'

The whistle and the boots halted, the sound of a musket being unslung coming clearly. '*Eh, merde! Qui êtes-vous?*'

MacDonald signalled them all to halt while he stepped forward. His figure was sucked away but his voice carried, magnified by the mist that allowed only the sense of hearing to function. Jack heard him tell the sentinel that he was at the head of a large command, come to relieve the Militia of their duty. And that the lucky man should call to his comrades along the cliff and bring them together – for Montcalm had sent a barrel of brandy as a reward for their vigilance against the bastard English this night. From the delight in the Canadian's reply, and his subsequent calling to his fellows, MacDonald's ruse worked. The darkness and mist must have hidden him, Jack thought, for there was no exclamation against a kilted Highlander. Instead, the voices moved away from them, and Howe and his men followed.

It took a minute, less, to reach the firelight and only a second for the Frenchmen there to recognize them. It was a second too late. MacDonald had his blade at his guide's throat and the circle of a dozen men who rose startled by their fire were unable to do more than exclaim before bayonets were levelled at their chests and they were thrust back down upon the ground, sacking in their mouths, hands tied roughly at their backs. Soldiers scattered back into the mist and sounds came from it. A cry of surprise, then of pain. A wail, instantly cut off. Wood striking bone.

Jack had rushed to the fire with the rest but once there became a spectator, watching the more experienced soldiers about their task. The sentinels were down and hog-tied before he'd drawn ten breaths. Now, in the returning silence of the night and the sudden intense heat of the flames, Howe came up to him.

'So, uh, Abbotsford, rumour is you are fast. See how quickly you can make it down to the beach and inform Captain Delaune that the path is under our control. And if the general is already there, my compliments to him. Tell him he may bring his army onto the Plains of Abraham.'

Jack hesitated.

'Go on, man,' Howe called.

Fumbling his bayonet off and into his belt, slinging his musket, he took a step, another. MacDonald joined him on the third. 'Wheesht, lad, and be wary. There's men we have nae t'aen. This is nae the jing bang.' With that he laid a hand upon his back, part pat, part shove. Jack followed the trajectory and was soon sliding. The path was steep and shale was again the base of it. It was no more than six foot across at its widest.

Jack had built up some speed, his musket once again jangling against his back, when he was brought up short, striking his knee hard against a tree trunk. The maple had been felled with its boughs facing outwards, down the slope. The path might lead to the Plains before the walls of Quebec but Wolfe would have to clear it if he wanted to bring up his guns.

As Jack was groping in the darkness for the best place to slide over, a sound stopped him. It came from below, from the direction of the beach. Not the reassuring march of several infantrymen. A single man coming, coming fast, scrambling and slipping on the shale, cursing as he came, using words Jack did not know, though the language itself was plain.

French.

Jack's jaw fell open, his hands gripped the trunk before him. Breath wouldn't come until he forced it to and then seemed to arrive in a huge and too loud gasp. But if he heard it, it did not deter the Frenchman in his climb; on he came, noisily cursing.

Jack forced himself away from the trunk, crouched, put his back against it while his mind jumped. He could hide there; the Frenchman might pass him in the gloom; the English at the slope's summit could deal with him. He had his orders after all, a mission, his first and his duty was to that. Let the enemy pass; MacDonald and the rest would snaffle him up.

And then, as the thought of the Scot and his other comrades up there, taken in the rear by even this one man, this man who would perhaps slip past them and run across the Plains to the walls of Quebec, rouse its garrison against this surprise assault . . . Jack knew he could not let him pass. So as the Frenchman reached the other side of the trunk, as he said, distinctly, '*Merde*', Jack drew the bayonet.

A leg came over, another, a body. The man sat for a moment on the trunk then shoved himself off. He landed a yard from where Jack crouched, took a pace forward.

Jack rose up, his musket butt striking the maple as he stood. The man turned sharply at the sound, staggered back. He looked at Jack's face and from it down to the bayonet in Jack's hand. At his shoulder was the hilt of a sword. His hand reached up to grasp its grip and the sound it made as it cleared its sheath was the loudest sound Jack had heard all night.

He pushed off against the trunk, his left arm raised high before him. The Frenchman's sword arm had gone back further, was about to bring it down in a killing stroke but Jack's arm reached the man's wrist before the force and the weight of the weapon was unstoppable. At the same time he thrust up with the bayonet. The man saw it come, deflected the weapon. It slipped past his right side and then the Frenchman grabbed Jack's wrist, wrenched it back, up. Both men now held the other's weaponed hand.

His opponent was big, as tall as Jack but wider and higher up the slope. He felt the weight disparity immediately, some wrassling instinct, so he let his body fall back and simultaneously jerked down with the hand that gripped the sword arm. The man fell towards him and Jack twisted away as he did, his own side jarring against the trunk; but the Frenchman hit it harder, just below his armpit. He gasped, tried to jerk his sword arm clear but Jack also felt a slight slackening on his own wrist. Wrenching back, he left the cuff of his coat in the man's clawing fingers. The bayonet butt banged against a branch, he nearly lost it but, grasping desperately, Jack now twisted his body, putting its force behind the upward thrust. The man's fingers could not deflect the blade.

Jack had not aimed anywhere but up. He could not see, could only feel as the point skittered along bone, opening cloth and flesh until somehow, somewhere it seemed to find a gap. The man screamed then, a terrible, high-pitched sound as the steel slid in.

Everything that had been tight was suddenly slack. The sword dropped from the fingers, Jack's twist and thrust and the man's falling taking them around so the Frenchman's back was now against the trunk. His hands, unencumbered now, reached to Jack's weapon, fingers grasping at the blade, trying to remove it. Blood ran between the fingers but Jack held it still, desperately, weight and slope bearing the weapon down. It took only a moment for something to falter in the man's eyes, some desire to fade. Jack knew because he was looking into them, so close the two of them could have been lovers. And suddenly those eyes rolled back and, with a shuddering exhalation, the man slumped back. As he did, Jack moved the opposite way, leaving the bayonet, his arms stretching out wide as if to deny their latest activities. Abandoned, the body crumpled, folding into shale.

Ecstasy! He didn't think he'd ever been happier! He was alive as he had never been before, felt as though he would explode with the joy of it. He wanted to throw back his head, laugh and laugh. He tried but could not get the air, the little that came allowing out a giggle which accompanied him as he sank down. Then, as breath started coming in whoops, joy slipped away. He was staring at a body, at a youth not much older than himself, wiping blood from his hands onto his black breeches, onto his red coat.

He didn't know how long he had knelt there when the sound of feet coming up the slope disturbed him. He knew he should reach again for his bayonet, should try to kill this next Frenchman who came over the trunk and the one after that. But he couldn't move, welded there by tears and another man's blood.

'Egad! Is that you, Absolute?'

Captain Delaune was perched with one leg either side of the tree trunk, caught where he'd first glimpsed Jack. He came fully over now, paused as he saw the body, then knelt. 'Are you hurt, lad?'

Jack shook his head, tried to make a word, couldn't.

'Your first?'

Jack nodded. Delaune put his hands under Jack's arms, helped him rise, held him while he steadied. 'They'll tell you it gets easier,' Delaune said quietly. 'In my experience, that is a lie.' More men were coming up the slope, halted now at the trunk, at the sight of the body. 'Do we hold the path?'

Jack nodded, at last found some moisture for his voice. 'Colonel Howe sent me to inform you so, sir. Says the general is at liberty to bring up his army.'

Delaune looked up the slope. Almost as he did, a cannon suddenly roared somewhere above them, its voice shocking in the silence. 'That will be the Samos battery above the cliffs here. They've wind of us now. I'm sure Colonel Howe could use some reinforcements for he'll have to take out those guns.' He looked at Jack again. 'Are you able to continue to the general with the news?'

'Yes, sir,' Jack shook his head hard. 'Yes, I believe I can.'

'Good.' Delaune slapped him on the back, picked up Jack's

tricorn from where it had fallen. As he handed it over, a corporal came up. In his hand was Jack's bayonet.

'Sir?' the corporal said.

Delaune took the weapon, wiped it on his sleeve, reversed it. 'You might need this.'

Jack hesitated only for a moment then took the blade, sheathing it immediately. 'I pray to God I do not.'

'Amen,' said Delaune, 'and *bonne chance.*' Turning back to his men he cried, 'Forward.'

Jack let the last of the Forlorn Hope file past him, each young recruit staring at the body as they went, then at him. When the last of them had passed, he looked at it himself. '*Bonne chance,*' he murmured then climbed the trunk. The darkness had yielded a little in the time it had taken for his blooding and he was able to move more swiftly.

The Plains of Abraham

13 September 1759

The last of the rain passed from the cliffs and ran, at an almost perfect right angle, over the long line of Redcoats. From where Jack stood on the army's right flank, on one of the few slight elevations that the flat plain afforded, he could now see across the thousand-yard frontage of the British ranks to the other slight rise opposite; could even, with his keen sight, note the muskets slung across the red backs of the soldiers there.

'I cannot tell. Has Townshend refused his battalions?'

General Wolfe had tapped the shoulder of his ADC and Captain Gwillim snapped his telescope up, scanned. 'Yes, sir. The Sixtieth is now formed along the Sainte Foy road.'

'Good.' Wolfe now glanced behind him. 'And our men here have similarly deployed.'

Jack followed the general's eyeline. Wolfe had ordered the Thirty-fifth to also refuse in a line roughly paralleling the cliffs. So the army was now drawn up like a square-sided 'U', with very short side arms. That this was necessary became immediately apparent for the cessation of the rain had brought a resumption of something other than clear sight – lead ball from the tree line along the cliffs. All ducked, as the first firing was directed towards their rise. All except Wolfe.

'Time, Gwillim?'

'It is approaching half past nine, sir.'

'Good. Good. Your glass, if you please. Absolute, a moment.'

Jack, who had been considering moving further away down the slope, now stepped up it. As he did, a sergeant he'd been standing beside cried out, fell backwards, clutching at his neck; blood pumped between his fingers.

'Tell the men to lie down, Gwillim.' Orders were bellowed, echoed down the long ranks. The British army, with some alacrity, lay down. 'All except you, lad.' Wolfe caught Jack in a half-crouch. 'I need your shoulder.'

Jack, uncomfortably aware that he was now one of the more prominent features of the bare battlefield, stood before his general, who laid his 'scope on his shoulder. Wolfe could no longer level one himself. He had been shot in the wrist earlier in the morning and a white bandage around it now paralleled the black one worn on his upper arm in memory of his recently dead father.

Jack tried not to flinch as bullets zinged by him, and failed. Wolfe, however, was completely steady. He had motioned Jack to face toward the east, towards the hills he'd heard called the Buttes à Neveu. Not far beyond them, yet out of sight, he knew stood the city of Quebec. On top of the hills was the French army, their white uniforms making the battalions appear like cumuli, massing. They were no more than half a mile away.

'Yes,' muttered Wolfe, 'I thought as much. Montcalm's placed his most experienced regiments, Bearn and Guyenne, in the centre. Forming into columns and . . . By God, that's himself! Do you see him, lads? He's mounted on a black horse, the swanky bugger. All right for some!' He sighed. 'Sit, shall we?'

With relief, Jack helped the general lower himself down then sat himself, scrunching his neck into his shoulders. He would have lain on his stomach but since none of the other staff officers who gathered around did, he could not.

'Do you think he will attack, sir?' Gwillim asked.

'I think he must and soon. We're astride his supply line

from the south and he'll think we're digging in, while every hour allows us to bring more men up from the ships. More guns too!' He inclined his head to the sound of an explosion. 'Williamson's six-pounders are nipping at him already. Ample compensation for these gnat bites from their Militia and their wild pets, eh?'

Jack looked again to the cliff-top scrub, to the ghastly shapes that moved within it – the enemy's Native allies, naked, painted beasts the lot of 'em! Their extended wail of a war cry caused the knees to weaken far more than the bullets they sent. It seemed to come not from the Damned but from their horned tormentors, unspeakable cruelties vouchsafed for anyone who fell into their hands. Jack winced as he remembered the call he and his Mohocks had unleashed in Covent Garden taverns. A schoolboy's pathetic whine! How had he ever thought he'd even come close to this chilling savagery?

Wolfe acknowledged the cries and the continuing snap of bullets overhead with little more than a shrug. 'And *le Général* knows that if he doesn't attack we'll swallow his reinforcements coming from Sainte Foy like oysters.' He smiled. 'No, gentlemen, he'll come, fast and in column. He personally forms his best troops around him there in the centre. So it's in the centre we'll break him.' He used Jack's shoulder and rose. 'Come, let's to it. Burton, you're in charge here. Keep your head down.'

Wolfe moved away fast, Jack, Captains Gwilliam and Delaune struggling to match his pace. Since he'd first appeared on the cliff top, and leaving aside the inconvenience of taking a ball in the wrist, Wolfe no longer seemed a sickly man. His long pigtail slapped and bounced on his back as he strode. In his good hand he clutched nothing more offensive than a black cane.

The standards of the 47th and 43rd Foot were planted at the very centre of the British line and it was by them that he halted. The battalion commanders rose from the ground as he approached, saluted, Monckton, the Old Westminster, among them. The soldiers, though remaining prone, gave him three huzzahs.

'All fair, George?' Wolfe addressed his brigadier.

'Seems so, sir,' Monckton replied.

As Wolfe and his officers conferred, Jack looked along the lines. The regiments, though recumbent, were dressed roughly in two ranks. There were gaps of about forty paces between each body of men and the next battalion up was the 78th, Fraser's Highlanders. Jack looked for and soon spotted Donald MacDonald. Not for him a seat upon the grass; he was striding about his men, his pipe clamped firmly in his teeth, waving and encouraging. Then his attention was caught by the conference taking place and, a moment later, by Jack. He marched over.

'How fare you, lad?'

'Tolerably.'

The Scot looked down. 'Ye might have cleaned yon bayonet.'

Jack looked too, shuddered. MacDonald stretched out a hand, rested it on Jack's shoulder. 'Delaune told me. It's a muckle powerful thing to take your first life and you chose the most direct method.'

'I had no choice,' Jack muttered, looking away. 'If I had—'

'If you had, you'd make the same one again. And again. It gets easier, trust me.' He indicated Jack's musket. 'It's easier with that. You don't fire at one man but at a pack of 'em.'

'Well,' said Jack, licking at his dry lips, 'it seems I shall soon find out.'

'Soon enough, aye.' MacDonald smiled. 'So long as Wolfe does nae intend to keep you as his pampered pet on the staff.'

It seemed Wolfe had other ideas. As they looked to the conference, Gwillim signalled him back and the Scot accompanied him over. 'Absolute, I am going to make use of your vaunted speed again. You will remain here in the centre and General Monckton here will send you with need or news.'

'Can I nae have him, sir? He can stand with me on the Seventy-eighth's right, with the Grenadiers. He's only a few yards from the brigadier's commands. And I can keep him safe.'

'Trusting a Highlander for one's safety is like trusting a whore with one's purse. But let it be so.' His men laughed and Wolfe smiled at the outrage on the Scotsman's face. 'You'll find me, lad?'

'I will, sir.' Jack smiled back. 'You may depend on me.'

'Depend on an Absolute? Mad Jamie's boy? Absolutely!' Wolfe raised his cane and touched the side of his hat. 'Gentlemen. To battle.'

He turned, striding back towards the little rise of ground that gave him the only slight overview of the field. They all watched him for a moment till MacDonald spoke. 'I never thought I'd say this, mark! For, dod, yon callant was cruel to many of my poor countrymen in the aftermath of Culloden. But he is a fine man and a good soldier and, if fortune favours, he will win much glory this day.' He turned to Jack. 'And speaking of Highlanders, let me introduce you to a gaggle.'

Introductions were brief, Jack hearing the names of but a few men, forgetting them instantly, distracted by the pace of the French drumming that seemed to increase even as he took his place. Then, a huge roar came from the white ranks opposite them, in three distinct shouts.

'*Vive le Général! Vive le Roi! Vive la Paix!*'

And on their country the white army surged forward.

'Rise the Seventy-eighth, rise!' Up and down the field, as their regimental commander called out their name, each regiment rose and dressed into their two lines.

'D'ye ken the use of your musket, man?'

Jack nodded.

'Then we're short a subaltern in the platoon here, with Archie MacDougal's guts despoiling the floor of his tent. So step in there and I'll step in beside ye. Every bullet will count today and my sword will have to bide.' He patted the basket hilt of his claymore then guided Jack to the end of the second rank.

Jack stared forward. A white wave was rolling toward them, eating the ground as if it were the sand of a Cornish beach before the tide, as steadily filling each wrinkle with its flood. Though it had seemed all one mass when it began to move, as it neared he could see the demarcations, the different facings of each regiment, the blue of the men of Rousillon, the red waistcoats of Guyenne. They marched in three main columns and between them were scattered men in a *mélange* of cloth and colour, the Militia of New France. The columns opposite the English right and left flanks seemed already a little blurred to Jack's sight, as if the ranks were melding as they came; not so the one straight ahead, made up of the regiments that Wolfe had proclaimed the pick of Montcalm's men. These marched as tight as on any parade ground, a white arrow aimed at the heart of the red-clad British who stood, their muskets shouldered, muzzles and bayonets pointed harmlessly toward the sky.

'Are you double-loaded, lad?' MacDonald's voice was low-pitched beside him, yet still startled him back to himself.

'Yes, sir,' replied Jack.

Wolfe's command had been to load with two balls and the powder to send them. It diminished the range of each bullet – and that told every man there what their commander intended: to wait . . . and wait . . . and wait . . .

The French drummers were increasing their beat and the regiments were responding in speed, their wings fraying further, their centre tightening. The soldier ahead of him in the first rank was praying, or cursing, it was hard to tell which for the language was certainly Gaelic. Jack swallowed, tried to work some moisture into his throat, tried to recall words himself, something to comfort him from the endless prayers he'd sat through at school and recited by rote. He cursed himself that he had not paid a greater attention to matters spiritual. Yet nothing came, in Latin, Greek, Hebrew or

English until . . . yes, there was something, some words, a pattern. He began to mumble them under his breath.

Of all the girls in town,
The Black, the Fair, the Red and Brown,
That chance and prance it up and down
There's none like Nancy Dawson.

He must have spoken them, even sung them, for the Highlander before him left off his prayer-curses to turn and glare. The look only added to a feeling that had been building in Jack for some while – he started to giggle. It was all so fucking absurd! Three months ago he'd been singing that song in the taverns of Covent Garden. And here he was, standing with a musket in his hands and a whore's name on his lips while four thousand Frenchmen ran at him with the plain intention of stabbing him dead.

And then they stopped. All the drums struck one loud exclamation and, a little over a hundred paces away, the whole white mass halted. For a moment Jack thought – and it only added to his hilarity – that they'd decided the situation was quite as absurd as he thought it and they were going to march off and leave the killing of him for another day. The joy that thought gave him lasted only moments, those it took for the Frenchmen to bring their muskets down from the port, ground the butts into their shoulders and, without seeming to wait for any command, fire.

There was a ragged roar like a drawn-out shout, the air suddenly filled with whistles and shrieks and, almost immediately, a sound like pebbles being thrown at a barn's wall as men around him were struck, on their muskets, on their cartridge cases and buckles . . . and in places that made no sound. The praying Highlander reeled back, dropping into the narrow space between Jack and the next man, one of his eyes a black and reddened hole.

'Seventy-eighth, advance three paces,' a Scots voice bawled.

All around him, the men moved on the command. Jack, unused to the drill, lingered a moment, long enough to see the red ranks clear the fallen, a dozen bodies perhaps, some writhing, some still. Then he too lurched forward and his momentum carried him beyond his assigned place, into the gap in the front rank. Before he could retire, another command came.

'Companies . . . lock!'

Like a door bolt shot into place, the two ranks melded, the space between men closed.

'Present your firelock!'

There was another movement, each man stepping forward on his front leg, leaning over it, raising his musket to parallel the ground. Jack, drilled relentlessly aboard ship by the foulmouthed Yorkshireman, did as all the others. Then he felt a leg behind him, a musket barrel rising beside his face.

'Good lad,' said MacDonald. Jack could feel the Highlander's breath on his cheek. 'Good lad.'

In their movements there had been distraction from what was before them; and the French volley had raised a cloud of smoke that hid the enemy for a moment. Now that smoke was thinning, pushed aside by men emerging like wraiths from the whiteness. The drums had started again, a faster beat, the voices calling again, '*Vive le Roi! Vive la Paix!*'

The French came on.

The voice that had commanded spoke again now, quieter yet still with the force to reach them. Jack could hear the same, single word echoing down the red ranks of the nearest regiments.

'Steady.'

The French came on. Less than ninety yards now. Some of them had reloaded, or held their fire, for bullets still zinged around and three men away from Jack a Redcoat cried out, fell forward, lay silent.

'Steady, lads! Aim low.'

The weight of the musket! Jack had always presented, fired,

215

shouldered, he had never held it out like this, for this amount of time, waiting, waiting. He could not help the shudder that came. He needed no encouragement to aim low; he thought he might discharge into the ground.

On it rolled, the white wave. Seventy yards now. Sixty.

'Come on, come on,' he whispered fiercely, 'Come to Nancy Dawson.'

MacDonald suddenly called out, 'Platoon, oblique right,' and Jack's company shifted and he with it, their left foot fixed, the right moving a half pace back. Now they were pointing their muzzles not dead ahead, where the French ranks were more frayed, but into the column sides of the Bearn regiment to their right.

Down the line on either side, platoon fire commenced, the smaller units of the regiments alternating their fire in well-co-ordinated drill. Still, the British centre held, both breath and bullet.

Fifty. Forty-five.

'Steady. Steady.' A terrible pause. 'Fire!'

With what relief did Jack squeeze the trigger. The pan flashed, he felt the jerk as the weapon recoiled, as the lead left his barrel. He had aimed at a specific man but the flash that seared his vision took away any chance of noting success. All was lost in smoke again, British smoke this time, and when that began to fray and separate into tendrils and wisps that rose and dispersed, it revealed carnage.

The front ranks of the French columns had been torn down, shredded full six men deep. All order was gone, those that still stood were isolated islands of white, three men here, one there. Jack saw an officer, hatless, blood running down his face, his sword-tip on the ground, mouthing commands that would not turn to sound.

It was a calm English voice that pierced the strange silence: 'Prepare to load.'

The sergeants' and subalterns' cries of 'Half-cock your firelock,' just preceded a wail from the French army that sounded as if it came from one voice, from one savaged animal. With it the men in white turned and ran.

'They are broken. By God, they flee!' Brigadier Murray had run up to the colonel of the Seventy-eighth, Fraser. He had lost his hat and his bald head was flushed. 'After them, sir. Rout them!'

The Highlanders needed no second bidding. 'A Fraser!' went the cry down the ranks, muskets were swiftly slung, claymores drawn. Jack, swordless, was nevertheless as excited as the rest and, as his platoon began to surge after the fleeing French, he took a pace forward with them. Only a pace, before a hand grabbed him by the collar, jerked him back.

'Absolute. Absolute!'

Jack wriggled in the grasp, wanting to be away. The French were fleeing and he had to be there to share in their slaughter. He might not have one of the Scots' fearsome swords. But hadn't that Yorkshireman told him that a bayonet had a better reach anyway? Hadn't he already killed a Frog bastard with one today?

But MacDonald's hand would not be dislodged. He jerked Jack round to face him. 'Listen to me. Listen! I was told to mind ye and I will. You've done your duty and had your share of the kill. But you were ordered to bear this news to the general, were you not?' He pulled Jack around till he could see the standards. 'To them, laddie. There lies your duty. Whereas mine . . .' He drew his own claymore and, with a shout of 'A MacDonald!', took off after his men.

'You there. You, Absolute!'

Colonel Hale of the 43rd had called him. Reluctantly, Jack took a step towards him.

'You must to the general. There he is, on his rise. Tell him the French flee everywhere and Murray leads the Seventy-eighth to seize the bridge on the Charles and cut them off. And tell him . . .' Hale stepped away, revealing a body on the ground. It was General Monckton, eyes widened in pain, his waistcoat a bloodied mess, bubbles rising from the oozing red.

'Tell him of this as well.' He slapped Jack's shoulder, startling him from his stare. 'Go on, Absolute. To Wolfe.'

Jack was reluctant on the first step, less so on the subsequent one. Suddenly, the joy of his mission came to him. He would tell Wolfe the news. The French flee. The battle is won. An Absolute would bring colour to that pale face.

Jack ran between the living and the dead, towards a cluster of red on Wolfe's Rise. When he reached it, he tried to pass between two men, but they closed together, stepped forward. Everyone appeared to be looking down at something fascinating at the centre of the circle.

A cry came. 'Room, gentlemen, I implore you. Step back!'

Jack slipped through. Beyond the backs of the crowd of men, there was a little circle of churned earth. In the centre of that lay Wolfe.

He was propped up against the legs of a kneeling grenadier, another of the same regiment standing near. A surgeon's mate was fussing at Wolfe's shirt, trying to part material soaked in blood; but even as Jack stepped through he saw Wolfe lift a hand and wave away the attempt, heard him murmur, 'I tell you, it is all done with me. Let be!'

Jack threw himself down. 'Sir! General! The French run.'

The eyes did not open but the slightest of smiles came. 'I have heard. God be praised, for I die in peace.' With that, his head rolled down, his body sagged, folding around the supporting legs as if all bone had gone out of it.

'But, sir! I bring other news. Monckton is wounded, perhaps dead and . . . and . . .'

The grenadier who'd supported the body now stood, laying Wolfe carefully down as he did. 'He's beyond your words, lad, good or ill. He's gone.'

'But I have a message for him, from Colonel Hale! He needs to know . . . to know . . .'

Another grenadier, an officer, now spoke. 'What's that? Monckton down as well?'

'Yes, sir. Badly wounded at the least.'

'Then that means Townshend's in command, God help us.' He hauled Jack to his feet by his cross belt. 'He'll need to be told. He commands on the left wing. To him, lad, and tell him of this,' he gestured down to Wolfe's body, 'while I carry out my general's last command to rout the enemy before it is countermanded. Drummer,' he bellowed, turning back to his regiment. 'Advance the Louisbourg Grenadiers! Come! Let's course these hares back to France! Halloo!'

The group around the corpse began to separate, dispersing to their duties, to the imperatives of victory. Jack took a step, then another, though he could not yet bring himself to look where he needed to go, still stared at Wolfe's face, calmer than he had ever seen it, less pale too. Colour had come to it in the time before he died though Jack didn't think he could claim the credit for that.

At last he turned, began again to run. Drums and fife were sounding the order for a general pursuit and the soldiers, reined in by discipline, now let out a roar. For near three months they'd got the worst of every encounter with their enemy. Now the foe had shown them their heels, they were all for treading on them fast.

Jack's own flew. The musket banged against his thighs as he ran until he grabbed its stock, his tricorn seemed determined to slide from his head so he let it, letting his free arm now pump, helping to drive him across the Plains of Abraham. Up ahead were the standards of the 15th and 60th Foot, refused along the Sainte Foy road. General Townshend would be under them.

He was. Jack had covered the thousand yards fast and was feeling it when he spotted the new commander of the British forces. He was standing on the cupped hands of two grenadiers, cursing them continuously as he tried to point his wavering telescope toward the chaos of the battlefield.

He came down instantly on hearing of Jack's arrival and listened while Jack tried to give him the news from the field and Wolfe's last commands. But the breathless delivery was not swift enough for him. Once he knew he was in command that was all he needed.

'Pursuit? Scatter my men between here and the city when we do not know what reserves Montcalm has waiting there? This runnin' off could be a ruse to lure us into an ambush.'

The Colonel of the 15th stepped forward. 'With respect, sir, General Wolfe seemed to believe that Montcalm had committed all his forces. He thought to—'

'Wolfe is dead,' Townshend barked loudly. 'Monckton is dying. So we cannot know what either would have thought. We can only know what *I* think! Eh? Eh?' He glared at the officer who dutifully dropped his gaze. 'We know that Bougainville and the rest of the French army will be marching to attack me in the rear from Sainte Foy. With my men scattered we could be caught between them. So call 'em back. Call 'em all back, by God, including Murray and those damned Jacobites of the Seventy-eighth.'

Officers nodded, commanded, men began to run along the road toward the gunfire. 'Who holds our rear?'

His ADC answered. 'Colonel Howe and his light infantry.'

'Not enough. Tell Ralph Burton to take his Forty-eighth to reinforce 'em. And you, Westminster lad.' He turned to Jack who'd been regaining his breath. 'Oh yes, I know you, you puppy. You were with Howe up the cliffs, weren't you?'

'Yes, sir, I—'

Townshend waved impatiently. 'Well, go find him now. Tell him to hold Bougainville till we join him. We're on our way. Go!'

Jack turned and began to run. Again. 'My kingdom for a horse,' he muttered. He'd thought he was there to fight but his superiors only seemed to want to make use of his legs.

At least Billy Howe had other ideas.

'Ah, uh, Abercrombie!' he drawled as Jack ran up to him, having sought him for above half an hour amongst the trees on the edge of the plain. 'What news?'

It was swiftly given, the fleeing French, even the word of Wolfe's death causing only the barest crack in the colonel's imperturbability. The only thing that ruffled him was Townshend's command.

'Hold? With what, pray?' He snorted. 'I've three companies of men scattered through this wood and that,' he cocked an ear toward the forest, 'is Colonel Bougainville approaching.'

Jack listened too, could indeed hear the drumming. The trees muffled the sound but they could not be far off. Clearer than that though, and thus nearer, were the high ululations Jack had heard intermittently throughout the day.

Howe observed him shudder. 'Yes, my man. Take care you don't fall in with those fellows. Your pretty hair will look very fetching at some squaw's lodge post.' He turned. 'Sergeant McBride?'

'Sir?'

'Send word to the Sixtieth to leave the head of the Foulon Road and join us here. We'll let these savages have the edge of the woods but the French regulars will have to come along the road. And that's where we'll take 'em.' He rose, lifting his musket. 'Coming, Archer?'

'That's Absolute, sir,' Jack muttered to the back moving away from him.

As they climbed the slight rise, the sound of the Native cries got fainter while the drum beats became clearer. Gaining the height, the road lay beneath them. 'First company onto the road. Second and Third up here. Open ranks, Sergeant,' Howe called. As the three companies, ninety men or so, spread out along the edge of the bluff and on the road, Jack suddenly tilted his head toward the sound of the drums. There was something else underneath it, a different sound.

'Sir?'

'Hmm?'

'Aren't those . . . hoofbeats?'

'Shouldn't think so. Not a cavalry regiment in Canada, more's the pity.' Then he suddenly looked quizzical. 'No, wait, I think someone did mention that Montcalm had perhaps a few . . .'

From around the wooded bend burst men . . . on horses. Not a few either; at least two hundred in blue coats and bearskin caps and each one brandishing a sabre.

'Present! Fire at will!' Howe shouted but his words were lost in the noise of the charge, of cavalrymen yelling, horses snorting, the English soldiers' ragged discharge and their screams as those on the road were ridden down. The shots from the rise drew the Frenchmen's attention but its puny slopes provided no protection, the horses were at the top in a moment.

Jack had fired, missed he was sure, dropped down and reached for a cartridge; but a horse cleared the ridge above him and he could feel the animal's heat as it passed over him. The rider slashed down at Jack with his sabre, just missing him, then his horse's momentum carried him past. There were easier victims for them there, six men had broken at the sight of the enemy and were seeking to run for the woods, which were too far away. They were hunted down, slashed, impaled, trampled. Then the cavalryman who had just missed Jack turned and began to gallop back towards him.

There was little time to think, enough only to run or to fight, and Jack had had enough of running for the day and had just seen what happened to those who did. Beside him, Billy Howe's Light Infantry now had bayonets fixed, the man himself waving two pistols. Jack remembered reading that cavalry against scattered light infantry usually led to the latter being massacred. But the Yorkshireman aboard ship had assured him that a man with a bayonet on his muzzle could outreach any man with a sword.

Even one on a horse? Jack thought, in the moment before the cavalry swept towards him. The French trooper who'd missed him before drove hard at him now, and Jack leapt to one side to dodge the horse's chest, then to the other as the sword swept down. Spinning round, he stabbed up with the bayonet at the man's leg, missed it, stabbed saddle. Jerking the point out, he was just in time to knock aside a second cut. Metal screeched on metal, the man cursed something unintelligible, jerked the reins, bringing his mount sharply up onto its rear legs. Hooves flailed out, Jack just dodging them. They crashed down and the rider fell slightly forward onto his horse's neck, just a little. Just enough.

'Yah!' yelled Jack, thrusting up, the triangular blade sticking the rider just below his waistcoat. He screamed, raised his sword to cut down at Jack once more, so Jack shoved harder, pushing in the bayonet point with all his force behind it. The scream went into a higher pitch, he jerked the reins and his horse's hoofs scrambled for purchase before powering him away, sucking Jack's musket with them.

Weaponless, he turned, looked along the line of the rise. Just below him, Billy Howe shot a man even as he raised his sword. The weapon fell backwards, stuck, point first, into the soft earth at Jack's feet. In a moment, he had it in his hand. The cavalryman followed his weapon, thumping into the earth, and suddenly, just beneath Jack, there was an empty saddle. All he had to do was fall onto it.

His arse hit the leather, his feet found the stirrups – a little high-set for he was taller than the Frenchman – one hand grabbed the reins. The horse tried to throw him, bucking and spinning. But he had had the mastery of horses since he was five and he soon had this one. To his left, three Frenchmen had surrounded the ensign and he was flailing his spontoon around him in a circle to keep them off. Driving his heels into the horse's flanks, Jack drove it along the ridge-line. He had spent three months in London with the Dragoons training for just such a fight.

'Bastards,' he yelled, drawing their attention, enough for the ensign to thrust the spear up into the chest of one of them. The two others jerked reins around to face Jack but he'd gathered speed, even in that short space and they were not ready for him. He passed between them, his sword whirling above his head; one ducked, one didn't. With a yelp, the survivor put heels to his horse and fled.

In fact, he joined the column of French troops as they hurtled back down the road. They hadn't been beaten – the red dead outnumbered the blue – but something else had clearly spooked them. And then, with gaps opened between them and the surviving light infantry, Jack saw and heard what it was.

'Sixtieth, prepare to fire. Fire!'

A solid red line had advanced. Several more horses and men fell, Billy Howe's command let out a cheer and Jack, waving his captured sabre around his head, carried on with huzzah after huzzah.

Until a nasal drawl intruded. 'Yes, that will do, Aspinall. That will do.'

Jack looked down. Howe was stood before him, distaste on his long thin face.

'That's Absolute, you donkey's arse!' he screamed. 'Jack Absolute! Mad Jamie's boy!' And with that he kicked hard at the horse's flanks and gave the beast its head. It took off after its companions.

He'd missed one pursuit and he was not going to miss another! If he was the only cavalryman King George had in Canada then, by God, he was going to honour his branch of the service! He yelled, 'View halloooo!' and the sound appeared to give the blue coats ahead some extra speed. Jack slapped the sword flat across his horse's rump and it responded, carrying Jack around the wooded bend just behind the nearest Frenchie. One more push and he'd reach forward and just flick him out of his saddle . . .

He rounded the bend. A regiment was drawn up there in open order. White uniforms. Their mounted countrymen streamed down between their files.

'Oops,' cried Jack, reining in so sharply he nearly flew over his horse's neck. Yelling men were running towards him and, whirling his sword over them, he just managed to regain control before they reached him. Kicking again, he drove into the tree line.

The wood was thin at its edge and he swiftly outdistanced the footed pursuit. It thickened more the deeper in he went, forcing him to walk, sometimes to stop to pick a way forward. It was dark, the maples' leaves, just beginning their slide to crimson but plentiful on the branch, blocking out much of the light. Clouds had come too, bringing a scent of rain.

He listened. The silence was deep, unsettling after the battle. In the distance shots came, some shouting; but it was as if he heard it all through a bolster. The horse pranced nervously to the side, jerking its head up and down, and he had to sheathe his sword now, use both hands to control it. He tapped his heels, steered the horse to his left. Towards the east, he hoped. It seemed to be a little fuller of the morning light.

Something called, a chittering cry. A bird or a squirrel, he wasn't sure, but it was loud in that cathedral silence, startling enough for him to reach down and half draw his sword. When the echo of the cry faded he let the blade slide back. There was nothing to do but move on. Ride to the sound of the guns.

The next cry was closer, much closer and though he was sure it was meant to sound again like a bird or an animal it had a human feel to it. Now his sword did come out and it was bending to draw it that saved him for he felt something pass over his back, heard it strike the tree beside him and looked up to see a tomahawk sprouting from a trunk. Wheeling, he sought where it had come from, saw two figures – naked, painted demons from a nightmare – sprinting toward him, each with hair in a single twist bouncing on their necks. They were yelling as they came, yelling something that was close to, yet nothing like the Mohocks' cry.

Yelping, he turned the horse, drove at what looked like thinner growth. It seemed almost like a path and his horse, as panicked as he, picked up speed along it. He felt, rather than saw, something reach for the horse's tail; he slashed back with

225

his sword, heard a shriek of pain, someone falling. He was free, moving faster. He could get away now. He could.

The suddenness of the blow surprised him, hitting him slap over his heart, lifting him from his saddle, his feet clearing the stirrups, throwing him back so fast that he missed the horse's arse entirely and landed flat on his back on the forest floor. That little air that had stayed in his lungs left now, though surprisingly he didn't pass out immediately. His head was partially propped up, on a root perhaps, thus enabling him to examine the war club that was resting on his chest. It seemed stuck to him, which was odd; yet he had no time to work out why, as a man ran at him, raising something on high. It may have been then that the lack of air finally told, because he didn't note a blow. Just darkness.

— FOUR —

Até

The dark that had taken him held him still; had done for three days, more or less; hard to tell as day and night had only been indicated by a slight shift from black to grey and back, seen through a blindfold. Denied sight, his other senses had grown acute; the touch of birch bark to cheek as, with Jack lying face down, the canoe was driven up the river; the sound of water against the bow; later, the scent of the forest where brief halts were made; the wet leaves and muddy earth he was thrown upon; the taste of the gristly, dried meat that was held for him to chew; the brackish water that washed it down. Under all the heightened feelings was the constant one of pain: at his head where he'd been struck and which was roughly washed and rebandaged above his blindfold; at his thumbs which were tightly bound together with a leather cord; up and down his legs and buttocks where he'd received the kicking when he'd tried to escape his blind by rubbing it along the ground of the camp. He'd desisted since, let himself sink into the oblivion thrust upon him. The fear was constant, an undernote to all other sensations, but panic had receded slightly when he'd accepted that there was absolutely nothing he could do.

Until now. This landing had been different. He'd been thrust ahead of his captors up a steep path, made to duck at an entrance of some kind. Warmth sucked him in, almost made him shiver more violently after his days of exposure on the water, for they'd left him only with his shirt and breeches, his redcoat, waistcoat, boots and stockings stripped away. This place also brought a raft of new smells to his sensitized nose, most of them unpleasant: wet dog fur; wood and tobacco smoke; humans who had been too close for too long. And beneath all these, a new-old scent – rum. The structure was awash with it.

The men who'd kidnapped him had barely talked, never to him, rarely to each other. Here, they and others gabbled, alternate voices rising and falling in passion. Both men and women were present and it was one of the latter who became the clearest, for after a long discourse from one of the men she began to wail, a low note at first, rising steadily to a keen of sorrow and pain.

Jack had been dumped on some sort of platform, his legs spilling over it to the earthen floor he could feel under his bare toes. His blindfold had been left on but someone had ripped off the leather cord that had held his thumbs together. Tentatively, he started to move his hands up the sides of his body. When no one shouted, or ran at him flailing, he carefully pushed up an edge of the blindfold.

He was at one end of a long, high-roofed dwelling. He was indeed on a platform that ran along the outer wall and was raised a few feet above the packed earth floor. At intervals down the length of the house were firepits, smoke rising from each of them to holes in the ceiling, though these vented only a portion, such was the haze that hung over everything. Some people sat or lay, singly or in groups, along the platform. Most, though, were gathered before the central and largest fireplace, around a body laid out there. Even through the haze and with sight accustoming itself again to use, Jack could tell that the warrior – he had the single top-knot of hair on his otherwise bald head – was dead. His body seemed frozen while a deep gash of congealed red at his throat proclaimed it as much as the blue tinge of his skin.

The woman who wailed struck herself repeatedly on the chest, pointing down to the corpse. Other women who tried to stop her blows were shrugged off. Another warrior was talking to her, telling some story that involved the dead man before him, violent gestures accompanying words that were almost sung. His volume increased, a bass note counterpointing the keening, as if they were caught in some hideous duet. Then, suddenly and together, they stopped. The woman fell, caught and held up by women to her side. The man had thrown his arm out, his finger pointing. At Jack. And everyone in the hut now turned and looked at him.

The warrior strode forward then, grabbed him, dragged him off the platform. Jack didn't try to resist. The man was twice his size and there were others there equally large and fearsome. There was nothing to do but let himself be dragged along the earth floor, to be thrown down before the fire.

The wailing woman instantly threw off her restrainers and struck him, her fists bunched, her moccasined feet jabbing. Jack rolled into a ball, knees up to stomach, hands over his face. The blows fell for a while, as the mob around her yelled encouragement and landed some hits themselves. When the assault finally stopped, the warrior bent to him, pulled his hands away from his face, began to jabber, waving from the corpse to Jack.

'I don't understand . . .' he said.

The man leaned in, thrust his face – heavily tattooed with blue lines running across it – and spoke even more rapidly, doubling his volume.

'No . . . understand . . . no . . . speak . . .' Jack gestured helplessly to his own mouth.

The man muttered something that could only be a curse then turned and spoke to a youth beside him – one who, Jack had noticed, had slid in a few, especially painful kicks of his own when the woman had attacked. He nodded, left the circle and silence came, Jack still lying there half-curled up, the woman weeping quietly, the warrior glaring. In a moment, the dispatched youth returned, dragging someone with him.

The newcomer was a Native of about Jack's own age, taller, thinner. His hair was even blacker and more unkempt than Jack's. What looked like the remains of a warrior's top-knot was at the crown, standing up from a sea of greasy curls. One eye was discoloured by an old, yellowing bruise. There were crusted scratches down one cheek. Unlike the bare-chested warriors, he wore a shirt of sorts, though how it still clung to the body Jack could not tell, so shredded and torn was it. Through the rents, he could see that the skin was mottled, filthy and reddened.

The fetcher threw the youth down with a vicious twist of the ear. Immediately, the warrior who had confronted Jack began to shout at the newcomer, who gazed forward and showed no real sign that he was hearing. Then, when the latest tirade stopped, the youth, without lifting his head, said, 'You kill this man.'

Already unused to hearing English, Jack wasn't sure if he had heard the words or made them up himself. 'What?' he said, startled.

In the same monotone, the words were repeated, accompanied by the faintest of nods toward the corpse.

'But . . . I didn't . . . I . . .'

The youth now spoke, in the same low-voiced way. The warrior let forth a burst of vowels, reached back behind him . . . and suddenly Jack's sword was being waved in the air above them.

'You kill him, with this. On horse.'

In the vagueness of memory, a little flicker came, of a sword swept backwards, a cry, just before the darkness had taken him. 'Ah,' he said.

The woman, who had been following the words, now leaned into Jack and screamed again. The boy translated. 'She is dead man's mother.'

'I am . . . very sorry.'

'Sorry, not enough. She wants . . . wants . . .'

Jack swallowed. 'Revenge?'

'Payment. You pay.'

Jack was relieved and puzzled at the same time. 'They have stolen all I possessed.' He reached up, touched the skin where Clothilde's half-shilling had rested. He'd known it was missing immediately, had felt its absence like a wound ever since.

His words were translated, producing another burst from the warrior.

'He say: You pay or you slave.'

Jack was sure he'd misheard. 'I'll do . . . what?'

'Slave.' The downcast eyes flicked up, only for a moment. 'Like me.'

'Slave!' Suddenly the meaning was all too clear and the outrage it brought overpowered the terror that had held him since he'd entered the hut. 'Now look here,' he said, rising up on his knees to stare straight at the warrior, 'I am a free-born Englishman and, by God, no savage can turn me into a slave. Tell them that if they take me to Quebec, to the British Army, I will see that they are not punished for what they have done. May even be able to get them some rum and . . . bead thingies.' He turned to the man beside him. 'Tell 'em.'

'I don't think—'

'Tell 'em, damn your eyes!'

The other man pushed his neck to one side as if stretching it then began to speak. He had only got a few words out before there was a roar from the warrior, a screech from the woman, and both immediately began striking Jack, knocking him back down to the floor where several kicks were delivered. Then they pulled away and began to jabber at each other.

'What did you tell them?' gasped Jack.

'Only what you say. How you were not a *savage*'s slave.'

'Next time, ignore me,' groaned Jack, holding his bruised ribs. As the volume and the gestures over him increased, he continued, 'How is it you speak English?'

'How does a savage speak?' There was a little gleam in the dullness of the eyes. 'Because I was not always slave to these Abenaki . . . dogs,' he whispered. 'I am Iroquois. Mohawk.'

'Mohock?' said Jack. It was a word from a better world, a civilized one; brought a memory of pleasure beyond the pain. 'That's strange. For so am I.'

The gleam grew. 'What you mean?'

'Friends and I. Back home, in England. A little . . . society.'

'So . . . soci . . .'

'Uh, gang. Of warriors, you know. Drinking, eating. Uh, whatchamacallit . . . whooping.'

'You . . . say you are warrior of my people? You . . .' The gleam was now a flame. 'You no Mohawk. You steal a name. You know nothing of honour—'

'Now look here, fellow—'

'Argh!' yelled the Iroquois, throwing himself on Jack, knocking him backwards. He was underneath, fending off the blows that fell for the short while before the others dragged them apart, only to beat each in a simultaneous assault in which everyone joined in. When it was over, both of them were thrown onto a platform, while the crowd went back to their debate.

Jack was now feeling pain in the few places where he had not felt it before. He lay curled up, finally daring to open his eyes again. He found himself staring into the eyes of his recent opponent. There was no dullness in them now as he whispered, 'I am warrior, not you. I am Mohawk, not you. I am Até of the Wolf Clan. Keep out of my way, White Face. Or you die . . . pretty damn quick!'

Slavery is a bloody slow way of passing the time, Jack thought, as he began his twentieth trip down the river path that day. He held the yoke away from his raw-rubbed skin, the birch-bark buckets jiggling before and behind him as he walked. On the return he'd have to lower the yoke onto his pain, it was the only way to get the full buckets back and only full buckets could be poured into the longhouse's trough. Anything less and he would get more kicks, less food at the end of the day. He'd tried folding the tattered remains of his lawn shirt

232

between the wood and the flesh but it had barely helped and the blue, cotton shirt they'd given him was proof against neither cold nor chafing. The meat fat he'd rubbed on, taken from his ration – *pemmican*, they called the foul conglomeration – had eased the hurt a little. Then someone had seen him doing it and he had been cursed, and struck, for wasting food. So now he just suffered, less on the way to the water, more on the way back.

Pain blurred the hours, toil the days. How long had he been there? He had tried to keep a rough calendar, gouged into the slats where he slept in the longhouse. But, exhausted, he'd forget to scratch the marks at day's end and was anyway unsure how long that darkened journey had taken to bring him here. If it was about two weeks since the battle, it was the end of September, beginning of October perhaps. The weather gave little clue except that it was colder than any autumn he'd ever known. There'd been some snow three days before.

If time eluded him, he had learnt other things, to be mused on as he dragged himself down the path. Some of the tribe – they were called the Abenaki – spoke French, albeit with an accent that had him always groping for meaning. Jack had been given as slave to the family he'd robbed of a son and one old man, Bomoseen, who lived in their longhouse, spoke it better than most. He treated Jack a little more kindly than the others, speaking to him each day and tolerating the occasional question. From him Jack had learned that he was in the village of St Francis though he was given no indication where that was. That the Abenaki were old allies of the French in the fight against the 'bastard *Anglais*' and that many of the scalps, both men's and women's, that decorated the lodge pole were taken by Bomoseen himself. He also informed Jack that what the tribe fought for was not land, the owning of which was an absurd idea, nor any distant king. The Abenaki fought for scalps – which proved prowess and brought glory – and prisoners, like Jack, who could eventually be exchanged for gold or goods to enrich the village. It was that 'eventually' which concerned Jack the most, yet further questions gave no answers, time an irrelevance in the Abenaki world. It was either before or after. Before the winter? A shrug. After? Another shrug. Running away was a fantasy. He had no idea where he was and was certain he would not last long alone in the forest. It had also been made clear to him what would happen if he tried. Bits of him would be cut off. Bits he was fond of.

There were white captives in other longhouses, men and women; Jack had tried to talk to them but it had proved frustrating. They were all either Dutch or Palatine German and spoke no languages but their own, though their weary gestures indicated they had been there a worryingly long time. There was only one other person there who spoke English and he had made it clear, from the first, that he wanted nothing to do with Jack.

As he lowered the buckets onto the shingle shore, Jack rolled his shoulders and mused on that person. The old man had spat that all Iroquois were demons and the Mohawk tribe the worst of all, their very name meaning 'cannibal'. This Até had been taken in war because the Mohawk usually sided with the British. But there was no profit to be had from such an uncivilized people. So the youth would live and, judging by his treatment, probably soon die, a slave.

That was something else Jack had learned about slavery. As in any society, there were gradations to it. There had been much of the same at Westminster where there was a form of slavery and boys lived in a hierarchy, the seniors catered to by descending ranks who each persecuted the one below them, down to the youngest boys who could only persecute each other. Jack had contrived to keep out of this Até's way and would continue to do so. A man who had no lower to fall was dangerous and his innocent claiming of Mohock kinship had obviously rattled the fellow.

Shivering, Jack bent to his buckets, wading up to his bare knees in the chill water, filling the bark containers as rapidly as he could. When the second was half full, an unusual sound from the village made him pause – a bell, tolling. It was the summons to church and that gave Jack the day, Sunday, which he should have noticed before because only the slaves were working. Yet even slaves would stop now, for an hour or two at least. Even slaves had souls, the French had convinced their allies, and might be saved if only they came to Mass. Thus once a week most of the villagers packed into the slat-boarded, shingle-roofed church, united in their adoration of a silver Madonna on the high altar. The Abenaki were Catholics of the most rabid kind and Jack had always been a casual Atheist. But not on a Sunday in St Francis. He had made the mistake of demurring the week before and so he had been assigned a task – he'd had to slit the throat of a dog, skin, gut and ready it for the longhouse pot. He would not demur again. Indeed, he looked forward to the hymns and prayers, would sing and chant with the most devout and display his superior Latin. Anything if it meant he would not have to carry any more bastard buckets for an hour or two!

The service was quite different from any that Jack had attended before. It had the solemnity of a communion at St Peter's Abbey in the procession, the hymns. It had the ecstasy of the Chapel in the Tottenham Court Road, the swooning, swaying, chanting congregation falling before certain sacred items, reverencing them, grabbing them from their robed bearers to shake at the crowd, staggering at their touch. The objects were different and went beyond what Jack would have expected even from Catholics. He knew they believed in the sacredness of relics, the living power resting in wood, metal and porcelain. The cross was worshipped from hand to hand, the small silver Madonna was carried forth to the beating of chests, to 'Hallelujahs' and 'Hosannas', but it was the other items that surprised Jack: hoes, flails and threshers; buckets and fishing hooks; tomahawks and muskets, flint and ball. Intricately carved masks with a variety of grotesque faces were also passed reverently down the nave, laid upon the altar around the Mother of God. But it was the last object that had Jack starting forward as it came through the doors.

'Leaping Christ!' he cried, and Bomoseen, who stood next to him and who'd used Jack's arms to be helped into the church, yelled out, 'Ave!' delighted that Jack joined in.

Held on high by the warrior who'd captured Jack was a trophy that elicited as much awe as any other: a war club. It was different from the more common ones, which were carved from a single piece of wood, the heavy end shaped into a ball. Only a few had this variation – a metal spike projecting from the head's centre, which in this case was only partially revealed . . . buried as it was in his mother's gift of *Hamlet*, which Jack had kept for luck in the pocket of his redcoat.

'*Orenda*,' Bomoseen was nodding beside him. 'Powerful spirit. It save life. Your life.'

Jack could only nod himself. It suddenly made sense of that last sight before oblivion took him in the forest at Quebec. A war club resting on his chest. The bruise that still discoloured his skin there, the indentation. The thrown club was meant to kill him, its spike to lodge. Instead he'd been saved by his mother, by the longwindedness of a Danish prince and the craft of Alexander Pope's printer on the corner of Dirty Lane, Dublin!

At the end of the service, with the sacred objects – including *Hamlet* and war club – piled before the Madonna on the altar, the congregation stepped out into the weak autumn sunlight. Jack was helping Bomoseen but the old man went to talk with other elders of the tribe, leaving Jack at the church's door observing another Sunday ritual, one seen in any village in England. His uncle, Duncan Absolute, had always done his duty as squire of Zennor in the parish church; then he would fulfil his other role as figurehead by getting utterly drunk in the village inn. Here the Abenaki had no less a love for liquor than their Cornish equivalents and drank it openly before their longhouses. In Zennor, the fuel would have been beer and cider, with the odd prized bottle of smuggled brandy. Here it was rum, of which there seemed to be a never-ending supply.

It wasn't just Sundays; there would be drunkards whatever the day. But Sundays, God duly propitiated, gave licence to all and amounts were consumed that would have disgraced no gathering in Covent Garden. Jack had seen the result the Sunday before, the joy of the first bumpers moving through songs on the fifth to arguments and fighting by the tenth. One man had been beaten near to death for some slight. And much as Jack could have used a snifter to set against the cold and fortify his thin, borrowed garments, he was unwilling to risk its consequences. As with the rest of his slavery, safety came with keeping out of the way.

His route to the longhouse where he slept took him close to a group of youths, occupied as any Cornish lads would have been of a Sunday – seeking trouble. A stone jug of rum was being passed round their circle. As he made to slip by, he saw what it was that they were yelling about. They were crouched over a large pit, a dozen paces across and the height of a man deep, in the bottom of which there was movement. Despite himself, the snarling below and the excitement above drew him.

Two dogs were down there, held at their necks, their hair up and stiff along their spines. The Abenaki kept two kinds of hound – for hunting and for eating – and these were of the latter kind and thus dispensable for this sort of game. As they circled, the youths yelled, bets obviously being made, called back and forth in their harsh tongue, accepted with grunts. Jack had often attended the cockfights – Marks was as fond of them as he was of dice – and the scene before him could have been exchanged for one in the Mall.

One of the dog-holders was a youth from Jack's own longhouse, the one who'd snuck so many kicks in when Jack first arrived and who had been his chief persecutor ever since, always ready with an extra task, an extra toe in the ribs. Segunki. Recognizing him made Jack duck down on the instant, begin to turn; but at that moment the dogs were released and the roar and snarling pulled him back.

It was over fast, one hound's fangs fastened in the other's throat. No attempt was made to save it, its scrabbling rear paws jerking ever more fitfully as it was shaken back and forth. Cries of triumph came from many around – but not from Segunki who responded to the final spurt of blood by stepping back into the pit and stomping on his dog repeatedly. The other dog was pulled off by its triumphant owner while the loser stood there and glowered all around.

Time to be gone, Jack thought, taking a step away. Too late.

'*As-ban!*' Segunki yelled the name he'd given him, that supposedly indicated both his status and his white man's smell. 'Racoon' was what MacDonald had called it when they'd chased one away from his tent.

Jack wasn't fast enough to elude the reaching hands of Segunki's friends. He was pulled back to face his tormentor whose features were twisted by the disappointment of his loss. His large hands twitched at his side and Jack prayed that he would observe the restraint that had been urged upon him by the longhouse matriarch. Though Jack spoke no words of their language, he understood clearly enough the meaning behind the kindness: the white man is property. Don't harm the livestock.

A rapid debate took place. Something was agreed and two of the group ran off towards the longhouses. Jack, meanwhile, was being pulled and poked towards the fields.

Segunki had a few words in French and was using them now to convey what he intended for Jack but perhaps because of the distracting prods that accompanied the words, he could understand none of them. Finally, when they stood at the edge of the rows of maize, whose ears had been stripped only the week before and lay now in huge piles that awaited carrying to the village, Jack at last caught a repeated word he understood.

'You want me to . . . race?' he asked in French.

'Race! Race!' Segunki shouted, moving to the ears of corn.

Beside them were the birch-weave baskets that were used to carry the produce to the grindstones. These had been left by those who worked here, no doubt at the summons of the church bell, because several were half-full. Segunki threw a few more ears in, then hefted the bucket, miming a run towards the village.

'You want me to run with this?' His French was accompanied by gestures that the Abenaki nodded at. But when Jack sighed and reached to begin this latest of his chores, the basket was jerked beyond his reach.

'You race!'

Jack just kept his tone within bounds – for only slaves could be yelled at in that society. 'Who? Who do I race?'

'Me.' The voice came from the edge of the group. 'You race me.'

The words were spoken in English and so, for a moment, Jack didn't understand them. He turned to see Até, the one man he'd been avoiding, thrust forward into the circle. 'You race me, we carry these,' Até gestured at the birch-bark containers. 'You carry more because they say you are stronger than me.' The eyes finally met his. 'They are wrong.'

Jack gasped, watching Segunki and the others haggling over the corn ears they were throwing into each of the baskets. 'You mean, they are . . . are handicapping me. Like some race-horse?'

Até shrugged. 'I don't know this word. You carry more. That is all.'

Jack felt his face redden. He muttered. 'I'm not a fucking horse. I damn well won't be treated like one.'

'Then they beat you.'

'Better that perhaps.'

'No. Not better. You win, you rest.'

'And if I lose.'

The shrug again, no words.

'So a beating either way,' Jack said.

'Unless you win.'

'Well, I better do that then, hadn't I?' The baskets had been filled and Jack walked to the fuller one, pointed at it. Segunki nodded and Jack bent, hefted it onto his shoulders. He staggered back slightly, which made the youths jeer. When Até lifted his, he did it with hardly an effort; the load, less than Jack's but not by much, seemed to trouble him less and Jack noted that though the Mohawk was thinner than him and had certainly suffered longer, his muscles were corded under his patched cotton shirt, his legs strong within his torn breeches.

One youth stood before Jack and Até, a hand in each of their chests. 'How far?' said Jack.

'To the church door,' same the reply. Then, to a shout of 'Aieeee!' the horses were off.

The weight! As Jack took a step, he felt the load pull him backwards. Até had immediately gained a pace, so Jack was able to observe his opponent reach behind him, pull forward a strap, slip it over his forehead. Reaching behind too, he groped until his fingers found some loose leather. Lifting it over his head, he mimicked the man now five paces before him. The strap instantly took some of the strain from the shoulders and back, while putting more on the neck but, dropping his chin, he was able to counter that. His speed built and he began to try to make up the ground lost.

The land sloped down from the fields and for the first hundred yards the going wasn't too bad. But then it began to climb, the path winding through a stand of spruce pine. Despite the slope, still Jack could not gain, the gap maintained. If anything, he dropped a little further behind, to the fury of Segunki and the joy of those who had bet against him. But it wasn't for him that Jack, when the ground levelled, began to pound harder. Even if he had seen the way the Abenaki youth had treated a dog that had let him down, it wasn't what drove him now. There was a rival ahead and rivals were there to be beaten. It was the Westminster way.

They had maybe two hundred yards to go when he saw the first flagging in the stride ahead. Not much, a misplaced foot, a slight stumble. But in any footrace there was a moment to be seized when a show of strength would add to an opponent's weakness. This was that moment. With a grunt, Jack sprinted the yards to come up beside, then pass, Até. Segunki, his cronies, cheered; those who had bet on the Mohawk screamed at him. And he responded, not with a burst of speed, but by reaching up into his basket, grabbing a corn ear and hurling it between Jack's legs. It was little, should have been nothing, but it caught just as his ankles were at their closest, lodged for only a second between them. Unencumbered, he'd have taken the stumble in stride, strode on. But here the pannier followed gravity forward, the top edge of it crashing into Jack's neck, turning stumble to fall.

The ground was hard, the basket pressed him into it, corn ears clattering around his head. Spluttering, he tried to force himself up just with his arms, then sank until he could pull his legs up underneath him. Heaving, he rose again to his feet. His opponent was at least thirty yards ahead now but Jack needed none of the curses or kicks. Nothing more than his own anger to drive after him.

It was too far. Despite the yelling, the encouragement turning ever more to threat – Jack, speaking none of the language, could at least hear the change in tone – he wasn't able to get any closer than ten yards. Até maintained that gap, speeding up to match Jack's final effort, which caused him to fall again. He raised his head in time to see Até touch the church door.

Jack took his time to rise, drawing in the breaths he knew he'd need. The men with the winning bets had clustered around Até, his slave status momentarily forgotten in the euphoria of victory. The losers, Segunki prominent, were spread between Jack and the finish. Despite their glares, they too were breathing deep after their run up from the fields. So no one tried to do anything more than curse him as he dumped the birch pannier and walked up to Até.

'You cheated,' he said quietly.

'Cheated?' Até turned his head quizzically. 'What mean?'

'You cheated to win the race. You didn't win fair.'

'Fair? Everything fair.' He hammered on the wooden door. 'Only win matters.'

Jack's voice dropped but something in it, though they did not understand the words, made even his disappointed sponsors, even Segunki, look closer. 'Then what I said here that first day was right. Like all of them, you truly are a savage. And the Mohocks of London know more about honour than all the Mohawks in Canada.'

Até flushed, the red running from his still-heaving chest up his neck, into his eyes. As the colour reached them he went for Jack, as Jack suspected he might. Thus prepared, he stepped sideways, seizing the Indian's reaching arm by the wrist, twisting his own body, bringing his other hand up into the armpit, using the force of the assault to throw Até past him. He fell hard but rolled up onto his knees on the instant, turning. Jack would have followed, pinned him to the ground, made him acknowledge his knavery, and he sensed that Até would have met him halfway, but others interposed, seizing each of them.

A hasty, fast conversation was had as they glared at each other. Then someone laughed and then all of them were running away from the church, dragging their prisoners with them. When they came to the dog pit, they were both lowered into it but still held. There was a slight wait, until one of the younger boys who'd disappeared, now returned with something Jack could not see. Segunki took what the boy brought, stepping up to the pit edge with the object behind his back. On a word, the two of them were taken to opposite sides of the rough circle, yet still pinioned there. Then Segunki threw what he'd been hiding . . . and two war clubs landed in the mud and the dog's guts. He spoke something to someone beside him, one of those who had bet on Até, and it was the way he said it that made Jack understand it instantly, even though he spoke none of their tongue.

'Double or quits,' the Indian clearly stated and, at his nod, Jack and Até were released.

As he dived forward, in the moment between thought and instinct, Jack realized that for the second time in just a few months he was going to fight a duel and that if he didn't hate this Até as much as he hated Craster Absolute, he hated him enough, hated him because he was one with all who'd made him suffer these last weeks. There was no fellowship amongst slaves. Reduced to an animal, he would fight, as the dogs had fought before him and on this same ground, for a higher place in the pack.

The slickness of the surface caused each to misjudge their leaps. Both slipped, slid, stuck together, one hand out to fend off, the other to grope for the weapon. Momentum made them spin in a half-circle, their conjoined bodies the axis. Jack grabbed a club first but he was holding it high up its shaft and couldn't swing it. Instead, almost as if it were a sword, he jabbed it into the face that grimaced close to his. Até turned aside, the blow glancing off his jaw. Drawing his legs up to his chest, Jack kicked out, too close to damage, close enough for the force to send the other man sliding backwards across the mud. Yet as he went, Até's hand trailed, grabbed the other club, taking it with him.

Both of them were now up, staggering back to the extremity of the pit. Jack shifted his grip on the weapon, swung it through the air. The weight was all at the top, in the heavy ball-head, these ones spikeless. He had never hefted one before and it felt awkward – as it obviously didn't to his opponent. In that instant, Jack knew the weapon couldn't be used as any sword he'd ever practised with, even the heavy cavalry sabre. But as Até moved away from the wall, circling left, and as he moved the opposite way, Jack grasped the shaft with two hands, raised it . . .

Well, kiss my arse, he marvelled, *it's a cricket bat!*

Wonder vanished as Até came for him, swinging the club in a high arc from behind him, aiming straight down for his head. Jack stepped into him, club raised square across, taking the blow before it had reached its full velocity. And yet the crack! It rang like a musket shot, sent a shock down his arms and on into his body, causing him to stagger back. Até followed, the club coming hard into Jack's left flank. He just blocked it in time but had to draw his feet awkwardly under him to do it. Spinning, the Mohawk took his weapon out, around, his whole body-weight behind it, and by the time it reached him its force was unstoppable; certainly the block Jack threw out barely slowed it. His club left his grip on impact. Only a leap back meant that his side was not shattered by the blow but what landed in the soft flesh just beneath his ribs was enough to knock the little breath he'd held from him. He fell into the wall, slipped to its base. On his back, the partisan cries from the pit's edge, of triumph and fury, came to him as if through a blanket. Jack looked back, expecting the killing blow that would at least end the terrible pain. But Até had paused to yell some Mohawk triumph to the sky.

It was a mistake.

When he came, Jack had taken a breath and it was enough to let him push himself from the wall, not off the ground, but along it, not away from his enemy but towards him, using the slickness of the surface for momentum. Até had stepped back to give himself room to run, to bring his final blow down and it was the blow he was focused on, not the target. He was half-turned away. He was running and Jack was sliding and the two met with Jack's one leg raised at an angle off the ground. Até impaled himself on it.

His groan was echoed around the edge of the ring, each man there folding in slightly to his centre. Até staggered back, clutching at his groin, while Jack snatched up his weapon. Both ended with their backs against the pit's walls, both sucking in rasping gulps of air.

Jack moved first. The pain in his side had a dullness he feared was only temporary. Before he succumbed to it, he had to end this. Grasping the club at shoulder height, he pushed himself off the wall, as if he were striding down a wicket to a short-flighted ball.

One stroke to win the match, he thought, grimacing at what the movement did to him.

Até came off the wall too, equally pained, equally determined. They met at the exact centre of the pit, both clubs descending for a blow, clacking above their heads, bouncing off, coming together again. Jack struck, Até blocked it; Até struck, Jack fended him off, both sucking air as they brought up their weapons, expelling it as they clashed.

It could not go on, exhaustion and pain had to make one slip and it was Jack. A blow hit his club from his grasp. But Até had not anticipated that giving and his whole body, which he'd put into the blow, followed it through. Suddenly they were side to side, shoulder pressed to shoulder, and Jack reached both his hands down to twist the Mohawk's wrist, jerking the weapon from his grip, his own hands coming around to grab. Fingers entwined, they spun round and around like a children's top, bouncing off the earthen walls, to their grunts, to the growing screams of those above them.

Then noise ceased, or at least dropped to only their harsh wheezing, the crump of bodies slammed into packed mud. Until a voice came, new, authoritative, roaring anger and commands. On the instant, the pit was full of bodies breaking them apart. And though he saw the fury and the desire in the Mohawk, Jack saw a glimmer of something else there too, that he suspected was mirrored on his face – relief. Death would not come to either of them that day. And they would not have to kill to avoid it.

— FIVE —

Deliverance

Jack lay listening to the night, wondering what it was that had woken him. He didn't think it was pain. Though he was beaten for his part in the duel, it wasn't any more than he usually suffered, the matriarch of the longhouse lacking the stamina and accuracy of even an under-usher at Westminster. It was the organizers who suffered more, Segunki and his cronies, unused to the punishment given to slaves and to the slave work that followed. And he hadn't rolled onto his side, which, for the first three nights after the fight, had pained Jack far more than the switch stripes on his arse; a bruise had spread in a profusion of purples and eventually yellow.

Of the deliverer of the blow, he saw little. If they had shared the briefest of realizations at the end of their fight, Jack had no desire to expand on the acquaintance. The fellow was still a cheat and he would prefer to keep from his company.

And yet it was from a dream of Até that Jack had awoken. At first he hadn't been there, hadn't intruded into the delight of a night at the Five Chimneys, the taste of the inn's fine Porter more exquisite than Jack had ever known, his comrades' banter more amusing. Then Mohawk had replaced Mohock at his side, though Até had retained some of Marks's features, his one knitted eyebrow startling beneath the brightness of the warrior's shaven head. There were tattoos upon his scalp which seemed to be leaking ink.

Até had led him outside onto a Tothill Fields more studded with trees than Jack remembered it to be. He'd thought the Iroquois wanted to renew their combat but instead he just stared, immobile.

'What do you want?' Jack had said and, for reply, the other man gestured toward the river that was the Thames and yet was not, for neither warehouses nor pleasure gardens lined its banks, only an endless forest. Até seemed to be inviting Jack to enter it with him.

'Now?' Jack had wanted to be back amidst the tankards and the laughter. Até had nodded, turned . . . and then Jack had awoken and lay there wondering why. It wasn't the cold, despite the slave's position furthest from the hearth. He had taken precautions against it, his thin blanket tucked around, one of the hut dogs pulled close despite its fleas and fetid breath. The hound was asleep, twitching but only slightly, in some dream of its own. No one else moved and the snoring, which could be as bad as at Porten's dormitory, was light. Pulling the dog closer, Jack was about to try to sleep again, suspecting dawn not to be far off and he would need to be about his chores soon enough. Then what had woken him came again, a whisper, through the thin birch-bark walls.

'Pass up to the junction there.'

Though the man's accent was harsh, the words were definitely in English. They were followed by the sound of several pairs of feet moving quietly away. Unfolding himself from the blanket and the dog's embrace – the animal whimpered but did not wake – Jack climbed carefully over the bodies on the platform, then stepped between those who'd lain closer to the hearths, all the way to the entrance, pausing there, his fingers on the deerskin flap. From another hut a dog started barking, ceasing on the sound of a blow, a sleepy curse. The wind that had been gusting throughout the night dropped now. Jack strained for more English words, which he did not realize till then how much he'd missed. He presumed that the speaker and his soft-footed companions would be trappers like the three Canadians who'd come through the village the week before and had stayed for a night of rum and trading. But they had spoken in their version of French and showed interest in Jack only as a commodity, to be taken off the Abenaki and sold on to the French Army for a suitable price. His captors had declined their offer. These fellows – they were probably from the Colonies to the south – though they might not be able to pay his hostage price, could at least take news of Jack's imprisonment to the nearest British fort. Contact with them might be his first step to freedom.

Gingerly, he stepped through, lowering the weighted flap behind him. He was immediately shivering, the tattered shirt they'd given him and the frayed buckskin leggings poor protection against a night which smelled of winter fast approaching. The ground was hard and he placed one bare foot atop the other, trying to warm each in turn while he turned in the direction he thought the men had taken. He could see a little, for the night was shading into dawn, the tops of the beech and maples showing what remained of their autumn reds. But there was no movement, no sign of those who had passed. Fearful now that they may already have been on their way out of the village, Jack took a step in pursuit. A bird called, shrill, piercing . . . and the night exploded.

Lanterns pulled from under overcoats illuminated men where only darkness had been, under the trees, in the shadows of lodges. Brands were lit, flared, and rose like shooting stars to plummet on to birch-bark shelters, barns, piles of drying corn. With the instant crackle came screams of terror from within. A man from the next hut burst from the entrance; gunpowder flashed and the Abenaki flew back as if jerked on ropes.

Whoever was killing his enemy was his friend. 'Heh!' Jack yelled, moving along his hut's wall, waving his arms, 'Heh, there!'

His reply came in ball, two shattering the bark walls each

side of his head. 'Heh!' He called again but not so loudly, dropping to the ground, crawling back the way he had come. Another bullet sprayed dirt up into his face and he froze, not sure which way to move, until five warriors ran from his own longhouse, the first two falling to shots, the other three crouching and firing in return, then sprinting away. A group of women emerged, pushing children ahead of them, and Jack took a step toward this crowd – until one of the women pitched forward, half her face ripped away. The children screamed, scattered, some running back inside despite the fire engulfing the wood, some fleeing after the men. The attackers began to whoop and, tomahawks drawn, give chase.

Jack ran too, from the burning longhouse, from the bullet or blade in his back. Yet every way was a variation of one he'd fled – flames, shrieks, gunfire, death. He ran towards a larger group who milled like sheep, until a ragged volley dropped half a dozen into the mud and the rest broke. He found himself running down an avenue of largely clapboard houses that seemed deserted – until another shot came, its wind passing close to his ear. He was looking back, even as he ran forward . . . and careened into someone.

Bouncing back, falling, he raised arms to ward off blows. Then, through his thrust-out hands, he saw someone doing the same thing.

'Até!'

The other's hands lowered. 'You!'

Another musket cracked nearby, someone shouted, a figure appeared, silhouetted in flame, pointing at them. 'Quickly,' hissed Até, leaping up. He disappeared between two houses and Jack followed. A path led through a copse of trees and leaving it, Até ran another dozen paces then threw himself behind a thick tree-trunk. Jack did the same, just as feet found the path and shouting men ran along it. Ducking his head, Jack waited till the earth stopped trembling before he looked up.

'They're . . . they're . . .'

'Rangers,' said the Mohawk.

Jack had seen Rangers with the King's Army at Quebec. 'They fight on our side, against the Abenaki,' he said excitedly. 'They've come to rescue us.'

'They come to kill.' Até nodded towards the sounds of terror. 'I tried to speak to them, for Mohawks and Rangers fight side by side.' He lowered his head. 'They give me this.'

Jack could see a dark furrow, gleaming red along the crown of the Indian's head. He swallowed. 'They tried to shoot me too. But we just have to wait till they beat the Abenaki—'

'They will not "beat". They burn, steal, kill. Then go.'

'So we must go with them.' Jack half rose, only for the Mohawk to reach out and pull him back down. A shout came from nearby, another two men ran down the path. When they'd passed, Até whispered, 'They kill all they see, anyone who look like Abenaki. Me. Even you.' He gestured to Jack's torn shirt, leggings, his straggly black hair.

'But . . .' Jack's desperation was overcoming his fear. 'I must try. I won't stay here to be a slave any longer.'

Até stared at him intently. 'Then we go other way.' His head indicated the forest, away from the river and the direction of the attack.

'We?'

'Abenaki maybe think we dead in raid. Maybe they wait for a day to come looking, give us start. We go. Find my people.'

'Maybe?'

'Better than here. Better than slave.'

He was right – especially if His Majesty's Rangers were going to blow his head off before they listened to him. So he nodded and, on Até's signal, they both rose, heading back down the path towards the clapboard houses. More were burning now but the shots seemed to be coming from their left, so they went right. Soon they came to more bodies, two men, a woman and a child in a huddle. The men had tomahawks which Até picked up, handing one to Jack. The road led them into the centre of St Francis, quiet compared to the noise of fight and terror that now came from the village's periphery. The doors of the church were thrown back and bodies were strewn up its steps.

Até made to go around, to follow the road out of the village. But Jack hissed, 'Wait!' and, despite his companion's curses, went inside. There were bodies in there too, sprawled over the upturned pews. He didn't look closely at any after the first one. Each one there, man or woman, had been scalped.

The altar was wrecked, the objects of veneration scattered around. The Silver Madonna was gone, the plinth that had held it, kindling. Beneath it, a moment's rooting gave him what he sought. Carefully tugging the war club, he pulled the spike out of the vellum and leather. There was a satchel lying in the wreckage on the floor and, dropping *Hamlet* into it, Jack slung it across his shoulder. There were offerings from the harvest festival too and some ears of dried corn followed the book.

'Now we can go,' he said to a glowering Mohawk. Tumult came from the road ahead, shrieks and gunfire, so they cut left and were soon under the canopy. They ran, until the sounds of massacre had faded behind them. And then they ran on.

'I think we've lost—'

Até's furious gesture halted Jack's hopeful sentence. He was peering back into the forest so Jack peered too, trying to pierce the thick strands of trees. Even though the canopy had grown thinner with the season, with most of the red and yellows of the maples now lying beneath them, it was still hard to see deeply into the forest, especially in the gloom of twilight. Hard to hear anything beyond the bubbles trapped in his ears that had hummed with every step. They had trotted most of the day since leaving St Francis and, since they'd glanced back from a hilltop an hour before to see sunlight gleaming on muskets, they had run again.

The Mohawk's hand was still hanging in the air when they both heard it – a distinct crack as something or someone trod on a stick, sounding like a gunshot in the sepulchral silence of the forest. They both looked where they thought it had come from – and there, just passing from tree to tree, a bald head moved, a blue feather, unattached to any bird, swaying across the brow.

Até signalled him down, and the two began to shimmy backwards through the leaves and undergrowth until they reached the scant path they'd stepped off to look. Then they were up, running. Jack felt his back tighten between his shoulder blades as if someone had sighted on a place that would soon hold a bullet or a blade. Immediately, his breath again reverberated in his ears, putting a blanket between him and the sounds of the forest, though it did not shut out the shout that came – the halloo of a hunter sighting his quarry.

Até was moving ever further ahead and Jack couldn't blame him. He had made it clear what the Abenaki would do if they caught them. It would be death for him, as painful and protracted as possible. Jack, more valuable, they might let live. But he would live without parts of himself he knew he needed.

The track widened, became the floor of a little valley, lined in white birch. He glanced up its steep sides, seeking any shelter to be had, but none was revealed. And since he was looking up, he didn't see that Até had stopped, just where the valley narrowed again. He ran into his back and both of them sprawled on the soft, leafy ground. The Indian was too winded to do more than gesture. Jack followed the hand, saw that the track didn't continue into another expanse of forest. It ended, dead, at a cliff. Forty feet below, a stream full of autumn's rains drove through boulders.

They rose, turned. Four figures were walking slowly towards them down the little valley. Their faces were painted in two colours, melding at the nose, blue and red. Two wore tricorns, beads strung from the brims. The other two, the ones that led, had their heads shaved to the crown, shanks of black hair dangling down their necks. One of these was Segunki, a blue-dyed eagle's feather swaying across his brow.

He was grinning as he came, the musket easy in the crook of

his arm. He stopped about twenty paces from them, said something, and two of the others laughed. The fourth, who was older and must have been the tracker, squatted down, muttering. Segunki nodded then took another step forward.

Beside him, Até had drawn his tomahawk, so Jack did too. The weapon felt awkward in a hand already slick with sweat. He knew it trembled as he raised it but there was nothing he could do about that. Suddenly, the little curiosities shop in Knaves Acre came into his head. He could not understand why, until he remembered that it was full of body parts that he had ogled and pawed and wondered at. Now, in the way that they were looking at him, he felt he was about to become an exhibit himself.

The two other men followed Segunki, and laid down their muskets. Each drew a tomahawk from their belt, a war club from a sling at their side. Até let out a scream of defiance, raising his own weapon high. Segunki laughed and said something to his companions. Instantly, the three of them leant back, then hurled the heavy wooden clubs. All were aimed at Até. He dodged one, knocked another away; but the third took him in the temple and he fell like a poleaxed ox.

The three Abenaki exchanged comments on their throws, the successful one running his fist over his head in some gesture of triumph, immediately emulated by the others. Segunki just continued smiling at Jack, reached into his belt and pulled out a long bladed knife before stepping closer.

Jack looked behind him, at the dark-green water pouring over the rocks below. The fall would probably kill him – which might be a better fate than the one the man advancing with the knife intended for him. But really, there was nothing for it. Setting his feet square, clutching the unfamiliar weapon before him as if it were a sabre, Jack prepared to fight, prepared to die.

The gunshot was startlingly loud. Everyone jumped, but no one more than the tracker. He staggered back, musket clattering to his feet, hands reaching to his chest, failing to contain the blood that instantly came there, spreading across the blue of his shirt in a moment. He was on one knee, and then he was cross-legged on the ground, his head sagging.

Everyone looked at him. For an extended moment, nothing moved. It was the cry that roused the Abenaki, had them leaping for the guns they laid down, a long drawn-out battle cry, similar to the one Jack and his friends had attempted in the tavern; very, very different: 'Ah-ah-ah-ah-AH-HUM!' It came with something thrown, a tomahawk that plunged into the arm of the second Abenaki. Shrieking, he fell, rose, began to stagger back towards the valley's end. Segunki and the other warrior, pausing only to snatch up their muskets, followed. All disappeared fast into the trees.

Jack had laid down, though he had no recollection of doing so. Now, as the Abenaki vanished, he got up, staggered a little, stabilized, just as three shapes disengaged from the white birch above and moved rapidly down to the valley floor. There was a man with thick grey hair tied back with a blue ribbon, a younger man, not much older than Jack, and a boy of about eleven.

The older man spoke, a rapid, incomprehensible sentence. Jack shook his head. 'I'm sorry,' he said, 'I don't speak . . .'

The man frowned. 'English? Rich Man, Poor Man, Beggary Man, Thief?'

Jack stared at him. 'I, uh . . .'

He pointed at himself. 'King George's Man.' Reaching into his shirt, he pulled out a medal, shook it at Jack, who could see, on one of its polished sides, a highly flattering portrait of His Majesty.

The younger man had gone to Até, the boy with him, both helping him rise to a sitting position. Até muttered something and the boy looked up and chattered excitedly.

The older man spoke again. '*Ga-ne-a-ga-o-no*?' He was pointing at Até.

'I do not . . . ?'

He thought. 'Mohawk?'

'Yes,' Jack said, 'he is a Mohawk.'

'Mohawk,' the man smiled, pointing again to himself.

The younger man had stood, came now and talked, gesturing back down the valley. The older man thought for a moment then nodded, and the younger, grabbing up the wounded Abenaki's musket, began to run in the direction they'd fled. The boy took a few steps after him but a word from the elder – Jack assumed he must be the father of them both – halted him, his disappointment clear.

Até was trying to stand and the boy went to help him. There followed a rapid conversation in what Jack took to be Iroquois, the older man asking the questions. When at last he seemed satisfied, he nodded again to Jack and signalled past him, up the slopes.

Até came to Jack, hand pressed to the side of his head where his ear was rapidly shading to blue. 'He is Jote. He has a camp over there.'

The man and his son had gone to the tracker's body, swiftly stripping it of clothes, weapons, jewellery and, in one swift motion, scalp. In a moment the corpse was naked, save for a little breech cloth. Clutching the prize of a new knife, Jote pointed with it back up the slopes.

'London, England,' he laughed.

'Don't I wish,' said Jack.

– SIX –

Castaway

Jack lay still, wondering if it was sound that had woken him again or the cold. One side of him was warm enough, pressed, under the deer skin, against Jote's youngest son. The other was against the hide wall of their forest shelter for, as the least important members of the party, he and Até took the extremities. His fellow former slave was against the far wall; a preferable position to Jack's, who was also up against the flaps where any breeze would penetrate. Between them, descending in order of age and importance to the chief in the middle, were the rest of Jote's family – the two sons, one daughter, a wife and his wife's sister, the latter two swaddling him. He was given to snoring most untunefully, in short, sharp grunts; but now Jack listened and heard nothing from any of his companions but gentle breaths. Perhaps it had been a noise from outside then that had roused him, an animal call from the vast forest? He tipped his head and, suddenly, he knew, the knowledge bringing a rush of excitement, memories of childhood, waking like this not to sound but to its absence, to the silence of a world wrapped and muffled.

Still caught in the thrill, the difficulty he had parting the hide flaps confirmed his belief. For it had snowed heavily in the night and a wall had drifted against their shelter. Soft, separate flakes, huge as cherry petals, were still drifting down from a sky showing a hint of dawn. Stealthily, Jack pushed out through the drift. He had always loved snow, the opportunities for play and mischief it created, and he wanted to have it to himself for a while, to not have to restrain his exuberance before the ever-solemn Mohawks.

He plunged out into the clearing. The snow came up over the moccasins they'd given him, to his ankles, bare beneath the deer-skin leggings. He shivered but it was less cold than it had been, for the icy winds that had swept against them on their three-day march – deeper into the forest, roughly south-westwards, he believed – had dropped. And some vigorous running on the spot soon warmed him, together with some slips and slides back and forth across the now-concealed track.

He didn't know how long he'd been observed in his frolics. He'd been spinning round a tree when he noticed the figures, dark against the tent. The whole family was standing there, in the same order they'd maintained inside, Até apart on the edge.

'Ah.' Jack coughed, brushed his coat. 'Snow, eh? Wonderful stuff.'

The family continued to stare until Jote said something. Then one by one they ducked under the flaps. Até was the last and he beckoned Jack to follow, waiting for him at the entrance to catch up. 'Snow,' he said, sourly, when he did. 'Not so wonderful.'

'What do you mean?'

Até just ducked inside, Jack following him. The family made a semi-circle, passing some dried meat between them. He sat eagerly, waiting his turn for his exertions had made him hungry. In their time with the Mohawks they had always been treated well, receiving equal shares; so he was much surprised when the ball of deer jerky halted with Jote's youngest son and was tucked away. He saw that Até, too, had received none and he felt the coldest flush of the morning.

'What's going on?' he asked, his voice suddenly raspy.

Jote began to speak rapidly, gesturing beyond the walls. Até nodded, waited till the man finished speaking, then spoke himself, in single sharp sentences. The man shook his head clearly at each of the questions, finally making a clear gesture, unmistakably conclusive. Até slumped back.

'What is he saying?'

Até faced him. 'They must leave us.'

'Leave us? What do you mean? They are taking us to General Amherst. For the many gifts they will get.'

'They said they try to do this. If snow did not come.' He tipped his head to the outside. 'It has come.'

'But surely . . .' Jack tried to keep his tone calm 'We can't be that far away.'

Até shrugged. 'Two weeks maybe, with no snow.'

'But this snow may melt. Will melt. We can press on.'

Jote had been following the conversation with his little English. He said something and Até nodded. 'He say, this snow not melting kind. Staying kind. Much more in sky. They are within three days of their winter camp. This is the way of many of our people, families go to their own hunting grounds. My family will be in theirs, many, many weeks away. Jote will go to his.'

'Then we will go with him.'

Jote, leaning forward, squeezed Jack's upper arm. He said something, shaking it, nodding around him. Até translated. 'He say that we are both big men. We eat like big men. At his hunting grounds, there will be little to eat, maybe enough for his family. Maybe not even for them. If we go with them, we will all die.'

Jack was suddenly remembering his happy life as an Abenaki slave, stewed dog for breakfast, the warmth of labour. He shook his head. 'Then you and I must continue. To Amherst.'

'We would never get there. It is too far when the snow covers all the tracks. And even if I knew them and could see them, we could not walk on them. Also they will not give us food for such a journey.'

'No food?' Jack could not help how shrill his voice became. 'By Christ, you don't mean they are going to abandon us here to freeze and starve?'

Jote was still squeezing Jack's arm. He patted it as he let it go, spoke rapidly to the two women who began to burrow among the piles of goods lining the tent's edge.

'They will give us what they can spare. They will leave us in a part of the forest that might have game enough for two.'

Jack could hear, behind the calm way he spoke the words, a real fear in the young Mohawk. It took away his own voice, the desperate questions he needed to ask, the pleas he wanted to make. He could only watch as a few items were pulled from pouches and bags and thrown onto the floor in the gap that was widening between them.

He recognized the ball of fat Jote's wife scraped from a birch tub, rolled between her hands, then placed on the floor because he'd been forcing himself to eat this ghastly *pemmican* whenever it was offered: reeking, crystalline bear fat and dried moose meat, studded with little dried berries that exploded bitterly when cracked. Next to it was placed a musket flint, and finally, and only after Jote overcame an argument from his sister-in-law, the Abenaki tracker's knife.

When the women sat back, Jack looked at Até. 'That's it? Food for a day, a flint and a rusted blade?'

'It is much for them, together with the clothes they have already given. My people live by trade and we have nothing to exchange, except the tomahawks that we will need.'

'Nothing . . .' Jack was still staring in shock at the three items upon the floor. Then he remembered something and, reaching into the bag he'd taken at St Francis, he pulled out the sole possession he retained from his English life.

'There,' he said, throwing down the copy of *Hamlet*, 'I'll trade that for the musket that goes with the flint.'

Até, despite the fear still in his face, laughed. He spoke and the family found it even more amusing, clutching their sides in their mirth. Jote picked up the book, held it upside down by a corner of its green leather binding. Through his laughter he said something to Até who nodded and turned to Jack.

'Jote says he likes your joke so he will take this. But it is not worth a musket and a musket will not do us much good anyway, when we have nothing to trade for powder and ball. So I have asked for something better.'

Jote's sister-in-law had returned to their belongings. She pulled a bigger item out, dropped it beside the other three. Jack was appalled. 'A k . . . kettle?' he stuttered. 'You've swapped *Hamlet* for a fucking kettle?'

Até nodded. 'A kettle will keep us alive, white boy. More than any gun. And he has no use for your book.' At Até's nod, Jote picked up the volume and swiftly ripped the paper from its cover, throwing the pages, still bound in one piece, back onto the ground. 'But his wife can sew the skin into a tobacco pouch.'

Jote led them slowly on, waiting patiently at various points for the two who struggled to keep up. Unlike him, they did not have what looked to Jack like elongated tennis rackets strapped to their feet. He and Até either plunged into drifts up to their knees or slipped on icy, bare rock amongst scrub brush. At least the deepening cold was banished by the exercise and Jote had relented about the jerky; once out of sight of his camp and his women's sharp tongues, he let the two boys chew a couple of fibrous strands apiece. Yet it was little enough to fuel their struggles and Jack was very grateful when, with a pale sun peeping through rents in the snow clouds indicating midday, Jote halted in a grove of beech. Jack dropped onto a pile of their leaves, leaned his back against the base of a trunk and watched apprehensively as Jote and Até conferred. Then, what he most feared, happened. He'd still hoped that Jote would suddenly declare it the sort of cruel joke the Mohawks were given to, would clap them on their backs, lead them back to the warmth of the tent and a meal. That hope ended when Jote raised his arm in a parody of an army salute and loped off down the trail. The snow swallowed the sound of his footgear slapping its surface and soon all that was in their ears was the wind soughing through the trees, beginning to bite now they were stationary, and their own deep-hauled breaths.

Jack looked up at Até. 'Where are we?'

The other shrugged. 'Here.'

Jack bit back a response. He'd learnt, in their brief acquaintance, that the other's taciturnity would only be deepened by anger. And he needed some reassurance now, anything to counter the rumbling in his stomach that was fashioned only partly of hunger.

'I mean, are we close to any settlement, any farms? Montréal?' The thought of surrendering to the French was suddenly very appealing.

'I do not know. This is not my country. But I do not think so. If anything was near, Jote would have left us by it.'

'Instead he's just abandoned us – in the middle of nowhere?'

'In the middle of somewhere. In the middle of . . .'

Até gestured around and the anger surged again within Jack. The young Mohawk had an air of glacial superiority that would have put a belted earl of England to shame.

'He's left us "somewhere" with nothing. Nothing!'

'No. He's left us with two more things.'

'Really? And what is this bounty, pray?'

Até moved to a tree beside the one Jack still squatted against, its far side out of his vision. Até pointed and, grumbling, Jack rose.

From the lower branches of the beech, skulls dangled. They were deer, small antlers still attached and they were hanging by what looked like thin string. He reached out to one and, at his touch, it dropped to the ground to join a couple of others already there. Até pointed to one still hanging. He ran his forefinger down the string and touched the tendon of his neck. 'They hang by this. It rots, skull falls, shows this animal has not been hunted here for a while, so will be plentiful. Many on ground here so . . . we can hunt it.' Jack was about to ask pointedly, 'With what? The kettle?' but Até now lifted a wooden ladle that rested, open-faced against the trunk. 'And this is for water, shows water here is good. If like this,' he closed the face, 'water bad. Must boil.' He pointed into the forest and, now he listened, Jack could hear the faintest tinkling there of an ice-choked stream.

Até pulled the ladle off and bent to the base of the tree. Gesturing to a piece of bone that looked like a shoulder blade, he said, 'Dig here,' attacking the ground as he spoke. Jack did as he was bid, the two of them scraping the snow away, the ground beneath not quite frozen solid, allowing them some purchase. They dug until a hole went the depth of Jack's lower leg before the note changed and his bone struck wood.

'Me,' Até said, and began to scrape around a shape that Jack soon saw to be some sort of container. It was quite large, a foot across and two deep, made of birch bark and woven with some reed.

'Buried treasure?' he whispered.

'Abenaki hunting post, left for their tribe if they are away from camp and in need. So, are we not their slaves? And are we not in need?' Jack saw the ghost of a grin cross the Indian's features before he set to prising off the lid.

The contents were meagre. No weapons, no snares, no real food save for a smaller container of bitter dried berries that they devoured swiftly between them. There were two small furs, threadbare but a little warming when shoved inside a deer-skin jacket that was doing little against the ever-deepening cold; and a long coil of rope, which Até seemed to consider the best discovery of all.

Jack sat back, shivering. The little exercise, the little hope, both passed now. He looked across at Até, whose face betrayed a similar disappointment.

'You said two things.'

'Yes.' Até's face had brightened again. 'Come.' He led Jack over to the trail up which Jote had disappeared. 'Look.'

Jack did. There were the marks of Jote's unusual footwear

there, beside the smaller imprints of Até's moccasins. He scanned back and forth. 'I can't see anything.'

Até pointed, his voice impatient. 'There!'

Jack followed the finger. There *was* something else, now he looked hard, another series of marks beside the footprints. They led away, into the trees. He looked up. 'Deer?'

Até snorted. 'You went to school, white boy? They never teach you difference of animals?'

'Only in Latin,' Jack muttered, bent again. Now he looked he could see that the prints were not cloven, as he had known deer tracks to be in Cornwall. These were not made by hoof then but by some big, five-toed paw. A claw's mark headed each one. But the cold was numbing brain as well as body, the name danced just out of reach. What other creatures lived in this strange forest?

'I give up,' he said, straightening. 'Why don't you tell me, brown boy.'

Another snort. 'This is made by *Ne-e-ar-gu-ye*. In your tongue it is . . . is . . .'

As Até searched his mind, Jack remembered the words. '*Ursus ursidae!*' he said, but for the life of him, he still could not think of the name in English. He knew no Iroquois and he was sure Até's Latin was just as poor. Then both of them suddenly remembered the word in English.

They said it together, 'Bear!'

If one should allow a sleeping dog to lie, Jack thought, how much more so a bear?

His shivering, which was ceaseless due to the cold anyway, only increased at this thought. But Até's logic had been incontrovertible.

'I track bear to hole, yes? I fix way to kill him, yes? What you do? Nothing!' he'd said, then added, a rare smile coming, 'And since you say I *cheat* in our race, now you show how fast you are.'

He didn't feel fast this late afternoon. A night freezing on pine boughs under a tree had yielded little rest and the morning spent trying to dig deadfalls (and then having to abandon all of them three foot down due to the granite seams), had left him with a headache worse than most sustained after a long night's carouse at Covent Garden and legs as wobbly as if he'd spent the whole afternoon notching a score on Tothill Fields. All fuelled by foul *pemmican*, fingerfuls of it scraped from the ball and deposited on the tongue, swallowing the rank grease, struggling to prevent it coming straight back up. Despite its loathsomeness, they had somehow managed to finish the whole ball between them. It was the last of their food. Thus Até's rejection of Jack's demand that they build themselves some sort of shelter for the night and tackle the beast on the morrow.

'We may be too weak then. You may not be able to run fast enough. And if the bear catches you, then eats you, he will leave no scraps for me.'

Jack thought he was probably not joking. Hadn't Bomoseen told him that Mohawk actually meant 'flesh-eaters'. And he wasn't referring to mutton!

Jack's shivering had become almost an ague. What was the blasted savage doing? He peered again over the lip of rock that was the entrance of the cave. He still could see and hear nothing down there but the smell was as rancid as the grease he'd lately consumed. The bear was there.

A whistle came and he turned to see Até beckoning him. Slipping off the rock, he ran down to him and the Native took his arm and pulled him into the canopy.

'You must take him only this way, pft! Straight! You understand? Grandfather *Ne-e-ar-gu-ye* will be very angry he has woken up so soon after he lie down for the winter. But because he is sleepy he will not think so good and perhaps he will not run so fast and so perhaps will not catch you.'

'Perhaps?'

Até ignored him, still dragging him down the faint trail till he jerked him to a halt about sixty paces from the bear's cave.

Pulling Jack with him to the ground, he pointed forward. 'You see?'

At first, Jack could detect nothing unusual, just another piece of foliage across the path. But looking closer he realized that the leaf-covered thing he took for a creeper or tendril was, in fact, part of the rope Até had pulled from the Abenaki container. It ran about knee-height off the ground, was wrapped around a birch trunk and tied to a stake embedded about four foot further on. Beside the stake a small birch sapling was pulled back to the forest floor, its end still rooted near the path, its tip straining under the rope. Something stood proud from that end and, stepping closer, Jack could see that another sharpened stake had been thrust through the sapling near its head, and bound tight in with further rope.

'But where—'

Até raised a finger to his lips, then parted the bush into which the rope disappeared, and pointed to a small hooped stake driven into the ground like a question mark. The end of the rope was held by another stick wedged against both curves of the hook.

'See?' Até grinned. 'Grandfather chases you. You jump rope, fall. He stops, hits rope, knocks the small stick, and . . . *wang*!' He made a flowing gesture of the sharpened stake flying up, showing it embedding in his own head. 'Dead bear!'

'This . . .' Jack was almost too astounded to speak, '. . . *this* is your plan?'

'What's wrong with it?'

'What's . . . ?' Jack could think of a thousand things, not least the idea of him 'falling' down and the bear obligingly stopping before advancing slowly onto the rope. But he decided to show Até an even more obvious flaw. So he just leapt up in the air and landed hard on the ground. The stick fell from the hook, the rope slackened and the released sapling surged up and juddered to a halt a foot from Até's face.

'Not now! With bear!' Até yelled, immediately going to the sapling to reset it, tugging the rope across it, keeping it taut as

265

he dragged it around the birch and back to the hook. Jack stopped him before he replaced it.

'I've just shown you! It won't work.'

'It will. My people use this snare all the time.'

'Oh, I'm quite sure. And have you? How many times?'

'Plenty.'

'You . . .' Jack pushed down his rising temper. 'My running will set it off. You have to make this,' he pointed to the hook, the trigger of the mechanism, 'harder.'

'It work well.'

'If you think it works so well, then you run it.'

Até shrugged. 'I fix. You run.'

Suddenly, all those other reasons, not least the bear's close pursuit of him, came flooding into Jack's mind. He shook his head. 'I can't,' he said softly.

Até didn't even look up from the rope as he whispered, 'Then we die here, white boy. Die pretty damn quick. You feel,' he jerked his head toward the sky, 'much more snow coming, tomorrow. Maybe next day. This is last chance for food before it comes.'

Jack shivered violently. Not just from the returning cold. From the knowledge that Até was right. If they didn't kill the bear, the winter would indeed kill them pretty damn quick.

'I'll do it,' he said, through his rattling teeth. 'Damn you for a brown-faced lunatic, but I'll do it.' He stood, stamped his feet and stared back to the cave entrance. 'How exactly does one wake up a bear?'

With fire. The musket flint they'd been given was for that purpose. Até struck sparks off it with a tomahawk onto some cattail down wrapped in a cone of birch bark. Once this torch flared it was thrust onto more bark, some twigs; soon a fair fire crackled away. Jack was reluctant to leave the first warmth he'd felt in an age, but Até was insistent.

'Here,' he said, handing Jack the kettle, and several branches of wood. Then he used the ladle to scoop embers into the metal bowl. 'You go now. These . . .' he gestured to the sticks, 'will burn. You drop into hole then run. But make sure bear is awake first.'

Jack looked at Até, looked at the kettle in his one hand, the branches in the other. Then, shaking his head, he moved up the trail to the cave.

It was one of several on that rocky hillside. Indeed the whole area was pitted with them, as if some giant had jabbed his fingers into the earth then dragged them away in lines. Some of these trenches had already half-filled with snow, making walking treacherous. Others were deeper, led to cliff faces like the one just beyond the cave, that tumbled into an ice-clogged rivulet below. Jack peered over the precipice, conscious of the slickness of stone beneath him, then looked in a circle all around. There was only one way for the bear to follow him – down the path on which Até stood now, waving him on. Beyond the beckoning Native, the land rose again in folds and troughs, more caves and cliffs and snags for fleeing feet.

Cursing, he turned to his task. Dipping the branch end into the embers he blew hard, watching it catch, leaves crisping into brief, yellow flame. Lobbing it over the edge of the hole, he set the kettle down and ran back a half dozen paces.

Nothing. Neither sight nor sound came to where he stood, feet pointed down the path. He looked back at Até. The Mohawk waved him on to another attempt. He blew again, watched the birch catch, stepped up to the hole. Was that the faintest whiff of scorching or just the embers in his pot? With the branch crackling well, he tipped it over, ran back . . .

Still nothing. The only noise came from the faint rippling of water under ice, the squeak as Até shifted his feet on snow. 'Go on,' he hissed, miming the tipping of the whole contents of the kettle into the hole.

Jack ground his teeth, shook his head, stepped forward, the metal bowl crooked under one arm, kindling this branch like the others, watching it flame. This was the biggest and driest of the three. If that failed to rouse the bear, well, Até could bloody well go down into the hole himself and invite it to a quadrille!

Because he was looking into the kettle he didn't see the trail of smoke rising from the ground. Because his nose was running from cold and fear he couldn't smell. Thus it was only when he bent over the hole that he suddenly was made aware that his previous efforts had been successful.

'NAAARGH!'

The roar was the worst thing he had ever heard; worse than the death rattle of the man he'd killed with a bayonet, worse than his uncle's screams, dying under his horse. It came from less than two feet away, from a head three times as wide as any man's. Though the eyes were small, they were entirely black, while the teeth were as big as dagger blades, yellow and lined in greenish slime. Jack took all this in during his long, slow fall backwards, while the predominant impression, before terror melded all of them, was of a reeking and terrible breath.

The dropped kettle rolled down the slope, a trail of sparks tumbling from its rim. Somehow he still clutched the flaming branch and it was this he thrust up as the bear exploded from the earth and ran at him as fast as he'd ever seen anything move. The animal, with a further horrible shriek, grappled the branch to itself, its jaws snapping the wood, scythe-claws ripping it into a cascade of sparks in seconds; seconds that yet allowed Jack to roll completely over in a backwards somersault, slide on the icy rock till his feet encountered the earth of the forest floor, somehow getting a purchase there. His first paces were to one side, then to the other; then, somehow, he was in the forest, stumbling forward.

He couldn't look, his vision blurred along with all memory – what the hell was he searching for on the path ahead? Then, just before he hit it, he remembered, his front leg rising to clear the foliage-covered rope by a foot, his trailing leg doing so by half that. He crashed down, slid along, contrived somehow to flip over, his legs scrabbling on contact with earth and snow.

The bear must have been a claw's flick away at that leap, for it was near on top of him now, rising on its hind legs, opening those horrific jaws to roar once more. It stepped forward, a pace, another, its shin pushing against the rope.

It's going to work, Jack thought. *Bugger, it's going to work!*

Then there came a snap, the whistle of tension released as the sapling shot up, the stake driving hard . . . into the bear's shoulder.

There was a moment of near silence. The bear suddenly looked almost human, puzzledly turning its face, paws rising to the wood embedded in its flesh. Then it jerked the stake from the wound, placed it in its mouth, shredded it. In a second, it had turned back to the prone man.

'*Jesus!*' Jack yelled, pushing himself to his feet, staggering back, colliding with a tree. Once more the creature roared, the note soaring higher . . . when a tomahawk suddenly sprouted from its back.

'Yah!' yelled Até, triumphant. Yet the bear just glanced in the direction the weapon and yell had come from, shrugged, as if it had been bitten by something small, then swung the huge head back to Jack once more.

As the bear moved forward, Jack pulled the leather bag from around his neck, hurled it. The bear batted it aside and came on. There was no time to curse, to do anything other than swing round the tree and run. His own tomahawk, thrust into his breeches, he did not even reach for. He thought of leaping into a tree, scrambling up, but even in his panic he knew that if the bear was twice the runner he was, he was assuredly three times better the climber.

The bear chased Jack, Até chased the bear, the three in a line back up the slope, Jack hurdling branch and bush, the only thing keeping him ahead of the bear, who crashed into the vegetation, through it, roared at it. He had no idea where he was going, was surprised when he saw the kettle again, when he leapt over the gash of the bear's cave. Beyond it was the chasm, wider, surely, than any leap. But the bear's breath on his back gave him no choice.

'Aah!' he yelled, sailing into space. He hit the lip on the far side, wasn't far enough on it to get a purchase; hands grabbed at tufts of weed, jerked them out by their shallow roots. He slipped off the edge . . . and his foot encountered a branch, some bush clinging to the cliff face; his other foot followed and one hand he wedged into the smallest of cracks up above.

The bear came. He heard it, felt it as it made the same leap he had, felt the vibration as its feet thumped onto the cliff's edge beside his hand. He closed his eyes. There were two ways to go now: up into the bear's mouth and claws, down into the chasm. He knew which he preferred.

Then, just before he released his grip, there was another roar, higher-pitched, along with the sound of claws scrabbling on stone. Then something banged into him, forcing him against the rock, nearly dislodging him. He felt a sharp pain in the back of one leg, as if someone had run razors down it. And then there was silence save for the sound of something snapping below him.

At first, all he heard then was his own gasping. Then footfalls slapped on the stone behind him and a voice came. Oddly, it took a moment to realize who was speaking because the Mohawk had never used his name before.

'Jack! Jack!' he yelled. Jack heard feet withdrawing, then running. In a moment, there was another thump from near his face and he looked up to see, first moccasins, then a hand.

'Jack!' Até was bending, grasping him by the wrist. He found it hard to dislodge his fingers, so tightly did they grip the rock, but Até pulled and soon he was sprawling beside the Native. 'We did it, Jack! We killed *Ne-e-ar-gu-ye*.'

'We . . . we did?'

Jack pulled himself up, peered over the cliff edge. On the fissure floor, about thirty feet below him, a huge shape sprawled, motionless. 'Well, kiss my arse,' he said.

'Maybe later,' said Até. It was a time of firsts: the name and then this grin widening on the broad brown face. Jack found one to match it and suddenly they were both giggling, then laughing, then roaring.

'I think I call you by Iroquois name from now on: "*Sagehjowah*." It means "Man Frightened". Your face, when bear pulled stake from shoulder . . .'

'Not very noble, is it? Can't you come up with something a little more . . . spirited?' Now he was laughing Jack didn't want to stop.

Até shrugged. 'You *were* fast. You run, you jump, you leap . . . this!' He pointed to the chasm whose width, contemplated, made Jack shudder. 'I know! I call you "*Daganoweda*".'

'And what does that mean?'

' "Inexhaustible". You like?'

'It'll do.' Euphoria passing, Jack realized it was a name he was already not living up to. He was exhausted . . . and very, very hungry. He may have survived; but the bear, whose death meant they might survive, was now lying far below them. 'So,' he said, 'what do we do with him now?'

Até rose, ran along the edge, down the slope, vanished. A moment later he reappeared, walking carefully beside the narrow stream along the chasm's base. When he got to the bear he bent and cautiously toed the animal before removing the tomahawk still lodged in the beast's back. Then he looked around him.

'Bad?' called Jack.

'No, good. Good!' Até waved his weapon at the rock face. 'I do not know how you call this . . . a place in the rock. With . . .' He mimed a covering. 'We can do what we need here, better than up there.'

Jack straightened, groaned. He hurt in so many places, not least beneath the blood-lined rents the bear's claws had made in his leggings. 'And what *do* we do?'

Até's grin returned. 'You may be "Inexhaustible". But Até-dawanete means . . . well, the closest in your tongue is "Clever Moccasins". Now I show you how *I* got my name.'

– SEVEN –

A Dozen Things to Do
With a Dead Bear

'Now what?'

Seven days after the slaying of the bear, and this was the first time he'd seen Até idle. Jack found it unnerving, especially since it was also the first time he'd been similarly unoccupied. He would have preferred another growled order, that he could grumble at, yet fulfil, for there was reassurance in every assigned task completed. Jack had begun to believe that they might, *might*, survive. The initial, terrible hunger had been sated. Yet now, with another storm wailing outside their shelter, Até was doing nothing. Except stare at him.

He stared back, awaiting a reply to his question, expecting none. Indeed, he'd have been shocked if the other had spoken. It appeared that casual conversation was not something in which an Iroquois indulged. Até was not exactly rude; with questions he would reply in as short an answer as possible. Yet he seemed to have no curiosity to match Jack's own. Jack had learned that his reasonable English was due to his being a nephew-in-law of a famous landowner in the Mohawk Valley, William Johnson, and that Até had been a favoured child, whose education Johnson had overseen and whose capture on the first raid of the war would have caused the white father much sadness. Beyond that, he was unforthcoming, with replies growing ever terser while questions simply never came.

Exhaustion contributed; but the euphoria they'd shared after the kill had evaporated rapidly. The growled order, the grumbled response had become their only communication.

It's going to be a long winter, thought Jack. He'd learned that the Mohawk regarded it as a matter of pride to stare him down and the night before they had remained locked for an hour until Jack had decided it was stupidity itself. So he looked yet again, around the walls, seeking anything to distract. Every square foot was filled with bits of bear. The Native had rendered the animal into an astonishing array.

'In Cornwall, we say, "use every part of the pig but the squeal." Reckon you don't even waste that much of a bear,' he'd said. Até had just grunted, as immune to praise as insult, another conversation still-born; but looking around now Jack realized that if the Mohawk had contributed the brain for what they'd done, much of the brawn came from the Englishman for it was his labour that had created the shelters in these two shallow caves at the foot of the precipice where the bear had fallen. While he did so, the Mohawk had turned the one into a charnel house, so besmeared with blood and body parts did it become. Once Jack had helped hang the bear's bound feet from a jagged outcrop on the cavern wall, Até had set him an endless succession of tasks. First, a fire was laid on the floor and a huge pile of fuel for it chopped and fetched. Then the entrance had to be closed off to keep warmth in and winter out, and Jack lost count of the trips he made, taking fire to the forest on the plateau above, using it to burn small balsam firs till he could hack through the charring and then drag the trimmed trunks down, to be propped against the cliff face and woven with thick hemlock boughs, gradually closing the butcher's cave off. It was hard work for both of them but they were goaded by a louring sky that warned of more snow. The hanging bear – a disturbingly human shape now it had been skinned – was full of winter fat that filled the kettle fast and was then ladled off to cool in hollowed birch trunks for *pemmican*. In four small oblong cedar frames, Até bored holes with bear tooth, then pulled through some of the stringy guts, knotted their ends, leaving them to dry in a webbing. Jack recognized the racket shape of them, knew that they were shoes like Jote had used, for the traversing of snow. Next Até had taken a supple piece of curved yew, cut notches in each end and fastened a length of drying gut into it. 'Bow,' he'd muttered. Then he began on the tanning of the hide, stretching it on a larger frame he bent from saplings. The two of them spent the whole day in their abattoir in silence, both naked, save for breech clouts, the heat inside so intense they often had to go outside and stay out there till the cold nipped their extremities. Then it was fast back to Hades.

On the third morning the snow had started, light enough flurries for Até still to send Jack out, clothed now, to gather some final necessities. 'For eating just meat will kill us, pretty damn quick,' he'd said, adding his favourite phrase. Cattails were dug up whole by their roots and brought back in sheaves; a root he knew no name for in English was gathered, along with thousands of tiny seeds, which Jack wrapped in giant leaves he found on the pond's edge. He'd pulled up whole plants with clover-like leaves and red berries, both tasting similar to wild mint. With the snow driving harder, he'd strayed up to a small lake, lured by another strand of cattails. By the time he'd gathered them, the snow was blinding and he stumbled in the rough direction he sensed he should take until he nearly fell off the edge that had doomed the bear. When he'd staggered into the living space, Até was stacking bits of bear against the wall. 'About time, white boy,' he'd grunted. Then he'd pulled the balsam door into place.

For seven days and nights the wind had screamed and driven snow against their shelter; they'd gone outside only to clear it from the entrance, relieve themselves, fetch firewood from their pile or duck into the other cave – for its flames had to be fed too, to continue the drying out of the hide, which Até rubbed every day with a rancid *mélange* of bear brains and wood pulp. Soon implements of every description awaited the day when they could venture out. Strands of the rope, peeled down, were tipped with small bones as hooks, for the lake might have perch to be fished for through the ice. Larger bones transformed to tools; a shoulder blade became a shovel, a thigh bone a hammer. Teeth became needles to sew the hide Até finally judged ready, which was transformed into two coats, the fur facing in, cattail down stuffed in for a lining, smaller teeth becoming toggles to close them.

But the bear provided hazards too. However useful its guts, their own seemed unwilling to part with any ingested till Até brewed up a concoction of berries and white cedar pulp that had them outside for freezing minutes, groaning in snowdrifts. And the coats were infested with fleas.

Aye, a very long winter, Jack now thought again, scratching hard at his chest, his head, his legs. Then he reached into one of his yew trays, pulled out a fingerful of bear grease, rubbed it on the worst of the inflammations. It soothed . . . and it warmed. What remained on his fingers, he sucked off. His detestation of the taste had only lessened because it was no more disgusting than many of the bear bits he'd eaten in the last few days. Indeed, compared to colon, it was positively bland!

He reached for another fingerful, heard a grunt. He looked up, again met Até's disapproving stare. Deliberately pulling up two fingers of the crystalline grease, he waved them at Até before he licked. Then he stood up, 'I am going out,' he declared.

'Why?'

'Why do you think?'

'Bring wood,' the Mohawk said, his most common order.

'Yes.'

Then Até surprised him. 'And don't get lost.'

'I won't,' he replied, lifting the bough door out of the way.

Well, Jack thought, that was almost a conversation.

He replaced the door, stood before it, shuddering. Though a bollock-puckering wind funnelled down the canyon, finding the many gaps in his attire, it was not snowing, though he suspected only a brief respite. They'd had to clear the front of their cave three times already with their shoulder-blade shovels to prevent entombment.

Usually a dried-out tributary, a short stagger from the entrance, acted as their latrine but it had lately become treacherous with icy turds and anyway, now he was out and the snow abated, he felt he'd like to venture a little abroad. Anything to be away from the cave and its taciturn inhabitant, whose stares and silences Jack was beginning to find threatening. Also, he was starting to experience some odd things in there. Only that morning he was sure his *pemmican* had tasted of 'curry cooked in the Indian way' while the stream water had a distinct savour of London Porter.

He followed the canyon out, climbed to the plateau above, the land where the bear chase had occurred. Putting his back to the wind, he began pissing, idly amusing himself by attempting to draw his initials in a snow bank.

Something drew his eye, something dark standing proud from the white. Tucking himself away, he moved to it. It would not come to a tug so he began scraping at the frozen snow with a stick. It took a little while but eventually the bag that he'd stolen from the church in St Francis lay before him. The frozen opening gave to his pressure with a crack; he reached within and pulled out an ice block.

'*Hamlet, Prince of Denmark,*' he read aloud. Under this was the inscription his mother had written in her strong hand.

'*All truths are within. Seek them out, sweet prince.*'

He smiled sadly, thinking of his mother dining alone at Curzon Street, waiting for news of her two men, gone to war. Then he suddenly remembered something else about the volume and, blowing carefully upon it, he peeled back its ultimate page.

There it was, where he had pasted it, the scrap of paper that had wrapped Clothilde's last gift to him, the half-shilling that the Abenaki had stolen, her last words written upon the paper: '*La moitié de mon coeur.*'

He looked up, eyes wide, careless of the freezing wind. He wasn't there anyway but back in Thrift Street, whispering secrets across the table while his feet met hers under it, concealing all from her father a room away; her father and the man beside him, Claude the apprentice . . . now Claude, partner in the house of Guen and husband . . .

He was back in the forest and his tears ran in icy trails down his cheeks. The wind began driving harder, bringing more memories and the new snow.

Até grunted as he came in. 'You forgot wood.'

He had. 'I'll g . . . g . . . go later,' he said, making for the fire, his fingers agonizing as warm blood returned. Then, flopping down on the boughs that served as his bed, he reached again into the bag. Holding the volume out to the fire, he sought to thaw both it and himself.

There was stirring opposite. Jack could feel the tension as the Mohawk strove not to speak. 'What's that?' he said finally.

Lawks, thought Jack, that is a question!

'Book,' he replied. The Mohawk was not the only one with monosyllables.

Silence again. He put another cedar log on, and the flames lapped it, needles crisping into flame. When the book felt pliable, he sat back. The page crackled as he opened it. He read Alexander Pope's first comment: 'The story was not invented by our author. Tho' whence he took it, I know not.'

The long silence ended. 'You went to book shop?'

A question *and* a joke?

'It was in the bag from St Francis.' He flipped another page.

This silence was shorter. 'What book?'

'It's a play. *Hamlet* by William Shakespeare. You know what a play is?'

'I know,' the Mohawk snapped. There was a longer pause. 'But I never seen one.'

'Really? Pity.'

Suddenly, Até leaned forward. 'You read it to me.' It was not a request.

Jack lowered the book, swiftly. 'Why should I? Did you agree to teach me Iroquois when I asked you to?' Jack had seen it as a way of passing their time but Até had scoffed at the suggestion.

'No. But since I speak English, you had nothing to trade.' He pointed. 'Now you do.'

Jack considered. The wind had increased in volume, snow was driving again against their walls. Winter was fully here, and far nearer its beginning than its end.

'I will read it to you. And you will teach me Iroquois.'

Até moved over to his side of the fire. 'I do not know much reading,' he mumbled. 'So you show me words, too?'

After a moment, Jack nodded and the Mohawk put out his hand, gently took the book. He looked at it from every angle, as if it hid secrets. 'What kind of story is this?' he said finally.

Jack considered. 'A ghost story,' he said at last.

Até dropped the book. 'Ghost. We call him "*Iakotianer-onhstha*". He comes from the Village of the Dead, to steal souls.' He shivered, hunched into himself. '*Iakotianer-onhstha* . . . ghosts . . . are bad.'

Jack picked the play up, dusted ash from the spine. 'You are wrong. For our purposes, ghosts . . . are good.'

The wind suddenly caught something, a jag of rock, a bough. A voice seemed to form out there, howled, trailed off. Another replaced it and another on a lower note. Até shivered but Jack knew it was not from the cold. The Mohawk never shivered from the cold.

Smiling, he looked down to the first line. ' "Who's there?" ' he whispered.

Até looked outside, startled still by the voices in the wind.

Then he saw that Jack's finger moved across the page. He peered closer.

'*Onhka non we*,' Até intoned in Iroquois.

'Who's there?' they asked, together, each in the other's language.

— EIGHT —

Undiscovered Country

From behind the silver birch, watching the near-naked man stride to the centre of the snow circle, Jack began to shiver ever more violently. Rubbing his hands together, shrugging deeper into his bearskin coat, he mused, yet again, on the power of words.

They had transformed the man before him. When engaged on the mundane tasks of survival Até was still taciturnity itself; here, in the arena they'd fashioned from tree stumps and snowmen, the Mohawk was verbosity incarnate. He had fallen in love with language.

'Words. Words. Words.' That's what Hamlet said to Polonius's enquiry as to his reading matter. Yet the joy for Até – and, it had to be admitted, for Jack, too – was in seeing how differently those words could be interpreted. Even that very line, that Jack saw as a weary dismissal, Até infused with individual meaning. '*Owen'na . . . Owen'na? Owen'na!*' he'd bellow, a statement, a question, a furious challenge.

It was only one of the many contrasts in their respective performances – as Até now began to illustrate with his stamping, clapping rendition of 'To be or not to be'; or '*Akwekon katon othe:non tsi ne'ken*' as Iroquoian had it. Jack recited the soliloquy as an internalized reflection both on death and the demands of action; Até played it directly to God, a summons to arms.

Jack sniffed. Até, as usual, was ignoring the verse, his voice swooping through octaves. Yet despite the fractured pentameter – as Até now began to question God directly, one moment prone in a whisper, then leaping with a shout – Jack found himself moved, as even David Garrick had failed to move him. Até had said that his people spoke exactly so in their councils and that Shakespeare was thus the most Mohawk of authors. And Jack had finally, grudgingly, come to admit that though he had made rigorous study of rhetoric at Westminster, he doubted if any Roman had ever harnessed the power of that art as skilfully as the shaven warrior before him now.

A large drop of iced water detached itself from the branch above him, ran down inside his bearskin. Is this the true thaw at last? Jack wondered. The one that sets us free? In the months they'd been there – Jack had again lost track of time, but believed it to be above five since his capture at Quebec – each time the snow had begun to melt, he would urge Até to prepare to leave; each time Até would bid him wait. Within a day, two at most, there would be another vicious drop of temperature, the world frozen again. Away from their shelter, on a path that led they knew not where, they would have died. So they would use the false dawn to scurry, finish the tasks required to survive, hunt, kill, butcher a deer, fish for perch through the ice, stockpile the wood needed for their fire, gather cattail, burdock and wintergreen berries. Then, as the wind again howled its mournful note, Até would pull the bough-door to, dust the snow from his furs, lift the, by now, much-tattered copy of *Hamlet* and say, 'Shall we play?'

Watching the man raise his arms to the sky, Jack smiled. *The Dane has kept us sane.* He had made them talk, argue, shout, sometimes – actually, often – laugh. Months of daily wrangling over words and meanings had taught Jack Iroquoian to quite a sophisticated – if somewhat specialist – level. And with the language, other aspects of the culture had come.

It had begun with the fleas. To reduce their habitation Jack had allowed his thick, black hair to be reduced to the single top-knot of a native warrior. Thus matched to the Mohawk, he'd begun to admire the delicate skin paintings Até rendered on himself – and on days when even *Hamlet* palled, other things were needed to stave off the boredom. He looked at his own tattooed forearms now, at the lines of blue-inked patterns: a diamond-backed snake; a wreath of beech leaves; a wolf's jaws curling up over his shoulder. The agony of their application had been appalling, Até dotting the trimmed porcupine quill rapidly into his skin, dipped in an ink made of ground rock, berries and blood. But, of course, he hadn't acknowledged that pain by even a grunt. You didn't give such a weapon to a Mohawk.

Jack watched him for a moment longer before slumping back. He truly was quite transported. The words had worked upon him and Jack felt he was not quite there, as if he was lost in one of his tribe's religious ceremonies – for though he claimed to be a baptized, indeed fervent, Christian, the antics Até described, and had got up to at various points during the winter, were quite unlike any service Jack had ever attended at the Abbey. Not to mention the praying he'd done over the dead bear. Thanking it, apparently, for sacrificing its life to them. If that wasn't pagan, he didn't know what was! Still, Jack had amused himself for a whole day with a vision of Sir James mumbling thus over a fox.

Jack pulled his bearskin tight, put his back against the birch, shivered once more. This would always distinguish him from the savage. They never seemed to feel any cold!

After a minute or so he heard Até stride again to the centre of the circle but he did not turn to look. It was the speech to the players next and both of them had decided that it could be delivered to tree stumps and snowmen; for the other actor, taxed with playing all the roles, needed time to prepare for the important ones to come: Claudius, the Player King, Gertrude, eventually the return of the Ghost. Jack started whispering Iroquois words to himself from the various guises he would assume. He liked the ghost best. Até was always genuinely terrified when the *Iakotianeronhstha* appeared!

It was the change of voice that halted Jack's mumbling. At first he thought Até was filling in the other parts.

Then he realized that someone just the other side of the tree was speaking French.

He lay, frozen in a different way now, trying to make out what was being said, who was saying it. It was difficult, his ear unattuned, and they spoke swiftly, two or three of them perhaps. The European tongue brought to mind one of Jack's fondest daydreams – that he would be captured by an honourable enemy, taken to the shelter and warmth of Montréal, treated well as an officer-prisoner, eventually exchanged as civilized warfare dictated. He nearly stepped from around his tree as those visions came back to him now. Then Até spoke, in a tongue he did not know but still recognized – the tongue of a slave. The Abenaki words were translated by someone else into French. Jack caught enough to know that Até was lying, saying that the English officer they'd heard about and sought had died at winter's start, that he had survived alone.

The sound of a blow followed, a harsh Abenaki voice shouted. Jack braced himself then risked a look past the tree trunk. There were three Frenchmen there, in coats of forest green – Coureurs du Bois. Até was lying in the snow at their feet, where the blow of the fourth man had knocked him.

That man was Segunki, cruellest of their St Francis' tormentors. He had come to reclaim his slaves.

Sounds came, of kicks, then of men moving away. Jack snatched another look. Two of the Coureurs had Até under each arm, were dragging him along the cliff top and down to the entrance of the little gorge, the Mohawk semi-conscious, his wrists already bound. The Abenaki, with one glance back, followed.

Jack's gaze moved frantically from tree to tree. Four against one! But what choice did he have? Surrender and there was a good chance they would fulfil his desire, take him to Montréal. He was valuable. It was one option . . . and none at all. For Até would still die, as escaped slaves did, as slowly as possible. Segunki would insist on it.

Jack rose quietly, skirting around to the left of their arena, thankful that Shakespeare was not the only thing he'd learned in the forest. Though Até rarely gave instruction, there had been competition between them from the beginning. Jack had observed the Indian, patterned himself on him, could move through the forest almost as silently now. And while he was not as accurate a thrower of the tomahawk, he was better with a bow and arrow, for Até was in love with gunpowder and thought the weapon primitive. Jack had hunted coneys in Cornwall with a bow and, in their time in the forest, had killed three deer to Até's one.

They had left their weapons to the side of the arena – performances would be interrupted if game appeared – and the enemy had not found them. Quickly slinging the bow and the deerskin quiver over his shoulder, taking a tomahawk in each hand, he moved parallel to the path through the trees. He could hear men just beginning the descent to the gorge. One man though had stopped, so Jack did too, the voices of the others fading. The Frenchman who remained went to the cliff edge, peered over.

Jack slipped from tree to tree till he was within ten paces of his quarry. He thought of the bow, dismissed it; even with a good shot the target would not die instantly, would scream, perhaps plummet over the edge, and Jack's only odds-lessening strategy – surprise – would be gone. Shrugging off the bearskin and quietly unslinging the weapons on his back, he laid them and one of the tomahawks down. Hefting the other in his right hand, he waited till he heard the voices from below disappear and, with the other men now in the first cave, he moved toward the cliff top.

He was three paces away when the man turned, so he covered those last three fast. The Coureur yelped 'Merde', not too loudly, not loudly enough, reaching to his belt, to his own tomahawk, too late. Jack struck him, not with the blade but with the blunt back of the weapon, high on the temple. The man spun backwards, instantly unconscious, following the trajectory of the blow. He was over the edge, about to plummet down, when Jack grabbed at his heavy belt. Sudden weight nearly pulled them both over and Jack desperately threw himself back, down, his feet slipping, seeking purchase in the melting snow. His moccasins ground into a lip of rock, the man swayed over the precipice . . . and Jack held him, dangling there, listening to the voices again rising up, to the feet moving along to the second cave. The sound came of the bough door being thrown down. Just when Jack thought his grip would break, he heard the last of them enter the rock face below.

He twisted the man back, tipped him to the side to fall. He didn't know if his one blow had killed, didn't take time to check. The man's fallen musket was choked in snow, and Jack didn't have time to clean it out. He thrust both tomahawks back into his hide belt, fitted an arrow to the string of the bow and dropped the quiver over his shoulder.

As he entered the gorge, voices came from their abattoir cave, sounds of more blows and a groan – Até was still alive. Whatever they'd found hadn't yet confirmed or denied the Mohawk's protection of Jack. He crouched, waiting, unsure. Then the two Frenchmen came out of their living cave. Jack waited, wondering if Segunki would also emerge. When he didn't, Jack began to run forward. Adept though he'd been with deer, he was no Robin of Sherwood, and had missed more than he'd hit. The closer he got, the better.

They heard his feet crunch on the ice and, as they turned, Jack shot. The arrows – they had made three altogether – were of shaved hickory, tipped with shaped stone. But they weren't the straightest, the crow feathers making the flights uneven. This one rose as it went, seemed to be bound for the first Frenchman's face. Then it deviated sharply right, missing him by a good foot.

Fuck. Jack reached back, fingers fumbling for the second arrow, too aware that both of his enemies had unslung their muskets, were swinging them down. He notched, pulled, let loose. There was little in the way of aiming but this arrow went straight where the other had not. It took the man on the left in the centre of his chest; he staggered back, colliding with his comrade, who was forced to step to one side before he could bring his musket to bear. Jack had dropped the bow, was running flat out now, tomahawk in hand. The man fired when he was three paces away, the noise deafening within the narrow, canyon walls. He missed.

Jack crashed into him, shoulder dipped, but the Militiaman was burly, thick-set and strong, and he braced himself, one hand flat-palming Jack in the chest, the other pulling a tomahawk from his own waistband. In a moment the two weapons rose, clacked over head, parted, rose again. His enemy's falling first, Jack ducked to the side, low, and struck at the man's leg. With an agility that belied his bulk, he dodged it, struck again, at Jack's shoulder. To save it, Jack spun out, his back colliding with the stone wall hard enough to expel air. The man, sensing victory, stepped back to give himself room to swing, stepped onto ice; weakened by the thaw, it gave and he sank to his knee. Off-balance now, he swayed and Jack, propelling himself off the wall, swung the tomahawk hard at the side of the man's head. It lodged there, and the bone-splitting force of the blow followed by the man's instant fall, sucked the weapon from Jack's grasp.

A shout made Jack, whooping great gasps of air, turn to see Segunki step out of the abattoir cave. He held a knife in one hand, its blade reddened; on seeing Jack, he dropped it, reached around and had his musket unslung and pointed in a moment.

Jack fell forward. The Frenchman with the arrow in his chest was curled around it, his hands grasping the shaft, cursing and weeping. Beside him was his musket. Jack couldn't remember if he'd fired it or not but he picked it up nonetheless and pointed it down the canyon at his tormentor.

They pulled their triggers simultaneously. Jack had no idea where the other's bullet went but he saw his own's course for it snapped the blue-dyed eagle's feather in the Abenaki's head-dress. The smoke curled between them as, almost slowly, Segunki reached up and pulled the half-feather from the headband. Jack moved quicker, first, running the three paces forward to his dropped bow, snatching out the last of his arrows, notching it. Segunki looked up from the feather at him, turned and sprinted away. He was gone before the feather had floated to the icy canyon floor.

Jack was suddenly hotter than he'd ever been. If he'd been wearing any clothes he'd have taken them off. As it was, he bent down to scoop up ice melt, rub it onto his body, his burning face. A bass drum was beating blood throughout his head and he suddenly found he was yawning, his jaw crackling with the width it was forced to. Yet there was not a trace of tiredness to him. He thought he might never be tired again.

'Monsieur? *Prend pitié. Par la grâce de Dieu, aidez-moi!*'

The whisper was startling in the silence. The Frenchman's lips were stained and bubbling with bright pink blood, he was reaching an arm out to Jack now, paralleling the arrow shaft sticking straight out from his chest. Blood made Jack think of the brightness of Segunki's blade when he came out of the cave and at the thought, he was up, weakened legs propelling him on.

He'd always thought that the bear, stripped of its hide, looked strangely human dangling upside down against the cavern wall. The body hanging there now seemed to have the same bluish-grey tone of flesh, similar sheets of blood.

'Até!' Jack cried, taking the weight on his shoulder, hoisting him so that the leather cords came off the promontory of rock above and the body slumped across his shoulder. Lowering him to the ground, he cut the ties, wincing at how they had gouged the flesh; yet looking at the deep scalp cut that gushed blood, Jack wondered if the Mohawk was not already beyond pain.

'Até! Até!' He went outside, into the other cave, grabbed a bark container, stooped to fill it with iced water. He washed away the worst of the blood, though more kept gouting from the slash. There was some deer skin tanning on cedar frames. Ripping a piece off, Jack wrapped it round the head and, as he did, the dark eyes opened.

'Daganoweda,' Até coughed, tried to sit up.

'Rest!' Jack tried to push the man down but the Mohawk resisted.

'He tried to . . . tried to . . .' Até raised a hand swiftly over his scalp in a cutting motion. 'Then he heard gunshots from outside. He said he would be back to finish . . .' Até suddenly gripped Jack's arm. It was the first time Jack had ever seen anything like fear in the Iroquois. 'Is he . . . ? Where is he . . . ?'

'Gone. For the moment, at least.'

'The others?'

'Dead. I think they are all dead.' He jerked his head to the outside.

'You killed them, Daganoweda? All of them?'

Exhaustion came then and Jack flopped down. One man on the Plains of Abraham had told him, when he'd killed for the first time, that killing never got easier. Another on that same field had told him later that it did. The second one had been right and the realization shocked.

'I did.'

They sat there for a moment, staring at nothing. Then Até

stirred, rose to his knees. Leaning forward, he took the second tomahawk from Jack's belt. 'This Abenaki . . . he may come back.'

'You cannot go after him. You are wounded.'

'This?' As he pointed to his own head, Jack saw the old Até return. 'I have had worse playing *otadajishqua*.' Tightening the bandage around his head, he got up, staggered a little, then moved to the cave's entrance. Reluctantly, Jack followed.

The Frenchman with the arrow in him had managed to crawl about ten paces, collapsing on a bank of snow, staining it red to a depth of several inches. He was still breathing, just.

As Até bent to examine him, Jack said, 'There's one above. I'm not sure I killed him. I'll go see.'

Out of sight of the Mohawk, halfway to the cliff top, Jack stopped, looked around once for any sign of Segunki, then leaned over and voided the contents of his stomach. Wiping his mouth, he carried on walking till he could see the first of the men he had struck that day, a short inspection revealing him to be definitely dead. The carnage made him think of how their day had begun, with Até's rendering of *Hamlet*. And if the Mohawk had not been allowed to finish his performance, at least this stage was as littered with bodies as any production of the tragedy.

Até returned from the forest when the sun was at its height.

'He flees fast, this Abenaki coyote, with the wind in his anus,' he said, leaning his snowshoes against the cavern wall. 'His tracks lead east, toward St Francis. But he did not come from there.'

'No?' Jack dropped another cedar shingle on the fire. He could not stop shivering.

'No. He came with *les Canadiens*. From the south-west. From Do-te-a-co, what you call Montréal. Their tracks come from there.' Até fell down beside Jack, re-tying the bloody bandage that had slipped across his face. 'I think he went to

Montréal to tell of you, a Redcoat officer in the woods, and they send these Coureurs du Bois to help take you.'

'How did they find us?'

'It seems we are close to one path from Montréal to St Francis. They cross our hunting tracks.'

'And the one with the arrow said that Montréal was two days' march.' He had sat by the Frenchman as he slowly bled to death. There was nothing Jack could do for him; but it was surprising how much the man talked, thinking that he might. 'He also said that a big army is gathering there.'

'To march north or south?'

Jack shook his head. 'No one knows . . . except Montcalm's successor, the Chevalier de Lévis and presumably some of his staff. General Murray is holding out in Quebec. Your General Amherst is mustering in the south. Who will Lévis choose to fight?'

Até sat up. 'I can go to Amherst. My uncle-by-law, William Johnson will be there. I can fight with my people.' He studied Jack's silence. 'You can come with me, Daganoweda. For we will fight your enemies too.'

'Yes.' Jack poked at the fire. 'But *my* people are at Quebec. If Lévis does march against the city, my fight is there.'

'So north or south, where will the war be?' said Até, lowering himself again. 'That is the question.'

Both young men now stared into the flames for a long moment. Then Jack spoke. 'You know, I've been sitting here thinking of another quote from that damn play. "There's a divinity that shapes our ends, rough-hew them how we will." Now I haven't suddenly converted, I hold ever to my non-belief—'

'And will burn in hell for eternity,' interjected Até placidly.

'But I do believe in . . . in destiny, in some force that propels a man along his path. All this,' he gestured to the forest outside, 'Canada, slavery, you, even bloody *Hamlet*, all have been shaping me for something. Look at me!' He ran his hand up over his shaved crown to the swinging top-knot, traced the wolfhead tattoo over his shoulder. 'A year ago I was still a schoolboy, pretending to be a Mohock. Now I am living as one.'

Até's voice was solemn. 'You have still to journey along that path before you are truly one of us. But you have come a way with my teaching. You have a name, Daganoweda. You can speak well and, in all but a bright light, you could pass for one of us. You have killed, even if you have not taken scalps as befits a true warrior. And you have saved a Mohawk's life – so now you owe a great debt to the tribe.' He overrode the objection Jack would voice to this logic. 'But you lack the one thing that would make you a warrior of the people.'

'The war cry?' Jack smiled. Over the winter, Até had tried to teach Jack the full-blooded yell that the Mohawk gave in battle, the one that his Mohocks in London had so singularly failed to render. He had not got it yet.

Até shook his head. 'You have not gone to war as one of them.'

'I know. And that's why I have been thinking about my destiny. If I went to Quebec alone, or south to General Amherst with you, I would have again to become Jack Absolute, the King's officer. A rather strange-looking one, for a while, perhaps.' He gestured to himself. 'But there is another path I could take, one where all this,' he waved again to the world outside, 'that has happened to me would make more sense.'

'A war path?'

'Aye.' Jack leaned towards the Mohawk. 'This war will be decided by which way the French march, which army they choose to fight, and neither your musket nor mine will affect that. But what if we went to Montréal and discovered the truth, then took that news north or south? Is that not . . . destiny?'

Até rose. It was rare for him to show an emotion but he was flushed with one now. 'What are we waiting for, Daganoweda? You have chosen for us a warrior's title: he who goes ahead and warns of the enemy's approach so that the warriors can gather and destroy them. In your tongue I think you call this man a scout.'

Jack rose too. 'In my tongue we also call it by another name. So I will go to war as a Mohawk . . . but I will call myself a spy.'

– NINE –

Single Spies

'There is a universal law,' declared Jack, as they walked down the Rue St Joseph toward the wharfs, 'and thus it applies as well in Montréal as in London. If you want a horse shod, you go to a farrier. To clear your bowels, you seek your emetic tartar from an apothecary. And if you want information,' he stopped before a set of wooden doors, 'you go to a tavern.'

Até grunted. It was not unusual for him to say little but his taciturnity had deepened ever since they'd first entered the city. He affected to look unimpressed, but Jack would sometimes catch his companion's wide-eyed regard for all about him. He knew that Até had visited nothing larger than a village before and though Jack could – and did – assure him that this young, provincial burgh was a shabby country cousin of his own glorious London, still the stone houses and flag-stoned courts, the Seminary Gardens, the walls and bastions, the heaving port with its thousands of civilians and soldiers, all intimidated the Mohawk. It pleased the Englishman; for no matter how advanced Jack's forest skills had become, Até was always the leader there. In the city, it was clearly the reverse.

Yet even Jack baulked at the tavern doors. For near six months the only humanity he'd seen – aside from the men he'd killed – was a single Mohawk, the loudest noises the crackle of a fire and the odd piece of shouted Shakespeare.

Here, those doors opening transformed a drone into a roar. Scores, possibly hundreds of men – and some women – shoved and jostled around barrels set upon planks. In one corner flames heated cooking pots; in another, two fiddlers sawed, the space before them cleared by the abandoned leaping of drunken men. For months, the main scents in his nostrils had been bear fat and wood smoke. Here he was assaulted by waves of intense and varied odour, chicken stew, perfumed bodies a season beyond a bath, heady shag tobacco, the monstrous sweetness of warmed rum. It was almost overpowering, even for a Mohock of Covent Garden; Jack hesitated, half-heartedly seeking some passage through the mob, until a shove in his back propelled him to a space barely there and he and Até became the head of a wedge of Canadian Militia in their distinctive knitted blue caps, all baying for booze, all shoving straight for the central table.

A silver coin secured them some rum and a plate of the stew. Prices were high in a city running low of everything after a long winter. Yet he had two more coins in his pocket, Até having shot a doe on their march in. The animal was the start of their fortune, sold to a harried army cook who had pointed them toward this wharf-side tavern; for while most in Montréal were reserved for townsmen, *habitants* and soldiers, and did not admit France's Indian allies, here the landlord was part Abenaki and wholly commercial. He'd let in anyone, the cook had told them, so long as they had silver and throw 'em out as soon as it was spent.

A portion of bench cleared as two men rolled onto the ground in the harmless fight of the very drunk. Jack and Até won the race to the hard wood and sat, laying their muskets and sacks at their feet. The first sip of rum, howsoever sickly sweet, was still like elixir to Jack. He closed his eyes, imagining himself back in London; opening them again, it took an effort to realize he was not indeed at Derry's Cyder House on Maiden Lane where, a lifetime before, he had fallen foul of Craster Absolute's schemes and too much arrack punch.

Fiddles whined, laughter brayed, men fought for women, for booze, for the hell of it. But the differences were clear: in the white uniforms of the regular French soldiers; in the caps of the Militia; in the top-knot bouncing over the plate of stew as Até slurped it back; in his own as he flicked it aside and bent to his eating. And there was a larger contrast between the taverns with an ocean between them, for here he had purpose beyond pleasure. It was this purpose that made him shake his head when Até indicated for another rum. One had made him light-headed enough after his winter of enforced sobriety.

Their brief time in the Iroquois camp outside the city's ramparts had yielded no more than conflicting speculation voiced as fact: the army was marching north against Quebec before the snows melted; it was marching south against General Amherst when they did; it was staying where it was. So Jack had gained little, except confidence. With his natural Cornish darkness, his tattoos, his clothes and a berry stain Até had concocted and rubbed over his head, neck and shoulders, Jack had successfully passed himself off as Mohawk. His accent was credible, apparently; even with its tendency to slip into iambic pentameter.

But it was his French he needed now. Somewhere in this crowd had to be someone who knew more or knew someone who did. Até moved off among the small groups of Natives with a jug of tongue-loosening rum, Jack taking its twin to some white-clad soldiers, who were both surprised at his speaking and contemptuous of his person. *Les Canadiens* were less prejudiced, many faces showing nearly as much Native ancestry as European. He was accepted among them, not least for the free liquor he dispensed. And once he'd listened to the inevitable stories of soldiers anywhere – the stupidity of officers, the poverty of equipment, the heartlessness of whores – he at last found someone happy to talk of other things. Indeed, boast of them.

In one corner sat a Frenchman who had obviously not spent the winter in a cave or under canvas. Corpulent and pink-skinned, his civilian clothes had been washed at least once in the last months and sported the odd dandified embellishment – a handkerchief protruding from a pocket, a silk collar. A horsehair wig sat atop a jowly and pockmarked face. Among the soberly clad and grimy *habitants*, he was a peacock among pigeons.

And he could talk. Not converse, just lecture, in an accent that was clearer to Jack than the guttural patois of the provincials; he was from the Old Country. And while he dispensed rations from the large jug sat before him, men were content to receive the words along with the rum. Jack was all set to pass the braggart by when a name, repeatedly flourished, drew him in. He was rewarded with a particularly large smile, a wink and a tot of rum, which he surreptitiously tipped to the floor. Then he just listened.

'You see, messieurs, while I would agree with you about most generals, the Chevalier de Lévis is different. He will listen to men of experience, men of intellect . . . well, men much like myself. Only yesterday he deferred to me over a matter of artillery. For you know, messieurs, that that was my branch. Before I received my wound.'

With a sigh of a martyr, he patted at his shoulder, stirring up a cloud of fine white powder there. He then tipped the dregs of the jug into his own pewter, raised it to the company. 'To the nobleman who has paid for our conviviality this night: my employer and, may I say, my friend – the Chevalier de Lévis!'

The audience barely joined in the toast to their commander before, sensing an end to hospitality, they went to seek it elsewhere. The dandy sighed as the crowd dispersed, reached to place his empty vessel on the table . . . where Jack intercepted it, slopping in some rum.

'Why, thank you, my lad.' He slurped, belched and refocused on Jack. 'My,' he said, his voice lowering to a whisper, 'but you're a handsome brute. Where do you come from?'

He spoke as an adult does to an especially dense yet

favoured child. Jack responded tersely to cue. 'Oswegatchie,' he replied, naming one of the main settlements of Canadian Iroquois who fought for France, then went on in a French he was careful to break up, 'I come to kill Englishman. Many kill I yesterday!'

The fat man gave an indulgent smile. 'I am sure you did. And the Great Father Lévis has paid you well for the scalps so you can buy rum, eh?' He nudged his tankard against the jug, and Jack nodded and duly poured a hefty tot, which was duly drained. The next words that came were still slower and more slurred. 'And may I be honoured with your name?'

'Daganoweda.'

'Hubert.' He inclined his head, shedding more powder. 'And who taught you such excellent French, *mon brave*?'

For a moment Jack was tempted to say, in his finest accent, 'A young lady above a goldsmith's shop in old London Town,' just to see the shock it caused. Instead, he replied, 'Black Robe, at village. Me, altar boy.'

'Altar boy, eh?' A gleam came into eyes already fired by rum. Then Hubert dropped a hand onto Jack's thigh, squeezed gently and spoke a phrase not directly translatable but understandable nonetheless.

Jack was not unacquainted with such advances. He doubted there was a Westminster boy who was. And though there had been the usual boarding house fumblings of youths stumbling into manhood, as soon as he was offered the alternative, Jack had wholeheartedly chosen women. Yet though the resting hand began moving up his deerhide breeches, Jack was careful to keep his face neutral. And when the hand reached his upper thigh, Jack dropped his own upon it.

'No?' The word came out on a purr. Jack shrugged, looked around. 'Yes,' the Frenchman continued, 'it is a little crowded here.' He gestured with his eyes to the door and Jack immediately got up and started to push through towards it. Até was moving to intercept him but, at the slight shake of Jack's head, merged again into the mob.

From fetid warmth they were plunged into a damp chill. It did not seem to affect Hubert. As soon as the door closed, he slid into Jack, his hand reaching to the place it had sought before. Jack's closed over his wrist, held him firmly a few inches away.

'My, but you're a strong one,' Hubert breathed. 'Shall we slip into that alley?'

'Too cold.'

The Frenchman looked annoyed. 'I thought you savages never felt the cold?'

Jack guided the hand to his upper thigh. 'Need present, too.'

'Present? Ah, of course.' Hubert reached into one pocket, then another, then sighed. 'Present later. Tomorrow.'

'Now,' Jack said, letting the hand slip up a little.

Hubert swayed there, caught. It was obvious he had spent all he had inside. 'Very well,' he said suddenly, straightening. 'You come with me, my handsome lad. But you'll be silent, yes?' He reached out, stubbed a grimy finger onto Jack's lips.

Jack followed the stumbling figure away from the tavern, aware that the doors opened and closed behind him. Até? The sky had cleared, a half-moon and starlight reflecting off the snow-packed street. As they advanced away from the wharf towards the Seminary, the houses began to get gradually grander. Soon, there were especially high walls, some impressive, ornate gates; they halted before a small postern. 'Quiet!' Hubert ordered, before knocking softly. After a moment, there was a shuffling from within. The lock screeched, the door opened, a lantern was swung out.

'Hubert?'

'It's me.'

Two soldiers in greatcoats stood there. The one in front yawned, stepped aside. 'Come in, then, and let me get back to my fire.'

'Is the chevalier still with his colonels?'

'Yes, gabbing away. And until he finishes we can't get any

sleep.' He yawned again then, as Hubert moved past, saw Jack. 'Shit! Who's that?'

'Just a friend.'

The lantern was raised and Jack squinted into a light that moved up and down him. 'What's the matter, Hubert? Navy not in town?'

The other soldier sniggered and Hubert came and drew Jack in. 'You know how the chevalier says we must reach out to all our Native children. I am merely obeying his commands.'

The hitherto silent soldier muttered, 'And our commands say no one comes in tonight.'

'Not even a friend?' Hubert reached inside his coat. Jack hadn't seem him secrete the jug of rum he now handed over. The soldiers only hesitated a moment. Taking it, the gruff one said, 'Twenty minutes, Hubert. That's all. Just make sure you bring him out to us then.'

A huge key was turned in the massive lock and the soldiers returned to a little hut beside the door. 'Come then,' said Hubert.

Jack, finding that he'd stopped breathing, started again. This was beyond anything he could have hoped for! Hubert, who had taken his arm, was drawing him up a path towards the side of a large stone house. From the talk at the gate, within that house lived the commander of the French army.

The side door opened onto a large kitchen, unpeopled, yet probably only recently so, for chickens dripped on a spit and something bubbled in cauldrons. Tugging still, Hubert led him up three flights of narrow stairs and into a low-roofed room that was well furnished with an armoire and a wood-framed bed. Hubert was obviously quite a senior household servant.

The Frenchman moved to the bed, threw back the coverlet. Turning back to Jack, reaching to his belt, he smiled. 'You must be swift, my savage,' he said. 'Brutally swift.'

'Oh, you may be sure,' Jack said in English.

'Eh?' was all the loquacious Frenchman could manage, just before Jack hit him.

He glanced back from the doorway. Perhaps Hubert would not have been averse to the arrangements – his hands tied to the head posts, his feet to the frame – though he might have objected to the gag, and he would probably have preferred to be conscious.

The slitting of sheets and binding had taken time, probably half the twenty that had been allotted for the act of love, so Jack did not hesitate. Servants' quarters were always elevated, in French houses as well as English; the masters' would be on the ground floor, so this conference of colonels the guards had spoken of had to be taking place there. Lurking inside the stair door, he waited till the kitchen was empty, following the servants who departed with their loads of chicken, stew and bread. He blessed his luck again, for the traffic was one-way, leading down a long passageway into a brightly-lit entrance hall. The main doors of the house gave onto it, as did three other sets of internal doors. As Jack eased into an alcove bulging with bearskin coats – a smell he knew well – one of these sets of doors opened, and a group of men emerged. At their head was a compact man in a tight-fitting blue-gold uniform.

'Supper first, gentlemen,' he declared. 'My rule is never to make important decisions on an empty stomach!'

Soldiers and civilians passed in hard debate. When the last of them had entered what must be the dining room, when the last of the servants had crossed back to the kitchen passageway, Jack moved swiftly across the room they'd come from.

It was empty. Stepping swiftly in, he pulled the heavy door closed behind him and turned. Shelves bearing sheaves of papers stretched up one wall; ledgers occupied the one opposite. A huge fireplace gave out some heat that yet could not account for how damnably hot he suddenly felt, with sweat on his forehead and his breath shallow. Moving to the tall windows, he found the catch, threw one up. Cool air calmed and he turned back to his study. At the room's centre stood a huge desk, chairs pushed back around it. The top of the desk was covered in parchment sheets, among which ornate silver candlesticks stood out like islands in a paper sea. With a nervous glance at the door, Jack moved to study the documents.

They varied from close scrawled, almost illegible sheets, to ones with barely a sentence upon them. Forcing himself to breathe and concentrate – he found he'd forgotten every word of his French – he bent to study one of the plainer ones. It seemed to be a tally of one of the *troupes de terre*, the French regular regiments. This one, the second battalion of the Régiment Languedoc, seemed to have about 480 soldiers with just 50 listed as *malade*. Since the date was 23 April – yesterday – if true, it meant this regiment was remarkably close to full fighting strength.

Other tallies provided similar figures. Though it seemed that some of the battalions had made up their numbers by drawing from the Militia, which would mean a consequent drop in effectiveness, if these figures were accurate, they gave account of an army that was remarkably strong after a brutal winter. The tally of regulars came close to four thousand. He suspected that the British at Quebec would muster considerably less. The French also had that Militia and, of course, their Native allies.

From the moment they'd entered Montréal, he'd had no doubt the chevalier was planning an offensive and soon. But where was this army to be aimed? North or south? Aware that his sand glass was fast running out, still hot despite the cold air from the window, Jack scanned the mass of paper with increasing agitation.

A shout of laughter startled from beyond the door, together with the noise of pewter mugs being clinked, then slammed down. Jack moved towards that open window. When the noise subsided to a rumble, he stepped back, began to search ever more urgently through the papers.

There were too many of them. He couldn't read them all, not in this increasingly foreign tongue, while place names he expected – Quebec, Ticonderoga, Oswego – all leapt out at him and confirmed nothing. Then, suddenly, the volume of voices doubled; the other door had opened and footsteps now moved across to his own. He half stepped to the window, glanced back . . . and saw it, the corner of an inked, wavy line. Jerking the parchment out from under all the others, sight confirmed his guess. It was a map, almost identical to the ones that had littered Wolfe's desk in September. For at that time, Wolfe was planning exactly what the Chevalier de Lévis was obviously planning now – a landing by boat to assault the city of Quebec.

The door opened, he dropped the paper back but even as he stepped again towards the window, Jack could not remove his gaze from the map. For at the top was scrawled in French what looked like a tide chart with various times and dates. One was circled. He may have felt his language skills to be failing him in recent moments but this was certainly clear: on the 26 April – three days' time – the French army would be landed at Point aux Trembles above Quebec.

'Sacred Jesus! What are you doing there, you dog?'

The young French officer had a tankard in his left hand and was trying to draw a sword with his right. Jack stared, caught between the desk and escape. Then, in a moment of pure inspiration, he seized one of the silver candlesticks and hurled himself out the window.

The cry that pursued him was of a word even his suddenly diminished French could recognize. '*Voleur!*' screamed the Frenchman.

Better thief than spy, Jack thought, sprinting down a path he hoped led back to the side gate. Though he was fairly sure that hanging would be the punishment for both.

The two guards had been drawn by the shouting from their shelter. Both had muskets. Jack kept sprinting towards them, partly due to the iced path – if he tried to stop he'd be over – and as he ran, he drew his tomahawk from his belt. All that practice with Até had to be good for something, yet while he was fairly certain he could incapacitate one of the guards he had no idea what he would do about the other.

At ten paces, as the muzzles before him levelled, he jerked to a sudden, sliding stop, bent back and hurled his blade. He watched it travelling forward and thought, for the tiniest of moments, how odd it was that the whirring of the flung weapon seemed to come from right beside his ear, oddity increasing as he saw two tomahawks fly down the path and strike home. Jack's hit the musket barrel even as the soldier pulled the trigger, gun exploding, bullet clipping a yew branch, man tumbling backwards. The second tomahawk embedded itself straight in the middle of the other guard's face.

Jack looked behind him as Até ran up. 'Where the hell did you come from?' he gasped.

Até jerked his head back. 'House. I climbed wall, followed you in.'

Before them, the soldier who was still alive was screaming as he ran back into his hut. Behind them, more men were shouting and bolts were being shot at the main doors.

'Time to go, Daganoweda.'

'I think you may be right.'

No key was in the gate lock so Até bent, clasped his hands. Jack hurled the candlestick over the wall, then placed his foot in the palms, scrambled up, reached down. Até grabbed and Jack drew him up and, as they were poised on top of the walls, the guard emerged from the hut and fired a pistol, the ball passing between their heads. Yelping, they fell into the night. Jack regained the candlestick and they sprinted away.

'Where we run to?' Até grunted.

'Christ knows. Somewhere to hide. I thought . . . the harbour?'

'Many white faces there. Not many brown.' Até jerked his thumb towards the hill outside the city walls, where the Native campfires glowed. 'Different up there.'

As Jack veered toward those lights he smiled. 'And maybe we can swap this,' he hefted the candlestick, 'for a canoe.'

'For many canoes.' Até slipped on a patch of ice, regained his footing, ran on. 'But which way do we paddle, once we have one. North or south?'

'North, my friend, north. And as fast as ever Westminster Sculler did scull. North, to Quebec.'

– TEN –

Encore une Fois

From the moment their canoe ground onto the shale at Anse du Foulon – the same shale he'd stepped onto from that barge six months before, just prior to the assault on the city – Jack had difficulty communicating. It wasn't that he'd latterly been speaking mainly Iroquois and some French; he remembered English perfectly well. It was just that the assorted Scots, Londoners, Ulstermen, Tynesiders, Welsh and Devonians (who Jack, ever Cornish, remembered to be a particular set of knuckly-downs) would not give him a chance to use it.

'Fucking scrounging savages!' was the term applied as soon as he and Até approached any of the piquet campfires on the beach. Each time, he'd call out, 'I'm English, damn ye!' only to be answered with thrown stones and more curses. They'd kept trying, until at last he was struck, a gash opened on his jaw. Clutching a piece of deerhide to the wound, Jack led Até back to the canoe, which they pulled up and hid beneath some bushes. 'Pox on 'em,' he said. 'If they won't let us up the Foulon road, I know another way.'

The cliff was as slippery as before but his moccasins gave better purchase than his boots had and a full moon helped. They made the cliff top in good time. But the British patrols were more frequent than the French had been, and the soldiers more vigilant, muskets levelled as they surveyed the scrub where Jack and Até crouched.

'I haven't come this far to be killed by my own army,' Jack muttered, dabbing blood from his chin. 'Let's wait till dawn.'

They didn't have to wait so long. Voices approached, speaking an unintelligible and guttural tongue, yet one Jack suddenly recognized; when he did, he also realized that the nearest figure lifting his kilt and exploding a stream of liquid into a moonbeam was someone he knew.

'For God's sake, Captain MacDonald, could you not piss somewhere else?' he asked, rising from the shadows.

The explosion of oaths, as men tumbled backwards, the struggle as those men had to decide whether to cease one activity before drawing steel made both Jack and Até laugh. Not so the indignant Scot. 'Come oot the scrog, ye bastards. Come oot or we'll plug ye, ken.'

They stepped forward and, on their appearance, the five-man patrol stepped back.

'Savages!' yelped a bulky sergeant to MacDonald's right.

'You don't seem pleased to see me, Captain MacDonald,' Jack said.

The Scot's claymore was yet aloft. 'Who the devil are ye?'

'Why, Captain, do you not recognize the man who stood shoulder to shoulder with you on the Plains of Abraham?'

MacDonald stepped closer, wonder creasing further the craggy face. 'I fought with no savages beside me, ken. No' even one who speaks English.'

'And French. Though you told me I had the accent of a Parisian whore.'

Recognition came, only increasing the wonder. 'Ja . . . Jack? Jack Absolute?'

'The very same.'

'But . . . but . . . you . . . died, out there. Howe said you cursed him most foully then rode off after the French. The only British cavalry charge that day.' The Scot gave a small smile. 'We've been singing a song about it, the whole winter through: "Mad Jamie's Boy". Needed something to keep us warm. And now you're here, raised like Lazarus and dressed like a devil.' The smile became expansive. 'By Christ, lad, ye've a tale to tell and no messin'.'

'I have and shall delight in recounting it. But there are more pressing matters to discuss now.' He took MacDonald's elbow. 'Such as the arrival of the French tomorrow?'

By the warmth of a piquet fire, made more loquacious by a tot of rum, information was swiftly conveyed, with Jack a little regretful. His plan had been to give the British a day's warning at the least; this had been reduced to hours by the French following fast in their canoe's wake.

'We made the mistake of trying to paddle against the tide and tired ourselves. We grounded to rest and wait for it to turn and then only just preceded the French upon it.' Jack held out his hands to the flames. 'But we lingered long enough to watch them begin to debouch upon the shore at Point aux Trembles.'

'Dinna fash, lad, for you've done well. We'd pulled a Frog boatman from a large piece o' floatin' ice who said he'd fallen off one of their landing bateaux. He confessed their army was landing at the Point. But some thought it a little too pat and were looking for signs o' 'em elsewhere. It's nae wonder you got such a reception on the strand.' MacDonald took Jack's arm, raised him from his crouch. 'But now I think ye must report this in person to Murray. He and I dinna get on so good since he remembers me being, first and always, Wolfe's man. If I say black, he says white and since I'd an opinion the boatman should be believed, he's chosen to think t'opposite. Come, let's to him.' They began to move away along the cliffs toward the city walls, bulkier shadows within the first light of dawn. 'And as we walk, ye can tell me of the enemy's strength. Ye mentioned ye'd scanned their tallies, nae right?'

By the time they entered through the postern by the Glacière Bastion and were marching up toward the looming mass of the

Ursuline Convent over which the Union Standard flew, Jack, with Até adding his observations from his own wanderings in the French bivouac lines, had appraised MacDonald of all they knew.

'That means Lévis has nigh on double our numbers. For many have died here during this awful winter, and most of those that remain are sick from the bloody flux and the bloody gruel we've called food. We're nae in a good state, ken.'

Jack had already noticed. Most of the soldiers they passed were urchins in uniform, gaunt limbs protruding from over-large coats. In contrast he and Até, with their winter diet of bear, deer and burdock root, appeared like town burghers to beggars. Yet if in some armies their leaders contrived to feast while their followers starved, this was not true of Murray. Jack remembered his features to be sharp but they had thinned to the point of caricature: his brother general, Townshend, would have made much of them upon a paper, no doubt. They reminded Jack of nothing so much as the gargoyle's mask Burgoyne had sported at the Vauxhall Pleasure Gardens, in that other life he'd led.

Murray's dourness though, had diminished not a jot. Jack's resurrection elicited no more than a grunt, his appearance in top-knot and tattoos only the muttered comment of, 'Fellow's gone Native? Seen it in India, of course. Shows a lack of Christian virtues and a weakness in the blood.' His shake of the head indicated that he'd expected nothing less.

Jack's report did, however, finally force the diminutive Scot's head up from his map table. He was silent as Jack repeated the French regimental tallies and only spoke when he confirmed those regiments' arrival. 'So the frozen Frog was being truthful. Hmm! Thought so all along.' Ignoring the obvious rolling of MacDonald's eyes, he continued, 'Then the Chevalier de Lévis will seek to cut off my outposts at Lorette,' he stabbed down at his map, 'and Sainte Foy,' he stabbed again. 'So we must sally out and withdraw them at dawn. And then,' a light finally enlivened the studiedly dull eyes, 'then we'll see if the chevalier has the balls for a real fight. MacDonald, summon my brigadiers.'

His sunken eyes dropped again to the map before him.

Jack and Até were halfway to the door MacDonald had left open when Murray spoke again. 'Cavalryman, ain't you, Absolute?'

'Dragoon, sir.'

'A dragoon without a horse is as much use to me as a cundum with patches. But your present garb and your companion,' he had failed even to look at Até during the previous conversation, 'might prove useful.' He looked up now, regarded them both keenly. 'One of the French advantages over us is their exploitation of their Native alliances. Only General Amherst in the south has many such Natives in his command, useful creatures who provide his eyes and ears and terrorize with their infernal yelps. I have only a few. Untrustworthy dogs, the lot.'

Jack was hoping that Até was not understanding all of the general's Lothian drawl. He doubted it, from the stiffening at his side.

Murray continued, 'But you and he, Absolute, you have already had a moderate success in that way. Perhaps you could continue it.'

'Sir, I would be hap—'

Murray cut him off. 'Stay outside the city. If I can, I will give Lévis a bloody nose, a quietus that may make Wolfe's victory of last September seem the paltry and fortunate thing it was. But these odds you speak of are heavy. So if I am forced to withstand a siege within these ill-prepared walls, then you must be my eyes and ears without them.' He reached up to remove his spectacles and pinch between his eyes. 'This, above all else, is your task: to give me a day's notice of any ship coming upstream and, most importantly, what colour that ship flies. For if it's the Union Standard then the Navy has won the race following the ice-melt and we will, by God and the Admiralty's good grace, be relieved. But if it's the fleur de lys at the main mast . . . well, then maybe I can get better terms from Lévis before he realizes. Is that all clear?'

It was barely a question. 'Yes, sir,' was all Jack could say.

'Good. Now go away. I've a battle to fight.'

Outside the walls of the convent, Jack turned to Até. 'I am sorry,' he began, 'about the reception that my countrymen—'

'I care nothing for that,' said the Mohawk, 'I only care that he is giving me what I missed out on when the Abenaki took me prisoner. What I most want in the world.'

'What's that?'

Até's eyes gleamed. 'A battle, Daganoweda. I am going to fight in a battle.' And on the word, he threw back his head and gave out that war cry Murray had referred to and Jack had failed to master. 'Ah-ah-ah-ah-ah-Ah-Hum!' It started on a high note, descended down the scale, then paused fractionally before ending in an explosive return to that first note. Jack, who'd heard it before, merely winced. But the town's people nearby began instant and frantic genuflections while Redcoats reached for their swords.

'"O that this too, too solid flesh would melt, thaw and resolve itself into a dew."'

Até's propensity for applying *Hamlet* to any and every situation was starting to annoy Jack. He was all for apposite quotes, but the sole connection here was the word 'thaw', evidenced by the continuous drip from the striped maples and cedars, the occasional sloughing of branches of snow that had already drenched more than one unwary soldier. The two of them, having moved away from the cliff top tree line for that reason, now rested halfway between the edge and the two blockhouses that dominated the flat ground. The soldiers could not move without orders but as the only two Iroquois fighting for King George that day, Murray's licence meant they could go where they chose, within reason. And MacDonald, in charge of the extreme right flank, had rapidly acknowledged Jack's strengths . . . and weaknesses.

'Ye're no infantryman, Absolute,' he'd said. 'So if ye've a mind to fight in feathers that's grand. Just so long as ye keep yer feet on the ground and don't go leading any cavalry charges, ken?'

Though Jack now grunted his displeasure at Até's versifying, the Mohawk merely grinned and jiggled the raven plumage he'd fashioned into a head-dress. He was as delighted as Jack had ever seen him, as much as when they'd killed the bear or when Segunki had been halted mid-scalp. If the Mohawk shook with pleasure, his wish, to take part in a pitched battle, having been granted, Jack, who had already experienced one, and on this same field, shivered. It wasn't the slush he was lying in to avoid fire so much as the dislocation. All through his life Time had played tricks on him – his inability to be punctual was just one sign of that. But that dislocation was even more clearly expressed in the scene unfolded before him now; for it was as if seven months had not passed and he'd just arrived from England.

Once more armies manoeuvred upon the Plains of Abraham. Once more he began the fight atop the cliffs above the beach. Yet what had been the British right flank then was now its left; it was the Redcoats who had their backs to the distant walls of Quebec, the white-clad French who assembled to assault them. And looking across the field now, Jack could not help but note the main difference between the days: the huge gaps between regiments and the thinness of what had anyway been a thin red line.

The windmill that stood on that far flank had been under sustained attack for an hour now, had been taken, then taken back. Their turn would be coming soon enough. MacDonald's volunteers – light infantry together with Moses Hazen's green-clad Rangers – were charged with holding the British left. They had learned from that first battle, where overlapping Canadians and Indians had caused such damage with their sniping, probably killing Wolfe himself. So they were part of a loose line that held the cliff-top scrub – Jack's second reason for

311

being there. For if the battle went badly, he needed to be close to the river, their canoe and Murray's mission.

Shouting from afar caused Jack to raise his head. Through breaks in the powder smoke and the snow that had started to come sporadically in big-flaked flurries, he could see Redcoats streaming away from the windmill, a standard with a white cross and red and gold bars raised. He saw the regiment on that far side – the 48th, he thought – 'refuse', swinging its ranks so they now formed a side to the British line, a front to the French beginning to overlap. And he saw a slight shifting in each of the regiments, passing down them in turn like a breeze disturbing rows of barleycorn.

MacDonald, ambling toward them along the line of prone bodies as if he were out for a Sabbath-day stroll in Edinburgh, distracted Jack from his bloody thoughts. 'The windmill's fallen, ye'll have seen?' To their nods he continued. 'Aye, weel, it'll be our turn next, nae fear. Lévis is no' the fool Murray thinks him. He'll no' charge our guns in the centre. He'll fold in our flanks and send us pell-mell back to town. In fact,' he raised his face into the wind and sniffed like a hound, 'if I'm no' mistaken, that's him coming now.'

The sniper fire had increased even as he spoke. Scattered figures had begun to run towards them, would squat, shoot, reload, run on. Some sported tunques, the knitted wool caps of the Militia, white and red and blue. Many, though, wore very different headgear.

'Abenaki,' said Até, pointing.

Jack could indeed see the shaved heads, painted in black or yellow blocks from crown to nose tip. Their top-knots were shorter than those of the Iroquois, with shanks hanging over their ears. 'Will our friends from St Francis be among them?' wondered Jack aloud.

'By God's grace,' said Até, fingering knife and crucifix at his belt.

Behind those darting, yelling men, more ordered ranks had formed. With a cheer of '*Vive le Roi! Vive la Paix!*', with drums thumping and standards dipping only to rise aloft, the French right flank advanced.

'Up, men,' yelled MacDonald, drawing his claymore for emphasis. 'Up and face them.'

The scattered line rose, their threadbare single rank at least meaning that the sniper fire had little effect.

'Cock your firelocks!' MacDonald bellowed. 'Present your firelocks. Now, steady, lads. Steady!'

Hazen's Rangers, out of earshot in the blockhouses, had already begun to shoot, from too great a distance to cause much harm. The French swept on.

'Fire!' MacDonald yelled.

Jack and Até discharged with the rest; several Frenchmen fell. But these were not the ranks that Jack had stood in that day in September. This was not a volley to halt an army. This was a hundred muskets at best. The white ranks merely flinched and marched on.

'*Le Roi! La France! La Paix!*'

'Thought as much.' MacDonald peered through the dissolving gunsmoke. 'I doubt the Rangers will bide long in those houses. So I'm off to bring Fraser's and Bragg's over to steady the flank. You lads take to the trees and harry them. Try to make them divert some men your way.' In a softer voice he added, 'Good luck, Absolute. There's nary another man can say he fought the Plains of Abraham twice, once as soldier and once as savage. It's too good a story for you not to live to tell it. Adieu.'

He turned, began to walk toward the red ranks some hundred yards away. He took perhaps ten paces.

'Ah-ai-ai-ai-ee-yah!' came the cry, seeming to split the mists of smoke just ahead of the running figures that actually parted them. A muddle of Militia and Abenaki ran at the gap that had widened between the cliff top and the 28th Foot. Ran at MacDonald.

'No!' screamed Jack. Already re-loaded, he dropped now, aimed, shot. A shaven figure jerked, tumbled; but he was only one of the horde that engulfed the Scot. He'd drawn his claymore again, the huge sword rising high, sweeping down, even as Jack took a step forward. But then the swirl split, the wave rolled on, leaving a body crushed on the ground like a broken Chelsea figure. For a moment, there was no one between Jack and MacDonald. He got up, ran, aware of Até following.

Donald MacDonald lay there. Or rather a part of him did, for it was obvious that the Scot's soul no longer inhabited his body.

As one set of drums beat the retreat, their sound moving away towards the city, another drew nearer, calling the advance, its rhythm punctuated by the terrible shrieks of the Native warriors. Jack now recalled what the old man at St Francis, Bomoseen, had once told him, what a Native warrior wanted from war: booty and glory. And the latter was represented by scalps. He could not let that fate befall the body before him. 'Até,' he hissed, 'play dead.'

Instantly, Até fell back onto the ground, mouth open, eyes half-shut. Jack sprawled across MacDonald's corpse. He decided to keep his lids fast. He could hear clearly enough what was happening.

French orders were bellowed. The regiment had halted where the British line had lately stood and their volley rolled over him, wrapping him in its roar. No sooner had its echo died than the advance was cried again, shod feet passing by him, over him . . . one, onto him, as an infantryman used his back as a stair, a moment of agony he managed somehow to withstand silently. Then they were gone, diminishing shudders as they moved away.

What had been a continuous roar started to break down into the individual sounds he realized he'd been hearing all the while but which had formerly been subsumed into the whole, like instruments in an orchestra. At first it was the real ones that dominated, French trumpet answering English bugle, drum for drum. Then, as these moved away with the Redcoat retreat, voices succeeded them in a variety of tones and pitches, from the bassoon-like groaning of one felled man, to the piccolo prayer of another. More joined, a chorus growing in disharmony, agony.

And then Jack heard some of those choristers cut off and he risked an eye.

Four Abenaki were moving through the bodies. As Jack watched, one bent, knife in hand. There was an increase in high-pitched prayer, a Cockney voice pleading, 'Nah! Nah! Please Gawd, nah!' then a sudden shriek, as suddenly cut off. The warrior rose, clutching something bloody, thrusting it towards the sky. 'Ah-ai-ai-ai-ee-yah!' he yelled the Abenaki version of the war whoop. Shoving his trophy into his hide belt, he and his companions moved on. Towards Jack. They were less than a dozen foot away.

Jack looked to Até, still maintaining his semblance of death, with one eye open and glazed. Now he winked it at Jack, who winked back and tightened his grip on his tomahawk.

Two of the warriors were already over them when both Jack and Até leapt up. Jack jerked his blade hard into the first Abenaki's calf. He screamed, fell back. In the corner of his vision Jack was aware of Até rising like a snake, striking.

Another Abenaki was raising a war club to strike down. Jack, on his heels hurled himself forward, arms wrapping around his opponent's legs, who struck down on Jack's back, the awkward angle sapping the club's force. Jack, with a grunt of effort, straightened his legs, lifting the man off the ground, then threw him back, his shoulder jamming hard down into the man's ribcage. Fingers reached for him, jabbing up into his face, gouging at his eyes. His hands and tomahawk pinned under the weight of them both, Jack did the only thing he could. Bit, and bit hard. The fingers pulled back, the body rolled, and Jack was free. Lifting his head back, he smacked it down on the bridge of the other man's nose. The body went limp.

A cry from behind him, something whirring through the air

above him, another body falling before him. The first Abenaki, who had held Jack's tomahawk in his leg, now had Até's in his chest.

'That's one I pay you back, Daganoweda!'

Jack, his eyes watering from the blow he'd delivered, looked through liquid to his companion. Até had taken a cut to his chest, the blood running freely to meld with the war paint. But the two Abenaki who'd come for him lay at his feet.

Jack wiped his eyes, looked swiftly around them. Others yet moved, fought, scavenged and scalped over the battlefield, none within a hundred yards. Anything beyond was hard to tell for the snow, that had drifted in occasional flurries throughout the morning, had returned in force. He suddenly realized how cold he was and he cursed his choice to imitate the Mohawk and fight with nothing but tattoos covering his chest. The chill removed all power to think.

'What now?' he said to Até.

'Now?' Até snatched up one of his recent opponents' knives, bent and lifted the Abenaki by the scalplock.

Jack looked, not to the man just about to receive the very thing he'd intended for them but to the other of Até's victims. There was something about him, something familiar. He had seen this man before.

'Wait!' he yelled, and Até paused, knife raised. 'Do you see who that is?'

Até looked where Jack pointed. It took a moment and then he dropped his intended victim stepped to the other, jerked his head up. 'Segunki!' he cried.

It was indeed their late slavemaster. The man who'd handi-capped him like a racehorse with corn cobs, who'd hung Até like meat and had begun trying to separate his hair from his head, that scar still bright on his forehead.

'So much the better.' The Mohawk's eyes gleamed. 'God has indeed favoured me.' He bent, lifted the prone warrior who gave a groan. 'Still alive! Good! Wake, dog. Wake so you know who it is who eats your heart.'

Jack, unwilling to look, was unable to look away. It was as if Até was silhouetted against a backcloth in some theatre, the smoke and snow so extraordinarily rendered it could only have been created by that young painter he'd surprised at Fanny's, Gainsborough. And how the artist would have loved the pose, the knife held just so above the scalplock, the power of Até's crouching body, the limp contrast of Segunki's. Then, just as the intended victim stirred to fulfil Até's desire, something moved behind them. The snowflakes were solidifying into snowmen.

'Até,' Jack screamed, again halting the rise of the blade. Até looked and saw too: the French reserve regiment seeking to march through them and on to the walls of Quebec.

'We must go, Até.'

'But . . .' Até had not moved, the knife still raised.

'Now!'

Reluctantly Até let the head fall. Then just as he was about to step away, he stepped back and slashed just the tip of the blade just below Segunki's scalplock. The blood was a sudden red fountain against the white.

'I will not kill him till he is looking into my eyes. But now, he and I bear each other's mark at least,' said Até, flicking the knife point up to where his own scar shone. 'And next time, one of us will die.'

The marching men were less than twenty paces away. He had no choice but to leave MacDonald's corpse and hope the French would treat it with respect. They ran, back towards the cliffs. They would have to take them again, for the enemy would have secured the beach path. If he was indeed no infantryman even he could recognize the sounds of British bugles and drum, calling the retreat. Murray had failed. Yet he had given Jack a mission should that happen. Their canoe was still hidden on the beach.

Twelve nights later, Jack and Até slipped back over the walls of besieged Quebec. They had less difficulty with the French, accustomed to seeing Natives in their camps, than the English who held the walls. But Murray had assigned an officer to watch for them at the St John Bastion and when he heard that an English-speaking Iroquois lurked without, he came rapidly.

Jack brought the news all wanted to hear. The first ship to appear in the upper St Lawrence sported the Union Standard at its main mast. And HMS *Lowestoft* was only the swiftest of the entire British fleet.

Epilogue

Montréal, September 1760

He'd always had a strange relationship with Time. And September was the month he felt that oddity most keenly. Até had noticed it, in Jack's increasing silences, in his brooding stares. He had tried to spirit him out of it on the game trail, for the British forces that now occupied Montréal needed endless fresh meat. But even hunting could not brighten Jack's darkness for long. It wasn't so much that the month was the bridge of seasons – though this autumn of 1760 had been a brief flash between a sweltering summer and the first sudden frosts of winter. It was more that memories came and refused to leave – of the September only a year before when he'd killed his first man; and of that September eight years ago when he'd still been a child and the English had finally accepted what Europe had known for two centuries – that a year had 365 days not 376. They had marked the sacrifice of those eleven days in flame and riot throughout the realm. Jack had marked it by losing an uncle and gaining parents he'd barely known he had. Eight years before, September had found him an illiterate wretch in Cornwall, wrenched him away to London. And this September found him in Montréal and took him . . .

Where? As what? He had no doubt that, with the war over in Canada, he would soon have to trade the garb of an Iroquois scout and spy for the redcoat and tricorn of an officer. But then to stay on as a garrison officer, to shiver another winter away in Quebec or Montréal? The thought made him feel nostalgic for the cave.

He sat where he always did when he was not on the trail, in the walled garden of the Seminary of St Sulpice. He liked to watch the monks moving through it, readying it for the winter that had hastened upon them. The regularity of the rows of vegetables being cleared, the ordered profusion of the herbal beds, their steady, slow movements, all calmed him, gave a respite from his thoughts. Though they had at first objected to a tattooed Mohawk in their sanctuary, his status with the conquerors – Murray had taken over half the seminary as his headquarters – and his quiet conduct within the walls had won them over. They had even started to bring him bread and stew. Sometimes he ate it, sometimes he didn't. Mostly he just sat, stared and waited for he did not know what. He knew these monks believed in Limbo, that place between heaven and hell. He had started to believe in it, too. Not as a place but as an aspect of Time. Perhaps that's what happened to those eleven days; they had come here, now, and he was stuck in them!

It had been twice that and more since the French had burned their flags and laid down their weapons in the Place d'Armes. Five months since Jack and Até had snuck over the walls of besieged Quebec and announced the inevitability of that surrender by informing Murray that the relieving fleet had arrived. The French had no choice but to raise the siege, to be chased by Murray from the north, harried by Havilland up from Lake Champlain, overwhelmed by Amherst coming down the St Lawrence. By the time he retired behind the insufficient ramparts of Montréal, the Chevalier de Lévis had less than three thousand men to oppose an Allied force of near seventeen.

Jack shivered and shifted, drawing ever deeper into his bearskin cloak. It was also coming up a year since the beast had sacrificed itself so that he and Até could live. Many times, harrying the French south, moving swiftly through the forests on horseback (they'd been issued with a precious pair because of their role as Murray's eyes and ears) he had thought of dumping the fur, for cold had been replaced by such a brutal heat, he'd thought he could never be cold again. Now he was glad he'd kept the rank thing. He didn't know what was intended for him now. It was one of the reasons he stayed close to the headquarters, so he could know of his future quickly and forsake Limbo; the general knew he was there. But if, as now seemed inevitable, he was to spend another winter in Canada, the bear might save him once again.

In the Tower, the bell sounded five and while its strident toll lingered in the air, a shape rose on top of the wall and dropped on the garden side of it. Até disdained gates, especially as the monks had once tried to prevent him joining his friend, fearing a Native occupation. He usually came to see Jack at this hour, as full of plans as Jack was lacking in them. He had met up with some of his own tribe when the Allies convened at Montréal. Jack had no doubt that, now the war was over, Até would rejoin them for the winter. Two things kept him close. Jack himself and another type of hunting. One that he was now eager to discuss when he threw himself down. He was not buried in fur, still wore only hide leggings and the blue cotton shirt he'd taken from a slain Frenchman. It made Jack cold just to look at him.

'I have found him, Daganoweda.' The Mohawk's eyes gleamed. 'I have found the Abenaki.'

This was news indeed. Ever since that second battle at Quebec, Até had regretted doing no more than mark Segunki with his knife blade. He had searched for him ever since.

'Where?'

Até, who had taken his dagger from his belt, now spat on a whetstone and began to run it down the blade, though Jack couldn't see how the weapon could get any sharper. 'My cousin, Ska-no-wun-de, tells me he sees Abenaki bringing deerskins to sell. I go look . . . fah! The dog is one of them.'

'How many?'

Até shrugged. 'He will be alone, sometime. Then . . .' Até threw the knife down into the earth of a bed of rosemary, pulled it out and began to strop it again. 'You come?'

'Yes.' At that moment, all Jack wanted to do was sit in the garden. But he couldn't let Até go alone. The Mohawk would get into trouble without him.

There must have been something in his tone that caused Até to pause in his activity. 'You . . . good now?'

'Why not?' Jack had made the mistake of trying to talk to Até about his feelings during this time of year and Até – inevitably, annoyingly – had quoted 'The Time is out of joint. O cursed spite/That ever I was born to set it right.'

Jack had glowered and said nothing. There was no contradicting the wisdom of *Hamlet* in Até's mind. But if Jack took anything from the blasted play it was that he was powerless to decide his fate. Destiny would have to decide for him. So he rose, followed the Mohawk towards the walls. He would not climb them though. The gate would do for him.

As he tried to leave, a young officer and a sergeant were coming in. They were not ones Jack knew – so many had come as reinforcements and these had the pallid faces of those straight from the boat.

The sergeant pointed at Jack, said, 'Is that 'im, sir?'

'Damned if I know. All savages look the same to me. Hey, you! Are you . . . Daga . . . Daga . . . what's the blasted name?'

'Daganoweda?'

'That's the damned word. All sounds like gibberish to me. You there, fellow, are you he?'

Jack stared for a moment. The man was both shouting loudly and speaking very slowly. Finally, he nodded.

'Then General Murray wants you,' he brayed. 'Now.' He clicked his fingers and the sergeant reached and grabbed Jack by the arm.

Jack disengaged himself, stepped away. His bearskin fell open, revealing the tattoos on his chest, the tomahawk at his

322

waist. At the same moment, Até, fresh from the walls, joined him.

'Egad, ugly brutes, ain't they?' Both the Englishmen looked nervous now.

'Do they arrest you, Daganoweda?' Até said in Iroquois.

'They summon me to Murray.'

'Do you wish to go?'

Jack sighed. 'Might as well.'

'Then I go keep watch on this Abenaki dog. He lurks on the wharf trying to trade with the sailors.'

'I will find you there. Don't begin anything without me.' Turning back to the officers he said, 'Lead on, fellows.'

Neither seemed to realize that Jack had spoken English, but this time Jack didn't shake off the sergeant's hand. The man was leading him to his desire, after all. To the general. Out of Limbo.

As usual, Murray was alone. He'd always received Jack thus; with MacDonald dead, there were barely three men in the army who'd been told of Jack's double existence. Also as usual, Murray spoke as if their previous conversation had ended a minute before and not the three weeks it actually had been.

'Why did you not tell me you were required to return in the spring?'

He was standing with his back to the window of the large cell he used as his command, pince-nez on the end of his nose, staring at a piece of paper held at arm's length.

Jack took a nervous step into the room. 'Sir? I did not know . . .'

'Orders, Absolute. The ones you brought from Pitt. You were to deliver them and bring news back as soon as the river thawed. Hmm?'

He glanced, and Jack shook his head. 'I am ignorant, sir, of any—'

'Course you are!' Murray glared then resumed his perusal. 'You arrived, let me see, day or two before the first battle, yes?'

Jack grunted but Murray wasn't interested in confirmation. 'And Wolfe wouldn't have taken time to read *all* the orders. Oh no! Too much work for that lazy turd!'

Jack stayed impassive. In each of their meetings Murray had conveyed how little he esteemed the dead hero of the first battle of Quebec. 'Still,' he sniffed, 'you stayed and became,' another glance, 'well, as we see. God knows how you talked me into it. Can't say it hasn't been useful. Can't say that. But you will obey those orders now. Especially as the King wants his messenger back. Or at least his favourite colonel does. Whatsisname?' He looked at a paper on the desk. 'Ah yes. Burgoyne. Popinjay!'

Jack's heart, which had begun to beat quicker at the beginning of the conversation, quickened again. Burgoyne had requested his return! He was going . . . home, if that's what it still was. Murray had indicated another paper on his desk but Jack's skills at reading upside down had not been tested since Westminster and anyway the general strode forward and covered one page with the other.

'So you are to return, sir.'

'When, sir?'

'When, sir. Now, sir! By the next available ship, sir. You are half a year late.'

Even by Jack's standards that was extreme.

Murray had seized another piece of paper. 'Too risky to try for Quebec with the ice due. Have to be Boston.' He scanned the sheet. 'Plenty of ships going from Boston end of October. You'll go from there.'

Murray read on and Jack waited. When he realized that the general had dismissed him, he spoke. 'Uh, sir . . . ?'

'Still here?'

'I have no uniform, sir, and no—'

'For God's sake, man, just speak to the quartermaster, will you? He has everything for you. Will fit you out with dead man's boots and full fig. Though you're a dragoon, ain't you? Well, you'll be a lobster-back on the way across. Give you gold, too, and your papers for the ship, together with the letters I require you to carry. Your hair will grow out on the voyage and till then wear a wig, sir. Wear a wig!'

An hour later he emerged from the quartermaster's. Murray had sent a note down that indeed arranged everything. Jack had a new fustian haversack stuffed with the full uniform of a man a touch smaller than himself, with a large blood stain under the armpit, inadequately patched. He had a horsehair wig, a tricorn hat, a sword, gaiters and shoes, and a rather fine silk shirt. He had a purse containing five guineas and a requisition for a third-class berth on the West Indiaman, *Accord*. Yet he still sported the single top-knot and tattoos of a Mohawk warrior so when a soldier shouted, 'Thief!' at him, he took the bearskin off and wrapped everything in it, suspending it from the end of his musket's barrel to be carried across his shoulder. Then he ducked into the sleet that had begun to blow off the river and headed for the wharf in search of Até. The cold and the news together numbed him to all but what lay ahead. Out of Limbo, bound for home, a hard farewell still awaited.

He didn't make fifty paces down the Rue St Joseph before a crowd blocked his passage. Men and some women were gathered, civilian and soldier, yelling at something before them. Taller than most there, Jack peered and winced as he saw four hefty Redcoats thrashing one of the townsmen, a balding man in his later-middle years. When a woman ran from an open door and slapped a broom-handle onto the largest assailant's back, Jack winced again as that man took the implement from her, reversed it to beat in his turn. He also noticed that the soldier thrust a hand inside the blouse he casually ripped.

Soldiers cheered or jeered, civilians looked on powerlessly. The largest soldier was still laughing cruelly as he groped, tugged, beat; and it was that cruelty that suddenly made Jack notice something familiar in this man's obvious enjoyment of pain. And in that recognition, in the moment before a detachment of soldiers began to stroll toward the fray from the guardhouse at St Sulpice, Jack suddenly realized what that something was.

The man with his hand in a defenceless woman's blouse was Craster Absolute.

He gasped, his legs gave. If his cousin had descended in lightning, he could not have shocked more. Jack had thought often of his former life through the winter in the cave, in the campaign that followed. Indeed, his dreams had become more urban the more his daytime life adapted to the forest. Fanny would come in heat and pleasure and, on waking, memories of her would linger happily. If he knew his actions had led her to her shame at the Vauxhall Pleasure Gardens, had caused the death of her patron, Melbury, he also knew that she would survive because she always had done. But Clothilde! Dreams of her came too, these swathed in sadness. She was innocent and he should have protected her and instead had opened her to the ravages of . . . the man before him now. Absolute gold had bought her off, paid for her to wed someone she could not love, all to preserve the family name. More gold had bought the uniform that Craster wore and disgraced even now.

He did not realize he had taken the five paces forward, arriving at the same time as the platoon, did not know his hand was gripping his tomahawk. Then he stood before his cousin, saw again that jowly face, little diminished by a campaign's privations, like a bear who had stored up fat; noted again those close-set eyes that only ever gleamed when there was pain to dispense, pain Jack had borne all his life.

Craster had stepped away from the fracas once the troopers moved in. He stood back now and let his comrades take the half-hearted blows, laughing and leering still. Then, suddenly, he turned and looked at Jack, and he said, 'So what do you think you are staring at, you poxed brown monkey?'

Jack had no words. And by the time he thought of the actions he'd promised himself a thousand times to take when this man stood before him again, his cousin was already being

326

pulled away by three Redcoats, already laughing with his captors. Jack, goaded by that braying laugh, still could not move. An order had been given to free him from Limbo but his body seemed still to be in it.

Slowly turning, he resumed his walk towards the river.

To a man in a trance, the wharf was an assault of sound and sense. The wind blew sleet off the water yet this did not stop the labours of men, hundreds scurrying over the sides of the ships. One army was leaving, the defeated French being readied for transport out. Another, their conquerors, continued to arrive. Both needed to be fed. So livestock bellowed in pens or swung in slings while men in every shade of coat cajoled and argued, hefted sacks of grain and vegetables, barrels of salted meat and rum. There were a number of Indians of the various tribes: Iroquois, Huron, Nipissing, Algonquin and Abenaki, a group of them seemingly hunting for something.

Tucked away in a tangle of fishing nets and old barrels, beneath a broken crane, Jack found him. Até was in the shadow of the upright, his bearskin on the planking before him.

'What are you doing here, Até?'

The Mohawk stepped back into the shadows, drawing Jack in. 'Watching them,' he said, gesturing back to the wharf, to the Abenaki still engaged in their search.

'What are they looking for?'

'Segunki.'

Jack felt a quickening at the name. He might not have suffered from their slavemaster as long as Até. But the memory of being handicapped like a horse, of fighting like a dog in a pit . . . He looked to Até's belt. 'Where's his scalp?'

'On his head.'

At his puzzlement, Até pointed to the bearskin at his feet. Now Jack looked closer, he could see the crown of a head poking out. There was a slight shifting, a muffled moan.

'You have not killed him yet?'

'I have not.' Até peered out to the wharf. The Abenaki were leaving it, their gestures indicating that they were going to search elsewhere.

'You are saving him for . . . something else?' Suddenly a vision came, of a body hanging naked from a rock wall, like a bear carcass stripped of skin. Até had hung like that, exposed to this man's knife. The idea made Jack a little queasy. Vengeance was something he could understand well. Indeed, since his sight of Craster, his own heart was full of it. But he'd heard many a dark tale in their winter cave of how prolonged vengeance could, should be. He had a feeling that Até had spared his enemy's life for such purposes – and that he would want to involve Jack in them.

'Something else, yes.' Até appeared distracted, by more than the departing Abenaki. Suddenly he turned back. 'Jack,' he said, which was unusual enough in itself. 'I was thinking of *Hamlet*.'

Jack groaned. 'Fuck, Até, not now, please.'

'Yes, now!' He had to raise his voice above a wind now whistling hard. 'Hamlet doesn't kill Claudius when he can. He doesn't take revenge.'

It was only the absurdity – and a certain gratitude for Time pausing – that made Jack take part in the discussion. 'He does. He kills Claudius—'

'But later! Only when he has to, when his uncle tries to kill him again. He doesn't, like the other wants to, "cut throats in a Church". He chooses . . . to accept fate, "the fall of a sparrow". And then fate gives him his enemy.'

An unconscious warrior at his feet. A pass to England in his pack. A blood enemy walking away, unpunished. Why not discuss a play? Why not?

'And fate has given you . . . him.'

'But now I can choose. Like Hamlet. Kill for vengeance. Slit his throat like a racoon in a snare. Take his scalp. Or . . .'

'Or?'

Até thrust his head into the icy wind, sniffed. 'You smell it?

Winter comes. The snow that buries.' Suddenly, that rare smile came, transforming the Mohawk's face. 'And Grandfather Bear will just have gone to sleep.'

Suddenly Jack saw and the lethargy that had settled upon him as he contemplated Time, the numbness that had descended when he'd had the man he'd vowed to kill within the swing of his tomahawk and he'd done nothing, both left him. Six months alone with the man before him meant he needed few words to clarify.

'Where?'

'We cannot take him to the cave, for he has been there and will find his way out. But my people have hunting grounds also . . . there.' Até gestured to the south.

'How far? By water or land?'

'Not far. By land.'

Jack looked into a sky swirling with snow. Até was right. Even Jack could recognize that a storm was gathering. And night was close. 'Then I will meet you at the horses at midnight.' Leaning forward, he pulled Até's ironwood war club from his belt. 'And I will borrow this.'

'Daganoweda?' Até called. But Jack was gone, the wind to his back now. It would blow him once more into the city. It would sweep him to his revenge.

In the six months since Jack had last supped rum in this tavern only a little had changed, the main difference being in the colour of uniforms, for the white of France had been replaced by the red of England. But the same half-caste landlord dispensed liquor and ejected troublemakers, the same whores disappeared to dispatch customers in the alley, the doors barely closing upon them before they were back, shrieking against the cold. Jack was sure that the English counterpart of Hubert sought solace this night with sailor or savage. And if there were less of the latter about, there were still enough, for Amherst had brought his Native allies, mainly Mohawk, north; enough top-knots and tattoos for Jack to remain unnoticed by the man he'd tracked to this place. Yet he need hardly have worried. Craster Absolute was noticing little save for the filling of his tankard and the groping of the maid who filled it.

Jack shifted as the door opened again, turning gratefully to the frosty air. The tavern was the usual fug of heat and smoke and Jack was wearing all his clothes. The scalplock and bearskin proclaimed him an Iroquois. But underneath it his skin was getting used again to the rub of linen and wool. It was uncomfortable yet he bore it; he needed his hands free.

He had waited and watched for an hour. Craster drank and groped and sang and drank more, yet showed no inclination to move outside. Jack was wondering if his bladder was unfillable. Yet it was another of his cousin's organs that gave Jack his desire. For one of the night-ladies had noticed Craster's constant touching of the tavern wenches. She had moved in, offered herself, been accepted and he was even now moving towards the door, passing within a foot of Jack, a dull gleam in those set-together eyes, a smirk on the lips.

The night air brought relief. The wind had dropped, the temperature gone up to just this side of freezing. Clouds were rolling over a half-moon. He could smell the coming snow. He stood staring up into the night sky, waiting. Sounds came from the alley, muttered curses, a woman's whimper of pain swiftly suppressed, a high-pitched groan. Then the whore emerged from the alley, shoving a coin away under her dress with one hand. She didn't seem startled to see a Mohawk there. 'Con!' she said, with a jerk of her head the way she'd come. The doors swung open and sucked her inside.

Most noise was cut off by their closing; he could just hear someone commence another verse from 'The British Grenadiers'.

Come, come my brave boys, let's away for the town,
Where the drums they do beat, and the trumpets shall sound.
Our bridge shall be laid, in order to storm 'em;
If they'll not surrender, so bravely we'll warm 'em.

Jack was softly humming it as he stepped into the alley. Craster, silhouetted against its end, his piss a stallion's spray in the moonlight, was humming too. Jack reached him before they'd finished the second verse.

He had thought of all the things he would say, in a speech born of a thousand cruelties, crafted over a lifetime. He had thought of recounting all his cousin's crimes from child to man, dwelling most on the most horrible of them all, the ravishing of Clothilde Guen. He had thought how he would make Craster feel some of the girl's terror in the moments before he revealed to the punished just who the punisher was. He had thought he would say and do all that.

Instead, he just hit him with the war club.

Até had said their destination was nearby, in a valley where he had hunted; but Jack had come to realize that the Iroquois had a very different relationship to both distance and time. So he was greatly relieved when Até dismounted towards evening of the third day of hard riding with a gesture to show they'd arrived. The driving snow had hindered and the swaying, hooded men riding before them had added to the exhaustion of all. They had little enough food, only what they'd gathered in their hasty leaving of Montréal and what they'd scavenged and traded for from sparse settlements along the way; not really enough for four young men. They also rationed that little because they'd need some for the return.

The two prisoners had remained under hoods fashioned of oat sacks, even to eat, to shit, to sleep, their hands bound. Now, in the clearing that Até indicated was their destination, having re-secured their hands around the trunk of a beech, Jack and Até simultaneously jerked the headpieces clear.

Both Craster and Segunki emerged gasping, their faces red and chafed from the material's rubbing, their lips rimed in the *pemmican* that had been their main diet. Both sported near-identical bruises where war clubs had struck them, though Craster's had a crust of blood at its centre. His gold hair was akimbo, a disordered profusion compared to the part-shaved scalp of the Abenaki, while Segunki's face-paint had been smeared into some indeterminate colour. Both, however, wore identical expressions of fear and outrage.

It was the latter that manifested itself first in the Englishman. 'How . . . dare you treat an officer of the Crown in such a manner? You will be punished for this, unless you return me instantly to my regiment! Instantly, do you hear?'

Até turned and said, in Iroquois, the only tongue they had spoken in the entire trip at Jack's instigation, 'He must indeed have your blood, Daganoweda, for he does not whine and beg but shouts.'

Jack nodded. 'I never called him a coward. He's too stupid to be one. But every other name I have given him is also true. He is a brute and a rapist and I cannot remember a time when I did not hate him.'

Something in the tone caused Craster's next tirade to abort. Instead he stared at Jack, studied the tattoos, the scalplock. Then he obviously shook the preposterous idea from his much-abused head and was about to embark on another rant when Segunki spoke. Jack had only picked up a few Abenaki words in his time at St Francis and the speed with which they poured out now admitted no understanding. The tone was clear, as Até rapidly confirmed.

'This one does not have your cousin's fire. He whines and begs and bargains.' Até uttered a short sentence in Abenaki before continuing, 'I have told him to rest easy. He will know his fate soon enough.'

Ignoring both plea and threat, they rose from their squat, the Mohawk leading Jack around the small valley, pointing out its suitability. Water there was, under a fresh sheet of ice created by winter's harsh return. New snow revealed deer tracks and, in one place, the unmistakable five-toed print of a bear.

'Good,' said Jack at the sight. Indeed, all was well. If there was no cave, there was balsam and hemlock a-plenty, assuming the Abenaki knew how to craft them into a shelter. Snow scraped up revealed the clover-like minty leaves and their red berries Jack had eaten before and, in a bog on their route in, Jack had noticed cattails thrusting up feathery leaves. There was just enough to survive on. Just as much, anyway, as he and Até had had.

The snow had started to fall again, heralding the long-anticipated big storm. Até was impatient to be away. He led the horses up to the last ridge they'd descended, then came back to Jack. Swiftly cutting two hemlock boughs, he handed one over. 'To sweep over our tracks,' he said. 'Don't want them to follow us out.'

When all was ready, they went and stood in front of the two bound men. The increasing cold had removed much of Craster's bluster, frozen Segunki's pleas. They stared numbly up at their captors now, eyes following as Até moved behind them, untied Craster, to his very temporary relief for he was swiftly rebound to the same tree as the Abenaki, their fingers almost conjoined. When he was done, Até once more took his place beside Jack and nodded.

Jack turned back to the captives. His voice was soft. 'Craster Absolute,' he said.

The gaze leapt to him. 'Eh?' he muttered.

'Do you not know me?'

The thought that had come before, that had obviously been dismissed as a phantasm, madness following suffering, now returned. The eyes narrowed into a stare of disbelief. 'No. No! It cannot be. Cannot be . . .'

Jack leaned down. 'It is. Exceedingly strange to you, I am sure. But true.'

For a moment, Jack wondered if he'd inadvertently spoken in Iroquois, so lacking in comprehension did Craster's face appear to be. Then suddenly he had it and something else came with it. Hope.

'Jack! My dear cousin! I am . . . amazed! You live.'

'I do.'

'By all that is holy!' Craster was nearly in raptures. 'Your mother, my aunt, will be so pleased. She asked me to look out for you before I embarked, she . . .' A memory of Lady Jane came that obviously didn't tally with the vision of family he was trying to create and Jack suspected why. His mother knew everything about the brute's behaviour. But Craster rallied. 'She will be delighted when I take her the news.'

'And why will you be the bearer of such tidings?'

Incomprehension, hope, still gripped him. 'Egad, Jack, you are in the right. We will take her the news together.'

'And do you think,' Jack spoke still more softly, 'that I have brought you here just to let you go?'

Craster's face, strained by its assumption of fellowship, slipped into more customary grooves. As Jack had told Até, his cousin was every kind of villain but a coward. 'Then why *have* you brought me here, sir? To kill me? It would be just your sort of poltroon's trick. Then why don't you get on with it, you turd? Our family shall know of it somehow and then, by God, you'll pay.'

If it was coming from anyone else, Jack might have been amused by the bluster. But Craster had never had the ability to make his cousin laugh.

'You raped Clothilde Guen.'

'Who?' He struggled with memory. 'What? That . . . that chit? I most certainly did not.'

Jack raised a hand. 'Take care.'

Craster gave, just a little. 'And if I did! She asked for it, the hussy. Enjoyed it, too, I'll be bound. Besides, society scarce notices such a thing. A child like that is not a woman.'

Até, who had watched soundless, now grunted in disgust. But Jack it was who went on. 'I noticed. She . . . *noticed.*'

'It ain't a hanging offence,' Craster blustered. 'So you can kiss my arse, Jack Absolute. Go on! Murder me, and have done with it.'

Jack leaned down, his voice near a whisper now. 'I could. I long to. To repay you for every kick you gave me, every slap and every switch your father laid upon my back. Most of all for what you did to that poor girl. By doing that, you changed all our lives. You did indeed turn me into a killer. Yet these hands,' he raised them and they shook slightly, 'have enough blood on them for now. Stained by worthy opponents and in fair fights. I do not intend to disgrace their memory by adding your blood to them.' For a long moment, Jack gazed into his cousin's eyes, Craster staring back. Then he rose, turned to Até. 'Ready?'

Até nodded, went to the edge of the clearing, fetched what they'd brought for the purpose; as he laid each item down, Jack named it. '*Pemmican*,' he said, pointing to the ball of grease. 'Enough for two days if you're not too greedy. A flint, a kettle, a length of rope and a knife.'

His cousin stared at the items dully. 'And what am I meant to do with these?'

Jack took his time before he said it. 'Survive.'

Craster's jaw went slack. 'You . . . you mean to leave me here? With these trinkets and . . . a savage?' On Jack's silence he continued, 'But what will we live on?'

'The savage will know. You'll just have to trade him something to share his knowledge.'

As he said this, Jack moved away to the faint outline of the path head. Até, who had bent once to whisper something into Segunki's ear, now joined him. 'You forget something, Daganoweda?'

Jack stared at his friend for a moment, then remembered. 'Of course.' He went back to Craster whose mouth was now opening and closing, no sound emerging. He reached inside his bearskin. 'I do have one last thing for you.'

Craster's eyes flickered with a little hope. 'A pistol?'

'Oh no,' Jack said, 'far, far better than that.'

And he dropped *Hamlet* upon his cousin's chest.

As they climbed from the clearing, Jack and Até were laughing so hard they could barely sweep the hemlock boughs across the path to obliterate their tracks.

A day and night found them at a junction of two valleys, one heading roughly east, the other southerly. There, as the snow eased again and a pale sunset shone through a rent in the clouds, they set up a night camp. While Até conjured fire from damp wood and constructed a birch-bark shelter, through the ice of a pond Jack had some luck with perch. These, and the last of their *pemmican*, made their meal.

At every halt, they laughed still about the men they'd left.

'How long will they take to free themselves?'

'With my knots?' Até smiled. 'If they work together . . . an hour. If they pull each their own way they could still be there when spring comes.'

Jack chuckled. 'And once free? Will they live? Die? Kill each other? Who would win that fight?'

Até shrugged. 'Fate decides. Not you or me. "If it be not now, yet it will come." '

Jack sighed. 'Do you think they'll read the play?'

Até, busy with wood, looked up. 'I think they will eat the pages one by one.'

That made them laugh again, then fall silent, staring into the heart of the fire they'd built between them. Both knew what was unspoken across it. Both had recognized what the two valleys – one going east, one south – meant.

'Até,' said Jack at last. 'Tomorrow—'

The Mohawk interrupted him briskly. 'Tomorrow we return to our own worlds, our own wars.'

'Unless you came with me,' Jack leaned forward, suddenly eager. 'You said you wanted to see England.'

'The land of Hamlet?' Até's briskness was replaced by a softness, a stare.

'Well, Shakespeare. Many other things too.' He stared across the flames. 'I could show them to you.'

Até looked away, up into the canopy. When at last he looked back, his gaze was firm. 'I have thought of this, Daganoweda. Thought of going with you.'

'Then do.'

'One day. One day I would like to see "what is dreamt of in your philosophy".'

'Will you stop quoting that bloody play?'

Até leaned forward, reflected fire not the only light in his eyes. 'And that is why I cannot go. Because I cannot quote from anything else.'

'What do you mean?'

'You have taught me some things. But there is so much still to learn.' The sadness went, replaced by excitement. 'But the French are beaten now; this war ends. And my uncle-by-law, William Johnson, each year he sends some boys to a school in Connecticut. Maybe he send me. Then I learn everything. Then I come to England.' Off Jack's look he added, 'I will come, Daganoweda.'

Jack nodded. 'So tomorrow we part.'

'Unless . . .'

'Unless?'

'Unless you come with me.' Até's excitement was building. 'You know your English ways. And now you know some of our ways, too. But your ignorance is as great as mine is of yours. I can lead you. You can truly become a Mohawk. You can join the clan of the wolf.'

For a long moment, Jack stared into the flames. *Why not?* The thought of London excited and appalled in equal measure. He had grown comfortable in the forest, there was game he hadn't hunted in this land he'd started to love, a friend to hunt them with, a man whose life he'd saved, who'd saved his. And there was still that damned war cry to learn!

Yet he shook his head. 'I cannot. I have orders and to disobey them, to go with you, I would become a deserter. And there is an oath I swore to my country, to my King, and a promise made to my father to honour the uniform he has honoured, the name we share. There is a land I love and people who love me there, blood of my blood.'

The silence came between them again, the flames' snap

suddenly loud. After a time, Até rose and came to Jack's side of the fire and there he did something strange. He took Jack's hand. 'Nothing is for ever. We will meet again. You will return to this land because you will be drawn by this,' he pointed to Jack's heart, 'and this.'

He had drawn out his knife and now he pressed it to Jack's palm, looking up at him. At his nod, Até slashed it in one swift motion down the flesh under the thumb. In a moment, he had matched the cut with one of his own.

'So this will bring you back, to the land where you will always be Daganoweda,' he said, pressing flow to flow, 'because blood of your blood is now here as well.' He gripped so hard he made Jack wince, that smile coming again. 'Also you owe me more chances to save you. Because without you last winter I would have died . . . pretty damn quick!'

It was not the last of Jack's blood that Até shed. At dawn, a dry shave and many nicks later, he no longer sported the scalplock that, more than anything, denoted him as a Mohawk. With the tricorn upon his head, and his body once more encased within silk and serge, he was again Cornet Jack Absolute of the 16th Dragoons. And if his skin was still stained with the dye Até had concocted for him to maintain his disguise, Jack could remember summers in Cornwall when he'd been nearly as dark.

They parted on the ridge where the valleys met. Snow lay before each of them, frozen hard yet not so deep it could not take the horses; yet both knew that, when the promised big storm came and the paths became impassable to hoof, they could skim across the surfaces on the snowshoes each had strapped to their backs.

They parted without words. All the necessary ones had been spoken the previous night, then sealed in blood. With a swift salute befitting the uniform he wore, Jack turned his horse, prodded it downhill through a drift till he came to an avenue between the trees where the snow was shallower. He picked up speed there, putting distance between the parting and himself. Soon he was out of sight of the ridge.

Yet not of sound. Suddenly, faintly, Jack heard the familiar, long, drawn-out ululation. 'Ah-ah-ah-ah-AH-HUM,' it came, echoing down the valley.

'Of course,' he said aloud, 'Of course! *That's* it.' Tipping his head, he gave it back, listened to the echo bouncing off the crags. It was . . . perfect! So good in fact that, if he wished to, he knew he would finally be able to teach the Mohocks of Covent Garden exactly how it was done. But in that moment, with the cry not yet faded from the valley's slopes, he knew he never would.

HISTORICAL NOTE AND
ACKNOWLEDGEMENTS

The campaign that climaxed in the Battle of Quebec is less taught now, the concept of Empire-building less kindly regarded. Yet that battle above those cliffs in 1759 is certainly one of the turning points of history. It won Britain Canada. It also conceivably lost Britain America for, by defeating and eventually disposing of our mutual French enemy, the Colonists no longer needed our protection. Sixteen years later they began to slip the yoke.

It was also one of the most dramatic of victories: a secret landing at 2 a.m.; the light infantry scrambling up sheer cliffs in the dark to silence the sentries and seize the cliff tops so the army could march up the hidden road; the French waking to find the red ranks drawn up outside their walls; the perfect volley that finished them; the deaths of both Wolfe and Montcalm in their respective moments of triumph and despair. There was almost too much drama for the pen and I had to select what to focus on or the battle would have occupied the whole novel.

Research narrowed it down. I wore out the pages of Osprey's superb *Quebec 1759* by Stuart Reid. Then there was C. P. Stacey's study with the same title, *Quebec 1759*, which had marvellous incidental detail, especially the conflicting tales of the reciting of Gray's *Elegy* prior to the attack and clarifying the calls the French sentries made as the English army drifted downstream with the tide. For native affairs, D. Peter Macleod's *The Canadian Iroquois and the Seven Years' War* was excellent and I also met him at the Canadian Museum of War in Ottawa where he kindly gave me his time and a 'eureka' moment – by pointing out that Rogers' Raid on St Francis took place just three weeks after the Battle.

I'd decided early that London – the city I live in, the city I love – was also going to be a major backdrop to the story. The more I read about that great metropolis and its inhabitants in the eighteenth century, the more I realized how little has changed. So much of the London we know was built in Georgian times and Londoners behaved then much as they do now, especially the youths. They caroused around the town, played games, gambled on anything, drank far too much, chased women, and always sought the sleaziest after-hour dens to end up in. The English don't change even if, by most standards, 2004 is tame compared to 1759. They also reacted just as you'd expect when, in 1752, the government finally decided to bring England into line with the rest of Europe – 200 years late – by adopting the Gregorian calendar. They rioted! I've always found the idea of those missing eleven days fascinating, hence the start of this novel.

Research once again gave me stories and their settings. For Cornwall, *West Country Words and Ways* by K. C. Philips was *proper*! It appeared that the British Museum put on a show especially for me, *London 1753*, but also for the 250th anniversary of the Museum's founding, full of texts, prints and artefacts. The catalogue was superbly detailed and I owe a great debt to its editor, Sheila O'Connell, and the curators. For debauchery, no one was a better guide to the taverns, bagnios, billiards halls and whorehouses than William Hickey in his *Memoirs of a Georgian Rake* while *Wits, Wenchers and Wantons* by E. J. Burford also provided lively detail. I again had great experiences in the British Library's Rare Books section, holding an original copy of that seminal Whores' Directory, *Harris's List of Ladies*; as well as the Alexander Pope 1731 edition of *Hamlet*, printed at Dirty Lane, Dublin.

Two period novels gave me the flavour of language and mores: *Humphrey Clinker* by Tobias Smollett; and the book that is one of the bawdy benchmarks in English literary history, *Tom Jones* by Henry Fielding. Any resemblance to that great work is entirely intentional.

Yet my favourite research is always on the ground and I owe a debt to many guides. My first were at a snooker hall in North Finchley where an old friend, Geoffrey Boxer, and his pool-hall-hustler son, James Boxer, helped me work out Jack's nigh-impossible winning shot. Then, in the forests of Killarney Provincial Park, Ontario, Steve Sanna of Pow Wow Wilderness Adventures took me by canoe into the wilds for three days and pointed out the flora, fauna, shelters and edibles that would enable Jack and Até to survive a winter.

My favourite moment came when I emulated my considerably younger creation and the British Light Infantry by scaling the cliffs that rise from the St Lawrence River to the Plains of Abraham at Quebec City. Though the battlefield itself is much developed and encroached upon, the cliffs are hardly altered. I cheated by doing it in running shoes and with a back pack in the afternoon, rather than in boots and carrying a musket in the middle of the night. But it gave me priceless detail – the shale cliff face slipping away, the deadfall of maples crumbling to the touch, the sturdier branches and trunks to be used as ladders. I climbed from the base where I calculated they might have begun, and came out on what was once the secret path and is now a road, exactly at the stone marker which testifies to Wolfe's midnight landing (and implies, in French, that he cheated!)

I went to the Georgian cricket match at Marble Hill House where I met two people: Christine Riding of Tate Britain, who kindly sent me the beautiful Gainsborough catalogue from the exhibition, great for faces and dress; and Andy Robertshaw of the National Army Museum who showed me how to use a musket and bayonet.

Of many other contributions, one stands out. I can give you 'To be or not to be, that is the question,' in German, Italian and Danish. For this book, I really, *really* wanted it in Iroquois. Fortunately I met a Mohawk at the Battle of Saratoga re-enactment in 2002 (as one does), who produced a card with e-mail address from within his furs and feathers. Wolf Thomas is the man to whom I am so grateful; the phrase worth repeating, in any language, '*akwekon katon othe:non tsi ne' ken*'.

Some others to thank. David Chaundler, Bursar at Westminster School, who showed me around and checked facts. Nat Heyden for her French. Alma Lee, Artistic Director of the Vancouver Writers' and Readers' Festival who gave me shelter when I first conceived Jack. As ever, my publishers at Orion, Jane Wood, Publishing Director, and Jon Wood, my point man there, editor, champion and friend; Susan Lamb who does such a great job on the paperback front; Henry Steadman, my excellent cover designer; Kim McArthur, my powerhouse Canadian publisher; Rachel Leyshon who does the line-by-line editing and, often annoyingly, keeps me honest; I also must mention my brilliant new agent, Kate Jones at ICM, who is busy revolutionizing my career. My wife, Aletha, who accepts the occasional weirdness to which writers are prone. And my son, Reith Frederic, born this year, who allows his father to work . . . some of the time!

C. C. Humphreys
London, July 2004